VAGABOND QUAKERS

Southern Colonies

VAGABOND QUAKERS

Southern Colonies

The Vagabond Trilogy
Book 2

OLGA R. MORRILL

Morrill Fiction

Madison, NH

FIRST EDITION

www.vagabondquakers.wordpress.com

Morrill, Olga, author. | Kirsch, Marina Dutzmann, illustrator, editor.

Vagabond quakers. Southern colonies / by Olga Morrill ; map illustrations and editing by Marina Dutzmann Kirsch.

Morrill, Olga. Vagabond trilogy ; bk. 2.

First edition. | Madison, NH : Morrill Fiction, [2021] | Series: The vagabond trilogy ; book 2. | Includes bibliographical references.

ISBN: 978-0-9984151-2-3 (paperback) | 978-0-9984151-3-0 (Kindle)

LCSH: Quakers--New England--History--17th century--Fiction. | Quakers--Rhode Island-- History--17th century--Fiction. | Quakers--Persecutions--New England--History--17th century--Fiction. | Quaker women missionaries--New England--History--17th century-- Fiction. | Women--New England--History--17th century--Fiction. | Puritans--New England-- History--17th century--Fiction. | Temporal power of religious rulers--New England--History --17th century--Fiction. | Freedom of religion--Atlantic States--History--17th century-- Fiction. | New England--History--Colonial period, ca. 1600-1775--Fiction. | Endecott, John, 1588?-1665--Fiction. | LCGFT: Historical fiction. | Biographical fiction.

LCC: PS3613.O755455 V34 2021 | DDC: 813/.6--dc23

This book is dedicated to my husband Steve

TABLE OF CONTENTS

PREFACE

ook 2 in The Vagabond Trilogy follows missionary Friends Mary Tomkins and Alice
Ambrose as they journey south from Newport, Rhode Island to the southern branch
of the Elizabeth River in Virginia. Their mission is to find John Perrot, a renegade who
has broken away from the mainstream of the Religious Society of Friends. Their search
takes them from the Eastern Shore of Maryland and Virginia across Chesapeake Bay to
the Patuxent River and the "Clifts," (original spelling for the Cliffs on the bay's western
shore) and on to the southern branch of the Elizabeth River in Lower Norfolk County.

In researching *Vagabond Quakers: Northern Colonies*, book 1 of The Vagabond Trilogy,
I was amazed to learn of the freeman system whereby prospective residents of any Puritan
New England town were vetted by the magistrate, the minister, and their "peers" (other
landowners and freemen). On average one third were granted this coveted status without
which one could not vote, hold office, or become a member of the church. Fully two-
thirds of the population of the northern colonies (Rhode Island excepted) did not make
the grade and were disenfranchised in their own communities. It was a theocracy that did
not tolerate any other religion. Attendance at the Puritan Congregational Church every
Sunday was mandatory. The residents were taxed to support the minister and his church,
and they were fined if they did not attend services. The Friends did not use "hireling
ministers" or "steeplehouses" thus taxes were not required to maintain them. In addition,
The Society of Friends welcomed all people as spiritual equals with community decisions
made by consensus. It was understandably a welcome alternative.

In book 2 the most noteworthy result of the research was the headright system, employed in the southern colonies of Maryland, Virginia, and Carolina. It was designed to
encourage immigration. Due to a struggling economy, over-population in Britain, and

England's Civil War (which erupted sporadically during the 1640s), many people wanted to leave England but could not afford the crossing. Through the headright system, established colonists paid the five-pound fee for an individual's passage and received a bonus incentive of between 50 to 100 acres of land per head. Even children counted. During the mid-17th century for those with means, it was an easy way to increase one's holdings in the Colonies while good land was still plentiful. Most who participated in the headright system kept the lion's share of the acreage for themselves, employing the newcomers as indentured servants with a promise of a few acres when their contracts were fulfilled—usually five to seven years.

Great numbers of these indentured souls died before their terms were up either from the climate, overwork, or maltreatment. Although 17th century statistics are sketchy, some seventy percent of passengers from England to the Colonies were indentured servants, and at least thirty percent of those servants died within a year after immigration.

In 1615 when John Rolf discovered that tobacco thrived in Virginia soil, over the next decades it became the staple of the Southern Colonies. In fact, it was used as currency as demonstrated by court fines calculated in pounds of tobacco. Anyone with a plot of land grew it, including Governor Berkeley of Virginia. Unlike New England, the Southern Colonies had very few towns, as everyone lived or worked on tobacco plantations strung along the riverbanks off the Eastern Shore of Chesapeake Bay. Unfortunately, tobacco used up the soil within three years, necessitating more land and making the headright system a roaring success.

Readers may wonder about black slaves. In the 17th century the Dutch had a monopoly on the African slave market, which they maintained into the early 18th century. Some blacks were brought to the Colonies from Barbados by their masters, and a few colonial entrepreneurs purchased small lots from Dutch business associates, but the slave trade did not go global until the next century. The majority of laborers in the American Colonies at the time of this story were white indentured servants.

The archaic spelling of place names such as "Plimoth" and "The Clifts" is intentional. Likewise, with words such as "physitian" for physician and "muskeetos" for mosquitoes. They are gleaned from older reference works and are included in the glossary at the end of the book along with other words and expressions of the time that enhance the atmosphere and authenticity of the text.

With this background established, the conclusion of Mary and Allie's story follows.

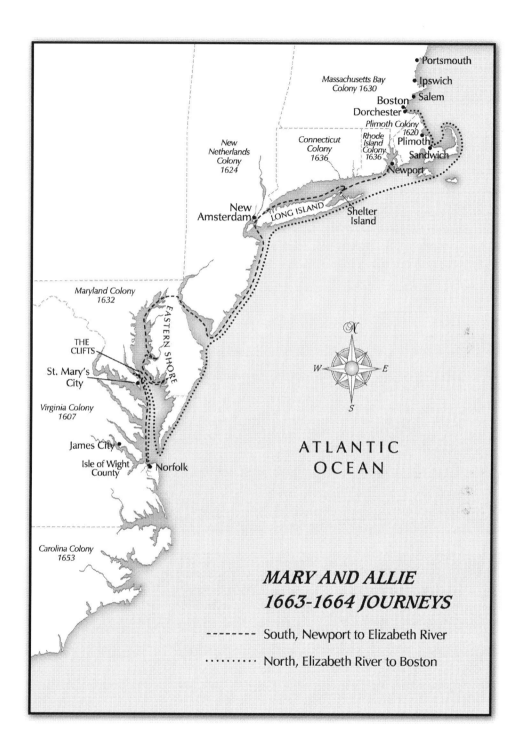

Portsmouth

Massachusetts Bay
Colony 1630

Ipswich

Boston • Salem

Dorchester

Plimoth Colony
1620

New
Netherlands
Colony
1624

Connecticut
Colony
1636

Rhode
Island
Colony
1636

Plimoth

Sandwich

Newport

New
Amsterdam

LONG ISLAND

Shelter
Island

Maryland Colony
1632

EASTERN SHORE

THE
CLIFTS

St. Mary's
City

Virginia Colony
1607

James City

Isle of Wight
County

Norfolk

N
W — E
S

ATLANTIC
OCEAN

Carolina Colony
1653

MARY AND ALLIE
1663-1664 JOURNEYS

-------- South, Newport to Elizabeth River

.... North, Elizabeth River to Boston

Prologue

THE CLIFTS, MARYLAND COLONY

December (10th Month) 1663

A wave of agony flung Mary Tomkins onto the cruel rocks of consciousness. She lay on her stomach, her upper body propped on pillows. She gasped, but even breathing hurt. Her back was afire, and the tiniest movement fanned the flames. A high-pitched whimper grew in the back of her throat. There was an immediate response.

"There, there, Mary." The voice was familiar, and a hand cupped her forehead. She had not realized she was fevered, until it touched her burning skin. "Thou art safe now. Be at peace."

It was a man's voice and kind, as reassuring as the cool hand on her brow. The source of the agony was her back, but the pain coursed from her feet to her temples. Her entire body hurt. A cold, damp flannel replaced the hand. She struggled to focus on it, a small anchor of comfort in a whirlpool of distress.

"It is I, Doctor Peter Sharpe, and thou art in my home at the Clifts. We met some weeks ago before thy journey to Virginia with thy companion Alice," the voice went on, turning the cloth to the cooler side. "Friend Dixon brought ye back here to recover. Dost remember being arrested and flogged? Both of ye were sorely beaten but fear not. Allie is here, too, and ye are safe now."

Images flashed in Mary's mind. Sheriff John Hill's fleshy face distorted with hate and a chilling avidity, as he stripped them to the waist and bound their hands with a running knot to a metal ring above their heads. Thirty-two stripes he laid upon their bare skin. She lost count and fainted, but High Sheriff Hill and his deputies took their time and revived her, so she felt every one of them. She remembered nothing after they cut the ropes binding her wrists, and she was at last allowed to escape into oblivion. She did not remember hitting the ground and had been unconscious until now.

"Please," she gasped, "The pain—"

"Certes, my dear," the doctor moved away. Seconds later he pressed a cup to her down-turned face and gently raised her forehead until she could drink. It sparked a surge of pain down her spine.

"Not too fast," he cautioned. The concoction was bitter, and the agony flared at each swallow, but she managed without choking. "Very good," he added, setting the empty cup aside.

"Allie is close by, but she is sleeping at present," the doctor went on, pressing the cold flannel to her forehead again. "This medicine will help thee to sleep, too, though it may take some moments."

Peter Sharpe continued to talk quietly, and Mary focused on his voice, desperate for distraction if not relief. Gradually the agony subsided enough to allow her to breathe normally. She sighed. The doctor's words faded to an indistinct rumble as the laudanum did its work.

She and Allie were safe. How far they had come since journeying south from Newport last spring! It had all started so well. The ten days with Edward and George on the *Sea Witch* had been idyllic. Anne Coleman was still with them. As the pain shrank, the events of the past months played out once again in her mind's eye.

Part I

SPRING 1663

Freedom of thought is the greatest triumph over tyranny that brave men have ever won; for this they fought the wars of the Reformation; for this they have left their bones to whiten upon unnumbered fields of battle; for this they have gone by the thousands to the dungeon, the scaffold, and the stake. We owe to their heroic devotion the most priceless of our Treasures, our perfect liberty of thought and speech; and all who love our country's freedom may well reverence the memory of those martyred Quakers by whose death and agony the battle in New England has been won.

—Brooks Adams, *The Emancipation of Massachusetts*

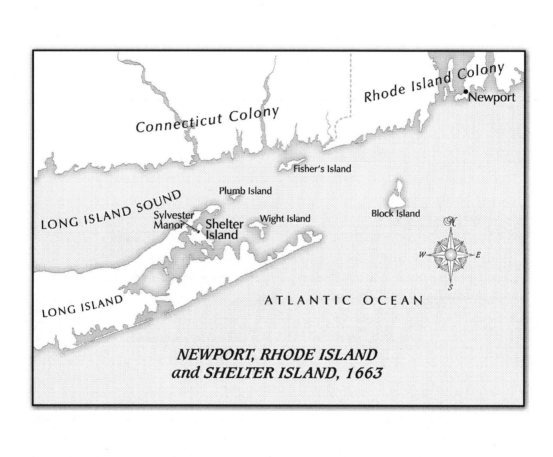

Connecticut Colony

Rhode Island Colony

•Newport

Fisher's Island

Plumb Island

LONG ISLAND SOUND

Block Island

Sylvester
Manor

Shelter
Island

Wight Island

LONG ISLAND

ATLANTIC OCEAN

**NEWPORT, RHODE ISLAND
and SHELTER ISLAND, 1663**

Chapter 1

NEWPORT, RHODE ISLAND COLONY

May (3rd Month) 1663

The Rhode Island coast slowly materialized from the overcast, as the *Sea Witch* made her steady approach. Rain kept Mary, Allie, and Anne below deck, and the weather reflected their mood. They packed and tidied in silence, for none had the heart for superficial chatter. In a matter of hours, they would be on shore. No doubt the Newport Friends would give them a warm welcome, but it was hard not to mourn an end to the informal ease and fellowship they had enjoyed the past ten days, since leaving Salem.

When nothing was left to preoccupy the women below, they donned their shawls and opened the hatch to catch a breath of air, moist though it might be. They watched the coastline grow from a dark line on the western horizon to a looming presence. Trees, rocks, and sand became distinct, then signs of human habitation—buildings, docks, fenced fields. A pall of smoke from the town's chimneys mingled with the low clouds and hung like a canopy over Newport.

As they neared the mouth of the harbor, traffic increased, and Edward maneuvered into the flow of vessels, putting the southerly wind astern. He angled for the wharf kept by his friend William Reape, whose merchant shipping business was similar to that of the Salem men though considerably larger. Will was an active member of the Religious Society of Friends and, like Edward, often ferried missionaries as well as goods along the New England coast. Will's faith was undaunted by his arrest at a meeting at Sandwich in the Plimoth Colony and the resultant flogging and imprisonment at Plymouth two years prior in 1661. He and his wife Sarah would give the missionaries a warm reception and be sympathetic to Mary's tender condition.

They docked smoothly, reefing the sails and sculling into a vacant berth at the pier. George secured the lines then hailed a lad and gave him a coin to take a message to the Reapes' home, alerting Will and Sarah of their arrival. The rain let up, and the Friends sat on deck, observing the activity of the landing while they waited. Several vessels were tied up at Will Reape's three piers, and one was being loaded for imminent departure.

"Will is here in Newport, at least, for that is his sloop," Edward said, nodding towards a handsome thirty-six-foot craft with three sails, bearing the name *Reapes' Gain* on its transom.

"Tell us something of the Reapes, Edward," Mary urged, her mood lightening as she contemplated meeting the Newport Friends.

Edward and George exchanged a glance.

"They are an energetic couple," he answered, smiling.

"Will scarce keeps his seat to eat a meal!" George added. "He is ever active."

"They came to Newport by way of Barbados in '55, the same year I immigrated to Salem," Edward said.

"Do they have children?" Anne asked.

"Yes, two," he answered but his face darkened, and he sighed before elaborating. "Their son, Little Will, is simple. They fear his mind shall never mature, though he live to an old age."

"What is his age now?" the little missionary pressed.

"Five years," George answered, "but he cannot feed or dress himself, and only his family can comprehend his speech."

"He is docile but requires constant care and supervision," Edward added quietly.

"Their daughter Sarah is but three and manages him better than any adult," George elaborated. "They are a loving family, and Dr. Cranston does what he can to keep the boy in good health, though he is prone to illness."

"It must be a constant trial for them," Allie murmured.

"They do not appear unduly tried," Edward said. "They take it in course and carry on with good cheer."

"God bless them for it," Anne added fervently.

"I believe He has," George smiled with a gesture to the busy landing. "They prosper well here."

Within a quarter hour the lad returned with the news that the Master was not at home, but Mistress Reape would welcome them. The Friends battened down the shallop and headed off, laughing as their legs adjusted to land. Edward and George were unburdened, as they planned to sleep on the boat. Providing overnight accommodation for three unexpected guests was quite enough to ask of their hosts. The women had few possessions left after their ordeals in the Bay Colony, and their satchels were light. Still, Edward took Mary's bag without comment, knowing her back was still tender from the flogging in Hampton ten days past. She gave him a grateful smile. The sun came out as they made their way up Maple Avenue, and the house was not far.

The Reapes' lot was pleasantly situated on the outskirts of the town's center and was surrounded by a brick wall, four feet high topped with ornate ironwork. A servant awaited them at the gate, greeting the guests politely and showing them into the house. Mary admired the broad lawn, ornamental bushes, and flower gardens bright with tulips imported from Holland. The glint of light on water from behind the house caught her eye before they reached the porch and the wide front door. Later she would learn it was Coddington Cove.

Sarah Reape greeted them with genuine warmth, particularly delighted to entertain female visitors.

"Welcome and well met!" she exclaimed, coming to greet them, as they entered the house.

Their hostess was as tall as Allie with a classic English complexion and delicate features. Mary was gratified that Sarah appeared unperturbed by Anne's abnormal appearance. People were usually taken aback by her humped shoulder, small stature, and long face with perpetually half-closed eyes, but Sarah grasped the little missionary's hands and bent to kiss her cheeks without hesitation; indeed, her next remark was addressed to Anne directly.

"Will's guests are usually men of business or sea captains, and they discuss ships and trade and taxes to the exclusion of all else," she laughed, rolling her eyes.

"Guilty as charged!" George replied with a grin.

"But in this instance, we women may ignore them and go our merry way," she finished mischievously.

"As is our custom," Allie responded. The missionary women smiled. Sarah Reape would be fine company.

William Reape joined them in the spacious drawing room as they were enjoying a sumptuous tea with lemon cake and pastries stuffed with dried apples, sugar, and cinnamon. The travelers savored the hot tea and fresh sweets, after ten days of cold fare at sea.

"Forgive my absence," Will said after greetings were exchanged. "I was at a meeting of investors to discuss the acquisition of land for a new settlement."

Edward was immediately interested. "Whereabouts?" he asked.

"The boundaries are not yet established," Will prevaricated, accepting a steaming cup from Sarah, "but it is an untouched tract across Achter Kol—a narrow strait west of Staten Island," he elaborated for his female guests. "Friend William Goulding lives in Flushing and is familiar with the area. 'Twas he who first told me of the project and sought my help in recruiting folk from Newport to settle there. He deems three points of land are ripe for settlement with lush marshland and virgin forests. The region is currently used seasonally for fishing by the Navesink tribe, so we must negotiate a price with them, but we need more investors. That is our first order of business."

"I may be interested, but I should like to see it first," Edward said.

George sat up. "Thou wouldst leave Salem?" he asked alarmed.

"As an investment only, George, I assure thee," Edward answered.

"And a wise one it is!" Will opined. "A number of Friends at Flushing and Gravesend are for it, as they say Long Island is becoming crowded, and they are sick of harassment on account of their beliefs."

"Are they not beyond the reach of the Puritans so far south? Who harasses them?" Mary asked.

"Their Governor Stuyvesant—or Director General, as the Dutch put it," Will answered. "All the townships on western Long Island are part of the New Netherland Colony and subject to Dutch rule. Robert Hodgson was the first Public Friend to visit Flushing in '57. Stuyvesant arrested him, and Friend Hodgson was severely flogged at New Amsterdam. They took him from a meeting at Henry Townsend's home and fined Henry for entertaining him. When Townsend refused to pay, they jailed him as well, and all of Flushing rose up in protest. Their clerk, Edward Hart, wrote up a document defining their right to religious freedom that was signed by their sheriff and twenty-eight others. They called it the Flushing Remonstrance."

"The Friends heard of it at Salem," George said, sitting forward. "It did state the right of all men to choose their religion according to their consciences."

"'Twas not unlike the Portsmouth Compact drawn up by John Clarke and the followers of Anne Hutchinson in '37, when the founders of Rhode Island were banished from Boston," Will added.

"But did the folk at Flushing prevail? Was their Remonstrance accepted?" Anne Coleman asked.

Will shook his head. "The town clerk and the sheriff were arrested, and Stuyvesant replaced them with his own appointees. Fiske—the sheriff—apologized to the authorities and was pardoned, but Friend Hart penned the document and would not bend. He was banished, as were many that signed it."

"But where could they go?" Allie asked.

"Any of the English towns further northeast on Long Island would accept them gladly. Although the Dutch claim that territory, they would not pursue them there, and the inhabitants consider themselves part of the New Haven Colony," Will answered. "However, most of those banished have ignored the order and remain at home with their families. Mark ye, even after the first wave of arrests, the Flushing Friends continued to meet openly at John Bowne's home, until he too was jailed. Governor Stuyvesant sought to change Friend Bowne's opinion on religion and sent a Puritan minister to his cell to sway him, but he remained steadfast, insisting upon his right to worship according to his conscience." Will chuckled. "They even left the door of his cell open, hoping the prisoner might leave of his own accord, but John refused to walk away unless guaranteed that right. Stuyvesant kept him all summer, thinking he would relent, but Friend Bowne proved more stubborn. There was no way to be rid of the man, short of banishment, thus in the end Old Peg Leg—that's Stuyvesant, mind you—put Bowne on a ship bound for England. His wife Hannah finally had word from him this past Tenth Month. He debarked at Ireland, avoiding England altogether." Will gave a bark of laughter. "No chance of a Friend appealing for freedom of conscience there! His letter said he would take ship for Amsterdam to appeal his case in person before the High Mightinesses of the WIC—the West India Company. They govern the colony of New Netherlands, mind ye. I only wish I could be there to see it!" He smiled and drained his cup.

"Do they still have meetings at Flushing?" Mary asked, concerned for the community of Friends.

"Oh yes!" Will told her. "The Friends of Flushing are not easily cowed. They meet secretly in the woods now. However, you can understand why many have invested in the Monmouth Project. They wish to be out from under Stuyvesant's Calvinist thumb."

Allie smiled, "Thou art well informed of opinions on Long Island, Will," she commented.

"Indeed, he is!" Sarah exclaimed. "He spends more time plying his trade there than he does in Newport. Ye are fortunate to have found him home!"

Mary studied her hostess for signs of resentment at this proclamation but found none. Sarah seemed amused, and Will nodded cheerfully and returned her smile.

"However, I warrant our guests would favor some time to rest before the evening meal. Shall I show you to your room?" she asked the three women.

"That would be lovely, and it please thee," Mary answered for even the short walk had tired her.

"And I must hie myself to the landing," Will said, setting aside his empty cup and standing. "The *Trident* is departing, and I would speak with the captain first. Shall ye accompany me, gentlemen?"

"We noted a vessel being loaded, when we docked," Edward said, as he and George rose.

The latter caught Mary's eye and raised an eyebrow as if to say, "As I said, he is never still for long."

She smiled, and George winked, as he passed her chair. The men left, and the women went upstairs. Sarah Reape noted the missionaries' small satchels.

"I assume ye have trunks aboard Edward's vessel," she said. "We can send a cart for them."

"That would be a fair distance for a cart!" Allie grinned.

"Our trunk is at Kittery Point with the Shapleighs," Mary explained. "We have no other baggage."

Sarah looked from one to the other in disbelief.

"We carry very little, when we travel," Anne elucidated.

"Each time we are arrested and flogged, our clothing is ruined, and they confiscate our things," Mary added. "These clothes were given us by the Hampton Friends two weeks ago."

"Ye have only what ye are wearing?" Sarah asked appalled.

"Oh no," Allie responded, upending the meagre contents of her satchel onto the bed. "We have extra smallclothes and stockings."

Sarah blanched. "One dress and..." Her voice trailed off as she plucked a shift from the bed and held it between thumb and forefinger. "But these are winter weight," she protested. "Ye require clothing for the summer weather—at least two of everything."

"Our wardrobe has been the least of our concerns," Mary told her with a gentle smile.

Their hostess marshaled her amazement. "I understand," she said, already imagining what she could spare and which of the Newport Friends might match her guests in size. "We shall soon remedy this sorry situation," she added, heading for the door. She turned and smiled. "As Will would say, it shall be our first order of business."

Chapter 2

NEWPORT, RHODE ISLAND COLONY

May (3rd Month) 1663

Two days later there was a meeting for worship at Nicholas Easton's home on Farewell Street, and Sarah Reape intended to make good on her promise to supplement the missionaries' wardrobe. It was a fine morning, and their destination was less than a mile away, so the Reapes and their guests walked. Little Will and three-year-old Sarah had taken to Anne Coleman, as all children did. They led the procession with the little missionary and their nursemaid Enna, holding their hands. The young woman was the daughter of one of Will's Dutch business associates at Gravesend. She had been with them since little Sarah was born, and the Reapes considered her part of the family. Enna was calm and strong—two essentials in Little Will's care—and most important, the children loved her.

The Eastons' good-daughter Mehitable welcomed them at the door and relieved them of their hats and cloaks.

"Merry is married to John, the Eastons' eldest son," Sarah Reape informed her guests quietly as they joined the assembly in the large main hall.

The Friends of Newport had been enjoying regular meetings without harassment for five years. They were well organized. There was no chatting as people congregated and settled into silence intent on connecting with the Light Within. Social interaction came after worship.

The meeting refreshed Mary's spirit, but once it ended, the three missionaries became the focus of interest. The Newport Friends knew Edward and George, so when Sarah Reape introduced Mary, Allie, and Anne as Public Friends from

England, they were barraged with questions. Everyone was hungry for news from the mother country.

While her guests were thus engaged, Sarah Reape drew her closest friends aside and told them of the missionaries' lack of proper clothing. She invited them for the noon meal after the fittings to make the occasion more festive. Nicholas' wife, Christiana Easton, accepted on the spot, and the others followed suit: her good-daughter Mehitable, whom everyone called Merry; Hannah, wife of Francis Brinley, an investor in the Monmouth Project; and Ann Brinley Coddington, William Coddington's wife and sister to Francis. Ann Coddington was in an advanced stage of pregnancy and was particularly enthusiastic. With eight weeks to her prospective due date, her confinement would soon begin. She welcomed an outing. Normally she was Mary's size and had several garments that had not been altered to suit her condition.

"May I bring my daughter Mary, as well?" Ann asked. "She is very mature for her nine years, and I would like her to keep company with these brave and dedicated women. They are an example to us all."

Sarah agreed readily, and the Reapes and their guests left the Eastons' soon after, when the children became restless.

Sarah's friends arrived at the Reape house late the next morning in a flurry of trunks and boxes, which took the servants half an hour to carry upstairs. Dresses, skirts, jackets, and blouses were spread across the missionaries' beds according to size—the largest for Allie, mediums for Mary, and the smallest for Anne, courtesy of nine-year-old Mary Coddington. The missionaries were not shy about stripping down to their small clothes to try on various articles, but the easy chatter died as their backs were revealed. All three bore the scars of repeated flogging, but Mary's more recent stripes were still a livid pink.

Little Mary could not contain her shock. "Oh!" she gasped. "Does it yet pain thee?"

The girl broke a shocked silence, and her mother made to hush her, but Mary Tomkins answered frankly.

"It itches, and the skin feels tight when I move, but it no longer hurts," she told the girl.

"All of Newport applauds your courage and fortitude," Christiana told the missionaries fervently.

"God is our courage and our strength," Anne responded. "Abuse to the body does not scar the soul."

"Brave words. Yet I believe I could not endure such pain and humiliation," Merry Easton said with a shudder.

"Nor should you!" Mary assured her. "As missionaries, we prepare for it. Our training took years."

"This one favors me, I warrant," Allie announced, bringing attention back to the matter at hand.

She had donned one of Sarah's dresses, for their hostess nearly matched her in height. The hem and cuffs needed letting down, but the forest green suited her eyes and dark hair, and exclamations of admiration ensued. There was no more talk of suffering.

Following the luncheon with Sarah Reape's friends, the missionaries received a flurry of invitations to social engagements. As Mary still tired quickly, they chose only one. Edward suggested accepting the Eastons' invite to dinner, as the women had already met Christiana and Merry.

"They are easy company," he told Mary. "Nicholas was persecuted by the Bay Colony authorities before he came here. He will be sympathetic to thy condition and will understand if we depart early."

The Reapes were included in the invitation, and the seven Friends walked the now familiar route to Farewell Street. The sun was lowering, but the air was mild and perfumed with the first lilacs. The lane was peaceful with the constant noise of the harbor muted by the buildings between. Mary relished the excuse to take Edward's arm, and they ambled along, enjoying the warmer weather.

When the guests arrived, they found the six Eastons already gathered. Nicholas and his sons had built the first house in Newport in 1638, but it had burned down three years later. The replacement started as a modest four-room dwelling, but a spacious wing had been added in recent years. The Eastons enjoyed entertaining socially as well as providing a location for the Newport Friends to meet.

Although he appeared younger, Nicholas Easton was seventy. He was an influential citizen of Newport, serving twice as President of the four major Rhode Island towns of Providence, Portsmouth, Newport, and Warwick; however, he was first and foremost a devout Friend and sympathetic to any who endured the wrath of the Puritans.

"A toast to our brave guests!" he proposed, as all held up cups of cider, ale, or spirits. They drank.

"I was saddened but not surprised to hear of your suffering in the Bay Colony," their host went on. "It would appear things have not changed these twenty years past. But I warrant John Norton's untimely death is proof that God does not approve their bloody laws." He shook his head ruefully.

"Who was John Norton?" Anne Coleman asked.

"One of the Puritan ministers at Boston's First Church," Nicholas answered darkly.

"Father misliked Norton from the first," John Easton explained, "even before he excommunicated Anne Hutchinson. He influenced both Winthrop and Endicott to uphold his zealous opinions and act on them."

"I wager 'twas his hand that writ the so-called Quaker laws," his father opined.

Mary was loath to dwell on that subject this evening and diverted her host with a question.

"I am curious, Friend Easton. How didst thou learn of our trials in the Bay Colony?"

"We received a letter from Dr. Walter Barefoote, describing your punishment at Dover and Hampton, and your release in Salisbury, thanks to Robert Pike. The message also called upon Public Friends to protest in the towns north of Boston," Nicholas answered.

"Mary assisted Walter with the wording, and Allie penned the copies," Anne Coleman told him.

"I thought I detected a woman's hand!" Christiana exclaimed. "I correspond regularly with Catharine Scott in Providence on this side of the Atlantic and Margaret Fell at Ulverston in England," she went on. "I also receive and send letters for our traveling brothers and sisters when they need to communicate with Friend Fox via Swarthmore Hall. But we learned of your third protest at Hampton from Isaac Perkins. His letter arrived just days before you. He said the Friends did stand witness to your punishment in that town."

Mary asked, "Lydia's father wrote thee about us?"

"Why yes," their hostess replied. "I have the letter, if thou wouldst read it after dinner."

"We are gratified that thou dost offer this means of communication, Friend Easton," Mary said warmly. "We must post a report to Margaret Fell ourselves, but I would also like to alert Catharine Scott of our arrival. She and I have corresponded for three years, and I am eager to meet her."

"Certes! The Scotts are dear friends," Christiana responded. "We entertain them whenever they come to Newport. But call me Christiana, and it please you," she said, smiling at each of the three women. "The use of my Christian name helps me imagine I am still of an age with you!"

They all laughed, and Mary did not remark the silent exchange between Nicholas and his son John at the mention of Lydia Perkins Wardell.

They settled around the large dining table, and after the blessing, the Easton men regaled their guests with anecdotes of their first year in the Colonies. Before the family moved to Newbury their neighbors at Ipswich had been Richard and Catharine Scott, Anne and Simon Bradstreet, and Anne's parents, the Dudleys.

"There were some fine folk at Newbury," Nicholas said, "and they welcomed us, as they had need of settlers. The Emery brothers and Thomas Wardell—Eli's father— helped us build and became good friends, but I realized I was no Puritan, when they excommunicated Anne Hutchinson later that year."

He paused, and his audience waited patiently. All of them had heard of the Antinomian controversy, but this was a first-hand account, and they were rapt.

"The spark that lit the tinder was a sermon that John Wheelwright preached one Sabbath afternoon in the late autumn of '36," he went on. "Although he spoke meta-phorically, Winthrop and his ministers took it literally as a call to revolt. Wheelwright was married to one of Anne Hutchinson's sisters, mind ye, so Winthrop thought they were in league to oust him from power. The young minister had no such intent, and many of us signed a letter declaring so in his defense, but the Governor was so threat-ened, he banished all who supported the Hutchinsons. 'Twas preposterous! Seventy men and their families were disenfranchised, stripped of freeman status and weapons, and turned out in March of '37. Most went south, following Roger Williams who was banished the year before, but the boys and I followed Wheelwright north. He went to consult the folk at Dover about land for a new settlement, while we settled at Hampton." He sighed. "However, within a few months they found us. We were summoned to appear at the Court in Boston, thus we left everything we had built—again—and came south to Portsmouth. We called it Pocasset then. Unfortunately, conflict devel-oped in the new settlement within the first year. We sided with Coddington's faction, which included John Clarke and the Hutchinsons, among others and removed to the southern tip of Aquidneck Island. Thus, was Newport born, and we have been here ever since."

"Wert thou with them, Christiana?" Anne asked.

"Only at the last. We married at Pocasset in '38," she answered. "My husband Thomas Beecher was lost at sea that year, and I found myself with three small children and a younger brother to care for. Our father did not survive the crossing from England thus James was my responsibility." She smiled at her husband. "Nicholas did not hesitate to take us all on."

"I enjoy children," Nicholas grinned. "My boys were grown by then, and I got a whole new family, as well as a wonder of a wife." The elder Eastons beamed at each other across the table.

The dinner plates were replaced with platters of cheese and bowls of nuts, and Madeira wine was poured for those who wished it. The talk turned to a windmill that Peter Easton planned to build.

"We need a gristmill near town," he asserted. "'Tis long overdue."

"How shall the cap be turned?" Will Reape asked, intrigued as always with the details of a project.

"With a gear wheel and chain mechanism rather than a tail pole," Easton's eldest son replied.

"Shall the building be of wood or stone?" Edward asked, equally engaged.

"There is local stone aplenty," Peter answered, "as well as lime and sand for the mortar."

Once this topic was exhausted, the company was quiet for some moments, as two servants cleared the table. When they withdrew, John gave his father a significant look, and Nicholas nodded.

The young man cleared his throat and said, "I recently returned from a journey north to conclude some business for my father, and I chanced upon your acquaintance, Friend Lydia Wardell."

All three missionaries straightened, surprised. "Lydia?" Mary asked.

John nodded. "'Twas the first Sabbath Day in May. I was breaking my fast at Trickey's ordinary in Newbury when she came in. She recognized me for a Friend, and we struck up a conversation."

"That was but a week after our protest at Hampton," Allie said.

John nodded. "She confided that she was answering a call to protest the false clergy. I offered my assistance, but she only wanted me to accompany her to the steps of the Newbury Church, where we parted ways." He paused. "I did not realize her protest would be so…extreme."

Mary's scalp prickled at his tone. She recalled her young friend's erratic behavior at their final meeting in April. Mary had assumed Lydia was upset at being forced to leave Hampton by the Puritan minister Seaborn Cotton. She had seemed distracted, both tense and melancholy by turns. Seemingly out of the blue, Lydia asked Mary how one recognized a divine call, but she had said nothing of making a public protest. Now Mary berated herself for not realizing her young friend's intent. Questions crowded her mind, but her throat constricted with dread, and she could not speak.

It was Anne Coleman who asked, "What did she do?"

John paused, placing his palms on the table before looking up. "She appeared sky-clad in the Newbury Church," he told them.

John had related the encounter to his father and stepmother, so the Eastons did not react as strongly as their guests, who stared at him in shock.

"I recall hearing of a similar instance back in England in my youth," Nicholas supplied, filling the heavy silence, "but it was two Puritan men. I believe 'tis meant as a protest against the spiritual nakedness of the ministers."

Mary was overcome with guilt and anguish. Had Lydia been influenced by their protests? Just the week before she had witnessed Mary's flogging at Hampton, and seen Allie and Anne stocked for speaking out against the Reverend Seaborn Cotton—and they had been fully clothed. How much worse had their young friend suffered for appearing naked in a house of God? Edward was next to her and took Mary's hand under the table. She looked at him, and he shook his head slightly as though sensing her guilt.

"What did they do to her?" Allie asked quietly.

John was loath to answer, but all eyes were on him, and Mary nodded, urging him to respond.

"A few days after I had met her, I concluded Father's business and stayed a night at the Emerys' inn at Newbury on my way home. John told me they took her to the Quarterly Court at Ipswich. He was there to pay a fine for entertaining Friends and witnessed her trial and punishment."

The missionaries exchanged horrified looks at this news. The Emerys had taken them in for two months that spring and refused any payment for room and board. Under John's roof they held meetings for worship and planned their protest to expose Reverend Cotton. Hampton's greedy minister had plagued the Wardells—both Friends—with fines for absences from his church. When they could not pay in coin, he confiscated valuable livestock, seed corn, and crops. After more than two years of this, the young couple was ruined. No doubt the minister's harassment spurred Lydia to act, but had their protests emboldened her, as well? In any case, the missionaries now knew that the Emery family had also suffered on their account.

"John Emery told me he tried to pay her fine," the younger Easton continued, "but the court would not permit it. Her crime was too heinous. The magistrates insisted she be publicly flogged."

"How many stripes?" Mary asked, recovering her voice.

John Easton eyed her warily and hesitated. The magistrates had ordered Lydia to be flogged "to the satisfaction of the crowd," but since the court met at noon in a tavern, most of the crowd were men and youths at their midday meal. They had become raucous with drink and made sport of her punishment. He could not bear to tell her that.

"Ten? Fifteen?" she pressed.

"John Emery said 'twas twenty-five," he told her reluctantly.

Mary's composure crumpled, and she covered her face with her hands. Allie rose to comfort her.

"Forgive me for upsetting—" John began.

"'Tis best we learn of it from friends," Allie smiled ruefully over Mary's head, as she embraced her.

"Lydia witnessed our punishments at Dover and Hampton thrice this past year. We cannot help but fear our example may have set her on this path," Anne Coleman added, reading Mary's anguish perfectly.

"She was determined." John shook his head. "Had I known her intent—" He broke off, then added, "I also feel responsible, although I doubt anyone could have swayed her. She did not even tell her husband."

"On a happier note," Nicholas put in kindly, "the Wardells are removing here to Rhode Island, as soon as Lydia can travel."

"Yes," John added eager to lighten the mood, "John Emery said as much. They are coming by wagon and should arrive by the end of Fourth Month, God willing."

Will Reape perked up. "Mayhap the Wardells shall wish to join our new settlement," he said.

Mary straightened from Allie's embrace, drying her eyes with the handkerchief tucked up her sleeve. She gratified her hosts with a brave smile. "They shall find good friends and a warm welcome at trail's end," she said.

As the dinner guests prepared to walk back to the Reapes' house, Edward helped Mary with her cloak and read the signs of exhaustion on her face. He knew she felt responsible for Lydia's suffering, and the guilt affected her keenly in her weakened state. When the wide front door closed behind them, he offered his arm, and she took it gratefully. Edward kept his eyes on the lane to avoid the puddles left by yesterday's rain, and they walked slowly in the muted light of the gloaming.

The others were soon some distance ahead, their voices drifting back on the still evening air.

"Are you quite all right, Mary?" he asked quietly.

She looked up at him, and he stopped to meet her eyes.

"I cannot say I am not tired," she said with a weary smile, "but my body has healed for the most part."

"And what of thy spirit?" he pressed. "Dost sleep peacefully?"

She looked down, placing her free hand on his arm. Her face was hidden by the brim of her hat.

"Thou hast come to know me too well, Edward," she said softly. Her hand tightened.

They were alone, and Edward took both her hands and waited for her to go on.

"Thou hast the right of it. 'Tis not just guilt over Lydia's plight. The ill dream has returned. It haunts me each night since—" she broke off, overcome by a flash of warmth at the memory of his embrace. She swallowed and pressed on. "—since we left the *Sea Witch*."

Without another word Edward opened his arms, and Mary took off her hat and stepped into their shelter, breathing in his scent. She had never felt so safe as when Edward held her. The nightmare of Richard Walderne had not plagued her, when she slept in his arms aboard the *Sea Witch*, cocooned in her own quilt but sharing his solid presence and warmth. Now they were back on land with all its social constraints and responsibilities. When exhaustion and guilt overwhelmed her, and she faced another sleep-addled night, she longed to return to that simpler existence. Edward understood this, but he also knew she would never abandon her call. Other men might press her to marry, but he did not. His patient understanding was one of the things she loved most about him. He held her gently, mindful of her tender back, and they took comfort from each other, then Edward stepped back to search her face.

"The Newport Friends mean well, but mayhap 'tis too soon for thee to revive thy suffering by the telling of it. Mayhap we should return to the *Sea Witch*. We could visit Shelter Island for a week or two until thou art stronger. It is peaceful there, a refuge for Friends. The Sylvester Family would welcome us."

"Shelter Island? Where our dear Mary Dyer spent her last months?" Mary asked.

He nodded and hope lit her eyes then dimmed. "But what of thy business, Edward?" she asked softly.

"I must speak with George first, but I warrant he will concur," he said. "We could go as soon as tomorrow, if it suits."

"I would like that," she answered slowly. "But what of the General Meeting?"

"That is two weeks hence. We can return for it if that is thy wish," he answered.

Mary leaned into him and sighed. "My thanks, Edward. It is a fine plan," she breathed.

He closed his eyes, savoring the rare moment of intimacy. Last winter the Puritan magistrate Richard Walderne had perverted the law and tried to murder Mary, Allie, and Anne two separate times, enlisting Dover's constables, the minister, and an elder of the church in his nefarious plans. Edward's outrage flared every time he thought of it. When he returned north, he determined to go to Dover and confront Walderne publicly, but he did not tell Mary of this plan. He would surely be arrested and whipped for it, and Edward did not wish to add to her worries.

Chapter 3

SHELTER ISLAND

May (3ʳᵈ Month) 1663

The distant boom of a signal cannon caused a brief hiatus in the cacophony of birdsong, continuous from dawn to dusk on Shelter Island. Nine-year-old Grissel Sylvester straightened, gazing across Gardiners Creek toward the deep-water harbor. Although she could not see the ships anchored there, she knew a boat had arrived. No doubt visitors would soon appear around the point of land that hid it from view.

"Giles, come out!" she called. "A ship has come!"

She headed for the landing, a causeway of rock and earth that bridged Gardiner's Creek, connecting the manor and outbuildings to the island's north peninsula with its crop fields and pastures. The rhododendron bushes trembled, and her six-year-old brother emerged from his hiding place.

"Verily?" he piped, clambering to his feet and running after her.

"Yes! Didst not hear the cannon? Now run and fetch Papa!" she commanded.

Giles scowled. His elder sister was always ordering him about. "Why must *I* go?" he challenged.

"Because thou art so much faster than I," she told him, sweetening her directive. She was adept at handling her younger sibling.

His face cleared at this concession to his superior speed, and Giles pelted off toward the manor with a will. Their father Nathaniel Sylvester was likely in his office, going over the accounts this time of day.

Grissel headed for the landing where a flatboat was being loaded with bundles of barrel staves bound for the family sugar plantations in Barbados. A line of six negroes passed the bundles from the wagon bed to the craft's wide deck, their dark skin gleaming with sweat. Mister Collins, the cooper in charge of the manufacture of the white oak staves, supervised the stacking, which was nearly done.

Hope came to Grissel's side holding two-year-old Natty on her hip. He squirmed to be let down, but the young Barbadian woman sang him a rhyme and jiggled him into submission with practiced skill. He would only get underfoot on the landing and might even run right off the narrow causeway that bridged Gardiners Creek into the water. There was no railing to impede loading anywhere along its thirty-yard length. Natty quieted and gazed at the activity, sucking his thumb. The flatboat headed for the deep- water harbor, and the wagon returned to the stable. Grissel leaned against the gate post, her eyes glued to the point, preparing to count heads as soon as a boat appeared. She hoped her Uncle Francis and Aunt Hannah Brinley might have come from Newport to see the new baby, bringing her young cousins Tom and Will. With Papa tending to the endless work of the plantation and Mama occupied with the new baby, it fell to Grissel as the eldest available Sylvester to welcome visitors, whoever they might be.

⌒⟶

A flatboat loaded with bundles of short wood passed the *Sea Witch* as Edward and George rowed into Gardiners Creek. Mary stared at the dark-skinned men poling the craft for they were a novelty to her. A white man at the sculling oar hailed them, apparently recognizing the shallop, and the Salem men returned the salute.

"That is Bernie Collins, the Sylvesters' cooper," George explained, as he and Edward resumed rowing. "Those barrel staves are on their way to Barbados. They shall be assembled there to store and ship the sugar from Constant's plantations."

"Constant is Nathaniel's elder brother," Edward added helpfully.

The *Sea Witch* rounded a peninsula, and the manor house came into view with its surrounding outbuildings. Smoke rose from several utilitarian fires, and the thwack of mauls and shouted orders reached them faintly across the water. Edward and George made for the landing, where two female figures waved a welcome. The taller was a black-skinned woman holding a small white child, while the girl at her side began to jump up and down and clap as they approached. Mary felt an unexpected pang of nostalgia, recalling her nephews. She had often hauled them around on her hip just so when she was a girl. Time and distance made the memory almost sweet.

"That is Grissel, the Sylvesters' eldest child," George informed them, as he shipped his oar and went for the bowline.

"And that is Hope, holding Nathaniel Jr," Edward added, moving astern to scull into the landing. "She and her parents came with the Sylvesters from Barbados when she was just a wee thing. Now she is near grown."

George and Edward secured the craft to the wooden posts closest to the manor and helped the three women debark by means of a conveniently placed set of stone steps. Grissel's exuberance at their arrival was tempered by commendable courtesy and warmth once they were on land. Edward embraced her and greeted Hope cordially over the little girl's head then introduced the missionaries. George plucked the wide-eyed toddler from Hope's arms and held him aloft.

"And how is little Natty? My goodness, thou hast grown like a weed!" he exclaimed.

The Salem men were no strangers to Shelter Island, and Natty was not shy. He giggled and seized George's nose, making them all laugh. As they started for the house, a male figure emerged and strode across the lawn toward them with Giles skipping at his side. Mary realized it must be their host.

"Edward Wharton and George Preston! Well met!" he greeted them heartily, shaking hands. "And who are these lovely ladies? Friends, I take it, from the look of you. Welcome, welcome to Shelter Island!" he went on, turning to the three women with a charming smile.

As Edward introduced the English missionaries, their host shook each of their hands and met their eyes with friendly curiosity. Nathaniel Sylvester was of medium height and strikingly handsome. His dark hair was going gray at the temples and his tanned face bore the lines of years in the sun and at sea, setting off strong, white teeth; however, Mary thought his most attractive feature was his air of confident good humor. He reminded her of Nicholas Shapleigh, and she liked him immediately.

They were soon comfortably seated in the family's parlor on the first floor of the large manor house. Hope settled with Natty and Giles on the floor, playing with a wooden top that Giles produced from a pocket. Grissel sat on a stool at her father's knee, and he smoothed her wind-tossed hair affectionately.

"Thy home is impressive, Friend Sylvester," Mary commented for the rooms were large and spacious, adorned with imported materials and appointments from the parquet floors to the high, corniced ceilings.

"My thanks, but I beg ye call me Nathaniel," he responded, flashing his rakish grin. "We favor informality here on the Island."

"Then thou must use our Christian names, as well, Nathaniel," Mary rejoined.

Their host nodded his agreement and went on.

"We built the house in '51, modeling the Jacobean style used in Barbados," he told them. "The bricks are Dutch made, and the manor is two stories plus an attic. The ground floor has four rooms—this parlor, a dining hall, our sleeping chamber, and my office. Cooking, laundry, bathing, and storage are in an attached wing, but we are planning to build a separate structure this summer, as the current facility is inadequate. We have grown apace since we moved here a decade ago; it seems we are always tearing down or building!" he laughed. "The entire second story is called the Long Room, where we hold more formal gatherings such as balls, concerts, and First Day meetings. Laborers who are unwed sleep in the attic, but those with families have their own dwellings. We also have a cottage for guests, as some visitors stay for weeks or even months. It is at your disposal for as long as ye wish to stay, although certes ye shall join us for meals—"

"Mama!" little Giles interrupted, jumping up.

He ran to the doorway, where a woman stood with an infant in her arms. The resemblance to her sister Ann Brinley Coddington was evident, as Grissel Sylvester had the same petite figure, creamy complexion, and dark auburn hair. She was the youngest of her siblings and serenely beautiful.

"Hello, my lovely," she crooned, cupping Giles' head with her free hand as he wrapped his arms around her waist.

All the men rose at her arrival. She smiled warmly at her guests, and Nathaniel introduced the women. Edward and George were old acquaintances, and they kissed her carefully on both cheeks over the swaddled infant she held.

"Welcome, all!" she said, settling with her husband on the settee. "I heard the signal canon and could not resist joining you." Nathaniel put his arm around her and gently stroked the baby's cheek. The tiny head swiveled toward his father's finger, mouth agape, seeking sustenance.

"This recent arrival to our family is constantly hungry!" he smiled, pushing his finger into the small fist. The baby gripped it instantly. "And he demonstrates the tenacity of a Sylvester already!"

They all laughed.

"When was he born?" Anne asked, approaching to look at the infant.

"April 26th," Grissel answered. "Near three weeks ago now."

"He looks perfect," Allie smiled, peering over Anne's head. "I hope it was a smooth delivery."

"Each one seems easier than the last, praise God!" their hostess replied.

"Yes, praise God! Our Little Miss Griss has three brothers to shepherd now," Nathaniel added, grinning at his daughter, who rolled her eyes.

There was a chorus of congratulations from the guests, as Anne and Allie resettled.

"What did you name him?" George asked.

"His name is Peter," young Grissel supplied, "but truly, Mama, a sister would be most welcome next time," she added gravely to the amusement of all.

A black woman entered with a full tray of tea things and set it on a sideboard. Her skin was so dark it seemed tinged with blue. Mary tried not to stare at this living novelty, but the woman turned and caught her gaze. She smiled and nodded once. The missionary was embarrassed to be find herself gawking like a child and blushed, but the woman's smile broadened warmly, her teeth bright against her dark skin then she turned to Grissel.

"Will there be anythin' else, Mistress?" she asked. Her voice was low and deferential, but her eyes sparkled with amusement. Grissel smiled back.

"That will be all for now, Hannah, I thank thee," she answered then turned to her daughter. "Shalt thou pour for us, my lovely? I am somewhat inconvenienced by the babe."

The girl flushed with pleasure at assuming this adult duty. She rose with dignity and hefted the steaming silver teapot with two hands, carefully pouring the first cup.

"Lemon or cream, Friend Tomkins?" she asked sweetly.

⌒⌒

The new arrivals took the time between afternoon tea and the evening meal to settle in. George and Edward rowed the *Sea Witch* away from the busy landing on the causeway and tied up to a small wooden pier that jutted into Gardiners Creek from the wide lawn on the north side of the manor. The Friends elected to sleep onboard as it was comfortable for them and less bother to their hosts. They stripped the berths to air the bedding, draping the quilts and blankets on every available space on deck. Then the travelers walked out to explore the area around the manor.

"When the weather permits, meetings for worship are held in the woods further along here," Edward told them as they took a westerly path away from the manor. At the far edge of the lawn, they passed a freshwater pond which supplied the household, and presently the path split off bearing left into the woods. Soon after Mary saw a rough circle of wooden benches in a clearing under the trees. Gardiners Creek was just visible to the right, glinting through the undergrowth. It was a tranquil spot, and Mary could easily imagine Mary Dyer sitting there, her head bowed in contemplation. Further along the path a tiny cottage nestled on the bank of the creek.

"This is where Mary Dyer nursed the Southwicks," Edward said, opening the door.

The one-room cabin appeared recently built and was simply furnished. Two narrow bedframes stood against one wall with a fireplace opposite. Across from the door a casement window with thick glass afforded a wavery view of Gardiners Creek. Mary placed her hand on the back of the rocking chair near the hearth, imagining her mentor sitting there reading to the invalids. Allie climbed partway up a short ladder to peer at a sleeping loft over the beds. It was barely wide enough for a mattress tick.

"Nathaniel had this built in the autumn of '59, when I brought Friend Dyer and the Southwicks here after our release from Boston prison. The manor is a busy place, and they needed rest and quiet, after their ordeal. The carpenters had it up in four days, and I made the window," Edward said.

"It is perfection!" Mary exclaimed, opening one of the casements and leaning out. Birdsong, droning insects, the faint lap of water at the bank, and the rustle of leaves were the only sounds.

"Peace and quiet, aplenty," Anne agreed joining her. "And to think your dear Mary Dyer lived here for a time."

"Not a very happy time, I fear," George said. "Lawrence and Cassandra did not recover from the illness engendered by regular beatings, poor food, and the noxious air of the prison. Friend Dyer and our hostess nursed them constantly, but they died within days of each other."

Mary turned. "I can think of no one I would rather have beside me in such case," she said quietly.

"The sun is lowering," Allie said. "We should get the quilts in, or they shall be damp."

The Friends withdrew, but Mary lingered a moment, reluctant to leave. Her spiritual mother's presence was so palpable, the hair on her neck prickled. She closed the door gently.

That evening the conversation ranged from the Sylvester's sugar plantations in Barbados to the ongoing struggle between Friends and the Puritan authorities. The Sylvesters were well aware of the brutality of the latter, for scores of Friends had sought refuge at Shelter Island since 1656, when the first missionary Friends came to the Colonies prompting Governor Endicott and his ministers to create the Quaker Laws.

"When we heard of the hangings, we were sore aggrieved," Nathaniel said, glancing at his wife.

Her usually serene expression darkened. "'Twas a perversion of justice! Certes, the King did not approve, once he was reinstated," she said referring to the royal mandamus of 1660 that had stopped the executions. "When William Coddington married my sister Ann in 1650, he also made me his ward. Our father urged him to take us to the colonies, as he thought it safer than England at the time. Parliament was in a shamble with Cromwell's army chasing King Charles around the country. No one could imagine how it would end. Father refused to leave our home and lands, but he lost everything when the Roundheads took over. He fled to France to serve the Prince, who, happily, is now reinstated as our monarch. Father has regained his status at court but not his properties as yet."

"My wife's father was the Royal Auditor for Charles I," Nathaniel explained. "As a Loyalist, he feared for his children. Friend Coddington was a Puritan but not a Separatist, and Father Brinley gave the union his blessing. He had the forethought to realize his daughters would be safer with him in the Colonies."

"What year didst thou come here, Grissel?" Mary asked.

"1650," their hostess answered. "We left England as soon as my sister was wed. Our younger brother Francis chose to go to Barbados to seek his fortune that year, but he joined us at Newport soon after, as the tropical climate did not suit him."

"He did stay long enough to become my friend," Nathaniel added, "for which I am ever grateful, for I met my wife through his acquaintance." He grinned at her, and she smiled back.

Mary spoke up. "Nathaniel, I would prevail upon thy knowledge of the southern colonies, as our mission takes us there. How is it for Friends in Virginia of late?"

Their host sobered. "We hear they are being imprisoned and sorely fined there, since Governor Berkeley instituted the anti-Quaker laws in '60. Also, Governor Stuyvesant has ever harassed the Friends on Long Island—surprising, as the Dutch are normally tolerant where religion is concerned."

"Maryland is different, though," Grissel put in. "There are new settlements of Friends there on the Eastern Shore. Cecil Calvert, the Second Lord Baltimore, encouraged their endeavor for he is more concerned with establishing the southern boundary between his colony and Virginia than he is with people's religion. He himself is Catholic, and the family endured religious persecution in England. Thus, people may worship as they please in his domain."

The three missionaries exchanged a glance, and Mary said, "Then we shall hope to visit there soon."

"Have a care, if ye do," Nathaniel cautioned. "Virginia yet contends its northern boundary with Maryland, and the Cavaliers are as fanatic as the Puritans of New England on religion."

"We came to the Colonies to take up Mary Dyer's cause," Mary responded. "She was our mentor, and we are called to stand against the abuse of justice, as she did."

"Oh! Ye knew Mary Dyer?" Grissel exclaimed, leaning forward.

"She was the instrument of our convincement and encouraged us to become missionaries," Mary replied.

"She was a spiritual mother to us both," Allie added.

"This visit is especially important to us because we know she spent her last months here," Mary went on, "and that ye nursed the Southwicks together."

Grissel's face clouded. "Poor Lawrence and Cassandra! Their advanced age did not spare them from abuse in the Bay Colony, and we were unable to save them. We put them to rest in the family graveyard."

"The Puritans have no regard for the elderly," Nathaniel said, shaking his head in disgust. "They were not only imprisoned and beaten, but they also lost everything they had built at Salem—house, land, Lawrence's glass business and animal stock. They were ruined."

"And whilst their parents were in prison, the Boston authorities tried to deport their two youngest children to Barbados to be sold as slaves!" Grissel fumed. "Can you imagine?"

"A tragedy worthy of the Bard!" George said ruefully. "But their villainous plan was thwarted, for no ship's captain would be party to so heinous an act," he added for the missionaries' benefit.

Nathaniel raised his cup. "Let us toast the integrity of good men!" he declared.

"And women," Grissel added with a smile and nod to her female guests, as they all drank.

Chapter 4

SHELTER ISLAND

May (3rd Month) 1663

On their first full day on Shelter Island the missionaries rose early, as Nathaniel had promised to take them on a tour. At the dining table over platters heaped with fried ham steak, steaming cornbread, warmed molasses, and pots of both coffee and tea, their host explained that although Shelter Island was aptly named as a refuge for Friends, he denied credit for the appellation.

"It was named by the Manhasset, the original inhabitants of the island," he said, spearing a piece of ham with his knife. "They called it 'Ahaquatawamok' meaning 'island sheltered by islands.'"

"Are they still here?" Allie asked in her direct manner. She was curious to see how these Indians might differ from the friends they had made at Kittery.

"Oh yes," Nathaniel answered. "There is a village on the southeast shore, and a number of the residents are employed here. Our stable master is a Manhasset. The men supplement our diet with fish and game, and the women are skillful tenders of the soil and gather shellfish for *wampum*."

"I have heard that word, *wampum*, but what is it exactly?" Anne Coleman asked.

Nathaniel leaned forward on his elbows. "'Tis a form of currency here—cylindrical beads carved from the central columella of clam shells. The Manhasset women are skilled at producing it. European coin is rare in the Colonies, so *wampum* is an alternative. The Dutch call it *seawant* and say 'tis the mother of the beaver trade because the Haudenosaunee of the northern territories are eager to exchange pelts for it, but the name comes from the Algonquian word *wampumpeague*. Our Manhasset pay tribute in *wampum* to the stronger tribes of the north, since the plague of '33 decimated their numbers and weakened them. The beads are strung on standard fathom lengths—six feet—each holding over three hundred beads. Among the Indians the more wampum one wears, the higher one's status. It requires some skill to manufacture."

At that moment, Hannah appeared, announcing the horses were waiting out front.

"Capital!" their host replied, and they all trooped outside.

The plantation encompassed the entire island of eight thousand acres, plus pastureland on Robert's Island. Nathaniel told them three hundred were cleared for pasture, cultivation, and buildings; the rest was woodland, marsh, and inarable coastline. The numerous outbuildings were clustered about the manor on ten acres of contiguous land, and the sounds of various labors rang in the morning air.

The weather was mild, and the May sun was a blessing on head and shoulders. Their mounts were saddled and ready, their reins held by three black-skinned youths. The area at the front of the house was paved with stone laid out in a pleasing pattern of alternating large and small cobbles. Mary thought it ingenious for avoiding spring mud or inconvenient puddles at the entrance. There were seven glossy horses, including one to carry a servant and refreshments, as they would be gone most of the day. The grooms assisted the women in mounting up. The missionaries had not been a-horse since the winter before on the grueling trip from Dover to Hampton. It was not a happy association, but they were soon distracted by the sights.

Nathaniel proudly showed off the warehouse, the stable, the grist mill, the sawmill, cider presses, the large two-story barn, and the salt house for curing fish and meat. They crossed the causeway and rode past recently planted vegetable gardens—one for the house, one for export to Barbados, and one their host called "the Negro garden." They smelled the hog pens before they saw them, but these soon gave way to orchards of fruit trees—apple, pear, peach, and cherry—blooming and a-buzz with bees. Beyond were new-sown fields which Nathaniel told them were planted in oats, wheat, and rye. Further on they saw a dozen Indian women planting corn in hills between stumps of freshly harvested white oak. The Manhassets straightened and watched the riders pass with grave expressions.

They rode on until cultivated fields gave way to extensive pastureland, and Mary noted sheep, cattle, and horses grazing in the distance. Then the lane entered woodlands thick with white oak, elm, beech, and locust trees. Nathaniel suggested they each break off a leafy branch to keep the insects from worrying their horses' ears and eyes, as the bugs were a plague in the woods. Soon a rhythmic sound punctuated the constant birdsong, and Mary recognized the whack of axes. The laborers soon came into view. Nathaniel kept moving to spare his guests being eaten alive, but he turned in his saddle to explain the process of harvesting white oak for barrel staves. Mary recalled the flatboat they had passed on arrival, bearing the bundles to a ship in the deep-water harbor.

As the sun reached its zenith, they came out of the woods at a crescent-shaped beach on the north side of the island. There was a cool breeze, and the mosquitos were not so fierce on the open strand. After a brief consultation, they decided to stop for refreshment. The Barbadian Jacquero set baskets and jugs on a rug on the sand, and the women unpacked the food and drink. The big man then began to lead the horses off to drink at a nearby stream. Without comment Edward took the reins of three of the seven mounts and accompanied him. Jacquero's eyes widened in surprise, then he inclined his head in thanks.

"Is Shelter Island part of a mainland colony?" Anne asked Nathaniel as they ate.

"Oh no!" he answered emphatically. "I should never consent to being governed by the English! I was raised in Holland, and my parents were quite content there. Technically, this island is Dutch, like the rest of Lange Eylandt." Mary noted his use of the Dutch name. "We pay Stuyvesant a tax of one lamb per year, and we have the same rights as any town."

"How much livestock do you have, Nathaniel?" Mary wondered recalling the herds they had seen.

"Interesting that ye should ask, since we just did an inventory this month past," he smiled. "There are four hundred sheep, forty horses (half of which are mine, and half belong to the partners), two hundred cattle, above an hundred swine, and a deal of domestic fowl. We are unsure of the latter, as they reproduce and move about so quickly, 'tis a chore to count them," Nathaniel laughed.

"Verily, the yield must be more than what is needed here," Mary said. "What dost thou do with it all?"

"We provision our plantations in Barbados, which are managed by my elder brother Constant," their host answered. "He has two and is considering the purchase of another. They require food since all arable land there is put into cane. And, as you saw earlier, we keep them supplied with barrel staves to store and ship the sugar—or the rum they make from it. Our white oak is the best in the world for that."

Once the horses were watered and secured to a picket line, Edward returned, helped himself to a leg of cold chicken, and settled on the sand beside Mary. She was considering the workers they had seen, dark-skinned slaves from Barbados, local Indians, and European immigrants at a variety of tasks—building a new dairy and cooking addition, finishing the spring planting, smoking meat or salting fish, shearing sheep, fishing, harvesting oak bolts, and manufacturing barrel staves. The skilled workers—coopers, sawyers, and blacksmiths—seemed to be English or Dutch, but they were a minority.

"Nathaniel, how many people are in thy employ?" Mary asked.

"Currently there are some twenty Negro servants, if one counts the children," Nathaniel answered. "The Manhasset come and go as they please—about a dozen can be counted upon. There are seven skilled laborers, not counting their families. They are Dutch, English, and one French Huguenot."

"It seems a daunting task to supervise them all!" Anne opined.

"Indeed, it is!" Nathaniel responded, "but I answer to no one except the partners—my elder brother Constant and Thomas Middleton. Excepting major investments, which must be approved by all of us, they trust me and give me free rein, which I do appreciate."

"Do the slaves not resent working alongside laborers who are paid?" Allie asked bluntly.

Nathaniel seemed unperturbed to Mary's relief, but he took his time formulating an answer.

"'Tis a peculiar mix of souls on this island," he began after a pause. "I took great care in choosing the servants that came with us." Mary noted he did not call them slaves. "There are two families—Jacquero and Hannah's is one of them—and some young men and women, who came with us as children but are now approaching marriageable age. Our association is long, and we have shared many hardships and accomplishments, but you must understand that the Barbadians are not capable of subsisting on their own, especially in this northern climate. Our children love them like siblings, and we provide their every need, so they do not require coin. God has entrusted them to my care. It is my duty to instruct them in productivity and the care of their souls. I believe success follows the approval of the Almighty. Certes we would fail without His blessing, thus I know He is pleased with our endeavors here.

"The Manhassets, on the other hand, were here when we came," their host continued. "They know this land better than I, and I have learned much from them. Their skills are of practical use—hunting, fishing, knowledge of the winds and tides, of the land and the climate, and perforce the production of *wampum*. Their assistance is crucial to the success of this plantation, but they are independent of us. They are not part of an existing system of labor, as the Barbadians are. Also, they sustain themselves and betimes provide game and fish for us, so I do pay them—in goods or *wampum*, as they wish.

"In addition, there are indentured servants from the Old Country that we employ for their skills—sawyers and coopers, joiners, blacksmiths, husbandmen, and masons. They are paid a fair rate in land or *wampum* for the standard of quality is defined by them, and they pass their knowledge on to others."

Nathaniel spread his hands. "'Tis a wondrous jumble of folk. I had thought to settle and run a provisioning plantation with ease, after ten years at sea in the employ of my family, but—" he laughed and scratched the back of his head, "I did not reckon on the complexity of managing such a diverse company. It is a constant challenge!"

"Thou didst mention the care of their souls. Do ye all worship together?" Allie inquired candidly.

Mary blessed her silently, for she had wondered, too. Were First Day meetings open to everyone?

"My immediate family follows the Society of Friends, as do ye. All are welcome to attend our meetings for worship," Nathaniel answered, equably. "but not all wish to attend, and we do not try to direct them, unless they seek guidance. Mark ye, your mentor reinforced this," he told the women. "Friend Dyer attracted more to our meetings than usual. The place in the woods was her idea, also. We share silent worship there or in the Long Room if the weather is inclement. We sing hymns and psalms. Betimes we read passages from the Bible or someone tells a story from their culture. We all appreciate some music and a good story! Both my Grissels love to sing."

"As do we," Mary responded with a smile, as Allie and Anne chorused agreement.

Nathaniel's eyes sparkled. "Then we are in for a fine service on the morrow," he said.

First Day was overcast but warm. Mary slept well on the *Sea Witch*, and her customary energy was returning. She was eager to worship at Mary Dyer's place under the trees. The Friends brought their cloaks with them in case of rain but did not wear them.

"I reckon the rain shall hold off until later this day," Nathaniel said after morning greetings were exchanged. "I for one welcome it for our newly planted crops."

The family and their guests set out for the woods as soon as they had eaten. Young Grissel and Giles took turns ringing a large cowbell along the way to signal the call to worship, and folk began to converge under the trees. The Barbadians came with their families, neatly dressed in colorful cotton clothing. As they sang the first hymn, five Manhantens quietly joined the group. Before worship Nathaniel introduced the missionaries as proteges of Mary Dyer, who was remembered with love and reverence. Her quiet dignity and deep spirituality had impressed everyone in the Shelter Island community. They had mourned her return to Boston in May of 1660, fearing she would be hanged. That fear had been realized, and now they responded to her spiritual daughters with warmth and respect.

The fellowship of their first meeting for worship and their affinity with the Sylvester Family refreshed the missionaries' spirits, while the island's lack of social pressure allowed them to relax. The many activities of the working plantation were a constant source of interest, but the five Friends also took long walks in company with Grissel and Giles, the two eldest Sylvester children, who had taken to Anne Coleman as children did. Hannah or her daughter Hope usually accompanied them. Picnicking on the banks of Gardiner Creek, they tucked up skirts or rolled up pants and went barefoot, wading in the shallows. Allie discovered that Hannah was a fount of information on local plants and their uses, and she replenished her store of medicaments with the Barbadian woman's help.

On rainy days they enjoyed conversing with their hosts and helping Grissel with lessons for the two eldest children. They admired the new baby and browsed through Nathaniel's modest library, sharing favorite passages aloud. In the evenings they sang rounds and popular tunes to the children's unbridled delight.

Even following Peter's birth, Grissel Sylvester was full of energy, laughter, and obvious joy at the liberties of life on her own island in the New World. The missionaries soon realized she was not as delicate as her cultured accent and small stature might lead one to believe. Despite being the mistress of the largest plantation in the northern colonies, Grissel nursed Peter herself. The infant needed frequent feeding and attention, but she was a devoted parent who clearly enjoyed the company of her children. Mary and Allie had an open invitation to join her in the family's chamber, so they could talk as she tended the babe. She encouraged them to hold him, evincing none of the sharp unease that Mary's sister Margaret had demonstrated with her three newborns. Their hostess was just as likely to get down on the floor and play with her children as she was to initiate a discussion about freedom of religion. The missionaries had found another sister in spirit. Nathaniel was also an enthusiastic conversationalist, but due to the endless work of the plantation, they saw him only at meals, in the evenings, and at First Day meetings after the tour of the island.

Chapter 5

PROVIDENCE, RHODE ISLAND COLONY

May (3rd Month) 1663

Catharine Scott put down the quill and flexed her fingers. Like Christiana Easton in Newport, correspondence demanded her attention nearly every day except the Sabbath. She employed a lad to deliver or collect the letters at Roger Mowry's ordinary on the waterfront. Her own sons had performed this task when they were boys, but they were in their twenties now and starting families of their own. Her five children were leaving the nest in rapid succession, it seemed, and it made her feel every one of her fifty-three years.

Her thoughts strayed inevitably to her eldest daughter Mary, living in England, and married to the dynamic young Friend Christopher Holder. Christopher was part of a group of eleven Public Friends that had come to Providence on the *Speedwell* in August of 1656. However, the ship's safe arrival turned tragic when the canoe transporting them to shore capsized. Young Sarah Gibbons drowned, as she could not swim. Her water-soaked clothes dragged her down so quickly her companions were unable to secure her body before it sank out of reach. Even in August the water was numbingly cold. Her pitiful corpse was recovered the next day at low tide, and they buried her under the willows on the Scotts' property bordering the Moshassuck River. The tragedy precluded the usual forms of polite association, creating an unusually close bond between the missionaries and the family.

Richard Scott was the first in Providence to be convinced of the new faith, and barring their son John, the family followed his lead. The Scotts' eldest daughter Mary was smitten by young Holder, and Catharine could not blame her. Not only was he confident and comely Christopher was also from an influential family and well educated in the law; however, he was committed to his calling and in no mind to settle down. He soon left to travel the Colonies initiating meetings for worship and bringing people to the Light.

When the Scotts next heard news of him, it was dire. He had gone to Boston in company with John Rous and William Robinson to protest the new law banning Quakers—a derogatory appellation for Friends used by their enemies—from entering the colonial capital. The three men were immediately imprisoned, each had an ear cropped, and they were beaten in their chains twice a week for nine weeks. Once their condition rendered them useless for labor, they were banished from the Bay Colony and released. Edward Wharton had brought the three invalids to the refuge of the Scotts' home at Providence. Their condition was deplorable, but during their convalescence, Christopher Holder and Mary Scott became engaged.

The abuse of the three young men only increased the Scotts' commitment to the Society of Friends. Outraged, Catharine had walked to Boston with Mary Dyer and her neighbor Hope Clifton to protest the new laws and the cruel treatment of her son-in-law to be. However, their plea to Governor Endicott fell on deaf ears and ended in their own punishment. The women were arrested, stripped to the waist, whipped ten stripes on their bare backs, and kept in the noxious prison at Boston for three weeks.

The next year, in the wake of their mother's punishment, Mary Scott and her twelve-year-old sister Patience made the same journey with a group of Newport Friends. They interrupted a session of the Great and General Court, and Patience amazed the Puritan authorities by entreating them to rescind the laws against Friends for their own souls' sake. In an unusual show of leniency prompted by her tender age, Patience was kept at the Governor's house, although her companions and her sister were imprisoned and flogged. The shared experience of abuse forged a strong bond between mother and daughters. Catharine loved all her children, but in her heart of hearts, she felt particularly close to Mary and Patience.

In Third Month, 1660 Catharine accompanied Mary to England for her summer wedding at the Holder Family estate in Gloucestershire. The ceremony in August was a joyous affair, but parting from her eldest daughter had been like losing a limb.

When Catharine returned to Providence, she learned of Mary Dyer's execution at Boston. Her dear friend had ignored the order of banishment a third time and was hanged like a common criminal. Richard Scott informed Catharine that Friend Dyer had stayed overnight on her way north, and Catharine was plagued by the notion that had she been home, she might have dissuaded her friend from that fatal course. At least she could have warned Mary of Endicott's evil intent, so clearly expressed, when Catharine had stood before him in '58. The Bay Colony Governor had threatened to initiate a new law to hang Quakers if they broke the law of banishment a third time. She had replied that if God called His servants, they would not shirk their spiritual duty out of fear.

"And we shall be as ready to take away your lives, as you shall be to lay them down," Endicott responded. His words were prophetic. William Robinson, Marmamduke Stephenson, Mary Dyer, and William Leddra had subsequently "swung from the halter" in graphic proof of his callous statement.

Since Catharine was absent at the time of the execution, her husband Richard Scott wrote to Margaret Fell of Friend Dyer's death. He sent a letter to Swarthmore Hall and received a response four months later from a young missionary in training there. Her name was Mary Tomkins, and Friend Dyer had been her spiritual mother. Once home Catharine replied to Friend Tomkins' anguished letter, confiding her own grief and guilt, and the two women had corresponded ever since.

Recently Catharine had received a note from Christiana Easton in Newport, saying Mary Tomkins and her companions were there to attend this year's General Meeting. The prospect of meeting the young woman face to face lifted Catharine's spirits. She yet struggled with the loss of her eldest daughter and her closest friend. She missed them both. When her daughter wrote of her first pregnancy, Catharine was thrilled to become a grandmother, but would she ever see the child? She mourned missing the birth, which occurred a year after the wedding. She worried whether the new mother was getting the nourishing foods that would bring in her milk, and she longed to rock the child of her child in her arms.

Catharine turned to look at Patience, as busy as her mother on correspondence of a different sort. She was engaged to young Henry Beere of Newport and was addressing invitations to the wedding planned for September. Catharine was relieved that at least this daughter would be closer to home.

Patience felt her mother's gaze and looked up from her lap desk, laying aside her quill with a sigh.

"We have earned a respite, dost think?" Catharine began. "I propose we leave early for the General Meeting at Newport this year."

Her daughter's face lit up. "Oh, may we? I should love to see Henry! Shall I write the Eastons to see if they might entertain us?"

Patience picked up her quill and laid a fresh sheet of paper on the blotter. It warmed Catharine's heart to see her serious girl so happy.

"Let us speak with thy father first," she smiled. "We can plead the case at table this night."

Chapter 6

SHELTER ISLAND AND NEWPORT, RHODE ISLAND COLONY

May/June (3rd/4th Month) 1663

After a second meeting for worship and two full weeks on Shelter Island, the five missionary Friends prepared to return to Newport. General Meeting would begin at the end of the week, bringing Friends together for three days of worship, Society business, and fellowship. After dinner on their last evening with the Sylvesters, they all strolled down to the *Sea Witch*. Edward wanted to show Nathaniel his latest renovations to the craft. Young Grissel and Giles ran ahead, two spots of color on the wide lawn lit by the amber glow of the lowering sun.

"I am sorry the new babe forbids us attending General Meeting this year," Nathaniel said. "I warrant ye shall have a following wind, going to Newport."

"We shall overnight at Fisher's Island as we did on the way down," Edward responded. "We can make Newport the next day before dark, I reckon, with an early start and a southerly wind."

"Capital plan," their host commented, "and we shall see ye well provisioned ere ye depart."

The four women walked with arms linked at a leisurely pace behind the men.

"I am so glad you came," Grissel said warmly. "The company of women is such a rare treat."

"We have enjoyed thy fellowship as well, Grissel," Mary responded. "This respite on your lovely island has lifted my spirits. Our thanks for receiving us so graciously with no warning."

"Yes, and thy children are fine companions, too," Anne added with a smile.

"I am gratified to hear it," Grissel said. "Betimes I am told they are allowed too much license."

"By whom?" Allie asked surprised.

Grissel smiled. "My elder sister Ann has said as much. Her Mary is of an age with our Grissel, but once their lessons are done, Grissel and Giles are constantly out of doors. Mary cannot keep up with them."

"I do not agree with your sister," Anne responded. "They are both capable and well behaved, and little Natty is so sweet."

Little Grissel and Giles had reached the pier but knew they were not allowed on the boat without the adults. They waited with barely contained excitement for their elders to catch up.

"I know how sisters can be," Mary said with a wry smile. "They would have us live by their opinions."

"Oh, I learned to agree with Ann long ago then do as I please," Grissel replied with a mischievous grin.

The next morning the Friends took their leave of the Sylvester Family and Shelter Island.

Newport bulged at the seams. Preparations for the third General Meeting of the Religious Society of Friends were well underway. Although officially the event would not start until the end of the week, folk were arriving early. Every inn was full; every home entertained guests; the streets were clogged with wagons, carriages, horses, and pedestrians; and the masts in the harbor were as thick as a forest.

Edward was glad of the slip at Will Reape's dock for the *Sea Witch*. With more vessels arriving each day, slips and moorings were at a premium. The five friends elected to stay on board overnight and return to the Reapes' in the morning to avoid inconveniencing their hosts at a late hour. Mary savored her last night on the *Sea Witch*. Reality would reassert itself on the morrow.

The next morning, they found Sarah Reape outside, a basket of freshly cut asparagus on her arm. She greeted them enthusiastically.

"Well met and welcome back!" she said, setting aside her basket and shears to embrace them. "I am so glad you are here! Christiana Easton had a letter from Providence last week. Catharine and Richard Scott are coming early for General Meeting with three of their daughters. They arrive on the morrow and shall be entertained at the Eastons."

Mary's face lit up. "Verily? Catharine Scott?"

"Yes!" Sarah confirmed, taking her arm. "She is eager to meet thee, Mary. Christiana has invited us all to dinner on Sixth Day," their hostess continued, leading them inside. "Oh, my thanks, George," she added, taking the forgotten basket from him.

"Is Christiana not hosting the Women's Meeting on Seventh Day?" Anne asked. "We do not wish to impose at such a busy time."

Sarah laughed—a lovely sound that made one want to laugh with her. "Missionary Friends from England are no imposition! 'Tis a privilege to enjoy your company. All of Newport is eager to meet you and share worship. Besides," she added, "both Catharine and Christiana are formidable organizers and cannot abide being idle. The Scotts' daughter Patience is betrothed to young Henry Beere and will likely be occupied with her fiancé and his family, but Hannah and Deliverance—their younger girls—are as active as their mother. They shall help us prepare for the Women's Meeting and the dame school. Did I mention that Christiana wants to open a dame school this summer? I believe we shall have more help than is strictly necessary with all of you and the Scotts as well. Oh, we shall be merry!"

The Friends exchanged smiles, as Sarah's enthusiasm was contagious. General Meeting was the biggest event of the year in Newport, barring the ceremony for Rhode Island's Royal Charter planned for November. The busy town was a far cry from Shelter Island.

On Sixth Day as the time for the dinner with the Scotts approached, Mary could barely contain her excitement. At last, she would meet Catharine. It was an idyllic evening for a walk, mild and windless, an auspicious start to Fourth Month and General Meeting. A servant received them and led them around to the back of the house, where the Eastons and their guests conversed on chairs and benches on the wide lawn. Catharine seemed to recognize Mary instinctively. She rose and went to the younger woman, grasping her hands before Christiana could draw breath to introduce them.

"Mary Tomkins! At last!" she exclaimed, taking in Mary's face then drawing her into a warm embrace.

The young missionary had never known a mother's love, and she was overwhelmed by the maternal gesture. Her eyes filled, and she could not speak. Christiana covered the awkward moment with introductions, but all were aware of Mary's reaction. The women were misty-eyed, and the men cleared their throats and looked away, embarrassed by the depth of emotion.

"How fares thy plantation on the Moshassuck, Richard?" Will Reape asked, launching a safe topic.

"Come, let us walk apart a little," Catharine said softly to Mary. They excused themselves and left the company arm in arm.

"Thou hast endured much this past year in the North Country," Catharine began as they paced slowly across the greensward. "When we received Dr. Barefoote's letter, I feared for thy safety."

"We had good response in the northern towns," Mary temporized, downplaying the pain and terror she had endured. "Many were brought to the Light by our efforts, and God did protect us in the end."

"Thy accomplishments are verily commendable, Mary, but I am grateful thy life was preserved." Catharine stopped and took the younger woman's hands. "I shall not press thee to speak of thy suffering for I understand thy reluctance. I never wrote thee of it but I, too, was whipped and imprisoned at Boston." Mary gaped. "'Twas three years ago," Catharine continued, "but I know pain and public humiliation wound the spirit as well as the flesh. Indeed, the unseen wounds take longest to heal."

Mary was moved by the older woman's perceptive empathy and fresh tears stung her eyes. Catharine cupped her cheek. "Poor girl! I know thou hast suffered much in God's service, but I also know from thy letters that thy spirit is strong. And Mary Dyer said as much whenever she spoke of thee."

"She spoke of me?" Mary asked amazed.

Catharine nodded. "My dear girl, she talked of ye both as though she were a proud mother—her Kingsweare girls. Ye are verily her spiritual daughters, thus I know ye shall prevail."

Catharine Scott had confirmed Mary's deepest feelings. Her gratitude was such that she could only nod.

Chapter 7

NEWPORT, RHODE ISLAND COLONY

June (4th Month) 1663

The next morning the third General Meeting of the Society of Friends in Rhode Island commenced at the Coddingtons' home. It was also the first meeting for worship that the English missionaries attended since returning from Shelter Island. The Reape Family and their guests walked the short distance, enjoying the warmth of a strengthening sun. Everyone wore their best outfits. The cotton dress Ann Coddington had given Mary felt light and clean against her skin, and she was grateful for the fine weather, the company of her friends, and her recovered strength.

Will informed his guests of the Coddingtons' background, as they walked.

"Ann Brinley is William Coddington's third wife and a generation younger. They met and married in 1650 when he went back to England to request a charter from the king. Two years before, mark ye, Roger Williams secured a patent for the Colony of Rhode Island which included the mainland towns of Providence and Warwick as well as the island settlements of Newport and Portsmouth." Will chuckled. "Old Cod did not like that! He wanted a charter for Aquidneck Island exclusively, thus he went to England to get Williams' document changed."

"That seems presumptive," Mary commented. "Had he the right to do so?"

"Certes, *he* thought so," Will answered, grinning.

"The issue was that the charter he procured named him governor for life!" Sarah added.

"Oh dear!" Allie commented with a short laugh.

"Whatever possessed him?" Mary asked.

"He mistrusted Roger Williams, who represented Providence, and he openly disliked Samuel Gorton, who founded Warwick," Will explained. "Coddington was a magistrate at Portsmouth—formerly Pocasset—when things came to a head. Gorton publicly expressed contempt for the authority of both magistrates and ministers, and Friend Coddington saw it as a threat to the peace of the new settlement. He had Gorton flogged and turned out."

"Verily? Flogged?" Allie was amazed that any Friend would resort to such brutality.

"Remember, none here were convinced by the Society of Friends until the first missionaries arrived in '56," Sarah put in. "This was near two decades earlier."

"Gorton left and founded Warwick, as a result," Will added, "but Old Cod did not forget the incident."

"Was Coddington's charter ever approved?" Anne asked.

"Cromwell's Parliament was in power, and since Coddington was a Puritan, they did approve it," Will answered. "But 'twas another story once he got home."

"It all occurred before we came here," Sarah went on, "but Nicholas Easton told us that the officials of the colony were outraged. John Clarke, William Dyer, and Roger Williams took ship for England at the earliest opportunity to have the offending document rescinded, and they did succeed."

"After that Coddington was in disgrace. His commission as governor was revoked by a unanimous vote of the Assembly, and he withdrew from public service," Will finished.

"Apparently he is not in disgrace now," Mary observed. "How was the rift repaired?"

"It took some years for tempers to cool," Will answered.

"I warrant it was Ann's influence on him," Sarah elaborated. "A young wife and the births of five healthy children can mellow a man." She grinned at Will who waggled his eyebrows in response.

"Or mayhap it was the influence of the Public Friends who arrived around that time," Will added. "Many in Newport became convinced, the Coddingtons among them. William made a public apology."

"Whatever moved him, he was forgiven, and his misdeed was expunged from the records," Sarah said.

Edward spoke up, as they turned onto Marlborough Street. "Speaking of charters, what news of Reverend Clarke's progress in England?"

"'Tis hopeful!" Will exclaimed, his eyes sparkling. "His efforts to secure a Royal Charter for the colony are about to bear fruit at last. Mark ye, John Clarke has been in England acting as our agent for more than a decade!" he told the missionaries, who looked appropriately impressed. "His latest letter says the wording is finalized, and he hopes to send the document before the end of this summer. Captain George Baxter is charged to meet the ship at Boston with an escort and see it safely delivered here."

"Will is on the committee to plan the reading of it at a public reception," Sarah told them proudly. "The colony entire shall celebrate that momentous occasion!"

"Friend Coddington has not quite smothered all his ambition, I warrant," Will said as they arrived at the Coddington's gate. "He is determined that Newport shall host the ceremony."

The hum of conversation ceased when the missionaries entered the Coddingtons' spacious drawing room. All eyes turned to the newcomers. Their rescue from a virtual death sentence was the subject of conversation at every gathering, second only to John Clarke's success with the colony's charter. Here, at last, were the brave Friends who had defied the repressive Bay Colony, risking their lives for the faith they all shared. Admiration generated an initial shyness, until Ann and William Coddington broke the ice by greeting their guests warmly.

William Coddington was now a respected public official in Newport, as well as a devout Friend. He and Nicholas Easton enjoyed a friendly rivalry, as influential members of the Society of Friends. This day his outward demeanor was humbly pleased, but inwardly he triumphed at hosting the first meeting for worship during the Third General Meeting at Newport—and with missionaries from England present, too! His drawing room had never been so full. As the weather was fine, the younger children were shepherded outside by their nursemaids and Anne Coleman. Older children and youths sat on footstools or on the floor. Men stood along the walls, to allow the elderly and women to sit.

"Friends! If we may begin," William Coddington announced. "We are all eager to hear from our guests, and they shall speak after worship. Questions may be addressed at that time."

Catharine Scott gestured for Mary and Allie to join her on a bench. Mary was thrilled. Even at Swarthmore Hall, where she and Allie had lived and trained as missionaries for two years, their gatherings had not been so large. They exchanged looks of happy amazement, as the room became quiet. Mary was transported by the fellowship of so many Friends in contemplation together. It seemed only moments before the shaking of hands ended worship. Friend Coddington took charge again, patting his bald pate with a handkerchief before addressing the crowded room.

"Our fair colony is unique. Many of us fled persecution in the north, and the Puritans would curb us yet, for we alone offer a refuge for freedom of conscience in the Colonies. We alone thwart their plan to bend all men to their way of worship and governance. We alone are guided by God Within.

"John Clarke has written that we shall soon have the King's sanction for our endeavor in the form of a Royal Charter for Rhode Island." Murmurs of approbation met this statement, and Coddington spoke over them. "On that illustrious day we shall cease to fear harassment when we travel in Puritan jurisdictions; the boundaries of our colony shall be safe from encroachment; and we shall govern and worship as we please for none may gainsay royal approval.

"Seven years past, the first missionary Friends came to these shores," he continued more quietly. "Those brave men and women did endure much to deliver their message of joy and bring us to the Light. Our visiting Friends prove they yet suffer in the Bay Colony. However, their sacrifice is validated, for our Society grows despite cruel opposition and ignorance. Certes, it thrives in Newport, as evidenced by this meeting." He smiled, and the worshippers beamed at each other in response. "Our guests have agreed to recount their trials in the north. Reserve questions until they have spoken, and it please ye."

Coddington gave way, and Mary stood. Once started, it was not as difficult as she had feared. She described the arrest and trial at Dover Point; Magistrate Walderne's brutal sentence, certes meant to kill them; Dr. Walter Barefoote's Christian act of accompanying the missionaries on medical grounds; the Friends' singing as the women were whipped, taken up by so many in the crowd; the long, cold ride to Hampton and the constable's reluctance to flog them publicly; Edward's appearance and the release at Salisbury by Robert Pike's order; the safe haven they found with the Carr Family on their island in the Merrimack River; the return to Kittery Point to recover at the Shapleighs'; and Mary and Allie's subsequent return to Dover at the end of Eleventh Month.

This last did not surprise their audience. It was the way of missionary Friends to challenge unjust laws and bear the punishments publicly. They hoped to arouse sympathy among the witnesses until public opinion censured the brutal laws. The four missionaries hanged at Boston for ignoring the order of banishment a third time were stark proof of this practice.

When Mary had finished, Allie spoke of the second arrest at Dover, for Mary had been unconscious during much of the incident, and Anne had still been recovering at Kittery Point. Four men led by Elder Hatevil Nutter had interrupted their meeting at the Emery's ordinary and dragged the two missionaries over a mile through the snow. They were left unconscious in wet clothing on the dirt floor of a root cellar without food or drink for sixteen hours. The next morning the men came for them, baldly stating that they intended to throw the women into the river, "So you shall trouble us no more." Unable to resist in their weakened state, the women were roughly dragged to the riverbank, where a boat was docked. The men intended to row them out to the middle of the river and drown them in the frigid water, a plan that would have succeeded, had not a raging blizzard prevented it. Their captors were forced to return to the house, dragging their unconscious burdens. Allie told of the missionaries' revival, thanks to Goodwife Canney, the woman of the household. After the men's exertions in the storm, she plied them a potent toddy that contained extra rum. The men slept in a drunken stupor while Jane Canney alerted Thomas Roberts and Walter Barefoote by a prearranged signal, and they managed to rescue the missionaries from the house.

Anne then related the third incident at Hampton just five weeks before, when Mary exposed Reverend Seaborn Cotton as a thief before his congregation. The minister stole valuable items from Friends who were absent from his services, justifying this avarice as "fines." He had deliberately ruined their young friends the Wardells. As a result of their protest, Mary endured fifteen stripes that day, while Anne and Allie shivered in the stocks until sundown. It had been worth it.

"Many in Hampton now follow our faith," Anne concluded. "Indeed, there are regular meetings on both sides of the Piscataqua River from Kittery to Quamphegan Falls on the east bank, and from Dover to Somersworth on the west. We count our efforts in the Bay Colony an unqualified success."

The Friends of Newport rose to applaud the English missionaries.

During the four days of General Meeting, the Reapes hosted a dinner party for their closest friends on Seventh Day. The weather was ideal, and tables were set up on the lawn behind the house. It was a large party. Coddingtons, Eastons, Scotts, Brinleys, and the five missionaries—over twenty adults and a confusing number of children who moved around so quickly Mary gave up trying to count them.

She and Catharine Scott were talking with Francis Brinley, Ann and Grissel's brother, and his wife Hannah, daughter of Caleb Carr, another Friend who was active in the local government. In 1652 William Coddington had sold the young couple land on the corner of Farewell and Marlborough Streets, where they built a home.

"What news of the Sylvesters?" Catharine Scott asked the Brinleys. "I had hoped to see them here."

"They would not miss it, but for the new babe," Francis told her. He corresponded with his sister on Shelter Island regularly.

"We are lately come from there," Mary put in. "The baby's name is Peter, and he thrives. Thy sister is well, also, Friend Brinley. We were refreshed by our visit with them."

"I am gratified to hear it," Francis replied, "We must plan to go soon ourselves, Hannah."

"Agreed! Another nephew for Tom and Will to play with! We love taking the boys there," Hannah added. "Grissel is fine company, and Nathaniel has worked wonders with the plantation."

Will Reape joined them, and the conversation turned to the Men's Meeting of that morning.

"Boundary disputes are a thorny issue," Will said, referring to the men's discussion. "Our neighbors harry Rhode Island's borders constantly. The Narragansett Territory on the western bank is particularly vulnerable as well as the settlements to the north. Connecticut and Plymouth have even attempted to tax Rhode Islanders, insisting they are on their land."

"We did reach consensus on the issue, however," Francis Brinley added. "After contemplation, we did appoint a delegation to survey the official boundaries once the Royal Charter is in hand. Our borders shall be safe with King Charles' seal to back us."

"We also elected to negotiate remuneration for those who have been unfairly taxed by the other colonies," Will added.

Mary admired these men. They were applying the precepts of the Religious Society of Friends in the governance of their community and in their daily lives. Rather than impotently raging against injustice or taking up arms, they turned to the Light and sought peaceful resolutions. They were proof that George Fox's tenets could be applied in practical ways to the benefit of all. Led by these men, the Newport Friends were thriving, and Mary was thrilled to witness their success. They would endure and prosper in Rhode Island.

Chapter 8

GREAT ISLE, MASSACHUSETTS BAY COLONY

June (4th Month) 1663

This same Cotton having heard that Major Shapleigh was become a Quaker, said "he was sorry for it, but he would endeavor to convert him," and afterwards, drinking in a house in an isle in the river Piscataway, and hearing that the Major was there in a ware-house, he went thither; but going up stairs, and being in drink, he tumbled down, and got such a heavy fall, that the Major himself came to help this drunken converter."

—William Sewel *The History of the Rise, Increase and Progress of the Christian People Called Quakers*

Reverend Seaborn Cotton of Hampton was plagued by a restless spirit. Ever since Mary Tomkins and her two cohorts invaded his church in April, accusing him of thievery, his congregation was dwindling. At least the Wardells had quit Hampton and were gone to the Rhode Island Colony—that hotbed of sedition, where heretics found shelter. The Quaker scourge was spreading, but the young Puritan minister was determined to fight it tooth and nail.

He knew the English Quakers had been protected by Nicholas Shapleigh. The man's wife was one of them, and the major welcomed them, allowing meetings and entertaining the heretics in his own home. It set a dangerous precedent, since the family had influence;

however, if the reverend could bring Shapleigh back into the fold, it would be a Puritan victory and might restore his damaged status.

Thus, he found himself at the Walton's ordinary on Great Isle in the service of the Lord and nursing a tankard of ale. It was not his first. The ferryman said Captain Shapleigh was at the warehouse close by, but Seaborn needed time to prepare. It was a delicate situation, and he labored over what to say.

"Would ye be taking another then, Reverend?"

Cotton twitched in his seat. He had not heard the barmaid's approach and was surprised to find his tankard empty so soon. God seemed reluctant to inspire his servant this day. Mayhap one more would serve then he would find the words to convince the major to repent. If he failed, he would inform the authorities in Boston of Shapleigh's converse with the Quakers. But he wanted this plum for himself.

"One more, I warrant," he answered then licked his lips. His tongue felt thick. Was this his second cup or third? He was unsure. The Reverend straightened in his chair and adjusted his neck cloth, glancing around. The ordinary was quiet this early in the afternoon. No one was looking at him, but he must exude authority as an ordained minister of God. He had not studied at Harvard for naught. He had married well. His wife's father was Simon Bradstreet, who was active in the colony's government despite his wife Anne's radical tendency to write poetry. Privily, the notion of a woman creating literature amused Seaborn. Thank God Dotty did not take after her unbalanced mother!

His tankard was topped up, and Seaborn took a long pull of the frothy ale. He noted the sun's progress through the open door. It was time to act. He drained the rest quickly, donned his hat, and stood. The floor tilted alarmingly, and he gripped the table until it righted. He dropped some coin on the stained wood without counting it. He was unsure he could and did not wish to confirm this suspicion.

The open door saved him fiddling with an unfamiliar latch, but the sun assaulted his vision, making him squint despite his wide hat brim. When his eyes adjusted, he looked around for the warehouse.

George Walton greeted Nicholas Shapleigh warmly. His friend had brought a dozen green planks from his sawmill on Spruce Creek to replace some rotten ones on the dock at Great Isle. George related his intention to extend the pier, while two hired men unloaded the boards and stowed them in the nearby warehouse, a large two-story building near the dock.

"Come upstairs a moment, Nicholas, and see the plans," George said once the boards were stacked.

George's office was on the second floor, accessed by a utilitarian stairway of rough planks with no railing. The innkeeper opened a drawer, taking out a bottle of scotch and two pewter cups kept handy for such occasions. The men toasted each other, then Walton brought out the drawings. During the past decade, custom on the island had increased along with the population, and the original dock was no longer adequate. They were discussing the extension when they heard a shout.

"Who the bloody hell is that I wonder?" George said, going to the top of the stairs and peering down.

The wide bay doors were open, admitting enough light to see a man walking—rather unsteadily, George thought—toward the stairs, but the brim of his hat hid his features from above.

"Hello there!" George called. "Might I assist thee, sir?"

Nicholas joined him, curious. The figure stopped and looked up, causing him to stagger.

"I seek Major Nicholas Shapleigh," he said, grasping a barrel to steady himself.

Nicholas and George exchanged a bewildered look.

"You have found him," Nicholas allowed.

"And who the bl—who might you be?" George asked, amending his habitual speech in deference to the man's clerical garb.

The minister reached the stairs and put a hand on the wall. His round face was flushed.

"I am the Reverend Seaborn Cotton of Hampton," he declared. "I know y'are bewitched by the Quaker heretics, Major Shapleigh, but I am prepared to guide you back to the True Church!"

George Walton and his wife Alice were Friends and had moved to Great Isle to distance themselves from the Puritan-dominated colony. George let out a curt laugh at Cotton's pronouncement.

"Which one? Several claim that distinction," he said.

Cotton looked offended and put a foot on the first tread. "I shall overlook your levity, sir. There is but one true religion in the Massashoosh—Mashashoo—" he stopped, belched softly into his fist, and started again. "There is but one true religion in the Bay Colony." He held up a finger. "The First Church."

His hand found the wall again, and the minister gained the second step.

"You journeyed from Hampton to save my soul?" Nicholas asked incredulous.

Cotton stopped his upward progress and put his free hand to his heart. "'Tis my sworn duty, sir. I am God's instrument on this Earth!" He had Shapleigh's attention. He must strike now while the iron was hot. Seaborn climbed two more steps as he spoke. "I am His Holy Shepherd, and you a wandering sh—"

His speech broke off, as the minister lost his balance. He bumped the wall, over-compensated with a violent jerk, and fell like a sack of meal off the open side of the stairs onto the dirt floor.

"At least he was not far up," Nicholas said, clattering down the stairs.

"And he did not hit a barrel or a box," George added, following more slowly.

They hauled him up between them, and George recovered Cotton's hat, replacing it on his cropped blonde hair. They half-carried him back to the inn and returned to the warehouse, leaving the dazed minister in Alice Walton's care. She plied him with strong tea and victuals until the ferry arrived then watched him board, moving slowly like an old man.

"What the bloody Hell was the Hampton minister doing here?" she wondered to herself.

Nicholas returned to Kittery Point unsaved.

Chapter 9

NEWPORT, RHODE ISLAND COLONY

June (4ᵗʰ Month) 1663

The fourth and final day of the General Meeting at Newport culminated in worship followed by a group picnic in the field near the Eastons' home. The fine weather held, and over a hundred Friends attended. The younger children played tag and hide and seek, supervised by Anne Coleman and Enna, while Peter Easton and Edward organized a game of quoits with the youths. Mary spoke with many people, but she favored her conversation with Francis Brinley. He had a library with more than two hundred volumes and invited the missionaries to tea the next day to peruse his collection. The gathering did not break up until dark.

Once General Meeting was over, Newport settled back into its customary level of industry. On Second Day Edward and George accompanied Will Reape to a meeting of the investors for the Monmouth Project. Anne Coleman set off early to help Christiana and Merry Easton plan activities and lessons for the dame school. The Scotts were returning to Providence on a sloop captained by their future son-in-law Henry Beere, and Mary and Allie went to see them off. They took a last cup of cider with the family as they waited for the tide to turn. The day was warm, and the ordinary was crowded with prospective travelers and seamen, so they sat outside on the benches that lined the front wall, facing the harbor. Catharine settled between Mary and Allie, while the rest of the family went off to shop for last-minute purchases.

"Where will you go from here?" she asked the missionaries.

"We must wait for word from Margaret Fell," Mary replied.

"You know you are ever welcome at Providence," Catharine said.

"Our thanks," Mary smiled. "We may hold thee to that, but we expect a letter from Swarthmore Hall any day now. It will determine our course of action."

"Will Reape spoke of going to Long Island to recruit more investors for his land project," Allie said. "We may accompany him and visit the Friends' settlements there, for we cannot rely on Edward for transport much longer," she added with a significant look at Mary.

Catharine took note. "Friend Wharton came to your rescue several times in the North Country, did he not?" she asked, searching Mary's face.

"Yes, he did," Mary answered, her cheeks flushing under the older woman's perceptive gaze.

Allie spoke up with rare enthusiasm. "Indeed, our mission would have failed but for Edward! He met us at Dover and took us to the Shapleighs; he prevailed upon Robert Pike to help us at Salisbury, which led to our release; he brought us back to Kittery Point from Carr Island in one day's sail! Edward Wharton is our savior, and we owe him our lives."

"His concern goes beyond friendship, I wager," Catharine smiled. "I thought he would ever remain single, but I remark the way he looks at thee, Mary. It puts me in mind of Christopher Holder and our daughter Mary ere they became engaged. Methinks thou hast succeeded where others have failed."

"I have done nothing," Mary answered stiffly, lifting her chin. "I do not intend to marry."

Catharine raised her eyebrows, noting discomfort cloaked in the sharp response.

"Ah, I see," she murmured. "Thy calling is paramount, is it?"

"Yes," Mary said definitively. "Standing against the persecutors of our faith and awakening people to God Within is far more important than serving a husband and children. Mary Dyer is my example."

"Mary Dyer did have a husband and six children, my dear, but verily, a divine call cannot be ignored," Catharine answered slowly. "I have experienced its power myself." She took Mary's hand in both of hers and held her eyes. "But remember, Mary, God does not only call us to suffer. Betimes He calls us to love. Indeed, 'tis His primary order."

Catharine's words plagued Mary's thoughts that night, as sleep eluded her. Had they accomplished enough to end their mission? Was God now calling her to join her life to Edward's? Would husband, home, and children fulfill her, after a life devoted to public speaking and missionary work? She dozed fitfully and woke no wiser, but happily, her mood was lifted the next morning by the unexpected arrival of Christiana Easton, as they broke their fast with the Reapes.

"Oh, thank Heaven ye are here!" she exclaimed upon seeing the missionaries. "Forgive me for barging in unannounced, but I reckoned this letter should be delivered in all haste," she went on breathlessly, tugging off her gloves. "It came this very morning on a ship from England." She placed a thick, sealed missive in Mary's hands. "'Tis addressed to thee, Mary, and it comes from Swarthmore Hall."

Mary caught her breath, recognizing Margaret's hand. The missionaries' future depended upon the contents of this letter.

The three Friends excused themselves to read the missive. It was long, written during several sittings and bore the Society's news. Most distressing was the death of their dear friend and fellow-missionary Edward Burrough with whom Mary and Allie had trained, preached, and subsequently suffered a six-month sentence in the dungeon at Lancaster. The local authorities had ignored Burrough's pardon by King Charles II, and the prisoner died at Newgate, when his weakened lungs failed him. Dear, eloquent Edward, who had written hundreds of treatises defending and explaining the Society of Friends; who had secured the mandamus from King Charles II that stopped the hangings at Boston; who had been like a brother to Mary and Allie; and who had died alone in a noxious prison before his thirtieth year.

They held each other and wept for their young friend, until the shock of loss—so incongruous in this sunlit place—abated somewhat. After wiping her eyes and blowing her nose, Mary read on.

Religious persecution raged at home, extinguishing all hope that the newly reinstated monarch would usher in a period of toleration. More Friends crowded the gaols than ever before, including George Fox who was again at Lancaster for refusing to swear to the new Act of Uniformity; however, Margaret Fell corresponded with him regularly and communicated the Founder's goal for their mission in the colonies.

It was devastating in its simplicity. Friend Joseph Nicholson reported finding John Perrot on the Eastern Shore of Maryland. Perrot was creating a schism in the Society by maintaining that it was not necessary to remove hats at worship. He deemed it an outmoded form. Furthermore, he eschewed regular meetings, maintaining that Friends were to gather only when prompted by the Light Within. The man was well spoken and comely, and many of the newly convinced were following him, creating a split in the Society. Mary and Allie were charged to find him and convince him to honor the Society's tenets or cease his missionary work. They were also to correct any damage he had wrought among the Friends in the region and bring his wayward followers back into the fold. The letter ended with Margaret's tender blessing and loving assurances. They sat for some moments before Anne broke the silence.

"Joseph Nicholson is one of the companions I crossed with. I parted company with him and his wife, Jane, and John Liddal last autumn when they went south. That is when

I joined you in the North Country. If they were unable to stop this man John Perrot, I fear it is a great challenge."

Mary shook her head slowly. "It requires contemplation. We cannot know unless we try," she answered.

"Even correcting his followers shall be difficult, if they have come to love and trust him," Anne added.

Allie sighed. "At least the winter shall not be so harsh further south."

Mary nodded absently, but she thought the weather would be the least of their concerns.

At table that night when the three missionaries expressed their plan to go south, Will Reape was quick to respond.

"I shall accompany you!" he announced. Sarah and Allie were not surprised, but the others gaped at him. "I was planning to go south in any case to speak with the investors in the Monmouth Project," Will went on. "Several of them live on Long Island, and I am eager to put together an exploration party. The land is but eight miles across Achter Kol from Gravesend. On top of that, my sloop is twice as fast as thy old bucket, Edward!" he finished, grinning.

George laughed, and Edward looked mildly offended, though he did not contradict Will. *Reape's Gain* was faster than the *Sea Witch*. It was also more spacious and comfortable with six berths. He inclined his head in tacit agreement.

"Excellent!" Will exclaimed. "We shall leave on the morrow!"

Two days later, after bidding farewell to their new acquaintances at Newport, the five missionaries and Will set out for Long Island. Mary relished the freedom of being at sea again. The six of them sang, laughed, and talked late into the night, sitting on deck with the stars blazing above them. Although she had chosen to follow her calling, Mary relished Edward's presence, sitting near him whenever the opportunity arose. As *Reape's Gain* tacked south against the prevailing summer wind, she put worries of the future aside and savored each day.

Part II

SUMMER 1663

*New Netherland was founded in 1624, just four years after the Mayflower
voyage and six years ahead of the Puritans' arrival in Massachusetts Bay. Its
capital and principal settlement, New Amsterdam, was clustered around the
wooden Fort Amsterdam, which stood where the Museum of the American
Indian is now located...When New Amsterdam was conquered by the English
in 1664, the city extended only as far as Wall Street (where, in fact, the Dutch
had built a wall). The main road Breede weg (Broadway), passed through
a gate in the wall and continued on past farms, fields, and forests to the village of Haarlem, on the north end of the island. Ferrymen rowed goods and
people across the East River to Lange Eylandt and the villages of Breukelen
(Brooklyn), Vlissingen (Flushing), Vlacke Bos (Flatbush), and new Utrecht
(now a Brooklyn neighborhood). The area had but 1,500 inhabitants.*

—Colin Woodard, *American Nations*

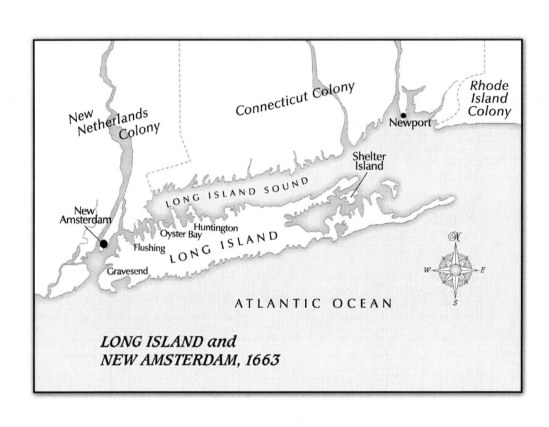

New
Netherlands
Colony

Connecticut Colony

Rhode
Island
Colony

Newport

Shelter
Island

LONG ISLAND SOUND

New
Amsterdam

Huntington
Oyster Bay

Flushing

LONG ISLAND

Gravesend

ATLANTIC OCEAN

N

W   *E*

S

**LONG ISLAND and
NEW AMSTERDAM, 1663**

Chapter 10

OYSTER BAY, LONG ISLAND

June (4th Month) 1663

Will Reape was glad of the excuse to visit Long Island. He spoke Dutch as fluently as English and was familiar with all the settlements, as he traded with them on a regular basis. The opportunity to meet with the investors in the Monmouth Patent and to recruit others, while helping his friends on their journey south, was a boon two times over. After three days at sea and two brief stops overnight, they approached one of his favorite destinations.

"We should reach Oyster Bay before dark," he announced, raising his voice over the rush of wind and water, as they tacked down Long Island Sound on a brisk southwesterly wind. "My friend Anthony Wright shall be glad of the company, and we shall be welcome for several days' visit, I warrant. He and his brothers are staunch Friends and resided at Sandwich in the Plymouth Colony for a time. Just shorten that spinnaker, wouldst thee, Allie?"

Allie scampered aft, bare feet and calves flashing white. At sea they all shed shoes, stockings, and head gear, and the women tucked their skirts into their waistbands. Allie was a nimble crew mate, and Will did not hesitate to put her to good use. George navigated, and Edward monitored the mainsail, content with Mary nearby. When Allie sat down next to Anne again, their skipper continued from his position at the wheel.

"The three Wright brothers came to the colonies in '37 and settled first at Saugus—now called Lynn—but they soon quit that Puritan stronghold for Sandwich on Cape Cod. Peter is the eldest." Will grinned at Allie. "Ye shall like his wife, I warrant—another Alice. She is a woman of strong opinions and one of the first to embrace our faith;

however, back to Sandwich. Peter is an energetic fellow and was soon restless. He scouted out land to the south and found a small party of Englishman at Oyster Bay. Their leader was Daniel Whitehead, and there were just three traders with their families. Technically it is Dutch territory, but Whitehead and his companions spoke Matinecock, and they negotiated with the Indians on their own, circumventing the Dutch authorities. Peter Wright found them eager for more English families to join the settlement, thus they readily agreed to help him purchase his own lot of land. A sizable group from Sandwich went there with the Wrights—mostly Friends. They increased the population at Oyster Bay so effectively that within a few years some of the original residents removed a few miles north and founded another settlement they call Huntington."

"When was this, Will?" Mary asked.

"Oyster Bay was settled in '53—Huntington some five years later. Peter Wright has expressed interest in the Monmouth Project and is likely to invest." Will chuckled. "He is happiest when exploring."

"Peter's eldest daughter Mary was in prison with me at Boston in '61," Edward added. "She was in the same cub with some twenty of us Salem Friends. Her younger sister Hannah was but fourteen thus the jailer kept her at his house."

"The girls went to *Boston*?" Allie asked amazed.

"Yes, to protest Endicott's laws, as so many of our faith did after the hangings," he answered.

"But over such a distance and at such tender ages!" Mary exclaimed.

"They are self-reliant, like their mother," Will grinned. "Ye shall see."

Mary, Allie, and Anne exchanged glances, impressed by the courage and commitment of Peter Wright's daughters. It appeared they would find good fellowship at Oyster Bay.

As Will predicted, *Reape's Gain* made port before sunset. Their landing procedure was second nature after four days at sea. They docked at an open slip; Edward and George secured the bow and stern lines; and Will went to settle up with the harbormaster, while the others battened down the sloop. Within half an hour the six Friends were headed for Anthony Wright's home.

It was not far. His house was at the south end of the harbor, overlooking the Sound, and served as a meeting place for the Friends in the area. During the ten years since its original construction, improvements had been added to the basic two-story dwelling.

The windows had leaded glass, and both chimneys were of sturdy Dutch brick. A long, covered porch faced the water with firewood stacked neatly at one end. Around the corner a wing had been added with its own chimney for cooking, laundry, and storage, allowing more space for meetings in the main house.

Will knocked on the door that fronted the lane, and a plain young woman answered. Her eyes widened as she recognized Will and invited them all in, welcoming them warmly. Will introduced her to the missionary women as Hannah Wright, Anthony's seventeen-year-old niece, who lived with her uncle.

Anthony heard their voices and came from his study. The Wrights were thrilled to have company and fresh news. They had eaten earlier but served their guests the remaining fish stew, cornbread, and cheese. They all settled at a large table at the kitchen end of the open room. There were no servants in evidence, and Hannah served them herself. Although their welcome was warm, Will knew them well and thought the Wrights seemed subdued. The travelers soon learned why.

"William, I am afraid we have sad news," Anthony began, when his guests had eaten. He glanced at his niece, and she nodded. "My brother Peter—Hannah's father—passed earlier this month."

"What! Peter gone?" Will exclaimed. "What a calamity! Was he ill or did some mishap befall him?"

"The latter, I fear. He was lost at sea. He went to visit a new settlement of Friends on the Eastern Shore of Maryland, and a squall must have overtaken him. Some fishermen found his skiff capsized, but there was no sign of Peter," Anthony answered.

"We know he is with God," Hannah said softly. Her eyes filled with tears.

Anthony covered her folded hands with one of his, and she looked up with a tremulous smile.

"We pray he did not suffer long," he added quietly.

"Our heartfelt condolences," Mary said. "We beg pardon for imposing at an inauspicious time."

"Oh no!" Hannah protested, blinking back tears as she straightened. "Your visit is most welcome! I am sure my uncle does agree that your company is a blessed diversion."

"Indeed," Anthony affirmed quickly. "We are glad to have you." He caught Mary's eye. "Ye are more lately come from England than anyone we know, and we would hear the news of our mother country, and how ye came to be here."

"Yes!" Hannah said, her face lighting up at the change in topic. "How did ye come to be missionaries?"

The three women looked at each other. How *had* it all come about?

"We cannot speak for Anne, as we became acquainted after arriving in New England," Mary answered, "but Allie and I became convinced when Mary Dyer came to our church at Kingsweare in Devon. She was with two men, also Public Friends. They spoke after the service and opened a whole new world for us. 'Twas Eighth Month of '56, and we enjoyed Friend Dyer's company for ten days before she sailed back to Boston. She encouraged us to become missionaries."

"But it took another two years of correspondence with Margaret Fell to arrange for our training and save the coin for the journey to Swarthmore Hall," Allie added.

"Ye knew Friend Dyer and have been to Swarthmore Hall?" Hannah's eyes were wide with wonder. "Oh, how I envy you! I hope to be a Public Friend one day. Have ye met the Founder, George Fox?"

Mary smiled at the girl's enthusiasm, so like her younger self. Hannah appeared plain at first, but she spoke well and exuded confidence. Her intelligence was evident, and her eagerness engaging.

"We met Friend Fox but once, and that briefly. He was on the panel that approved us," Mary answered with a smile.

"We should like to hear all about that," Anthony put in, "but we must alert the family of our guests' arrival, Hannah. Shall we host a dinner for everyone here tomorrow evening?"

"Certes, Uncle," the girl said, popping up from her seat. "I shall go forthwith, before 'tis full dark."

"I would accompany thee, Hannah," Will said, standing up. "I wish to see thy mother and offer my sympathies."

The Salem men rose with him. "As do we," Edward added.

Will turned to Anthony. "We three shall sleep on my vessel and see you on the morrow."

"But we would be happy to accommodate you all here," Anthony protested.

"Our thanks, but I shall rest better, watching over the sloop myself," Will responded. Edward and George concurred. "The women shall be glad of a bed on dry land, I wager," he added, turning to Mary.

"We do not wish to inconvenience you," Mary demurred.

"I should be terribly disappointed, if ye do not stay here with us," Hannah assured her.

Anthony rose and shook the men's hands warmly. "As ye wish then. We rise early. Come break your fast with us as soon as ye wake. We shall be looking out for you."

After the men left with Hannah, Anthony led the three missionaries out to the porch. A cool breeze came off the water, and they sat in silence for a time, enjoying the view of the harbor and Long Island Sound beyond. Smoke from cooking hearths perfumed the air, and Oyster Bay was settling down for the night. As the twilight deepened, mothers called children; animals were corralled or stabled; chickens roosted; and wavery candlelight glowed through thick glass windows. Across the Sound the clouds on the western horizon glowed pink and orange with the last rays of sun.

"I realize we have only just become acquainted," Anthony began slowly, "but I am curious…"

"Concerning what, Friend Wright?" Mary asked.

She had taken to their host immediately. Anthony was a slight man, but the only sign of his sixty-three years was the thick, white hair that fell to his shoulders and contrasted with the perfectly round bald spot atop. His face was clean shaven with few signs of age; his carriage was erect; his gray eyes sparkled with intelligence; and his voice was deep with an educated accent. He reminded Mary of her father.

"It appears you travel unescorted but for your fellow Friends. 'Tis uncommon for such lovely young women to be single," Anthony commented.

"We have dedicated our lives to God and taken up Mary Dyer's cause against injustice," Mary answered. "Marriage would mean abandoning that mission."

"I find that quite remarkable," Anthony rejoined, "for, mark ye, my niece and I are in accord."

"Thou hast never married, Friend Wright?" Anne asked, surprised by this revelation.

"My brothers provide me with family," he answered, smiling, "Hannah is like mine own daughter."

"Then we need not explain—for a wonder," Mary smiled back.

Anthony chuckled. "Not in this house, at any rate. Society may look at us askance, but the state of matrimony is overrated, in my humble opinion. I have dedicated my energy to my faith, as ye have."

"Just so," Mary murmured, as the others nodded.

"And Hannah shares this opinion, as well?" Anne posited.

"'Tis hard to credit in one so young, I warrant; however, she is a most unusual child— 'twas ever so. Did Edward tell you of her protests at Boston?" he asked.

"He told us that he shared a cub in prison with her sister Mary, but little else," Mary answered, wanting to hear Anthony's version of the extraordinary undertaking.

"Yes, Mary did accompany her," Anthony went on, "but it was Hannah's idea."

"How far is Boston from here?" Allie asked.

"Over two-hundred miles," he said.

"Did not her family try to prevent her?" Anne wondered.

"Prevent her?" Anthony raised his eyebrows. "Quite the contrary! They encouraged her to follow the inner light that prompted her to go." He smiled.

The women exchanged a glance. The Wrights were, indeed, an unusual family.

"Were they flogged?" Allie asked quietly.

"No, Praise God. The officials were impressed by Hannah's eloquence and tender age—at least, initially." He sighed. "But not enough to heed her. She returned the next year, after Friend Dyer's hanging, but again her pleas fell upon deaf ears. The Puritans at Boston have hearts of stone."

"We have not been to Boston as yet," Mary said, "but certes, the authorities at Dover meant to kill us."

"Verily? Keepers of the law attempted murther?" he asked, alarmed.

Anthony was a good listener, and the women related their experiences in the Bay Colony. It was full dark by the time they finished, and the four of them sat without speaking for a time. At length Anthony broke the silence.

"My dear girls, 'tis a wonder you are here to tell the tale," he said quietly.

"Only by God's Grace working through our friends," Mary replied. "Thus, we choose to serve Him and not to marry. We stand against injustice, wherever it is found, and carry out His work."

Anthony nodded solemnly. "I understand," he said, "and I commend you for it."

Chapter 11

OYSTER BAY and HUNTINGTON, LONG ISLAND

June (4th Month) 1663

The next morning was clear and unseasonably warm. The men took Anthony out for a sail in Will's sloop, while Hannah showed the missionaries around the village, introducing them to some of the Oyster Bay Friends as they went. They ended the tour at Alice Wright's home where they met Hannah's recently widowed mother and three sisters.

"We commiserate with thy loss, Friend Wright," Mary began, as they shook hands.

Alice held up her free hand. "My dears," she said to the three missionaries, "my thanks for your sympathy, but my husband died as he would wish, on an adventure at sea. Better that than to become infirm and take to his bed. Peter could never endure that. His loss is a blow to the family, but at least God spared him that indignity. I rejoice in the life we built together and our seven strong children."

"Thy fortitude is an example to us all, Friend Wright," Anne said fervently.

Alice Wright smiled and took the little missionary's hand without hesitation. "Then as thy paragon, I beg ye use my Christian name and call me Alice," she said to her new acquaintances.

"I am Alice, also," Allie told her, "but my friends call me Allie. I hope thou shalt as well."

Alice and Allie took to each other immediately. As they all enjoyed a refreshing cup of cold mint tea, the two women planned an outing to collect local plants, and Alice took them outside to see her herb garden. She soon had them picking greens and packing baskets of foodstuffs for the gathering at Anthony's home. Hannah explained that Nicholas, the youngest Wright brother, would join them with his family later, when the workday was done. Alice tallied up their number to plan the meal.

"I reckon we shall be sixteen at table this evening," she said.

The English missionaries were beginning to realize what a force the Wright Clan was in the community.

Laden with baskets of food, a jug of cider, and extra trenchers, the women walked to Anthony's house. As the sun lowered, the breeze died, and they were all overwarm by the time they got there.

"Anthony's lean-to is a deal cooler for cooking than my hearth in this weather!" Alice Wright asserted, as they unpacked the food and fed the banked coals of the cooking hearth.

"How can we help, Alice?" Mary asked.

"Ye may begin by rinsing those greens, and it please thee," Hannah's mother directed, pointing with her chin. Within minutes they all had tasks, and Mary understood why there were no servants in evidence—there was no need in this close-knit clan.

The women worked together so efficiently they were all lounging in the shade of the porch drinking cider by the time the men returned from their sail. Soon after, Nicholas and Ann Wright arrived with their three youngest daughters, bearing pies for dessert and two jugs of buttermilk. Introductions were made, but Mary and Allie were hard pressed to keep all the cousins straight. Peter and Alice's daughters were Mary, Hannah, and Elizabeth, who were twenty-one, seventeen, and ten; Nicholas and Ann's girls were Sarah, Mercy, and Deborah—sixteen, thirteen, and eleven, respectively. The family resemblance added to the confusion, but when the missionaries got a name wrong, as they inevitably did, the girls corrected them with good humor.

The meal was simple but delicious—two large baked halibut stuffed with savory herbs and lemon slices (the latter a gift from Will Reape), three fresh loaves, a round of cheese, dried pease porridge, pickled radishes, and greens from the garden. Jugs of sweet cider and buttermilk graced the table, as the Wrights did not drink spirits. The trenchers and cups were pewter or wood, and the guests brought their own. All used their belt knives and fingers for eating. Although Anthony's table seated a dozen, they managed to squeeze four more around it. They joined hands as Anthony said a blessing then tucked in with gusto.

"So, when did you come to the Colonies?" Alice asked, dabbing buttermilk from her upper lip.

"We landed at Dover in the Bay Colony last Fourth Month, as we would have been arrested at Boston," Mary answered. "Edward and George met us there and kindly transported us to Kittery Point in the Territory of Mayne, where we were entertained by Nicholas and Alice Shapleigh for the summer."

"Friend Wharton is ever there when needed," Hannah said, smiling at Edward.

"Verily, he helped us many times over!" Anne Coleman agreed, as Allie and Mary nodded, mouths full of the delicious fish.

Edward nodded once, acknowledging the compliments with a modest smile.

"We have heard tell of your journeys to Boston," Allie said between bites. "We applaud thy courage."

"Indeed, Mary and Hannah both went to protest the executions," Alice Wright said proudly.

"I wanted to go, too," Elizabeth piped up, "but Mamma said I was too little."

"As indeed thou wert at the age of seven, Poppet!" her Uncle Nicholas put in, chuckling.

"When we heard of the hangings, we were compelled to go," Hannah elaborated, and her sister Mary nodded gravely.

"What happened when ye arrived?" Allie inquired with customary directness.

"The Great and General Court was in session, and we interrupted it," Mary Wright answered. "Hannah was most eloquent, pleading with the officials to forgo their brutal ways for the sake of their own souls. She gave them pause for she was but fourteen. The chamber went completely quiet, but in the end, they did not heed her. They kept Hannah at the gaoler's house because of her tender age, but I was taken to the prison. It was crowded and smelly—above twenty of us in one cub, all Friends. Most were from Salem. Friend Wharton was among them."

"How long did they keep you?" Allie asked the sisters, fascinated by their pluck.

"Three weeks. We were released when Friend Shattuck served the King's mandamus to Governor Endicott," Hannah answered. "I wish I had seen the governor's face, when a Friend he had banished put the royal order in his hands."

"As do I!" Edward agreed. They shared a smile.

"And thy uncle said ye were not flogged," Mary Tomkins prompted.

"No, praise God!" their mother exclaimed.

"When they released us, we were made to witness two of our fellows being scourged. It is an ugly thing," Hannah said with a shiver.

"After that they marched all of us to the southern border of the colony and bid us not return," Mary Wright finished.

"But it did not stop our Hannah," Anthony added. "She went back the next year to protest Friend Dyer's execution."

"I hoped to awaken That of God in their hearts, but they would not be swayed," Hannah sighed.

"We heard the Reverend John Norton died this spring," her Uncle Nicholas said. "Is it true?"

"Yes, 'tis true," Will confirmed. "They say he was stricken of a sudden, as he stood by his hearth. Many Friends in Newport believe 'twas God's Hand. He and Endicott contrived the Quaker laws together."

"I fear divine wrath shall smite them all in time," Hannah mused without rancor.

The scar on Allie's cheek made her smile look rakish. "Amen to that," she said.

"On a happier note," Alice put in, "Our Mary shall be wed to young Sam Andrews at the end of Sixth Month. We shall be occupied this summer making the preparations!"

The talk turned to lighter topics, but Mary was impressed with the fortitude of the Wright sisters.

On First Day they woke to rain, but the weather did not deter the Friends from meeting. They crowded into Anthony's large common room, eager to share silent worship with the visiting missionaries, and they stayed long after to converse and hear the news from England.

Second Day dawned clear and cool, and Ann Wright came to Anthony's home as they broke their fast.

"Forgive me for stopping in so early," she began as Hannah poured her a cup of tea. "I thought to visit my eldest daughter Rebecca this day. She lives in Huntington and birthed her first babe this Tenth Month past. The rain has cooled the air, and 'tis a fine day for a sail. Would ye like to accompany us?"

Will and Edward declined, as they were meeting with several Oyster Bay men, who were interested in the Monmouth Project; however, George Preston opted to join the women and offered to skipper Nicholas Wright's shallop for them. They made an impressive group—the four visitors plus Ann and Alice Wright with their six daughters.

They boarded in high spirits, for the outing was a welcome alternative to daily chores. Everyone carried something—baskets of prepared food and fresh fare from the gardens; a sack of baby clothes and extra linens for diapering; a crock of laundry soap; several skeins of newly spun wool; and bread, cheese, and cider to sustain them on the way. There was mild chaos as the bounty was stowed and everyone found a place to sit, but at last they were all settled. George and Allie rowed out of the harbor until they picked up some wind then Alice Wright hauled up the sail, and they were underway.

They reached Huntington before noon, and Ann Wright distributed the baskets, crocks, and bundles for the walk to Rebecca's home half a mile north of the harbor. George gallantly took the heaviest. As they walked through town, folk recognized the Wrights and greeted them. When they learned that four English missionaries were with them, they followed to hear them speak, and their number swelled.

Ann Wright's daughter Rebecca was married to Eleazar Leveredge, the eldest son of Reverend William Leveredge. The two families had been neighbors at both Sandwich and Oyster Bay, and no one was surprised when Eli asked for Becca's hand. Everyone knew he had been sweet on her for years.

Eli's father was one of the original founders of Huntington and the town's Puritan minister. His congregation loved him, and although there was no meeting house as yet, they had built him a parsonage and deeded him the meadowland on both sides of the creek at Cow Harbor—enough to give a portion to his eldest son, when he married. Rebecca and Eli had a small farm just down the lane from the minister.

Reverend Leveredge left Oyster Bay because the preponderance of Quakers discomfited him. Despite the lack of a proper church, he was content at Huntington, for he was used to preaching in primitive conditions. In 1633 he immigrated to the Piscataqua region with Thomas Wiggin as the first minister at Dover Point, going on to Sandwich in '38 and Oyster Bay in '53. Leveredge was tolerant, for a Puritan. In his younger days he preached to the Indians around Sandwich and on Long Island in their own languages. He had lived at Huntington for five years and prospered above and beyond his religious duties through land speculation and by providing the only grist mill in town. On this fine June day, he had just inspected the quality of the flour and was heading home for the noon meal with his wife Ellin.

Upon arriving, the maidservant Suki informed him that Ellin had gone to visit their good-daughter Rebecca and the babe. Usually, they ate the noon meal together. More curious than put out, he decided to postpone eating and walk to his son's house to find her.

As William approached, it was evident something was afoot. Women's chatter and laughter spilled from the front door, which stood open. He hesitated to intrude uninvited and went around back, looking for his son. He found Eli with his younger brother Caleb in the shade of the barn, splitting rails for fencing.

"What passes, Eli? Is your mother in there?" William asked, nodding toward the house.

"Becca's relatives are here," Eli answered, putting down the maul and arming sweat from his brow, "and they brought visitors from England, Father."

"Visitors from England?" Leveridge queried. "But I hear only women." He felt uneasy. God-fearing women did not make the crossing from the mother country unescorted. Who were these people?

"Well, when Becca brought us refreshment, she said they are come with her family to see the babe," Caleb answered, shrugging. "We have not met them."

Eli was surprised by his father's suspicion. Normally he was hospitable to strangers. "The visitors are guests of the Wrights—" he began but was interrupted, as the back door opened and women spilled out, talking and laughing. Some twenty of them gathered near the barn under the shade of an old oak. A man and a woman stood facing the group, and she began to speak. Her clear voice reached the men easily.

"Good people, our thanks for this warm welcome! If you have any questions concerning the Society of Friends, we shall be glad to answer them."

The reverend rounded on his son. "They are Quakers," he seethed, "and your wife has welcomed them into your home!"

Eli and Caleb exchanged a glance, as their father strode toward the gathering. He was becoming more belligerent with age, and they did not share his antipathy toward Friends. In their experience, Quakers made good neighbors, and Rebecca was an exemplary wife. The brothers trailed after him, hoping he would not make a scene.

"God's Light dwells within us all," Mary was saying, as Leveredge approached, "and by this Light, every one of us is capable of a personal revelation, a direct experience of divine—"

"Here now! What nonsense is this? Revelation is found only in the Bible!" The clergyman's tone was peremptory as though speaking to a child. His wife and daughter-in-law stared at him, horrified by his lack of courtesy, and the other women were rapt. How would the Public Friends respond?

George Preston stood with Mary. "Friend, thou art welcome to join us. What is thy name?" he asked.

"I am the Reverend William Leveredge, and I am not your 'friend.' I am the ordained minister in this town, and ye are interlopers, poisoning these folk with false religion! There can be no revelation in these days!" he spat.

"If there is no revelation presently, *from* what then dost thou minister and *to* what?" George posed.

"From the Spirit of the Lord to the souls of the people!" Leveredge responded definitively.

"Is there not revelation there?" the Salem man pressed.

The elderly minister was flustered to find himself debating theology with a heretic in his son's back yard. He wanted to appear confident, but words eluded him. He groped desperately for a riposte.

Seeing him hesitate, George added, "How canst thou profit the souls in thy care, if thou deniest revelation?"

"I think as much as Quakers profit the people, which is not at all!" the minister spat back, flushing.

"Good people!" Mary said, raising her voice to include all present. "Let us pray that your minister may discover the revelation of God's Light in his soul."

She knelt on the grass, and others followed suit. William was taken aback, but his confusion quickly became fury. How dare she, a heretic, pray for him, an ordained minister! His temper broke.

"Blasphemer!" he bellowed, advancing on the kneeling missionary.

He seized Mary by the shoulders and shoved her so forcefully, she fell to the ground. Eli and Caleb grabbed his arms and pulled him away, but the damage was done. Red-faced and panting, the Reverend Leveredge was overcome by choler, and those who witnessed his unbridled attack on a woman in prayer would not soon forget.

Chapter 12

OYSTER BAY AND GRAVESEND, LONG ISLAND

June (4ᵗʰ Month) 1663

Mary was shaken but unhurt. Eli and Caleb took their father home, and after apologizing for her husband's behavior, his wife Ellin followed. The Wright women fussed over her, but the missionary quietly suggested they all join in silent worship to calm themselves. Half an hour later most of the gathering dispersed except for the Wrights and their guests. The rest of the visit went without incident, although the women's former high spirits were subdued. They focused on practical matters, chatting superficially as they helped Rebecca clean and launder. Ann Wright doted on her grandson, playing patty-cake and ride-a-cockhorse with him tirelessly until he fell asleep in her arms.

It was late afternoon when they returned to Oyster Bay. There was more room without Rebecca's gifts, and the two-hour sail sped by as they took turns sharing ballads and rounds. They sang "John Barleycorn Is Dead" and "Barbara Allen," and George launched into "The Coast of High Barbary" in his strong tenor just as the shallop turned into the entrance to the harbor at Oyster Bay. The westerly breeze took them right to the town wharf, where the Wrights had several slips. Allie steadied the tiller, while George leapt to the dock to secure the lines. The Wright women rolled and tied the sail and gathered up the empty baskets, but their casual chatter died as they passed the empty slip next to the shallop. Mary realized it was the spot where Peter Wright's skiff would have been docked, now ever empty.

"There is Will's sloop," Alice Wright said breaking the heavy silence and picking up the pace. "We shall find the men at home then."

"Sitting on the porch, drinking Uncle's cider, I wager," Hannah added, reading her mother perfectly.

When they parted ways at the lane to Anthony's home, Alice Wright embraced Hannah, saying, "We shall come help with *thy* laundering on Third Day, daughter."

Mary Tomkins was touched by the love in her eyes. How wonderful it must be to have a mother's help.

The men were indeed sitting on the porch, but Will had purchased a keg of ale, and they were talking animatedly. While the women and George visited Huntington, Edward, Anthony, and Will had met with potential investors in the Monmouth Project at Nicholas Wright's home.

"My friend William Goulding from Gravesend arrived this morn. Nicholas is entertaining him, and there is news from John Bowne in Holland," Will said excitedly, as the women joined them. "He arranged an audience with the High Mightinesses of the Dutch West India Company, and they sided with him on the issue of religious toleration! As a result, they have sent Stuyvesant a letter, ordering him to cease arresting the citizens of New Netherland on matters of faith, so long as they do not disturb the peace."

"That is fine news!" Hannah exclaimed.

"They realize it would discourage immigration and thwart trade," her uncle added wryly. "'Tis a rare privilege to worship as one pleases. Certes, most emigres did not enjoy it in their homelands."

Will gave a bark of laughter. "A fine assessment and, no doubt, a true one! The crux of the matter is the Directors of the WIC are businessmen, and persecution is bad for business!"

"Hear, hear!" George laughed, and they all raised their tankards in a toast.

Rather than assuaging Will Reape's restlessness, the meeting with the investors spurred him to act. He still had not walked the land to determine a location for the Monmouth Project, and both he and Edward were eager to do so. At dinner that night he expressed his intention to enlist more potential settlers from the towns on Long Island. Before he returned to Gravesend William Goulding had offered to entertain them there, and Mary and Allie readily agreed to this plan. Much as they were enjoying the company of the Wright Clan, the women wanted to visit as many communities of Friends as possible to assess their progress for Margaret Fell. The next morning, they thanked Anthony and Hannah for their hospitality and were underway at first light.

During the next week *Reape's Gain* was the missionaries' base, as they cruised the coast of Long Island, stopping at any sign of habitation to spread their message of God Within on their way to Gravesend. They were always welcomed warmly, even at the Matinecock and Carnasie villages, for visitors provided the best entertainment—news of the wider world. Regular ferries connected New Amsterdam and the western Long Island towns, and as a result, the area was unusually diverse. In addition to the local Indians there were French Huguenots, Belgians, Swiss, Finns, and black-skinned Negroes from Africa or Barbados, as well as Dutch and British. Although each community had its own characteristics, the residents generally adopted the most useful practices of their neighbors. The result contrasted sharply with the autonomous towns of Puritan New England. Mary thought the Long Islanders were stronger for it.

At Gravesend, the missionaries found good fellowship with Friends who had established regular meetings in each other's homes. William and Anna Goulding had a small family—just two sons, William Junior and Joseph, eleven and nine years old, respectively. Half of the Gouldings' large sleeping loft was reserved for guests, and the three missionaries stayed there while Will, Edward, and George slept on *Reape's Gain*. Anna Goulding was Dutch, and William was Irish, confirming Mary's concept of the area's diversity.

"I was two-and-twenty when I joined George Holmes' party on the *George*," their host said in his lilting Irish accent. "Once I reached my majority, I put Eire behind me and never looked back. 'Twas near a year before I could book passage from London, though. There were several groups emigrating in '35, but none wanted another randy young bachelor, until I chanced to meet Holmes. He planned to settle on a river named for the Baron De La Warr, who was Governor of the Virginia Colony at the start. We were to be the first English settlement there, y'see." He chuckled. "But Stuyvesant would not have it. He considered that region to be Dutch, and within weeks he appeared with a company of troops and hauled us all off to New Amsterdam. It was stay and swear allegiance to the WIC or leave. I had not yet been convinced so I swore, rather than get on a ship so soon after the crossing we had!"

"And I am fortunate that he did," Anna Goulding put in with a smile. "When first we met, he was Welem Gelder." She pronounced the W like a V. "A fine Dutch name, and he spoke our language like a born *Nederlandertje*. 'Twas weeks before I learned he was Irish!"

"I'd been there eight year, when we met, wife. Verily, I should have mastered the language by then, I hope!" her husband added, grinning. At sixty the Irishman was still vigorous and handsome.

"When did you marry?" Anne asked.

"On Fourth Day of Fourth Month in '44," William replied. "Annatje held it would bring us luck," he reached for his wife's hand, "and it worked," he finished, smiling.

They were sitting on the Gouldings' porch after the evening meal. The boys sat on the steps, whittling. The couple's daughter Margrietje was seventeen and had married the year before. As they described the wedding, Mary's mind wandered. She realized that porches were few and far between in the northern colonies, but nearly every house from Rhode Island south seemed to have one. Was it due to the warmer climate or to the Puritan aversion to encourage leisure? she mused. Mayhap a bit of both.

"Who shall accompany us on the morrow, William?" Will Reape asked at the first pause in the conversation. He was eager to discuss the details of their exploration the next day.

"Richard Stout will guide us, for he attempted settling there in '55." William answered, "He knows the choicest ground and will save us blindly thrashing through miles of wilderness. Also, young John Tilton speaks the language of the Leni-Lenape Indians who live along the river over there. If we negotiate with them directly, we can avoid the Dutch."

"Is that wise?" Edward asked, frankly.

William Goulding leaned forward to answer. "We have reason to believe King Charles plans to take over the Dutch territories early next year. Several Gravesend men are deputized to keep an eye out and report to an agent of Colonel Richard Nicolls, preparatory to taking action." He smiled. "Richard Stout and I are among them."

Young Will rose at the mention of exploration and stood patiently at his father's side, waiting for permission to speak.

"What is it, Will?" his father asked, straightening.

"Might I come too, sir?" the boy asked quietly.

His father looked at him, considering. Anna opened her mouth to protest, but William spoke first.

"Yes, my boy," he allowed, "but thou must follow orders without question and do whatever task falls to thee without complaint."

Anna inclined her head in acquiescence and made no comment in front of their guests.

Young Joseph was listening to their exchange and jumped up. "I would go, too, Father!"

William chuckled and shook his head. "Thou art too young yet, Joe lad. We know not how the Indians will receive us. 'Tis too dangerous," he said to his wife's evident relief.

"I have need of thee, Joseph. Thou shalt be the man of the house, whilst they are gone," she assured him.

"How far is it from here?" Allie asked, as Will rejoined his downcast little brother on the steps.

"Just eight miles across the sound, and the blow is usually southerly of a morning, to our favor," their host answered. "We are taking Richard Stout's shallop. It is large enough for all of us with a shallow draft that can maneuver the river as well as handle the crossing. I wager it will take about two hours. If we leave at first light, we shall have most of the day to explore."

"Mayhap one day is not enough," Will Reape mused. "We do not know how far up the river we need to go—and there are several tributaries."

"Ye shall need provisions and bedrolls then," Anna said, standing. "I will pack some baskets."

"We can help thee," Mary said, rising with her.

"Shall you missionary ladies not join us?" their host asked with a mischievous twinkle.

Mary and Anne looked surprised, but Allie grinned back at their host.

"Land speculation is beyond our provenance at present," she said wryly to the amusement of all.

In truth Mary hoped to talk with Penelope Stout during their stay at Gravesend. Will Reape said her husband Richard was among the first to sign on as a Proprietor for the Monmouth Project, and when Anna Goulding introduced them at First Day Meeting the day before, Friend Stout's wife intrigued Mary from the start. Penelope's head was bound with a linen band beneath her dust cap, giving her a nun-like appearance. Her demeanor was grave, and her grey eyes assessed the missionaries with striking candor upon meeting. Her handshake was firm, but her left arm hung uselessly at her side. Mary was curious.

"Anna, was Friend Stout's arm injured recently?" Mary asked, as they packed a large cooking pot and two baskets of provisions for the men's expedition.

Anna froze in the act of wrapping a round of cheese then turned to her guests. "Ye have not heard Friend Stout's story, I take it," she said. The missionaries shook their heads.

"Penelope Stout is the strongest woman I have ever known," Anna began. She finished wrapping the cheese and placed it carefully in the basket, as she gathered her thoughts. "She was sorely tried and survived by God's Grace. Verily she is among His chosen."

"I sensed that upon meeting her," Mary murmured.

"What happened?" Allie asked.

Anna sighed and wiped her hands on her apron.

"She and her first husband, John Kent, made the crossing from Amsterdam in 1640 shortly after they were married. Their destination was New Amsterdam, but their ship foundered off the very coast that the men shall visit on the morrow—a trackless wilderness but for savages. All managed to get ashore, but John Kent had broken his leg and could not go on. Penelope refused to leave him, and the captain promised to send help, once he reached New Amsterdam, but they left the Kents there alone." Anna shivered at the thought. "They were attacked by a brutal party of young warriors. They killed John and almost served Penelope the same." Her listeners gasped. "They took everything, even their clothing! In the struggle they slashed her belly, broke her arm, and attempted to scalp her. Something must have distracted them for they did not finish this last and left her for dead."

The three missionaries were too shocked to respond and stared at Anna wordlessly.

"But God did not abandon her, and for a wonder, she survived. Seven days she sheltered in a hollow log, eating moss and drinking rainwater, until two Indians found her. She entreated them to end her pain and kill her, but the elder stayed his young companion's hand. He wrapped her in his blanket and carried her back to their village. Under his care she did recover, and when she was strong enough to travel, they took her to New Amsterdam, hoping for ransom. She was recognized by a couple who had sailed with her. They paid the ransom and took her in, moved by her suffering and mayhap their own guilt.

"She met Richard Stout soon after. He had debarked at New Amsterdam, after serving seven years on an English man-o-war. They married within a year and attempted to settle on the western shore of Achter Kol, but Kieft was Director General then, and he kept stirring up trouble with the Indians. Penelope's native friends counselled the Stouts to leave. She spoke their language, and they had good relations, but they feared what others of their race might do to the Stouts, if war broke out. Thus, Richard procured a patent from Kieft for land on Lange Eylandt. A dozen other families at New Amsterdam came with them, and they helped Lady Deborah Moody settle Gravesend.

"But to answer thy question about Penelope's arm, it is an old injury that never healed properly after the attack. She has no strength to grasp things, and she binds her head because the hair did not grow back where they tried to scalp her. The scar is—"

"We understand," Mary broke in. "Our thanks for telling us her story, Anna. 'Tis not easy to speak of such horrors."

"Makes our trials seem paltry in comparison," Allie murmured.

For a few moments no one spoke, considering Penelope Stout's fortitude. In silence they covered the baskets with cloth and put them on the table for the men to take in the morning.

"We are tempered by suffering, like hot metal under the blacksmith's hammer; thus, does God shape us to His purpose," Anna said quietly.

"Amen," her guests chorused.

Chapter 13

GRAVESEND, LONG ISLAND

June (4th Month) 1663

The next morning Will was eager to make an early start and did not even break his fast before going over his gear. The men expected to be gone for two or three days, and he had come prepared with iron tools and cooking pots, dried food, English greatcoats, and blankets. Some was for trade, as well as their own use for they hoped to curry favor with the Navesink Tribe of the Leni-Lenape living along the river.

The Goulding household rose before the sun. Edward and George helped William and his eldest son to haul Anna's supplies to the town dock along with their equipment. The Elder Goulding carried his fowling piece. They found Will Reape among stacks of trade goods on the pier next to the Stout's shallop, and they were eating their morning fare of bread, cheese, and ale when Richard Stout appeared with his fifteen-year-old son James. As the sun cleared the horizon, others joined the group until it numbered twenty. Most had fowling pieces, bedrolls, and some dried meat or fish.

It took nearly an hour to pack it all into Friend Stout's 30-foot shallop. Mary, Allie, and Anne joined a crowd of wives and daughters gathered to see the men off. Mary was disappointed that Penelope Stout was not among them. The women chatted as the sun climbed higher, and the wind picked up. It seemed a good omen. The atmosphere was festively chaotic. The men got in each other's way, but finally everything was stowed, and they boarded. The sun was warm on their backs as the shallop set out. Four men manned the oars, while Richard Stout took the tiller.

Once away from the lee of the land, Friend Stout's son James raised the lateen sail. The canvas bellied, and the shallop picked up speed. The men would have a fine sail across Achter Kol.

The missionaries returned to the Gouldings' with Anna and her youngest son Joseph. The boy was downcast at being left behind, but his mother knew a remedy.

"I reckon we must celebrate this day with a fine pudding," Anna said brightly. "Wouldst thou fetch us some eggs, Joe?" She handed him a small basket.

The boy perked up at the prospect of this sweet treat. His mother made the best puddings in the village.

"Yes, Mam!" he agreed and was out the door.

The Gouldings' hired servant Lotte was kneading bread dough at one end of the big table. She smiled as the women entered the house, blotting her forehead with her sleeve. Banked coals heated the brick oven for the bread, and the room was already over warm even with the window open.

"Yesterday's bread is perfect for pudding," Anna said, unwrapping a day-old loaf. "Lotte is just at the second kneading, thus there will be fresh loaves for the noon—"

A shrill shout from outside interrupted her. "Mam! Come quick!"

"That is our Joe!" Anna said, heading for the door. The missionaries hurried after.

Indeed, it was Joe, and he was not alone. Three Friends stood with him by the gate. When Anna Goulding burst out the front door, they all turned. Anne Coleman gasped then ran toward them.

"Jane! Joseph!" she exclaimed. "And John! Well met!"

"Dearest Anne!" the woman cried, hastening to meet her.

The three strangers embraced the little missionary warmly, moved to tears of joy. Mary realized these must be Anne's original companions with whom she had crossed from England—Joseph Nicholson, his wife Jane Millard, who had kept her maiden name, and John Liddal. Would Anne now wish to rejoin them? She looked at Allie and saw the same question in her eyes. They linked hands and went to meet the new arrivals.

Once introductions were made and the initial excitement of the reunion had abated somewhat, the Friends settled on the porch. Their hostess left them alone to catch up, while she made her pudding.

"I would hear everything that has happened to you since we parted last autumn," Anne said eagerly.

"We spent most of the winter in Maryland on the Eastern Shore," Joseph Nicholson began.

Mary leaned forward. "Did you encounter John Perrot?" she asked hopefully.

"We did treat with Friend Perrot," Joseph responded gravely, "but with little success. Some few of his followers heeded us, but he has a core that will not budge. He is devilishly adept at convincing folk of his superior spirituality. They deem him to be God's chosen, because he survived three years of torture at the hands of the Inquisition. He is a veritable danger to the Society."

"How does he justify keeping on the hat for worship?" she asked.

The young missionary shook his head. "He says he had a revelation. He claims his ordeal in Rome brought him closer to God, and that his conscience directs him."

"He does not stop at wearing hats during worship," John Liddal said darkly. "Now he declares the shaking of hands and regular meetings unnecessary forms, as well."

"What! No regular meetings?" Anne Coleman asked.

"The man is unbalanced," Joseph explained. "At the first, when he returned from Rome, his suffering aroused admiration and sympathy among Friends in London, but the attention went to his head. In a matter of weeks, he alienated most of them—even Edward Burrough, who was his mentor."

Mary spoke past the grief her old friend's name revived. "Friend Burrough convinced Perrot?"

"Yes, in Ireland," Joseph answered. "Edward visited there in '56. Perrot left a wife and two children and followed him to England. After three years of missionary work there, Perrot felt called to speak with the Pope at Rome, and John Luffe did accompany him. They had the Founder's approval, and the enterprise was funded by the Society. A group of missionaries journeyed to France and thence to Greece. After some months, Perrot and Luffe left the others and went on to Italy. Perrot arranged an audience with the Doge in Venice, proving his powers of persuasion. They exchanged books, and Perrot wrote up a treatise for him. He and Luffe were questioned by the ministers of the Inquisition there, but they were released, and all was well—until they reached Rome." Joseph paused, shaking his head.

John Liddal went on. "We know not what passed exactly, but they must have offended the Pope, for next we heard, Luffe and Perrot were imprisoned by the Inquisition. Sadly,

Friend Luffe died under torture, although the officials claim he starved himself to death, but Perrot survived. His zeal was such that they could not break him, thus they confined him to their madhouse—the *Pazarella* they call it. He was tortured for three years before he was released."

"Three years," Allie commented.

"The London Friends believe the experience left him deranged," Joseph said.

"Small wonder, but were they not able to help him?" Mary asked.

"At the first, George Fox himself along with Friend Burrough worked mightily to bring him around, but he ignored their counsel. Perrot wrote a pamphlet entitled *Epistle for Unity and Amity* wherein he said he felt more fellowship for Seekers, Baptists, and Independents than he did for 'Quakers,'" Joseph told her. "Friend Fox was outraged, but Perrot refused to retract his words."

Mary, Allie, and Anne stared at Joseph in shock, and he confirmed, "Yes! He used that derogatory term 'Quakers' and sided with the critics of our Society! Even Friend Burrough could not countenance it."

"At the same time, Perrot began wearing his hat during worship and encouraged others to do likewise, saying it was a mere form," John Liddal added. "The London Friends shunned him entirely after that."

"Is that why he left England for Barbados?" Mary asked, recalling Margaret Fell's letter about Perrot.

"In part, mayhap," Joseph answered, "but he was also arrested twice after his return to England—once at Canterbury and a second time at London. Mayor Browne presided at the latter. He abhors followers of our faith and set a brutal sentence. Perrot took ship for Barbados soon after his release."

"But, Friend Nicholson, do the Friends in Maryland follow Perrot now?" Mary asked, appalled.

"Not all," Joseph temporized. "The leaders of the community did heed us, but I fear common folk are seduced by his show of spirituality. They enjoy the drama, and he has a glib tongue and is comely."

"His influence is pernicious," Liddal added ruefully.

Jane spoke up for the first time. "Especially among women."

Anne's former companions were staying with John and Mary Tilton, an older couple whose children were grown and gone from the house for the most part. Anne Coleman went to help them settle in. With an entire day to do as they pleased, Mary and Allie elected to visit Penelope Stout.

They found her supervising a soap-making project in the yard behind her house. Penelope seemed initially surprised by their visit, but when they offered to help, she soon put them to work.

A leaching barrel sat atop a large kettle next to the open fire, and two servants poured boiling water over the layers of straw and wood ash it contained. The hot water absorbed the lye in the ashes, and once it drained, the resulting liquid was mixed with tallow, which had been rendered earlier. The mixture was then heated over the fire and constantly stirred with a wooden paddle until it thickened, and Penelope deemed it ready for the candle molds.

Mary and Allie spent the rest of the morning feeding the fire and taking turns at stirring, while getting to know Penelope, her two young daughters Mary and Sarah, and the Stouts' live-in serving girls Fenna and Martje. It was a welcome diversion from thoughts of John Perrot. As noon approached, their hostess surprised them.

"Fenna and Martje can finish this up, I warrant," Penelope said, eying the sun's zenith. "'Tis time for the midday meal. On such a fine day I reckon we should pack a basket and eat on the dunes."

Seven-year-old Sarah clapped her hands. "Oh, shall we, Mamma?"

"Yes, we shall," her mother allowed with a rare smile. "I wish to see if the beach plums shall be plentiful this year, as well."

They left the hired girls to finish the soap and were soon on their way to the shore with a basket of cold lamb, cheese, and bread. Mary carried a jug of cider, and Allie borrowed a basket for foraging.

Penelope's knowledge of local plants was soon apparent. She explained their properties and uses to Allie, as they walked through field and forest, but she suggested harvesting the plants on the way back to preserve their freshness.

In the woods the muskeetos buzzed around their heads but did not bite due to the salve of lavender, pennyroyal, mint, and bear grease that Friend Stout provided for hands and faces. It was a joy to gain the shore for once they cleared the dunes, the wind was a blessing, bringing relief from the heat and the insects. They all shed their shoes and stockings immediately and tucking up their skirts, waded in the waves. The beach plums looked encouraging. Many of the low-growing bushes had tiny green clusters of fruit, and Penelope declared it would be a good crop. They had their noon meal at the base of a large dune, facing the sea. The girls ran back to the surf, as soon as they had eaten, and the three women enjoyed a companionable silence, as they ate more slowly.

"Have you been long in the Colonies?" Penelope asked her new friends at length.

"We landed at Dover in the Bay Colony about a year past," Mary answered.

"What prompted you to leave your homes and make the crossing?" she asked, frankly.

"Our mentor was Mary Dyer," Allie explained.

Penelope knew of the executions at Boston, as all Friends did, and she was impressed.

"You are called then," she said, turning her intense gaze directly upon them.

"Yes, we carry on her work," Mary said, grateful for her new friend's quick understanding.

Penelope looked gravely from one to the other. "What is your mission?" she asked.

"Of late we are charged with finding a Friend named John Perrot, who was last seen on the Eastern Shore of Maryland," Mary answered, "but in general we hope to awaken folk to God Within and protest the injustice directed against those of our faith."

"I doubt they welcomed you in the Bay Colony," Penelope commented wryly.

"They did not," Mary affirmed. "We were arrested and sentenced by the Whip and Cart Act."

Penelope winced. "The brutality of these laws against Friends and their supporters must be made known. They are no King's laws, and public censure is an instrument of change."

"One hopes," Allie added, quietly.

"Ye are battling Evil," Penelope stated simply. She looked at Allie. "It has marked thee."

Allie returned her gaze and nodded, unperturbed by the reference to the scar on her face, acquired at Dover when Constable John Roberts' whip went high.

"I, too, am marked," Penelope went on. "It serves to remind me that folk often speak of Evil, but they do not understand it. It is not inherent in any one race or nation, though they would have it so for simplicity's sake. 'Indians are brutal savages,' they say, or 'The Spanish are cruel tyrants.' But Evil is not confined to any one race, as ye discovered in the Bay Colony. 'Twas Indians killed my first husband and near served me the same; however, I was rescued by other Indians and restored to health through their care. They were kind to me and generous with their knowledge. I learned much living among them. Kindness and cruelty exist among all people."

The women were silent, considering her words. Mary thought of the Anglican apothecary Walter Barefoote, who accompanied them and tended their wounds after the first arrest at Dover; the open-minded Puritan, Robert Pike, who arranged their release from a fatal punishment; the Carr Family that took them in and nursed their bodies and souls even though they did not share their faith; and, of course, the Shapleighs, who received the missionaries like family, whenever they needed refuge. She said, "'Tis true we suffered in the Bay Colony, but we did find kindness in unexpected places, as well, people who risked their own safety to help us."

"If Evil has no boundaries, neither does Goodness," Allie added.

"Thus, we must encourage it in every person we meet," Penelope replied gravely.

Chapter 14

GRAVESEND and FLUSHING, LONG ISLAND

June (4th Month) 1663

The explorers returned two days later, tired, grubby, and covered with fresh mus-keeto bites but elated. The Gouldings' table was crowded that evening, but no one minded. The atmosphere was festive.

"Such potential!" Will Reape exclaimed repeatedly.

"A good investment," Edward opined. "I shall verily join your proprietors, Will."

"Untouched timber right up to the riverbanks just waiting for the axe," William Goulding added, refilling his cup with ale from a pitcher on the table. "Good soil and flat stretches of land for crops. Our greatest challenge is negotiating with the Indians. Both the Navesink and the Raritan tribes claim ownership, but any we hap-pened upon ran away even when Richard and John called out to them in their own tongue."

"And what of the Dutch?" Joseph Nicholson asked. "Do they not claim that territory as their own?"

"I wager the Dutch shall have more pressing issues to address in future," Friend Goulding said, referring to the rumor that King Charles planned to take New Netherlands as a gift to his brother James next year.

"I hope they shall, indeed!" Will Reape exclaimed, helping himself to more meat from the platter. "Stuyvesant has persecuted our faith long enough, beginning with Friend Hodgson's flogging in '57."

"There were conflicts with him before that, mind ye," Goulding said. "George Baxter, Lieutenant Stillwell, and Adam Mott were arrested in '56 for raising St. Andrew's flag on our palisade here at Gravesend. He kept them in prison near a year, while the WIC deliberated over what to do with them."

"But in the end, they were released," Anna added, attempting to calm the rising indignation against her native country. "Elbows off the table, Joe," she added to her youngest in the same calm tone.

"Stuyvesant could use some instruction, methinks," John Liddal said. "Shall we take up the challenge?"

All but the two boys stopped eating and looked at him.

"What is thy meaning, John?" Joseph Nicholson asked.

"I mean that we should go to New Amsterdam and exhort the man to repent!"

Goulding snorted. "Old Peg Leg shall never repent, and ye shall only get yourselves arrested, if ye make a commotion in his town," he warned.

"Let him!" Liddal said heatedly. "We are not deterred by arrest or punishment!"

His words resonated with Mary. To confront the man who had been harassing the English Friends of Long Island for years sent a thrill of excitement up her spine. She was ready for another challenge, but they would need a plan to be effective.

"Tomorrow is First Day, and we anticipate enjoying good fellowship with our Gravesend Friends. Let us contemplate the idea in worship and discuss it after," Mary suggested.

"Words of wisdom," Friend Goulding said, wiping his belt knife with a handkerchief. "Now, let us repair to the porch. It is a fine evening, and I have a bottle of port to celebrate the initial success of our project for any who would like some," he added, effectively changing the subject.

Edward caught Mary's eye and nodded as they rose from the table. His approval was gratifying. Once they had all settled outside, the conversation returned to the men's explorations.

⸻

On First Day Edward, Will, and George rose early from their berths on *Reape's Gain*. It was a dim morning with light rain, and they battened down the sloop before heading for the Gouldings' home. The six visitors and the family broke their fast together with leftovers from the night before then helped William and Anna set up for the meeting for worship. By midmorning, the Friends of Gravesend began to arrive, their cloaks and headgear beaded with moisture. The large, open room was soon crowded.

Anne Coleman's three companions arrived with their hosts John and Mary Tilton. They were an older couple with three of their eight children still at home, so they had room for guests. In fact, the three missionaries had stayed with the Tiltons on their way south the autumn before.

John Tilton served as Town Treasurer and was instrumental in organizing the governance of Gravesend from the start; however, once he became convinced and welcomed missionary Friends to his home, his position of authority in the English settlement did not protect him from the wrath of Director General Stuyvesant. Three times Tilton was fined for opening his home to traveling Friends, and three times he ignored the order. His eldest son John Jr. had readily signed on as a proprietor of the Monmouth Project, and his parents considered moving with him. Like many English Friends, they chafed under the Director General's Calvinist thumb.

The meeting was less formal than those at Newport, but the fellowship moved Mary profoundly. Apparently, John Liddal agreed for just before the shaking of hands began, he stood and spoke.

"Friends, I would share a revelation that came to me during worship this day!" he called, commanding everyone's attention. "Stuyvesant's persecution of our faith has gone unchecked for too long. My conscience calls me to bring him to the Light! Who will accompany me to New Amsterdam to speak with him?" He looked around the room.

"We will!" Joseph Nicholson said, grasping his wife's hand and raising it.

"And I," Will Reape and Anne Coleman said at once.

"We will accompany thee," Mary said, including Allie with a nod. She had hoped this would be decided more privily, but if the Light was prompting John Liddal to take this course, she would follow.

"I shall go," Edward affirmed, catching Mary's eye.

"And me!" George put in hastily.

After a brief silence, the room erupted in applause. The Gravesend Friends approved the mission, and soon after the meeting broke up. John and Mary Tilton lingered, and once all had left but the Gouldings and their visitors, the older couple revealed that they also wished to join the venture.

"But what of the children?" Jane Millard asked. "Are ye able to leave them?"

Mary Tilton answered. "Our Esther has sixteen years and can supervise her sisters, and the Drakes—our indentured couple—will be there, as ever, to do the heavy work."

"I reckon we shall only be gone for a day or two," John added. "I shall ask our eldest son John to look in on them, as well. He lives nearby."

"'Twill be crowded on my sloop with eleven of us," Will began doubtfully.

"Oh, 'tis simpler to take the ferry from *Vlacke Bos*, if one is going to New Amsterdam," Tilton said.

"And there is an inn hard by, if we miss the last crossing," his wife added.

"'Twould cost ye dear to dock at New Amsterdam!" William Goulding warned. "The harbor fee is hefty, as the Dutch seize any opportunity to add to their coffers."

"Also, the officials would inquire as to our business," John Tilton reminded the Newport merchant.

"I doubt they would welcome a shipload of 'Quakers' bent on convincing their Director General," Edward said dryly.

"Welcome or not, by land or by sea, we shall bring Petrus Stuyvesant to the Light!" John Liddal declared exuberantly.

Chapter 15

FLATBUSH AND NEW AMSTERDAM, NEW NETHERLANDS TERRITORY

June (4th Month) 1663

"The first folk to settle *Vlacke Bos*, or Flatbush as the English call it, were employees of the Dutch West India Company from the Netherlands," Will told them as the eleven Friends started out on the lane to the ferry town the next morning. "There were not many of them to start, but by '34 there were enough to necessitate naming the village. However, they could not agree. Some called it *Vlacke Bos* for the flats that extend south from the hills on the north side of the town. Others preferred *Midwout*—or Midwood in English—for the large swath of forest that runs west to east across the village."

"'Tis the seat of justice for King's County," John Tilton informed them. "Most of the public officials reside there, whatever they call it."

"Verily, they have the finest market on Long Island," Mary Tilton told them enthusiastically.

"The ferry landing is just north of the town," her husband added.

It was near noon, when they reached Flatbush, and the Friends were hungry. They decided to stop for refreshment before going on to the ferry. The Tiltons suggested a tavern run by Annetje Van Borsum.

"Van Borsum's has fine fare," John Tilton told them, raising his voice over the clatter of traffic in the busy dock area. "The widow is well known for her cooking. We are in for a rare treat."

"Her son runs the ferry," his wife added, "and we are assured passage if we eat at his mother's establishment. Betimes it is full, and one must wait."

The eleven travelers wove their way through the throng of vehicles and foot traffic around the harbor but staying together proved difficult. Mary was unaware that John Liddal had fallen behind, until they reached the tavern and realized he was missing.

"I will go fetch him," Joseph Nicholson said.

"I shall accompany thee," Will Reape replied.

"We shall procure a table and meet up with you inside," John Tilton suggested.

"Should George and I come with thee?" Edward asked Joseph quietly.

"My thanks, but John is wont to engage folk in conversation," Nicholson replied with a smile. "No doubt we shall find him thus. Just see the ladies comfortably settled and refreshed. We shall join you anon." He squeezed his wife's hand and left.

The two men found John Liddal soon enough. They heard his voice before they saw him. He was engaged in a heated exchange with some laborers at the town dock.

"—is at hand! Open your hearts and repent past ignorance! God's Light will reign in your conscience and inform all your deeds!" Liddal was declaring.

The men laughed and jeered at him in Dutch, but John only spoke louder. Heads turned as people around them took note. When Joseph and Will came to John's side, the workers' laughter stopped abruptly.

"*Meer van dat!* (More of them!)" one of the men growled, and they glowered at the Friends.

Will held up his hands, smiling. "*Wees niet haastig, vrienden* (Be not hasty, friends)," he began, but John, now encouraged by the support of his companions, resumed his exhortations with gusto.

"Forgo wickedness and sin for salvation is at hand!" He pointed at the largest of the laborers.

The man raised his fists and stepped forward threateningly. "*Ga naar huis, Engelsman!* (Go home, Englishman!)"

Their escalating exchange attracted more attention, and a crowd began to form. Never one to ignore an opportunity, John Liddal leapt onto a crate and spread his arms to include everyone within earshot. "Salvation is at hand for all of you!" he shouted. "Put aside your hireling ministers and their steeple houses for they are false—"

Will looked at Joseph. Things were getting out of hand. The Dutch were tolerant on religious issues, for the most part, but a public disturbance was grounds for arrest. Will thought Friend Liddal was crossing that line, but Joseph appeared calm, so Will kept quiet, though he looked around nervously.

John's ringing voice claimed more attention every minute, so Will was not surprised to see a Dutch *schout* shoulder his way through the crowd toward them. The source of the disturbance was obviously the *Engelsman* on the crate. He promptly pulled Liddal down and arrested him for disturbing the peace.

Will tried in vain to ameliorate the situation, but Liddal was no help, continuing to exhort the crowd even as his hands were bound. The *schout* deputized two of the laborers on the spot, and they marched the noisy Quaker off to the ferry landing north of town.

"We must alert the others and follow," Joseph said.

"We may yet be able to intervene on his behalf. They shall have to wait for the ferry," Will suggested, as the two men hurried back to the tavern.

The ten Friends caught up to Liddal and his escort at the ferry landing. John smiled with relief at seeing his companions had not abandoned him. Will tried to reason with the *schout*.

"What is thy name, Friend?" he began.

"Pieter Tonneman," the officer answered curtly.

"I am William Reape, merchant of Newport," Will began, offering his hand. The sheriff ignored it, and Will soldiered on. "*Schout* Tonneman, I beg thee reconsider this arrest. Thou hast my solemn pledge—"

"He broke the law, harassing these men at their business and creating a public disturbance," Tonneman huffed. "Keep your distance and save your speeches for the court."

"*Certes*, there is no law against us following to insure he is treated justly," John Tilton said.

The man shrugged and turned his back on them.

"Well, we were going to Manhattan in any case," George Preston said, grasping at the only positive straw in the tangle that engulfed them.

Fort Amsterdam sat northwest of the docks on a rise at the southern tip of Manhattan Island. It had four turrets at each corner and overlooked the confluence of the East and North Rivers. Within its walls the steeple of the Dutch Reformed Church rose into the clear, blue sky like a beacon. Although it was a short walk from the ferry landing, the little procession attracted attention. The *schout* led; the "deputies" followed with the prisoner between them; and the ten Friends trailed behind. The Quakers' plain dress and peaked headgear stood out in this city of diversity, commerce, and fashion. Curious townsfolk trailed after, and by the time they reached the north gate of the fort, the procession had become a parade.

Pieter Tonneman was embarrassed by the attention. He was a seasoned sheriff who had made many arrests, but there had never been a group of vagabonds attached to any of his former prisoners. On top of that John Liddal did not go quietly. Inspired by the size of the crowd behind, he tried several times to address them, repeating the very offence for which he was arrested. The dock workers hustled him along, practically carrying him between them. Tonneman wished he had a gag.

The sheriff was relieved to reach the warehouse and turn Liddal over to Provost Marshal Loockermans, but customary procedure proved inadequate to the bizarre situation. The prisoner's companions crowded into the room behind him. The Dutch officials tried to maintain some semblance of control, but while the Quakers were respectful, they refused to leave. They insisted on seeing where Liddal would be confined; they demanded to know when and where his trial would be; and they asked who would preside over the proceedings. *Schout* Tonneman's patience snapped.

"Enough!" he shouted, silencing the questions. "You must leave or join him then!"

Provost Marshal threw up his hands. "*Tonneman, wat moet ik doen met al stellingen mensen?* (Tonneman, what am I to do with all these folk?)" he asked more bewildered than angry.

It was a good question for the "prison" was a storeroom in the basement measuring ten by twelve feet.

"*Het is te gevaarlijk hen vrij te laten,*" ("It is too dangerous to let them free,") the *schout* replied.

Writing down the names of the accused took Loockermans some time, but at last all eleven Quakers were recorded and locked up. The room barely contained them, but at least it would keep the motley crew from contaminating the town's citizens with their nonsense about "God Within."

The Friends made the best of a bad situation. They made a bed of their cloaks and took turns lying down. They pooled their coin to pay for food and drink to sustain them for the two days and three nights until the trial. When they were not sharing silent worship, they talked and sang. Loockermans was a gentle jailor, and he allowed them to stretch their legs in the fresh air twice a day within the confines of the Fort, guarded by four soldiers. John Liddal attempted to convince them, but in this he was frustrated as they did not speak English. He asked Will Reape to speak for him, but Will refrained from adding to the case against them. He spoke, but only of ships and trade, and the soldiers warmed to the Rhode Island man and were soon calling him *Willem*. Their cell was always swept clean and the buckets for waste emptied by the time the prisoners returned. The Dutch prized order and were as efficient as circumstances allowed.

Although civil cases were normally heard on Mondays, *Schout* Tonneman was eager to be rid of the Quakers and arranged for them to be tried at the Thursday session held in the Director General's house at nine of the clock. Tonneman, Loockermans, and two soldiers escorted the Quakers to trial, making sure they spoke to no one. It was a short walk for Stuyvesant's dwelling was also inside the fort. The morning sun seemed glaringly bright after the windowless cell, but the prisoners were not bound as they crossed the compound. Edward took Mary's hand while Allie grasped the other. A troop of militia was drilling, and three wagons rumbled through the gate, raising dust and making for the warehouse, laden with cargo from a West India Company ship. Mary looked up and saw soldiers patrolling the ramparts of the fort. On the opposite side of the compound the Dutch Reformed Church looked impressive among the utilitarian buildings.

In his position as *schout* Tonneman would also act as prosecutor at the trial. The court officials included two burgomasters and five *schepens* (aldermen) along with Director General Petrus Stuyvesant as judge. Their expressions changed from dignified boredom to open amazement, as the crowd of Friends trooped into the room. Word of the Quakers' trial had spread, and the benches were full. Court was fine entertainment for those who had no stake in the outcome. The usual bench for prisoners was inadequate for eleven, and there was some confusion as spectators were moved to make room for the Friends.

The court was bilingual for many of New Amsterdam's residents spoke English, and the officials conducted the proceedings in that language in deference to the prisoners' nationality. For the sake of space and order in his court, Stuyvesant took up the Quakers' case first.

"What is the charge against these people, *Schout* Tonneman?" he began.

"They created a public disturbance on the High Street at *Vlacke Bos, Edelachtbare,*" Tonneman said.

"Are there any witnesses to give testimony against them?" Stuyvesant asked.

Tonneman had ordered the two dock laborers to attend court this day, but predictably, they had not taken time from their workday nor assumed the expense of the ferry crossing to be here.

"I myself was present, *Meinheer,*" he answered. "I heard this man, John Liddal, making a disturbance in the vicinity of the docks. When I arrived, he was engaged in an altercation with two citizens."

John opened his mouth to protest the veracity of this statement, but Joseph Nicholson put a hand on his arm and shook his head slightly. For once, John stayed silent.

"You speak of one person," the Director General noted. "What of all these others?"

Tonneman's face flushed. He himself did not understand why all the Quakers insisted upon sharing their companion's fate and was hard put to explain it to his superior.

"They insisted upon following, *Meinheer*, and their very number attracted notice on the way from the ferry to the fort. A crowd followed us, and I feared if I let them go, the Quakers would infect our citizens with their heretical ideas and further disturb the peace of our city. Loockermans and I deemed it best to confine them all."

Stuyvesant's keen gaze turned to the Provost Marshal, who snapped to attention.

"It seemed a public risk to release them, *Edelachtbare*," Loockermans confirmed.

The Director General sighed. "Then if I understand you correctly, but one of these vagabonds created a public disturbance, yes?"

Tonneman reddened. "Well, the lot of them walking behind us attracted a great deal of—"

Stuyvesant cut him off and addressed the Provost Marshal. "*Meinheer* Loockermans, do you deem our facilities adequate to hold eleven prisoners at one time?"

Loockermans avoided looking at Tonneman. "Not for an extended period, *Edelachtbare*," the Provost prevaricated, although in truth the storeroom was grossly inadequate even for three days.

The Director General perused the paper bearing the prisoners' names then looked up sharply. "John and Mary Tilton, identify yourselves."

The Tiltons raised their clasped hands.

"You are John and Mary Tilton of Gravesend on *Lange Eylandt*?"

"We are," John confirmed.

"You owe outstanding fines to this Court several times over for harboring Quakers at your residence. Will you now consent to pay them?"

"No, sir," Friend Tilton replied calmly.

Stuyvesant flushed at the blatant refusal. "Why not?" he asked, piqued by the man's attitude.

"'Tis an unjust law," John answered. "Thy employers, the High Mightinesses of the West India Company, promise freedom of worship here in New Netherlands. Thou dost overstep thy authority to persecute us against their dictates. The Flushing Rem—"

"Enough!" Stuyvesant interrupted. *Damn these Quakers and their protests!* The last thing he wanted was a reminder of the Flushing Remonstrance and all the trouble it had caused. "This is irrelevant! The Court shall now deliberate upon this case and come to a decision."

The officials rose and left the room, which was becoming uncomfortably stuffy. They were back in minutes, which Mary feared was not a good omen. The Director General announced the verdict.

"William Reape, Edward Wharton, George Preston, Joseph Nicholson, John Liddal, Jane Millard, Anne Coleman, Mary Tomkins, and Alice Ambrose: you are hereby banished from the Colony of New Netherlands. If you stay beyond sunset of this the twenty-first day of June *anno domini* 1663 or are found in said colony within the next five-and-twenty years, you shall suffer arrest and punishment."

Mary felt a flood of relief that there would be no public flogging, but Stuyvesant was not finished.

"As for John and Mary Tilton," he continued, "you shall remain until the fines against you are paid."

John Liddal began to protest, but the Director General overrode him.

"Marshal Loockermans, return the Tiltons to the gaol. Tonneman, take the rest to the harbor and find a ship to remove them from this colony forthwith!" he ordered. "Next case!"

Chapter 16

NEW AMSTERDAM, NEW NETHERLANDS TERRITORY

June (4ᵗʰ Month) 1663

Outside the Director General's residence, *Schout* Tonneman gave John Tilton little time to ask his companions to inform his son John of the situation, before sending the older couple back to the basement cell with Loockermans and two soldiers. The sheriff then enlisted four more of the military to assist him with the remaining prisoners on the march to the docks. He prayed there was a vessel leaving this day that would take the Quakers off his hands. Their plain dress and sheer numbers—nine all bunched together— still attracted notice in the streets along the way, especially with an armed guard. However, he kept them moving at a brisk pace straight to the harbormaster's office and left them outside under guard with strict orders that they were to speak to no one. Then he set off to assess the possibilities for transporting them out of New Netherlands.

Dodging wagons, handcarts, and laborers, the *schout* searched the busy wharf for a ship or a captain he recognized. When he saw *La Grace* at one of the merchant slips, he breathed a sigh of relief. He knew her skipper for the man had lived in New Amsterdam during the '40s and '50s. Currently Augustine Herman resided in the Maryland Colony, but business often brought him back to the Dutch port.

Like many of the ambitious young men who immigrated to the Dutch outpost of New Amsterdam, Herman had eventually run afoul of Director General Stuyvesant. He was on the Council of Nine Men formed in 1647 ostensibly to help the Director govern the colony, but the members soon realized Stuyvesant had no intention of conceding any power to them. They rankled under his iron-fisted autocracy for two years, for all their proposals fell on deaf ears. In desperation, Augustine persuaded the Nine to initiate a complaint against Stuyvesant with his employers, the High Mightinesses of the West India Company back in the Netherlands. When he learned of their subterfuge, Old Peg Leg was furious. He disbanded the council and took revenge on Augustine by ruining him financially during the next three years. By 1652 Herman was imprisoned for debt, and everyone in the colony knew who was responsible. *Schout* Tonneman hoped Herman's former experience in the gaol would make him sympathetic to the Quakers. He hailed a sailor on deck, and the captain soon appeared.

Augustine Herman was forty-two, although his vigor and dark good looks belied his age. He came from Prague and was the only Bohemian Pieter Tonneman had ever known.

"I beg a word, Captain Herman!" the *schout* called up from the pier.

"Pieter Tonneman! Well met! Come aboard and welcome!" Augustine boomed, gesturing to the gangplank.

At this friendly greeting the sheriff's hope rose, and once aboard, he was politely ushered into the captain's cabin. The *schout* explained the situation over a cup of Madeira that his host pressed upon him despite Tonneman's initial refusal. Although it was not yet noon, he accepted the wine gratefully. The Quakers were more trouble than they were worth, and he longed to be rid of them. As he talked, he tried to read Herman's face. The captain seemed genuinely friendly, although his age was more evident up close. His dark curls were graying at the temples, and fine wrinkles lined his sea-weathered face.

"Quakers, eh?" he commented, refilling their cups when Pieter finished. "How many did you say?"

"Nine of the original eleven," the *Schout* said. "Two are being held until their fines are paid."

"And where do they wish to go?" the captain asked, leaning back and toying with his pewter cup.

"It matters not, so long as they quit the colony this day," Tonneman answered with a shrug.

"Shall I be recompensed for their passage?" Herman's eyes narrowed over his cup.

The Sheriff's fair skin was flushed from the wine, and now his rosy blush deepened to red. "You do a service for the city, as would any good citizen."

"But" the captain smiled and held up a finger, "I am no longer a citizen of New Amsterdam."

"That is beyond my purview," Tonneman temporized. *Why had he not asked the Director General about coin for the passage?* He had drunk the wine too quickly and felt a headache coming on.

Herman regarded him steadily without comment until the *schout* squirmed. The Bohemian was a consummate negotiator and knew he had the upper hand. In truth, he was intrigued and wanted to meet these miscreants, but it amused him to let this self-important officer sweat a few moments more. Tonneman had been the one to arrest him six years ago, for the *schout* had ever been a sycophant to Stuyvesant. Although he did not hold a grudge, Herman was enjoying this.

After a lengthy pause, the captain took pity. He sighed heavily and slowly nodded. "I make no promises, but I shall speak with the Quakers," he allowed. "Come, drink up, my friend. Proost!"

"Proost!" the sheriff managed, overcome with relief. The pewter mugs clunked, and Pieter Tonneman drained his in one gulp.

"We must hope for passage to Gravesend," Will Reape said quietly to his companions, as they waited for Tonneman to return. "I must retrieve my sloop." He turned to Joseph Nicholson. "Shall the three of you travel north with us?" he asked.

Joseph nodded. "Yes, we plan to go north, but how large is thy vessel? Hast thou room for us?"

"It is a thirty-six-foot sloop," Will answered. "'Twill be a tight fit, but not as bad as that storeroom, I wager! We can reach Newport in two or three days with a good wind. Once we get to Newport, we shall have Edward's shallop, as well."

"Yes, George and I must return to Salem," Edward agreed. "We should be glad to transport you and your companions north from Newport, Joseph."

"Ye can take all eight of us?" John Liddal asked doubtfully, scanning the group.

"We have a mission in Maryland," Mary said, indicating Allie and Anne. "We shall not be going north."

Anne Coleman began to respond but was interrupted when Tonneman appeared accompanied by a tall man with large, intelligent eyes and dark hair curling to his shoulders. He was impeccably dressed and had an impressive air of authority, as well.

"This is Captain Augustine Herman," the *schout* said without preamble. "He owns the vessel *La Grace* and wishes to speak with you."

"Augustine Herman!" Will Reape exclaimed, extending his hand. "Well met! I am William Reape of Newport, and I have heard of thy work with cartography! Is it true thou art mapping the Chesapeake?"

Herman's face broke into a smile that had swayed both men and women on several continents. It was so warm and genuine Mary felt an immediate liking for the man.

The captain shook Will's hand warmly. "Indeed, I am!"

"I should love to see thy work and hear how—"

"Gentlemen," Tonneman interrupted impatiently, "I beg we keep to the matter at hand. These soldiers must return to their duties and I to mine."

"Certes, *Schout* Tonneman," Herman replied wryly. "I agree to transport these 'dangerous criminals' from your jurisdiction. Methinks their company shall be a fine diversion. You may leave them to me."

The Sheriff was stunned by the abrupt realization of his fervent wish to be rid of the English vagabonds. If Herman did not wish to discuss the price of passage further, he would not bring it up. He masked his relief, bowing stiffly to the captain then turned to his charges.

"*Vaarwel*," he said shortly. "Stay out of New Netherlands." He started to leave then turned back. "At least we do not hang you like your countrymen in the north," he added and left.

After three days packed like salt fish in the storeroom at Fort Amsterdam, the frigate *La Grace* seemed luxurious to the Friends. The First Mate and the Bosun gallantly surrendered their cabin to the women, as it had two bunk berths large enough to accommodate all four of them. The men were given hammocks in the crew's quarters below the foredeck.

Their host understood what his guests required, having endured imprisonment at the Fort himself. He provided hot water and French soap to wash three days of grime from their hands and faces; he ordered a noon meal of cold meat, cheese, and ale to refresh them; then he bid them rest until the evening when they would dine in his cabin. The hold was already packed with bales of beaver skins and sassafras from the upper Hudson River. They would sail with the morning tide.

"We shall ride at anchor this night," he said as his guests devoured the food and drink. "If you feel movement, 'tis *La Grace* being towed out into the harbor for an early departure on the morrow. Be not disturbed and rest well." He left them to tend to the crew and his ship.

Mary was impressed by their host's consideration. They had snatched only fitful periods of rest during their three nights in the ten-by-twelve-foot storeroom, taking turns lying down. It was Heaven to wash with warm water and soap. The ale was fortifying and the meat passing tender and flavorful. Mary thought no feather bed could compare to the comfort of the horsehair mattress, as she stretched out her legs on the berth she shared with Allie. They settled back-to-back and were immediately asleep.

When she woke, Mary felt refreshed and eager to explore the ship. She and Allie left Anne and Jane still napping in the lower berth and went up on deck. The ship had left the dock and rode at anchor in the harbor. The high stern deck afforded a fine view of New Amsterdam, its rooftops gilded by the setting sun. It was beautiful at this distance. Mary felt a wave of relief. Once again God had rescued them in the form of Captain Augustine Herman, and the two women joined hands to share a moment of silent gratitude. Dinner that evening was a celebration.

"We shall reach Gravesend by noon on the morrow," Herman told them, lifting his cup. "Let us drink to freedom!"

Even the missionary women took some watered Madeira to celebrate their deliverance with a toast.

"What is thy destination after Gravesend, Friend Herman?" Mary asked, using her belt knife to cut into the rib of beef on her plate. She had not enjoyed such sumptuous fare since visiting the Shapleighs.

There were fresh greens and new peas from the local gardens, as well as two loaves of rich, black rye, a favorite with their host and a staple in his homeland of Bohemia. Herman had stocked up on good Dutch butter and cheese, too, and encouraged his guests not to stint themselves. The captain insisted they use his Christian name, and his guests returned the courtesy.

"My friends call me Gus," he announced, "and I would be honored if ye would consider me such."

"'Tis we who are honored by thy hospitality," Edward responded for them all. He had shaved his three-day beard and looked relaxed and handsome. Mary pushed away the thought of parting with him.

"Indeed!" Will Reape added. "We owe thee a debt of gratitude for transporting us from our troubles. Mark thee, we intend to pay for our passage."

The captain waved his hand, dismissing the subject of coin. "'Tis no hardship," he said. "To answer your question, Mary, we are bound for my home in Maryland, and we pass by Gravesend *en route.*"

"Where is your home, Gus?" Will asked.

"'Tis on the north shore of a river I named the Bohemia in honor of my homeland. The Proprietor Cecil Calvert granted me land there three years ago in exchange for charting the Chesapeake region."

"Thy project is the talk of the nautical world!" Will enthused. "I am fascinated to see it!"

Gus smiled. "I believe it is my life's work. Captain John Smith and Joost de Hondt made a good start of it, but one cannot depend upon the older maps for they omit many hazards, and the soundings are not accurate. A deal of the waterways flowing into the Chesapeake were never charted. Now that the settlements are increasing and the traffic on the waterways with them, I see a need, as does my patron."

"Might we see thy work after we have supped?" Edward ventured.

"Certes!" Gus responded, pleased with their interest. "I have divided the area into four quadrangles, and I am nearly finished the first. Are you a mariner as well, sir?"

"Will and I both engage in imports," Edward answered with a nod to his friend, "but my business is more modest than Will's. George here is my partner, and we have but one vessel, a small shallop, as I often navigate the rivers of New England as well as the coast to make deliveries. But of late we have spent more time transporting missionary Friends and spreading word of our faith than turning a profit."

Gus smiled. "Then I am pleased to reward your sacrifice by assisting you." He turned to Will. "You say your business is based at Newport, Will?"

Will nodded, his mouth full. He was enjoying the beef, the wine, and the company enormously. He chewed and swallowed quickly. "At present I have two barques and a frigate, as well as my sloop which we left at Gravesend," he replied. "George, Edward, and these three ladies accompanied me in visiting the Friends' settlements on Long Island these past weeks. In fact, most of this party, except the two Salem men and myself, are come from England this year past. They are all active Public Friends for the Society and have sacrificed much more than I."

"We three recently returned from the Eastern Shore of Maryland," Joseph Nicholson explained. "There is a new settlement of Friends on the Annemessex River. No doubt thou art familiar with that area."

"Why yes," the captain replied. "I know it well for I do business with Levin Denwood, who has a plantation on that river, among others. A group of them settled there two years ago, fleeing persecution in Virginia."

"Thy trade routes are extensive then," Will commented. "How didst thou start?"

"I immigrated from Amsterdam in 1640 with my brother-in-law, Joris Hack. I was nineteen. We were employed by the WIC—the West India Company—and we also acted as agents for a mercantile house called Peter Gabry & Sons. We did passing well in land investment and the export of peltry and tobacco, but Joris and I recognized an opportunity when we saw it. Investment in our first ship was 'inspired' by the Navigation Act of '51." He smiled ironically. "It was a blatant attempt to give English vessels an unfair advantage in international trade, thus the WIC encouraged its employees to engage in privateering. We bought *La Grace* in partnership together, and I spent more time at sea."

Gus waited as the cabin boy refilled their cups then he went on.

"My wife Jannetje is an independent sort with a good head for business, praise God. We were newly married that same year. She keeps our accounts to this day. In truth 'twas tobacco made us wealthy and acquiring it is safer than beaver pelts. I dealt with the Wappinger Tribe on this trip, as the Esopus are becoming resentful of the Dutch again. They wreaked havoc among the settlers three years past, and the Wappingers tell me the Esopus are preparing to attack again. I shall not go back, I reckon."

They were all silent, for Indian attacks were devastating for both Dutch and English.

After a pause, their host changed the subject. "Joris and I have exported tobacco for two decades now. They clamor for it in the old countries, and it has served us well. Ye must realize there are no towns to speak of in Virginia or Maryland, unlike New England. Just the capitals at James City and St. Mary's. Each plantation has its own dock, and they are located along the riverbanks where the soil can support tobacco. Within two years I was familiar enough with the route to realize the existing charts were inaccurate. Thus, I determined to make my own."

It was full dark by the time the cabin boy cleared the table. The rich food and sweet wine made Mary sleepy despite her nap, and the other women were in accord. When they rose to retire, she took Gus aside to ask him about passage to Maryland.

"You would go on alone, just the three of you?" he asked surprised.

"Allie and I made the crossing and spent six months in the Colonies alone, before Anne joined us," she answered, smiling to cover her irritation at this predictable reaction. "We are charged with a mission on the Eastern Shore."

He regarded her in silence with his large, perceptive eyes.

"We can pay for our passage," she added, reading his silence as the preamble to refusal.

"'Tis not coin that concerns me," he responded. "The Eastern Shore is a dangerous place for unescorted women. As I said, there are no towns with ordinaries like the Bay Colony, only isolated plantations along the riverbanks. I am happy to entertain you at my home in Maryland. Jannetje shall be thrilled to have female visitors from England, but I worry how you shall manage, after leaving us."

"By the kindness of Friends," Mary answered promptly. "In New England we rarely stayed at public establishments. People entertain us in their homes."

"Well, I reckon you are women grown. I do not mean to prevent you," Gus allowed. "You are welcome to stay on board and visit my home as my honored guests for as long as you wish."

Mary expressed her gratitude and bid her host goodnight. On deck she found the three other women admiring the distant lanterns of New Amsterdam, glowing from the shore. After taking some air, they retired to their cabin.

The men stayed up with their host, eager to see his work. The captain cautioned his new friends to set aside their cups of wine then spread his parchments on the table.

"Oh! West is at the top instead of North," Will commented at first sight.

"Yes," Gus affirmed. "These are working charts for mariners. Access to the river plantations and decent places to anchor are clearer if they are not written sideways as usual. I have roughed out the other three quadrants, but this first is nearly finished. It has taken me most of three years."

"Thou hast a fine hand," Edward said, admiringly.

Their host accepted the compliment, inclining his head and smiling. "My thanks, Edward. I trained as a surveyor in Prague, which schooled my eye to assess distances, and even as a child, I sketched on any workable surface I could find. 'Tis a great joy to me."

"It is a great labor," Will noted, impressed, "and will benefit many."

"And I am handsomely rewarded for it," Gus answered. "Calvert has enabled me to realize another lifelong dream—to be Lord of my own domain."

It was late when the men thanked their host and bid him goodnight.

"We sail with the morning tide," Gus told them. "Rest well."

Chapter 17

GRAVESEND AND AT SEA

June (4ᵗʰ Month) 1663

Mary woke to shouts and thumps of activity overhead on deck. The sensation of movement told her *La Grace* was underway, and she roused the others. They joined the men on the high stern deck to watch, as the frigate was towed out into the Hudson River to catch the wind. Captain Herman ran a tight ship, and they were soon tacking south at a good clip. It was thrilling to be on a large ship again. She could feel the power of the wind through her feet on the deck. It was cloudy, but the rain held off, and the southwesterly wind generated by its approach sped their passage.

Hunger drove the men inside to break their fast, while the women lingered a few moments longer.

"I spoke with Captain Herman last night about taking us on to Maryland," Mary said to Allie and Anne.

Anne exchanged a look with Jane Millard. "I shall not be going south with you," she told them gently.

Jane put an arm around her misshapen shoulders. "Anne is rejoining us," she announced.

Mary and Allie were not surprised. They realized the bond Anne had with her original companions upon witnessing their reunion at Gravesend and their interaction since.

"We understand, dear Anne," Mary said, masking her dismay with an embrace. Despite a rocky start to their relationship, they had shared triumph and misery. Anne had become a spiritual sister, and Mary would feel her loss keenly.

"We shall miss thee," Allie whispered, bending to hug the little missionary.

Anne's eyes misted as she returned their embraces, and for once, she could not speak.

Their host was occupied with getting *La Grace* underway, but the other men were at the table, partaking of a simple but hearty meal. There were platters of cold meat and cheese, fragrant loaves, a pot of pease porridge, and plenty of strong English tea with fresh cream. The bread was still warm. Anne shared her news with Will and Edward.

"Thus, thou shalt be coming north with us," Will Reape smiled. He turned to Mary and Allie. "And ye shall go on to Maryland then?" he asked.

"Captain Herman agreed to take us, yes," Mary replied. "We must find John Perrot and treat with him."

"He was not well received at Annemessex," Joseph told her. "Especially once we arrived and talked with the Friends. He may have gone on to the settlement at Nassawadox on Virginia's Eastern Shore."

Mary nodded thoughtfully. "Methinks we shall start at Annemessex in any case," she said. "We would like to visit the Friends at the new settlement there. The more they can tell us of him, the better."

When they had finished eating, Edward caught her eye. "Wilt thou walk with me, Mary?" he asked.

On deck they went to the starboard side and watched the western bank slip by. Edward struggled to master his fear for her safety and his anguish at parting. He would have proposed marriage, if he thought it would change her mind, but he knew it would not. She would only refuse him, and he preferred to live with a possibility rather than an outright refusal. He had no idea when they would meet again. Edward turned to face her and took her hands.

"Mary, I love thee with all my heart and soul," he began. "I know I cannot dissuade thee from thy mission, but I prithee, have a care for Allie's sake as well as thine own. Avoid Virginia. There are laws against our faith there, and they are as brutal as those of the Bay Colony. The swamps and the heat breed disease, as well. Many have died of it, coming unseasoned from England. I fear for you both."

Mary studied his face, touched by his earnest concern and longing to reassure him.

"Anne's companions had no trouble with the swamp sickness, and they were there for months," she pointed out. "If Perrot is influencing people to follow his misguided ways, as Joseph says, then he is spreading dissension among Friends. We are charged by the Founder himself to stop him or at the very least to undo the damage he has wrought. I cannot abandon this mission, Edward."

He closed his eyes briefly, the slim hope of changing her mind gone. "I wager Friend Fox does not fully grasp the difficulty of the assignment he has put upon you, especially for two women alone—"

"I wager our Founder knows that women can be better negotiators than men, whose pride and need to dominate surpasses their patience and understanding," Mary shot back. She was tired of this argument.

Edward looked hurt. "I meant no insult," he said softly. "I beg thee, Mary, let us not spend our last moments together at odds."

She nodded, and Edward drew her into his arms.

"Dear Edward," she breathed, holding him tightly, "I love thee as well, but this must be done. John Perrot must be stopped before his contagion infects more of our faith."

He spoke over her head. "May I hope thou shalt return to me, when thy mission is accomplished?"

His question both thrilled and frightened her. It was the closest he had come to proposing marriage. She drew back to see his face, and they stared at each other intently. For a moment Mary allowed herself to imagine a life with Edward. She did not pull away but laid a hand on his cheek and slowly nodded.

"Yes," she answered. "I shall send a message, when we return north."

Edward released the breath he held, gently kissed her lips, and gathered her close again. She concentrated on his warmth, his scent, and the solid feel of him. It was a memory that would sustain her in the turbulent months to come.

All too soon the frigate approached the harbor at Gravesend. The Friends stood together on deck, as *La Grace* dropped anchor, and the longboat prepared to take passengers ashore. Conversation faltered as they realized the time of parting was at hand and their merry band would disperse.

Although Anne was glad to rejoin her original companions, she wept as Mary and Allie embraced her for the last time. Parting moved all three to tears, for they had shared suffering and triumph together.

"God be with thee, Anne," Mary said, kissing her cheek and holding the little missionary tightly.

She and Allie shook hands with Jane, Joseph, and John. "God be with you in New England," Mary cautioned. "They seek out Friends to punish. There is yet much work to be done there."

"I wish you success on your mission," Joseph said, taking both their hands. "God keep you."

Will Reape was next. "What a fine adventure we have shared!" he said heartily, hugging Mary and Allie in turn. "I am right glad Edward brought you to us. Ye are ever welcome at Newport."

"Our thanks, Will," Mary returned warmly. "We may hold thee to that and give Sarah our regards."

"Good luck with thy land investment," Allie added. "Mayhap we shall visit there one day."

Ever jolly, Will laughed. "I hope ye shall," he responded.

George shook their hands, kissing them on both cheeks and wishing them well. Then it was Edward's turn. Allie embraced him.

"Keep safe and bring her back to me, Allie," he whispered for her ears only. She nodded.

"She loves thee, too, Edward," she whispered back then gave way to Mary.

Edward took Mary's hands, his face intent. "I shall wait for thee, Mary. It matters not how long." He kissed her forehead. "God keep you both safe. Send notice when ye return north."

Mary did not trust her voice. She squeezed his hands and nodded. Then he was gone.

Mary and Allie stayed on deck, watching until the longboat returned, looking forlornly empty. The crew stowed it efficiently, hauled up the anchor, let out the sails, and *La Grace* moved away from Gravesend. Anne Coleman had accompanied them for nine months then Edward and George had taken all three of them to Newport, where Will Reape had joined them. As a result, it felt strange being just the two of them again. As soon as they were underway, Gus invited them to his quarters for a fresh cup of tea and, as though sensing their mood, diverted them with the story of his clash with Stuyvesant, his imprisonment for debt, and the bizarre circumstances of his release.

"Stuyvesant commuted my sentence on condition that I meet with the governors of the English colonies to assure them that New Netherlands had no intention of attacking them," he related.

"When was this, Gus?" Mary asked, comfortable now using his Christian name.

"It was '53," he answered. "Verily I had no choice, for my wife, Jannetje, was with child and living on the charity of our friends the Van der Doncks. I was frantic with worry about her, and here was my nemesis, old Petrus Stuyvesant, offering me a diplomatic post as well as my freedom," he grinned. "Happily, I discovered I have some small skill at it. I managed to convince the English governors that the Dutch were not thirsting for their blood or hungry for their land. The mission was a success, thus Stuyvesant called upon me in '59 in the same capacity."

"To New England a second time?" Allie asked fascinated by this gifted man who had experienced imprisonment and hardship earlier in his life and now appeared so confident and successful.

"No, this time Old Peg Leg sent me to Maryland in company with Resolved Waldron, a Dutch Burgher, originally from Amsterdam. We were to treat with Cecil Calvert, the 2nd Lord Baltimore, concerning the boundary between his province and the Dutch territory on the De La Warr River—a source of contention ever since the first King Charles granted it to George Calvert, Cecil's father in 1631. Your King did not realize—or did not care—that he was patenting territory the Dutch had claimed for over a decade.

"To further complicate things, that same year the *Zwaandael*— the Swiss—established a settlement there, unaware that there were already two conflicting claims to the same ground. Eventually Petrus lost patience and personally ousted them with a troop from Fort Amsterdam in the early '50s.

"Thus, Waldron and I were sent to plead the Dutch claim." Gus chuckled. "Calvert was charming, well-spoken, hospitable, and absolutely immovable. He refused to recognize the WIC's authority, but during the negotiations, Cecil and I found much in common and became friends. Maryland agrees with me. Ye shall soon see how beautiful it is there! At the earliest opportunity I visited Cecil again, unofficially, and proposed mapping the Chesapeake and its waterways in exchange for a grant of land. He accepted with enthusiasm and gave me four thousand acres bordering the river I named 'Bohemia.' I hired skilled workers to build the manor, a dock, and a stable. They had done similar work for Joris and Anna and proved most efficient. I moved my family that same year. This is our second growing season, and although there is yet much work to be done, the tobacco flourishes. Ye may stay as long as it suits you."

Mary and Allie exchanged a glance.

"Might we find passage to the Friends' settlements on the Eastern Shore from there?" Allie asked.

Augustine laughed. "I think you are as single-minded as my friend Cecil."

Mary drew breath to apologize for Allie's blunt request about moving on, but their host held up a hand.

"I understand your tenacity, and I admire it," he assured her. "Ye are rare women, like my wife Jannetje; however, I know what it is to have a 'mission,' as mapping the Chesapeake is mine." He turned to Allie. "No doubt passage can be arranged, but ye must know that although Maryland is tolerant, Virginia has laws against your religion. Captains are fined an hundred pounds of tobacco for each Quaker discovered onboard, but even if ye find one willing to take you, I would caution ye not to go. My Jannetje and I are happy to entertain you whilst ye determine where to start. We can introduce you to some business acquaintances who are Friends. They may have heard of this Perrot man ye seek. Will that suit?" he finished with a smile.

"Yes, perfectly," Mary answered quickly. "We are flattered by thy hospitality and grateful for thy help," she said with a sharp glance in Allie's direction.

"Our thanks, Gus," Allie added sincerely.

"Excellent! Jannetje shall verily be pleased!" Gus exclaimed. "God and a good wind willing, we shall be there in three or four days."

Chapter 18

BOHEMIA MANOR, MARYLAND COLONY

June (4ᵗʰ Month) 1663

On the third day at sea *La Grace* put in on the west bank of the De La Warr Bay. In addition to his dock on the Chesapeake, Augustine Herman had built a sturdy wharf for his merchant vessels at this eastern access, as it was considerably closer for ships coming in from the Atlantic. Bohemia Manor was ten miles west overland, but Gus maintained a wagon route for the transport of goods to and from his plantation. His laborers kept the ever-encroaching vegetation cut back and repaired the frequent washouts caused by rain on a regular basis to insure efficiency.

It was just after noon when they debarked, and the missionaries were struck by the heat and humidity. The quick-footed cabin boy was sent to fetch a wagon to transport the captain and his guests to the manor. The crew stayed on board to prepare *La Grace* for her trans-Atlantic voyage in two days. The frigate would be cleaned, small repairs seen to, and provisions loaded from the plantation in the interim.

"I hope my eldest son Ephraim shall join me as cabin boy next year, when he turns twelve," Gus told his guests, as they watched the boy lope off down the road. "We have a few hours before the wagon arrives. Would you care to walk about, ladies?"

They did for it gave Allie a chance to peruse the local plants, and the woods afforded some relief from the sun. The area around the wharf and the warehouse had been cleared of vegetation, but elsewhere the woods were lush and alive with birdsong and the rustling of small animals. Allie recognized oak, elm, maple, chestnut, beech, and several varieties of pine, but Gus named others that were new to her—sycamore, paw-paw, hickory, black cherry, white ash, red cedar, and tulip poplar. The taller trees towered over the lavish undergrowth of holly, magnolia, alder, rhododendron, and prolific ferns, vines, and groundcovers. Herman pointed out that sassafras was the height of a tree here, sometimes reaching fifty feet. Butterfly weed and Black-eyed Susan were both in bloom, and the purple and yellow blossoms seemed to blaze against the green foliage, especially along the road and at the edges of the forest.

At length, the heat overcame Allie's curiosity, and they stopped in a relatively open space under the canopy of a large tulip poplar. Muskeetos found them instantly. Gus broke off two leafy branches from a nearby sapling, and the women used them as fans and bug deterrents. Then he removed a clay pipe from his belt pouch and, clamping it between his teeth, took out a strange-looking iron tool and a piece of flint. In seconds, a thick, fragrant cloud of smoke rose around them, repelling most of the bugs.

"How didst thou light thy pipe so quickly, Gus?" Mary asked surprised and impressed.

"Have you not seen a smoker's companion before?" he asked, holding up his tool. Both women shook their heads. "I bought this in New Amsterdam some years ago. One uses a piece of tinder fungus called *amadou* to catch the flint's spark. Once lit, one grasps it with these little tongs, holding it over the bowl, and voilà!" He puffed anew to keep the tobacco burning. "'Tis convenient when there is no flame about. As ye have seen, I do not smoke on board, as we are ever mindful of fire, but I find it useful on land to ward off the biting insects."

"Is it usually this hot?" Allie asked, blotting her forehead with her handkerchief.

The captain laughed. "This is warm," he told her. "July and August are hot, but we shall stay in the shade until the wagon is come."

Gus was curious about their lives and families back in England, and he asked such perceptive questions the wagon arrived sooner than Mary expected. The captain had a small sack with presents from New Amsterdam for his wife and four children, and the missionaries had no luggage, except Allie's bag of medicinal herbs. Their extra clothing had paid for their food in the prison at Fort Amsterdam.

Mary was grateful for the protection of her broad brimmed hat in the full sun, although sweat gathered under the brim. She had to blot her forehead often to keep it from running into her eyes. The trees had been cleared for the roadway, and there was little shade. The women's dark clothing intensified the sun's heat which seemed to intensify with every passing mile. At first Gus kept up a running commentary, but eventually even his proclivity for conversation lagged. When the two horses broke into a trot, the wagon jerked forward, rousing Mary from a heat-induced torpor. The animals knew they were approaching home, and soon after, Bohemia Manor's smoking chimneys appeared above the trees.

The Herman plantation was three years old and seemed a beehive of industry to the newcomers. Smoke from several utilitarian fires rose straight up in the still, hot air. The brick manor and the stable looked new, the materials still fresh, and another building was under construction. The thud of mallets and the rasp of saws was punctuated by the ring of a blacksmith's hammer and shouted orders, but these gave way to greetings, as the wagon pulled up in front of the house. As the travelers climbed down, two boys came from behind the house at a run, shouting gleefully.

"Papa is home!" and "*Welkom, Vader!*"

They threw themselves at Gus, who matched their enthusiasm, embracing them and laughing.

"Now, mind your manners, my boys," Gus chuckled, disentangling himself. "Practice your English and greet our guests like proper young gentlemen. Alice Ambrose and Mary Tomkins, these are my sons Ephraim and Casper."

The boys snapped to attention and bowed politely, but once the formalities were observed, they assaulted their father with questions.

"How long are you staying?" "What did you bring us this time, *Vader*?" "Did you get lots of beaver pelts?" "Did you see Indians?"

This barrage was interrupted as the front door opened, discharging a little girl with her father's dark curls, followed by a pretty woman with light brown hair. Her dress was simple but perfectly tailored, and she carried a smaller girl on her hip. She looked clean, cool, and confident, causing Mary to blush at her own rumpled condition.

"*Ma mala Anna* (my little Anna)!" Herman cried, sweeping up the child and kissing her.

Despite the children each of them held, Gus managed to embrace his wife warmly.

"And this is my wife Jannetje and my daughters Anna and Judith." Gus smiled proudly as he gently set the former on her feet.

Janet greeted her guests enthusiastically. Her English was perfect. "Well met and welcome to our home! 'Tis a rare treat to have women visit! Such a long, hot journey from the wharf! Come in, come in out of the sun!" Their hostess continued to speak, as she led Mary and Allie into the relative coolness of the manor. "Ye must be parched. We shall have *switzel* with plenty of ginger to guard your stomachs from the cold water."

"What is *switzel*?" Allie managed to insert, as a smiling maidservant took their hats and shawls.

Janet turned to her, surprised. "Oh! Do ye not drink it in England? 'Tis quite refreshing! Cold water from the spring and a dash of cider vinegar sweetened with molasses. It is common in the Caribe islands where 'tis certes hotter than here. Gus dotes upon it," she added, smiling at her husband as she passed Little Judith into his arms. "Now Gerda shall draw some warm water. Come with me. No doubt you wish to remove the dust of the road with a quick wash. Gus will see to your things."

Their hostess turned and headed for the stairway to the second floor.

"We have no bags but this," Allie informed her, indicating her shoulder bag of medicaments.

Janet stopped short, turning to them with raised eyebrows.

"The sheriff took our extra clothing to pay for food at the gaol in New Amsterdam," Mary explained candidly, bracing herself for censure, but their hostess surprised her.

"Well then, you have tasted Old Peg Leg's justice as did my husband. Small wonder Gus took you in!" She continued up the stairs. "We shall find replacements, and I look forward to hearing all about it once you are refreshed. You have had some adventures, I wager."

"Indeed," Allie confirmed.

The warm water and cedar-scented soap revived the travelers. When they came downstairs again, Gerda led them out to the veranda at the west side of the manse, where the Hermans sat in the shade. Little Judith was asleep in her father's arms. Undaunted by the heat, the boys and little Anna played on the lawn with a ball their father had brought from New Amsterdam. Beyond the children, rows of new tobacco plants sloped down to the confluence of the Bohemia and Elk Rivers. Most of the stumps had been burned or pulled, though several large ones remained. The view across the water to Hack's Point was unimpeded. The *switzel* was refreshingly cool, and Mary sipped it gratefully as she told Janet a brief version of the past year, ending with the imprisonment at New Amsterdam.

"So, my husband tells me you are on your way to the Eastern Shore," their hostess commented, when Mary had finished. "Mind you stay away from Virginia. They have laws against your religion there."

"Yes, Gus warned us of that," Mary answered. "We seek a man called John Perrot, who was last seen at Maryland's Eastern Shore. We are bound for a new settlement of Friends there along the Annemessex River in the hope that they have seen him or know where he is."

"What has he done that you must travel so far to find him?" Janet asked.

"He flaunts the tenets of our Society and encourages others to follow," Mary told her. "Our Founder has charged us with finding him and correcting any wrong practices he may have initiated."

"Just the two of you?" Their hostess was amazed.

"We shall have help, I wager," Mary answered. "We hear he was not well received at Annemessex."

Gus sat forward. "We have business associates who are Friends—the Denwoods. Levin, the father lives on the Annemessex now, but his sons Luke and Levin Jr. keep the family farm at Nassawadox," he said. "Mayhap they know of this Perrot. Shall we arrange passage for you to visit them?"

"We would be most grateful," Mary replied. If she and Allie might speak with Friends who had met Perrot, their insight would be invaluable and might enable a speedy resolution.

"Yes, and what of the Hacks, husband?" Janet turned to Mary. "My sister Anna is married to our cousin Joris Hack." She pronounced the J like a Y in the Dutch way. "He is a physitian and constantly busy with his rounds, so Anna manages the family's merchant trade. They encouraged us to remove here, closer to them. They have land just there on Hack's Point." She gestured to the south bank of the Bohemia River clearly visible less than a mile away. "Nine-hundred acres in tobacco and wheat at the Point as well as their plantation called Evergreen in Virginia. Anna's ships sail up and down the Bay regularly. We can send a servant across on the morrow to determine when the next ship goes south."

Mary looked at Allie, and her friend nodded once.

"Our thanks. That shall be a fine start," Mary said gratified to have a clear destination and the names of people in the region that might help.

"May we ask what religion ye do observe here?" Allie asked, changing the subject.

"We are Dutch Reformed Church, as are Joris and Anna," Gus answered promptly. "In fact, my brother-in-law is godfather to Ephraim, our eldest boy."

"Maryland is passing tolerant of one's choice of worship, unlike Virginia," Janet added.

"Now, yes, but 'twas not always thus," Gus interposed gently. "The Puritans persecuted the Catholics here, during Cromwell's Protectorate in England," he informed his guests, "but that stopped when Charles II was reinstated, as He honored Lord Baltimore's original claim as proprietor of the colony."

"And even before the Restoration of 1660, many of those Puritans were converted to the Society of Friends by that brave woman. What was her name, husband?" Janet asked.

"Elizabeth Harris, I warrant," Mary supplied, having learned of her work during missionary training.

"The very one," Janet agreed. "Many former Puritans on the Eastern Shore are now Quakers, and they are coming to Maryland to practice their faith freely. It flourishes here. Just two years past a group of Friends fled Virginia, when the Assembly there enacted the anti-Quaker laws. They established two settlements—one on the Annemessex River and the other at Manokin. Also on the Patuxent River across the Bay a large community of Quakers is led by Richard Preston, and they also meet at the Clifts in the home of Doctor Peter Sharpe. No doubt there are more, but those are the ones we know of."

"Ah, yes! The Good Quaker Doctor, as folk say it," Gus added. "Our Joris is a physician as well and has a deal of respect for Peter Sharpe. In any case, 'twill be no hardship to find transport south, wheresoever you wish to go. The ships are ever busy, supplying the plantations or transporting their crops."

"Our thanks to ye both for your hospitality and your help," Mary said fervently.

"We are all strangers in a strange land," Gus replied. "It is mete that we help each other."

They saw the captain off the next morning with good cheer for his family was accustomed to his frequent absences. The missionary women thanked him again profusely, and he kissed them fondly on both cheeks and wished them Godspeed in their endeavors.

That afternoon the women went through Janet's wardrobe for clothing their hostess claimed she no longer used. Mary and Allie were so relieved to change the dresses and smallclothes they had been wearing since leaving Gravesend, they did not even pretend a polite protest. Gerda whisked away the filthy articles to be washed, and Allie helped the household seamstress Missus Block alter the items Janet gave her. It would not do to flash her ankles for all to see.

At supper that night Janet informed the missionaries that a ship would be leaving Hack's Point in two days, and the captain agreed to take the women to the Annemessex River.

It was all coming about so smoothly, Mary thought. Certes, God was with them.

Chapter 19

DOVER POINT, MASSACHUSETTS BAY COLONY

July (5th Month) 1663

E dward Wharton secured the *Sea Witch* to the dock at Pomeroy Cove and strode up the lane toward Emerys' ordinary. Since the previous December when the three female missionaries were tied to the back of an ox cart and publicly flogged, Quakers drew attention in Dover. Edward's long hair, peaked hat, and plain clothing marked him as one. All eyes followed his progress, but the tall figure looked neither right nor left consumed with purpose.

Anthony Emery greeted the Salem man with warmth at his ordinary on the High Street. He and his wife Frances were independent-minded people and sympathetic to Friends, no matter the consequences. Edward recalled the missionaries' first meetings in this common room last June before the authorities had coalesced against them. The day he had met Mary Tomkins had changed his life irrevocably. It seemed longer than just one year past.

It was mid-morning, and the ordinary was quiet on this sunny summer day. Edward had stayed with the Shapleighs on Kittery Point the night before, leaving early that morning to catch the tide, and he was hungry. Anthony drew him a pint of small beer and called Frances from the kitchen for food.

"Why, Edward Wharton!" she exclaimed, her homely face lighting up. It faded quickly. "What brings you here? Are the missionaries with you? Certes, the constable shall arrest you on sight!"

Edward shook hands and smiled down at her. "Mary and Alice have gone to Maryland, Frances," he assured her.

"Yes, Walter did say you took them south in May," Anthony said.

"I am glad they are not with thee!" Frances declared. "'Twas a dark day when those girls were dragged from this ordinary by those so-called constables! We thought never to see them more!"

"Aye, we did fear for their lives," Anthony agreed. "But fetch our friend some bever now, wife. He is come from Kittery Point and has not broken his fast this day."

Frances hurried back to the kitchen, and the two men sat at a table. The hearth was dark, and the windows were open to the summer air. Anthony leaned forward on his elbows and lowered his voice, although the room was empty.

"Why *have* you come, Edward?" he asked, his brow furrowing with concern.

"To address some unfinished business," Edward answered, evading Anthony's eyes by taking a pull from his tankard.

The innkeeper sighed and changed the subject. "You heard what happened to the Wardells?"

Edward nodded. "John Easton chanced to meet Lydia at Newbury that fateful day. He told us of her arrest when we were at Newport. He said they took her to the Quarterly Court at Ipswich, but who pronounced that brutal sentence that she be whipped to the satisfaction of the crowd?"

"The old captain, Thomas Wiggin, and Samuel Symonds, the Ipswich magistrate," Anthony told him.

Frances appeared with a warm loaf, a generous wedge of cheese, and a bowl full of tiny wild strawberries, and Edward removed his hat and closed his eyes in a brief blessing before tucking in.

"As a matter of fact, Wiggin is presiding at the court here this day," Anthony added.

Edward looked up. "Not Richard Walderne?" he asked around a mouthful of bread and cheese.

"We rarely see Captain Walderne on the Neck anymore—praise God," Frances told him. "He is at Boston for court sessions or at Cocheco, building his fine new house."

"This is delicious, Frances. My thanks," Edward said.

She nodded brusquely but returned to the kitchen, humming. Anthony was staring at Edward.

"Tell me you did not come to seek out Walderne," he said slowly.

Edward drained his tankard, wiped his mouth with his handkerchief, and stood up.

"I think 'tis a good day to attend the court," he said, donning his hat.

"Then I shall accompany you," Anthony stated firmly and fetched his own.

⟜⟝

The meeting house on Dover Point was relatively new. Richard Walderne had supplied the materials, inspiring his Puritan friends to finance the rest of the project, which was completed in April of 1654. It was a fit addition to the growing community, measuring twenty-six by forty feet with six windows of real glass and roofed with tile rather than shingles or thatch. It was a testimony to Walderne's wealth and power, and it sat on Nutter's Hill with a fine view of the Neck to the south. Horses drowsed in the July sun at the hitching posts or in their traces. The court was always well attended, providing as much entertainment as justice for the hard-working colonists.

The double doors were propped open with bricks to admit some air, and the afternoon session had just opened with the customary prayer intoned by the Reverend John Reyner. The magistrates sat at a table in the nave. Anthony took a seat near the door and noted the Salem magistrate, William Hathorne was presiding with Thomas Wiggin. Walderne was indeed absent to Anthony's vast relief. Edward would not have hesitated to call him out publicly, exposing Walderne's attempt to kill Mary and Allie last winter. The day would still end badly, most like, but at least his friend would not be publicly accusing the most powerful Puritan in the region of murder.

Edward did not pause but strode up the aisle, shouldering past two men who stood before the judges. He wore his hat, and the room fell silent in anticipation of a scene. William Hathorne recognized his fellow townsman. Wharton had installed glass windows in his manse at Salem, and Hathorne's wife appreciated the wares he imported from England. Unfortunately, the man was a damn Quaker—a loquacious one, too.

"Edward Wharton! What is your business here?" Hathorne huffed, his eyes narrowing.

"I come to bear my testimony to the truth against miscarriages of justice committed by the elected officials of this town," Edward declared.

The magistrates conferred in hushed voices, while the room buzzed at this statement. The spectators would not be disappointed this day, and any afternoon torpor was dispelled.

Hathorne straightened and said slowly, "That is a serious charge that must be proved; however, you are not on the docket, and this court has many cases to—"

Edward interrupted, his deep voice ringing from the rafters. "Woe to all oppressors and persecutors, for the indignation of the Lord is against them! They have no regard for the law, inflicting deadly harm as they please with unbridled malice!"

The buzzing increased. Everyone had witnessed the flogging of the three Quaker women at the cart's tail last December, and some had seen them bodily dragged from the Emerys' ordinary in January by the town's constables. The magistrates stared at the Salem man in shock, as he continued.

"Therefore, friends, while you have the time, prize the day of His patience and cease to do evil and learn to do well." He glared at the judges. "Ye who spoil the poor and devour the innocent!"

Wiggin was first to recover. "You are out of order, sir!" he responded hotly and gestured to Constable John Meader, newly elected that spring. "Clap him in irons, Constable! He disrupts these proceedings!" He rose to his feet in agitation. "You, sir, are a heretic and a rebel and deserve to be flogged!" he shouted, his face attaining a glorious beet red.

Meader moved toward Edward, who addressed the distraught magistrate calmly, "Thomas Wiggin, thou shouldst not rage so. Thou art an old persecutor and grey-headed. 'Tis time for thee to give over for thou mayest be drawing near to thy grave."

His words were like oil on fire, incensing the old captain.

"Do not 'thee' and 'thou' me like a child!" Wiggin roared. "You evidence no respect for court business and shall suffer for it!" His eyes protruded, and spittle flew from his lips.

Hathorne laid a restraining hand on his fellow magistrate's arm, and Wiggin started at his touch then seemed to recall himself. He sat down and mopped his perspiring brow with a handkerchief.

"Confine him to the stocks for now, Constable," Hathorne ordered evenly. He knew from previous incidents at Salem that Wharton was not a man to be trifled with. People respected him. His eloquence was dangerous, and few could match his tenacity. The miscreant must be removed to regain control.

"We shall sentence him on the morrow. And see that you write the order in the King's name," he added to Elias Stileman, who was acting clerk of the court.

Stileman was a Salem man also, and Edward admonished his fellow townsmen. "Friends, you do wrong the King and abuse his name for I believe he never gave you such an order, so to abuse his subjects."

"Remove him *now*, Mr. Meader!" Hathorne ordered, a note of urgency in his voice. He knew this argument had merit. The laws against Quakers were not the King's laws but were devised by Governor Endicott and his ministers Wilson and Norton. Inexplicably, the latter had died just two months ago, and Hathorne's mind shied away from the implication of divine wrath at work. Wharton must be silenced forthwith. Constable Meader hastened to comply, and Edward allowed himself to be led away.

They left him in the stocks overnight, an unusually long duration. Anthony knew it was Wiggin's revenge. The innkeeper alerted Doctor Walter Barefoote and the Dover Friends. Once Constable Meader went home for the night, they brought Edward food and drink and some spiritual comfort, but they were helpless to relieve his pain. As the hours crawled by, discomfort became agony. Edward's muscles cramped, and if he tried to move his limbs to get some relief, the rough wood abraded his wrists and ankles. The Friends eventually went home to their beds, but Walter stayed, massaging his friend's calves, draping a cloak over his shoulders to keep off the chilling dew, and distracting him with conversation. Sleep was elusive and brought little relief. There was none for Edward's bladder, and he was chagrined when he lost control.

At long last a dim glow lit the horizon, and Walter left to fetch sustenance and fresh clothing. Anthony Emery returned with him, and Edward drank thirstily but ate little, for his limbs were in agony. He had never felt so humiliated and helpless. He was not released until the constable had broken his fast. Then Anthony and Walter all but carried their friend to the gaol to prepare him for court.

Once he had changed his soiled clothing and could walk unaided, Edward was brought before the magistrates. He was not allowed to speak. They sentenced him to the Whip and Cart Act—ten stripes each at Dover, Hampton, and Newbury, thence to be remanded into the custody of Constable Daniel Rumboll at Salem.

"I fear not the worst you may be suffered to do unto me; neither do I seek any favors at your hands," Edward responded calmly. Wiggin glared but kept his temper.

However, an ox and cart proved impossible to find on such short notice. It was haying season, and none could be spared. Edward spent the night in the gaol, while the officials worked out an alternative.

The next morning the entire town watched as Edward was stripped to the waist and whipped at the post outside the gaol. Hathorne and Stileman had returned to Salem, but Wiggin presided, savoring his revenge. He also provided a horse so the prisoner could be pilloried to the saddle after each whipping and led half-naked from one town to the next—normal procedure for common criminals. Wiggin aimed to humiliate Edward, as well as see him bleed. He smiled during the flogging, but when it was done, Wharton stood erect and evidenced no pain.

Catching Wiggin's eye, he said, "I rejoice that I am counted worthy to suffer for righteousness' sake."

The crowd reacted, repeating his words to those who had not heard them. His scoured back bleeding, Edward Wharton was pilloried to the horse and removed from Dover as quickly as possible.

Part III

SUMMER/AUTUMN 1663

John Perrot, when he found he had lost credit and standing in England, had gone over to the West Indies and America, and to both places promulgated his peculiar views. Here he took a step further than in England, and beside objecting to taking off the hat in time of prayer, as being a mere form, he declared it wrong to have regular times appointed for offering public worship to the Almighty, and that it was not right for a Friend to attend at meetings for worship, unless feeling a special call therein.

—Charles Evans, *Friends in the Seventeenth Century*

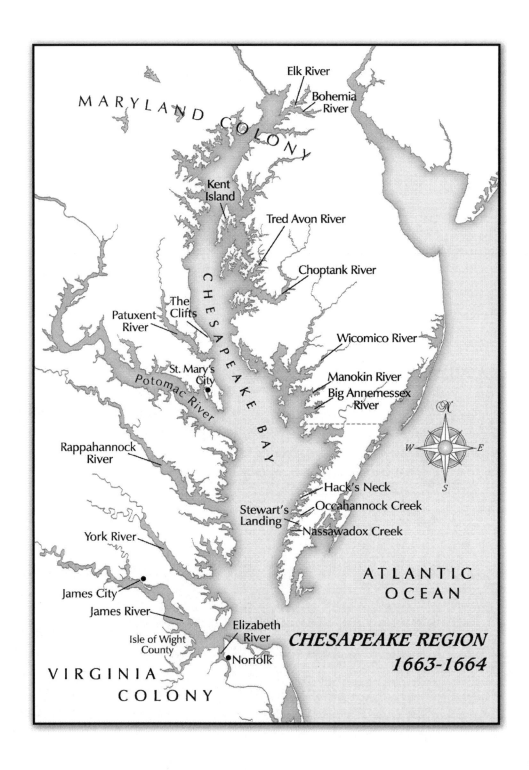

Elk River

Bohemia
River

MARYLAND COLONY

Kent
Island

Tred Avon River

Choptank River

The
Clifts

Patuxent
River

CHESAPEAKE BAY

Wicomico River

St. Mary's
City

Manokin River

Big Annemessex
River

Potomac River

Rappahannock
River

Hack's Neck

Stewart's
Landing

Occahannock Creek

Nassawadox Creek

York River

ATLANTIC
OCEAN

James City

James River

Isle of Wight
County

Elizabeth
River

Norfolk

CHESAPEAKE REGION
1663-1664

VIRGINIA
COLONY

Chapter 20

ANNEMESSEX SETTLEMENT, MARYLAND COLONY

July (5th Month) 1663

The missionaries stayed another two days with Janet Herman. Their hostess spent several hours each day in her office, tending to the family's trade business. Her guests took the time to replenish their clothing with bits and pieces from her extensive wardrobe. Gus's travels supplied a range and quality of material unavailable to most colonists, and Missus Block was kept busy making clothing for the family.

"The children grow so fast, it is a constant labor to outfit all four of them," Janet explained. "My time is taken up with business concerns, and in truth, I have no skill with handiwork," she added with a laugh.

Missus Block loved to converse and was grateful for both the help and the company. Their garments were altered and ready the night before they left. The gift of light weight skirts and blouses was a godsend in the southern climate. Mary and Allie repaid the household with an evening of song, and Janet invited everyone who worked and lived at Evergreen. The children and adults were delighted with the rare entertainment.

Early the next morning Janet and the children saw them off, as one of the Hermans' servants rowed the English missionaries across to Hack's Point. There they met Captain Samuel Groome of the ship *Dove*. Initially he seemed young for a sea captain, but, surprisingly, he was a Friend, and he welcomed Mary and Allie with warmth and respect.

The *Dove* was a cargo ship weighing forty tons. She had crossed the Atlantic many times since her first voyage in 1631, bringing Lord Baltimore's first settlers to the

Maryland Colony. However, she was small enough to maneuver the various rivers off Chesapeake Bay, as well. Her three traditional masts were augmented by two Lateen sails, affording speed and adaptability. Later the women learned that Samuel Groome had been her captain for five years, assuming the post when he was just twenty-one.

"I am honored to aid you on a mission for our faith. Where d'ye wish to go?" he asked the missionaries.

"We would visit the Friends on the Annemessex River," Mary answered.

"There is no town there, mark ye," he said. "Did ye have a particular Friend in mind?"

"Captain Herman mentioned Friend Levin Denwood, as they are engaged in business," Mary answered, "but as thou art a member of the Society, we would defer to thy knowledge of the community."

Groome answered without hesitation. "Then I suggest Ambrose Dixon. He is the driving force behind the settlements on the Annemessex and is respected by everyone, Friends or no. Several families followed him from Nassawadox when he removed to Maryland. He is a skilled mariner, as well, and has transported other Public Friends from prison in Virginia to the safety of Maryland. We are scheduled to stop at his plantation Dixon's Choice to deliver some tools. It is near the mouth of the Annemessex."

"Then we shall follow thy advice and go there," Mary said. "Our thanks, Captain Groome."

After three days and several stops at plantations up the rivers off Chesapeake Bay, the *Dove* approached Ambrose Dixon's wharf on the south bank of the Annemessex River. The plantation was still a work in progress, for the former caulker-turned-planter had come from Virginia just two years before, escaping persecution against Friends. This summer was the first season he had been able to plant tobacco.

At mid-morning, the *Dove* docked at Dixon's sturdy pier which jutted out into the river to accommodate larger vessels. With so many plantations growing the popular weed it was small wonder that Anna Hack's ships were kept busy delivering tools and goods from England or New Amsterdam and collecting the colonists' harvest or livestock for transport.

Mary and Allie stayed out of the way, waiting on deck with Captain Groome as a group of laborers began to unload crates of tools. A young man with chalk and slate accompanied them, and Captain Groome introduced the women.

"Henry Pennington, may I present Friend Tomkins and Friend Ambrose, lately come from the northern colonies." He turned to the women. "Henry is Friend Dixon's stepson," he informed them.

"My stepfather is helping a neighbor at present," the young man told them smiling and shaking hands courteously, "but we expect him back well before dark."

On closer inspection Mary realized Henry was not yet twenty. Frontier living apparently provided opportunities for those with youthful vigor.

"Mother shall be delighted to welcome you, Friends," the young man continued. "Just follow that road, and ye shall gain the house."

"Our business here shall not take long," Captain Groome added. "We shall join you presently."

The lane ran roughly parallel to the river, and the missionaries followed it. The land showed signs of recent clearing, a portion of which was planted in tobacco. Laborers were hard at work on the rest, pulling stumps with a team of oxen. A two-story house appeared around the next bend, modest by plantation standards. The new brick looked rosy in the sunshine. As they approached, the now-familiar evidence of industry increased—the thud of mauls, the rasp of saws, the ring of a blacksmith's hammer. The ever-present smoke from several fires spiraled into the hot, still air above it all. Behind the house Mary caught a glimpse of sheep grazing in a meadow. Although Dixon's Choice was more modest than the Hermans' holdings, progress was evident. New plantations were sprouting like mushrooms in Cecil Calvert's colony. Any arable land was planted in tobacco or corn, and the rest was used for pasture. Most of the yield would be exported on ships like the *Dove*.

As Mary and Allie approached the house, a woman turned from a large kettle suspended over an outdoor fire pit and saw them. She set down her wooden paddle and approached smiling and wiping her hands on an apron blotched with blue stains. She seemed about their age and wore a simple brown dress. Mary assumed she was a servant, until she spoke.

"Well met and welcome, Friends," she greeted them, cheerfully holding out a hand, also stained blue with vegetable dye. The dark curls that escaped her dust cap were plastered to her forehead with sweat. "I beg you, pardon my appearance. We are at dying wool. I am Mary Dixon, mistress here."

Mary and Allie introduced themselves, and Mary Dixon's enthusiasm grew, when she realized they were Public Friends visiting from England.

"My husband Ambrose is upriver, helping neighbors fell some trees, but he shall be eager to speak with you!" she exclaimed, as she ushered them indoors for some refreshment.

Ambrose was indeed home before dark and greeted his guests warmly. He was a big man with dark red hair and an open face. His blue eyes were discerning, and Mary understood immediately why folk followed him. The missionaries soon learned that young Henry Pennington was Mary Dixon's fifteen-year-old son by her first husband. His stepfather appeared to trust him with considerable responsibilities and encouraged him like his own. The family dined with all six of their children at table. The Dixons' five offspring—four girls and a boy—ranged in age from Mary, who was thirteen, to four-year-old Gracie. John and Martha Combs, an indentured couple, were included, too. With Captain Groome and the missionaries their number was thirteen, and Martha ate sitting on a stool by the hearth, insisting thirteen at the board was bad luck. Ambrose asked Mary to say the blessing, and they all joined hands before tucking into Martha's savory lamb stew.

"I hope ye might tarry a good while with us here," Ambrose said, filling trenchers and passing them around, while his wife sliced a loaf. "Folk are thirsty for news of England, and they shall be eager to worship with you on First Day. We hold meetings here."

He lifted his chin, indicating the large hall that was the entire first floor of the house. The space was open and bright even as the sun was lowering outside for the Dixons had real glass windows. It made Mary think of Edward Wharton. He would have liked their host.

She wanted to ask about John Perrot, but the family peppered the missionaries with questions about England. She and Allie were so busy answering, they barely had time to eat. Mary relaxed, biding her time, and enjoying the easy interaction at the Dixons' table. All ages were encouraged to talk.

At a rare lull in the conversation Mary Tomkins asked, "How did ye both come to be convinced?"

Ambrose responded. "Elizabeth Harris came to Nassawadox some years past. When was it, wife?"

"'Twas the spring of '57," she answered promptly. "Lizzie was a newborn at the time, I recall." She smiled at the six-year-old, who had red hair like her father. The girl was shy and blushed at the notice.

"Then the year following, I brought Friends Coale and Thurston up from Virginia. They stayed several weeks, refreshing us greatly," Ambrose went on.

"And we had need of it for many of us were fined and called to court at that time for not paying tithes to Reverend Teackle at Hungar's Parish," his wife added.

"Aye, 'twas when they first introduced the new laws against Friends in Virginia," Dixon elaborated. "Thomas Price, Levin Denwood, George Johnson, Stephen Horsey, and I were all summoned to court to make us pay—all neighbors on this river now."

"Stephen does not worship as a Friend, although he is in sympathy with us," Mary Dixon clarified.

"Cecil Calvert welcomed us for he is eager for settlers to secure his southern boundary," Ambrose continued. "'Tis an ongoing issue with Virginia. They ever seek to extend their colony by appropriating Maryland land."

"Were ye arrested for not paying the tithes in Virginia?" Allie asked.

"They tried," Ambrose replied with a rakish smile. "We removed here before they could enforce the summons to court. Now we worship as we please."

"Certes, this river bottom land is rich indeed," his wife added. "We planted five acres of tobacco in Third Month, and our first crop is thriving. It shall be a fine yield if we can keep the beetles from the drying racks. But our Indian friends say that after three years, it uses up the soil. Then one plants corn for three years, as the roots go deeper; however, if we continue to grow tobacco, we must constantly clear more land to keep up."

"The best market for us is New Amsterdam. The price is steadier than London tends to be, and 'tis a deal closer." Ambrose nodded toward Captain Groome. "Samuel here will ship it for us at the end of Seventh Month when 'tis dry and packed in hogsheads. All the plantations on this river cultivate it."

"But if everyone grows tobacco, shall it not affect the price?" Allie asked.

Friend Dixon gave her a keen glance, and Captain Groome chuckled. "An astute observation, that," he said admiringly. "In time that may indeed be the case, but for now the demand exceeds the supply. Also, some folk turn to husbandry if their land does not support tobacco. There are ready markets for meat and livestock in New England and Barbados," Ambrose added.

"Though they are more work and expense to ship than hogsheads of the stinking weed," Samuel added with a sea captain's perspective.

Once they had eaten, the visitors rose to help clear the table, but Mary Dixon protested.

"Ye are guests," she insisted with a smile, "and the girls are accustomed to this chore. Go sit with the men out of doors. There is like to be a breeze on the porch. I shall join you once the little ones are abed."

The missionaries found Samuel Groome, Ambrose Dixon, his twelve-year-old son Thomas, his stepson Henry Pennington, and Mr. Combs outside on a stone-flagged veranda that faced the river to the north. It was cooler as the sun had set across the Bay to their left. Dixon's Choice was on flat and fertile ground bordered by water on three sides. Two smaller streams emptied into the Annemessex to the east and west of the house, and the latter was near enough to provide water for the house their host explained.

John Combs smoked a pipe, which kept most of the muskeetos away, and the breeze Mary Dixon had mentioned was indeed a blessing. Even banked, the cooking fire warmed the house, and the air outside felt cool in contrast.

"Ye are brave traveling unescorted," Ambrose commented. "Are ye on a mission for the Society?"

Mary seized the opening. "Yes, Friend Dixon. We seek a Public Friend called John Perrot. Hast thou heard of him?" she asked.

Ambrose sat up. "Indeed, I have!" he exclaimed. "He was here this spring until a month or so past. Are ye in accord with him?" he asked cautiously.

"On the contrary," Mary answered, "our mission is to stop him preaching false doctrine and to correct the damage he has wrought among Friends."

Dixon leaned back with a sigh of relief. "I am glad to hear it. His influence is pernicious, and ye are not the first to seek him out. Other Friends were here—"

"Joseph Nicholson, his wife Jane, and John Liddal?" Mary posed.

"Ah! Ye are acquainted then," Ambrose replied, nodding.

"We recently parted company at Gravesend after our release from prison at New Amsterdam," Mary told him.

"Stuyvesant imprisoned you?" Samuel Groome exclaimed indignantly, straightening.

"But briefly," Allie said dismissively, "and they did not flog us."

"Augustine Herman kindly transported us away from Dutch territory to his plantation on the Bohemia River," Mary elaborated. "His wife Janet arranged for us to meet Captain Groome at Hack's Point, and he brought us south." She smiled at the young sea captain.

"It was a treat to have Friends aboard," Samuel smiled, "and I thank you both for your patience. We were obliged to stop often to deliver this latest shipload of tools from England. Certes the crew benefitted from the evening meetings, and we all enjoyed your singing."

Ambrose smiled, too. "I do admire resourceful women." He sobered, returning to the issue at hand. "Mind ye, your companions did try to bring Perrot around but to no avail," he finished gravely.

"As Joseph said," Allie affirmed.

"Dost know where Perrot went from here?" Mary asked.

"To Nassawadox, I wager, as the Friends here spoke of it, being our former home," their host replied.

Mary looked at Allie. "Then we must follow," she said.

"I do not recommend that course," Ambrose cautioned, leaning forward. "Virginia has laws against Friends, itinerant ones in particular. 'Tis why we quit there. Samuel here would be fined an hundred pounds of tobacco each for transporting you; folk are prosecuted for entertaining Friends in their homes; and meetings for worship result in fines for residents—flogging and banishment for vagabonds."

"Sounds like New England," Allie commented.

"But is there not some way to journey there undetected?" Mary insisted, "Overland, mayhap?"

Ambrose drew breath through his teeth and shook his head. "That way is challenging for men. In good conscience, I would not advise it!" Mary opened her mouth to protest, but he held up a finger. "But a small craft can land at a private dock undetected. I have done it many times, since first bringing Friends Coale and Thurston to Virginia's Eastern Shore, and now I think on it, Levin Denwood's sons Luke and young Levin are yet at Nassawadox on the family's original holding. They have a private dock, where we could put in."

Mary's eyes shone. "Thou wouldst take us there thyself? We are willing to work for our passage—"

"Ye need not," Dixon interrupted. "'Tis enough ye are come. Your mission is important to our faith, and I shall aid you in any way possible, but I beg ye call me Ambrose," he finished warmly.

Mary agreed, gratified that she and Allie had found an able companion and helpmeet.

Chapter 21

EASTERN SHORE of MARYLAND
and VIRGINIA

July/August (5th/6th Month) 1663

First Day came two days later, and after the meeting for worship in the Dixons' hall, their neighbors the Prices stayed to share a noon meal. Their plantation Cheap Price bordered Dixon's Choice to the east, and they had removed to the Annemessex River together. Now they all settled at the big table, sharing platters of cold meat, cheese, salat from the kitchen garden, and yesterday's bread, as baking was not permitted on the Sabbath. Drawing cider for the table fell to six-year-old Elizabeth Dixon as the youngest child in the family capable of the task, but her elder sister Sarah helped her carry three jugs to the board. The Prices' nine-year-old son Thomas Jr. thoroughly enjoyed the company of other children, as he was an only child. Mary waited until the young ones had left the table to raise the subject of John Perrot. Price was a reticent man but did not hesitate to express his opinion.

"He put me in a pother, to be sure," he replied gravely.

"How so?" Allie asked with a keen glance. Friend Price seemed unshakable to her.

Thomas considered his answer carefully, as he wiped his belt knife with a handkerchief. "At the start he appeared sober and committed to the Light, but soon he began to speak so contrary to our faith, we could not credit him. Is that not the right of it, Ambrose?" he finished, deferring to his friend.

"Yes, Tom," Dixon affirmed. "His spirituality was impressive at the first. As he tells it, he was sore tried at the hands of the Inquisition for three years and survived. It gave him credibility among us for God must have lent him the strength to endure. But then he insisted on wearing hats at worship and further shocked us by abolishing regular meetings, as well. It led us to suspect his ordeal unbalanced his mind."

"Friend Nicholson suggested as much," Mary agreed.

"And Friend Perrot is too taken with the comforts of this world," Mary Dixon added. She counted his faults on her fingers. "His hair is overlong; he keeps a beard; he is vain and dresses like an Anglican; and he is too fond of food and drink. He deemed our fare was plain and lamented that we had no French wine." She rolled her eyes. "He may appear comely, but I mistrusted him from the first."

"He said 'twas an empty form, removing the hat at worship," Thomas Price added, morosely.

"And we were to gather only when 'the spirit moves us,' says he!" his wife added with mounting anger. "What if some are moved to worship but not others? What of fellowship?"

"Indeed!" Mary Dixon affirmed. "He said 'tis enough to be 'upright in our hearts,' whatever that signifies."

"Aye, he often used that phrase," Ambrose confirmed, turning to Mary and Allie. "He travels with John Browne, and they stayed here for two weeks. We feared they would never leave." He glanced at his wife, who nodded vigorously. "I called a private meeting at Tom's place with our neighbor George Johnson, and we were all in accord. Together we told him he must move on."

"And did he so with good grace?" Mary Tomkins asked, fascinated. She had wondered how Perrot would react to a confrontation. These men had faced him down and could tell her.

The four local Friends exchanged a look.

"He was furious," Ambrose said quietly.

"At the first he was serene as an angel, but by the time we finished, he was the Devil himself," Thomas Price elaborated. "Friend Browne eventually calmed him. He appeared accustomed to doing so."

"It shook us, I tell you," Ambrose went on. "Certes, it confirmed our fears. I have transported Public Friends for six years now, but none ever spoke so harshly or abandoned the tenets of the Society. They left that very day in Browne's skiff. I reckon they went to Nassawadox to try their luck there."

"John Browne's younger brother Thomas lives there, as well," Katherine Price put in. "He is married to Luke Denwood's sister, and 'tis likely Perrot and Browne are being entertained at their home."

"I had forgot that," Ambrose said, nodding. "More reason for them to go to Nassawadox."

"We saw nothing of his choler, until we crossed him," Tom Price added, apparently still affected by the encounter despite his slow and steady demeanor. "Verily, it rattled me. I was that glad when he left."

"Our thanks, Friends," Mary said. "Your observations help us immeasurably."

Mary and Allie stayed with the Dixons longer than intended. The Friends living on the Annemessex River were so grateful and welcoming that the missionaries extended their stay through a second meeting for worship. The fledgling community was shaken by Perrot, but Mary and Allie reaffirmed the tenets he had dismissed as "empty form." Although Mary was eager to confront the man and accomplish her mission, she and Allie agreed it was time well spent. Their friendship with the Dixon Family deepened, and their only regret was that Anne Coleman was not there to share it with them.

During the first week of Sixth Month Ambrose took Mary and Allie to Nassawadox in his thirty-foot sloop. The summer heat was punishing, and they were all glad to get out on the water. Ambrose's stepson Henry came along as crew, and it was well he did for the wind was fitful, now blowing southwest, then gusting northeast, at times dying altogether; however, Ambrose was capable and knew the Bay well. Everyone was in good spirits.

"That is Smith's Isle to starboard," he told them, pointing with his chin, as he prepared to come about again. "We shall put in at the Hacks' plantation Evergreen tonight for we cannot make Nassawaddox with this fitful blow but fear not. I know George and Anna Hack well, and they are sympathetic to Friends. Being Dutch, they tend to be more tolerant on religious matters than our own countrymen."

"Captain Herman spoke of them," Mary said over the rush of wind and water. "His wife Janet is sister to Anna Hack, is she not?"

"Aye, she is," Ambrose replied. "I forgot you are acquainted with the Hermans. All the better."

"We do not put thee in danger going to Virginia, Ambrose?" Allie asked yet again.

The big man chuckled. "Fiddle-faddle!" he grinned. "I know these waters better than most, I reckon. We shall avoid the authorities, and the Hacks shall welcome us. Now prepare to come about, ladies!"

The plantation of Evergreen was just north of Hacks Neck on the west coast of Virginia's Eastern Shore—not to be confused with Hack's Point on the Bohemia River, although the family was the same. Two merchant vessels were docked at a long pier, and the activity from a distance reminded Mary of an anthill. As they drew closer, she realized one ship was being loaded, and the other was being cleaned from stem to stern. Sailors dangled from ropes, scraping the hull down to the waterline, which was exposed with an empty hold. As Henry and Ambrose secured the sloop, a foreman strolled over to confirm their identity. He recognized Friend Dixon and informed them that the Hacks were at home. The four Friends battened down the hatches then followed the lane to the house.

The manor soon appeared, silhouetted against the lowering sun. Mary and Allie were impressed for this plantation was more established than any they had yet seen on the Eastern Shore, having been established over a decade before. Had Ambrose Dixon not been with them, they might have felt intimidated by the three-story brick manse with its colonnaded front entry, glass windows, and numerous chimneys; however, their new friend did not hesitate to rap boldly on the wide front door.

A servant girl opened and recognized him immediately.

"Why, Mister Dixon!" she exclaimed, "What a pleasant surprise! Come in, come in. The Master and Mistress are to home. I shall alert them ye are here." She looked at the women curiously. "With guests."

"My thanks, Martje," Ambrose said as she took their hats and scurried off.

George Hack soon appeared. Ambrose made introductions, and the doctor welcomed his unexpected guests warmly and led them out to a veranda, where the family gathered in the evenings. Anna Varlet Hack resembled her sister Janet but with darker hair and a fuller figure. The Hacks' two young sons left off rolling a hoop back and forth on the lawn to meet the newcomers. Introductions were made, and in the lull following the younger boy could not contain his curiosity.

"What happened to your face?" he blurted, staring at Allie's scar with fascination.

"Georgie! *Dat is gemeen* (That is rude)," his mother admonished. Her son blushed. She continued in English without missing a beat. "I beg you, pardon our youngest. He is yet learning the social graces."

"He is not the first to ask," Allie replied, meeting the boy's eyes. "We were scourged in New England last Tenth Month, and the whip went high," she answered, frankly.

Georgie's mouth fell open until his elder brother pinched his arm. "*Stop met staren!*" he hissed.

"Ouch! *Vader!*" the boy wailed, turning to his sire. "Peter pinched me!" he reported indignantly.

"Enough, George," his father said firmly. "I shall serve thee worse, and thy manners do not improve. Return to your game, boys, and allow us to talk."

The boys obeyed, and Henry joined them much to their delight. Refreshments were ordered, and the adults settled, facing a fine prospect of the river.

"How do things fare at Annemessex, Ambrose?" George Hack asked.

"Our first crop of tobacco appears to have taken well," Dixon answered, "The soil is rich along the river. There is yet much work to be done on the place, but I reckon we shall have a decent harvest."

"How long have you been in the Colonies?" Anna asked the missionaries while the men spoke of crops.

"We landed at Dover on the Piscataqua the summer past," Mary said, "but most recently we came from Bohemia Manor. I have a letter for thee from thy sister."

She handed Anna the missive from Janet.

Anna Hack's face lit up. "My thanks!" she said warmly, pocketing it then leaning forward. "Does she fare well?" she asked with evident concern.

"Why, yes," Mary answered, surprised. "She seemed in good health. Has she been ill?"

"A catarrh plagues her from time to time," Anna said then smiled. "No doubt I worry overmuch. But tell me, what brings ye all this way from the north?"

"We seek a man, a member of our faith, who was last seen among the Friends on the Annemessex," Mary said with a nod towards Ambrose. "Friend Dixon believes he may now be at Nassawadox. His name is John Perrot. Have you heard aught of him?"

"I fear not," Doctor Hack replied upon hearing Mary's question. "Most of our acquaintances who are Friends removed to Maryland, thus we are not so familiar with that community as we once were."

"Nassawadox is not far from here, though," Anna told them. "Did you bring your sloop, Ambrose?"

"Yes, so another day's sail," he replied. "We make for the Denwoods' landing. The boys still manage the old family place, do they not?"

"As far as I know," the doctor replied. "I was last there in February—or Twelfth Month, as you call it— when Luke's sister Susannah Browne birthed her first child. She and Thomas live a few miles northeast of the Denwoods," he explained to the missionaries. "Luke and his younger brother Levin stayed in Virginia, when their father moved the rest of the family to Maryland two years past. The elder Levin donated materials for a meeting house for the Friends before he left. 'Tis on the Nassawadox River within easy walking distance of the Denwood farm. Luke, like his father before him, is the unofficial leader of your faith in that community. He is a sober young man."

"Mayhap he knows of this Perrot person you seek," Anna added.

After a restful night with the Hacks, the travelers were on their way at first light.

Chapter 22

NASSAWADOX, EASTERN
SHORE of VIRGINIA

August (6th Month) 1663

The Denwood Family's Virginia holding was situated between two estuaries of the river north of Stewart's Landing. They left Henry to batten down the sloop, and Ambrose led Mary and Allie up the lane to the farm.

The house was modest compared to the Hacks' manor—two stories with glittering glass windows and a central brick chimney—but it had a lovely view overlooking the river to the south. The Denwoods raised beeves for meat and export. The usual outbuildings surrounded the main house built close for convenience. The odor of smoldering coal came from a forge near the stable, where horses were being shod. It competed with the fragrance from a smokehouse out back, where meat was curing. Yet another column of smoke rose from the behind the house, soap-making or laundry, Mary supposed. She glimpsed cattle grazing in neatly fenced meadows beyond the cluster of buildings.

Ambrose strode purposefully to the front door, and a middle-aged woman answered his knock.

"Good day to thee, Friend Waters," Ambrose greeted her, proffering his hand.

"Friend Dixon! Well met!" the woman smiled, shaking it warmly. "The lads are out and about, working on the place, but they shall soon be here for the noon meal. Come in, come in!" She continued speaking as they followed her into the house. "'Tis the Devil's anvil out there at midday! Certes ye did not come all the way from Maryland this day."

"No, we left from the Hacks' plantation at Evergreen this morn," Dixon said to her back.

"Ah, not so far then," she commented, flapping a hand.

The entry opened into one large room twenty by thirty feet, comprising the entire first floor. Two casement windows on the south side were shuttered against the heat, so the room was dim and only slightly cooler than outside. Light from an open window on the north wall revealed a central brick fireplace with two hearths. An older woman stirred a kettle while a young girl set trenchers on a sturdy oak table. Allie's mouth watered at the delicious smells of beef stew and fresh bread. Ambrose made introductions, explaining that Mabel Waters was the Denwoods' housekeeper, hired when the rest of the family went to Maryland. Luke was twenty-three, young Levin was sixteen, and both were unmarried.

"Sit, sit! Ye look in need of refreshment," their hostess went on, pointing to the table. "I knew ye were from away, as your faces are new to me."

Mary and Allie sank down on a bench at the table, fanning themselves with their hats.

"Not accustomed to the heat, are ye," their hostess noted with sympathy.

"Indeed," Mary sighed.

Mabel smiled. "Took me months to get seasoned. We treat fevers often at the *infirmaria*, mind ye."

"There is an *infirmaria* here?" Allie asked, perking up.

"Near the meeting house on the creek. 'Tis for the indentured," Mabel told her. "Folk ignore their servants' ailments and expect them to work regardless, like beasts. It riles Susannah—that's Luke and Levin's sister. She is wed to Tom Browne and lives hard by. 'We must minister to their bodies as well as their souls,' says she. Some of the local women help her. Friends all, certes," she added proudly.

"I should like to see it," Allie said.

"Thou shalt see it, when we go on the morrow," their hostess added.

"What happens on the morrow?" Mary asked.

"Ye are here for the meeting, are ye not?" Mabel asked, slicing a loaf.

"We know of no meeting," Ambrose replied, blotting sweat from his broad brow with a kerchief.

Mabel looked surprised. "Did ye not come to hear Friend Perrot?"

Her guests stiffened and exchanged glances.

"John Perrot is here?" Ambrose asked.

"Ah, ye do know of him then," Mabel smiled, mistaking their shock for awe. "He and John Browne have been here three weeks, staying with Tom and Susannah. Friend Perrot has brought the Light to many. People flock to hear him, thus ye have come in good time."

Before they could respond, a young man's voice called, "Halloo, Mabel! Is dinner on the board?"

Mabel rose to greet the young Denwoods, and Ambrose gave the missionaries a cautionary shake of the head, indicating it was not the time to take exception to their hostess's enthusiasm.

Mary's mind reeled. Had all the Denwoods fallen under John Perrot's spell?

Chapter 23

NASSAWADOX, EASTERN SHORE OF VIRGINIA

August (6th Month) 1663

The next morning, the Denwood household rose early to pack the wagon for the meeting for worship. The missionaries would at last meet the man they sought. After the morning meal, Ambrose and Henry took their leave, saying they must return to duties at home. Mary and Allie accompanied them to the landing to see them off.

"I would not thwart your mission. Perrot will recognize me and knows I oppose him," he said once they were away from the house. "If he sees me with you, he may oppose your council out of hand. When should I return for you? If things take a turn for the worse, ye must ask Luke to send word—"

"Our thanks, Ambrose," Mary interrupted gently. "We are indebted to thee for bringing us here safely, but we must proceed as God directs. We cannot know not how long this may take."

He glanced at Allie, who indicated her solidarity with Mary by nodding once. He sighed, shook their hands, and wished them success in their mission then he and Henry set sail for home.

When the missionaries returned to the house, it seemed the entire household was going to the meeting, including the hired help. Everyone was in high spirits released from daily chores even though it was not a First Day. Mabel sat on the bench with Luke, as he drove the wagon. Young Levin and half a dozen servants walked alongside, and the missionaries joined them rather than squeezing into the back of the wagon with the elderly cook, baskets of food, rugs to sit on, jugs of *switzel*, and kegs of small beer. The mood resembled that of a fair day rather than a meeting for worship.

"'Tis not far!" Mabel told them cheerily, as the wagon lurched off.

Torn between anticipation and dread, Mary struggled to prepare herself for the confrontation with John Perrot. Ever since speaking with Joseph Nicholson, she had tried to imagine what she would say to persuade him to abandon his "revelations." Certes, God approved this mission for she and Allie had found the man, but Mary felt confused. How could the Friends here abandon First Day meetings so easily? How had Perrot garnered such complete trust and admiration? Could she convince them he was leading them astray or would they continue to be blind to his faults? Around her everyone was elated, singing, bantering with each other, and bubbling with happy anticipation. It set her on edge and made her feel more isolated and uncertain.

In less than an hour Luke guided the wagon under the trees at the edge of a large field, drawing up alongside other conveyances and mounts. There was a confusion of greetings and introductions. Folk crowded close to meet the English missionaries. She and Allie shook the proffered hands politely, but Mary 's nerves were strung tight. She scanned each face, searching for Perrot. She was not sure she would recognize the man, having never met him.

"Dost see Friend Perrot here?" Mary asked Mabel at the first opportunity.

The housekeeper looked surprised. "Oh no," she said. "He comes once all are gathered."

"But how can he know, if he is not present?" Allie asked.

"Friend Perrot is among God's chosen. How could he not?" Mabel answered, smiling.

Her words made Mary's scalp prickle with dread, but before she could respond, Mabel was introducing Luke's twin sister Susannah and her husband Thomas Browne. The young couple carried a curly-haired baby girl of seven months named Sarah, their first. The little family lived on the Machipongo River at a plantation called Brownville eight miles to the northeast. They were soon engaged in conversation with the Brownes.

Time flew by during the social interaction, but during a lull in the talk, Mary realized the sun was nearly at its zenith. They had arrived more than an hour ago, and Perrot was still absent, but no one seemed concerned. The children played; the men discussed crops and livestock; the women nattered. Mary hid her exasperation with increasing difficulty.

Then another cart arrived, and everyone surged toward it, calling out greetings and blessings. John Perrot was here at last.

Mary and Allie stood back, watching. The two men remained on the driver's bench of the cart. Both were bearded and in shirtsleeves. Perrot was indeed comely with dark brown curls that fell to his shoulders and a neatly trimmed beard. His prominent cheekbones and deep-set eyes gave the impression of an ascetic, but his frame was as sturdy as any common laborer. His well-muscled chest and arms pressed against the fine material of his collarless shirt, as he reached to shake hands from the cart's bench. He smiled benignly at the adoring crowd, but his eyes were shrewd, assessing the size and content of the gathering. In so doing, he remarked Mary and Allie, standing apart. His gaze sharpened, and he stood up slowly and began to speak, his eyes on the missionaries.

"Beloved Lambs, we gather this day in the presence of God at His prompting and in His time." His voice was sonorous with a slight trace of his Irish origins. It was deep and compellingly pleasant to the ear. "Though some mock me, yet am I uplifted by ye who know the truth and are upright in your hearts."

There were murmured assents from his audience, but Perrot's eyes were fixed on Mary.

"I am not brought down by the reproach of doubters with your sweet love to nourish me. Let them sneer and say I am a wonder to sundry minds, but I say it is a wonder that I yet live! Glory, glory, unto His Name!" His voice rose to a joyous shout, and Perrot spread his arms wide.

"Oh, praise Him!" a woman exclaimed, and other voices assented.

"For three long years was I tested—beaten and reshaped on the anvil of the Inquisition at Rome. My companion John Luffe was unable to endure the torture and was called to God, but I—" he drew a ragged breath, and his voice shook with emotion, "—I took that bitter cup and drank it down."

His head bowed, as though weighed down by this responsibility, and his audience murmured sympathetically. The allusion to Jesus was not lost on anyone, and Allie nudged Mary at this evidence of delusion. The people were rapt. Even the children had gone quiet. The silence was absolute but for the drone of cicadas, the stamp of a horse's foot, and the soft swishing of their tails. Allie took her hand, and Mary realized she was holding her breath. She took in air, squeezing back, but kept her eyes on Perrot.

His head snapped up, and he scanned his listeners' faces. "Why?" he posited. No one spoke, knowing he would answer himself. "Why was I able to endure what my dear friend could not?" He paused, taking in the upturned faces then spoke slowly, emphasizing his next words. *"Because Almighty God was tempering me to His purpose.* Yea, the suffering I bore strengthened my connection to the Light! My soul became as yeast to leaven the spirits of others, like you, my dear lambs. I am come to free you from the forms of worship, for what is a form? An outward appearance, a crutch for those whose spirits are crippled. If one is upright in one's heart, no forms are needed. We speak with God direct. Is He of a sudden deaf to us if we wear the hat in prayer? Can He hear us only if we worship on First Day?"

Chuckles rippled through the listeners, and some shook their heads.

"The Almighty cares not for these paltry things. They are superficial! That of God resides in our hearts and guides us daily. *This I know.* The upright in spirit need no forms to tell them when and how to commune with the Divine."

Perrot's gaze took in every upturned face, and the worshippers smiled and nodded agreement. He held them in the palm of his hand, and Mary shivered despite the heat, realizing his skill. She must wait to speak with him privily rather than attempt a public confrontation in the face of this blind support.

"Friends, let us join together in silent worship that we may be refreshed in the Lord," he finished.

Men and women separated into two groups, facing the cart where Perrot stood, as though it were the pulpit in a steeple house. John Browne climbed down to join the men, but Perrot stayed up on the cart. Susannah Browne and another young woman each carried a baby, and they led the younger children off some distance to a stream at the edge of the field.

"That is John Browne with Friend Perrot?" Mary asked Mabel quietly, as the women settled.

"Aye," she whispered back. "He is elder brother to Thomas, Susannah's husband."

The midday heat was too strong for any insects save the biting flies around the horses and the ever-present cicadas. The crowd of people could not all fit in the shade under the trees, and the missionaries stood in the full sun. Mary tried to escape the heat by connecting to God Within, but peace eluded her. The piercing drone of the insects seemed overloud and distracting. How could she convince these people that Perrot was leading them astray? They obviously trusted and admired him, and she was but a stranger. She had finally stilled her roiling mind and was waiting for inspiration when Perrot ended the contemplation. It was abrupt for he eschewed the shaking of hands, and it was the shortest period of worship that Mary had ever experienced. Mayhap he was as uncomfortably hot as she. The instances were rare when she did not feel refreshed by a meeting, but this was one. She needed confirmation of her faith this day more than ever, and her failure to connect with the Light rattled her.

Perrot jumped down from the cart and was immediately assailed by a knot of admirers, Mabel and Luke among them. He placed his hand on their heads, blessing them, and Mary turned away from the cart, outraged by his gall. She and Allie moved off a little, seeking some shade.

"Didst thou see?" Mary began when a mellifluous voice came from behind them.

"Who might ye be, Friends? I do not believe we are acquainted."

They turned to find John Perrot standing behind them. Mary met his piercing gaze.

"Well met, Friend Perrot," she said, relieved that her voice was steady for his sudden proximity unnerved her. "I am Mary Tomkins, and this is my companion Alice Ambrose."

"Came ye lately to the Colonies?" he asked lightly, though his eyes glittered with suspicion.

Mary realized he was on alert under the veil of polite interest. Might he suspect they were sent by the Society to curb him? She struggled to return his gaze with equanimity.

"We landed at Dover in the Bay Colony the summer past," Allie answered, trying in vain to turn his keen gaze away from Mary.

"What moved ye to come so far from home? A mission, mayhap?" he pressed, holding Mary's eyes.

The tension was mounting. In desperation Allie thrust out her hand.

"I admire thy eloquence, Friend Perrot, and would shake thy hand," she said, smiling. As ever, the scar on her cheek became more pronounced.

He looked down at her proffered hand then up at her face. "The shaking of hands is a mere form," he said loftily, "and I would free thee from it." He looked from one to the other. "Ye are Public Friends, I wager. Why have ye come?" he demanded abandoning all pretense.

"We were convinced by Mary Dyer at our hometown in Devon, and we trained as missionaries at Swarthmore Hall upon her recommendation," Mary explained. "When we learned of her execution, we determined to continue her fight against the unjust laws of the Bay Colony." As ever, Allie's presence calmed her and bolstered her confidence. She would not dissemble, but she would not reveal their purpose if she could manage it.

The diversion worked, and Perrot's expression changed radically. "Mary Dyer!" he exclaimed with reverence. "A sainted martyr for our faith, indeed! I never met the woman, but all know of her. She is an inspiration to us all! I, myself, was convinced by Edward Burrough when he visited Ireland in '56."

"Our first mission in England was in company with Edward Burrough. We endured six months at Lancaster Prison together," Mary told him, hoping the connection might allay his suspicion.

"Edward was like a brother to us," Allie added helpfully.

For the first time his smile reached Perrot's eyes, but at that moment young Levin Denwood came to invite them to share some refreshment. The food had been brought from the wagon by the servants, and Mabel and Susannah Browne were setting it out on rugs laid down in the shade.

"I see thou hast met our guests, Friend Perrot," Luke said, as they all settled to eat.

"Indeed, I have!" Perrot smiled disarmingly. "We have much in common, and I am eager to hear more of their travels with my mentor Edward Burrough," he added with a significant look at Mary, who smiled back.

However, even this small connection was cut short, as everyone was vying for Perrot's attention. Others crowded near the Denwood party, engaging him in discourse, as they ate. There was no opportunity to speak with him further, but as the gathering broke up, and they repacked the wagon, she heard Luke invite Perrot and the Brownes to dine with them that evening. She lingered near to hear the response.

"My thanks, Friend Denwood," Perrot replied, turning to Tom Browne, "but I must defer to my host."

"We are ever eager to visit with thy brothers, are we not, Susannah?" Thomas responded cheerfully.

"Certes! Our thanks, Luke," Susannah replied.

"Then we shall follow along with you now," John Browne answered.

"Excellent!" Perrot exclaimed, beaming at Mary.

She felt the power of his approval and inclined her head in agreement, but she was aware of the danger posed by the man's comely looks and fine speech. She must guard against falling prey to his charm.

Chapter 24

NASSAWADOX, EASTERN SHORE OF VIRGINIA

August (6th Month) 1663

It was late afternoon by the time they returned to the Denwoods' farm. Mabel supervised unloading the wagon, but when Mary and Allie tried to help, she shooed them away.

"Friend Perrot is come to enjoy your company. I have plenty of help here," she insisted.

This was evident as the servants were efficiently emptying the wagon and tending to the horses except for Missus Smith the cook, who hurried off to prepare dinner.

Susannah and Thomas Browne approached Mabel and the missionaries. Lulled by the wagon ride, Little Sarah awoke when they stopped and was fussing. Susannah went indoors to nurse her, and Mabel went to help Missus Smith, while Luke took the rest of his guests around to the veranda for some refreshment.

Although the sun was lowering, the heat was still stifling, and they were all relieved to sit in the shade. Young Levin appeared bearing a tray with a bottle of Madeira, a jug of *switzel*, and pewter cups. The missionaries and Levin preferred the latter, but the four men took wine.

"To the fellowship of Friends!" Luke proposed, lifting his cup.

"Hear, hear!" Perrot responded. He drank deeply then sighed with content. "That is a fine Madeira, Friend Denwood," he smiled, ostentatiously setting down his empty cup.

Luke was an attentive host and promptly refilled it, saying, "Ah yes, the 'Vinho da Roda.' It is the only wine that travels well in the warmer climes and the only cargo that is exempt from the King's latest Navigation Act. Anna Hack's ships keep us in good supply."

"Blessings upon her," Perrot toasted, and the men drank again.

Mary and Allie exchanged a glance. Perrot's enthusiasm for the wine confirmed what Mary Dixon had told them. Friends—particularly Public ones—rarely imbibed anything stronger than ale or small beer. Cider, buttermilk, or *switzel* seemed to be the usual beverages of choice in the southern colonies. There would be no serious discussion with the man if he continued drinking wine at this pace. On the other hand, John Browne nursed his first cup, taking small sips. He was a man of few words but now made a rare contribution to the conversation.

"We must also thank the South American sugar trade in part," he said. "It drove down the market price, forcing the Isle of Madeira to cultivate vineyards instead of cane, hence Madeira Wine."

Perrot laughed. "Thou art a fount of information, John. To the South American sugar trade!" he exclaimed, draining his second cup.

Mary scrutinized the others for some sign of censure or unease, but they evidenced no concern of Perrot's seemingly unquenchable thirst and increasingly merry behavior.

Allie, however, had no patience for the man or for Mary's cautious overtures. "I reckon that was the shortest meeting for worship I have ever experienced. Shall there be another on First Day?" she asked brightly, addressing Luke.

Their host did not answer but looked at Perrot. There was an awkward silence as John Perrot stared at the tall missionary. His celebratory manner had fled, and his face was grave.

"I know not, as yet," he answered slowly. "The spirit has not prompted me. We meet in God's good time."

Perrot had found that even his mild disapproval usually cowed people, but Allie was immune.

"Does the Bible not tell us that time is the Sabbath?" she pressed, unflinchingly.

John Browne glanced at Perrot and cleared his throat, as he set down his cup. "We are not constrained by that particular form," he said stiffly, frowning at her.

"Yes, so ye have said, but I wonder then how folk do know when to gather?" Allie asked innocently.

"Friend Perrot tells us," Luke answered quickly, discomfited by the sudden tension between his guests.

Allie did not respond to this statement but looked at Perrot and pointedly raised her eyebrows.

"My conscience prompts me, Friend Ambrose," he said gently. "I do not blame thee for thy skepticism for 'tis difficult to compass what exists beyond mere reason.

I shall attempt to explain. During my suffering under the Inquisition in Rome, God did sustain me in His Light, and that connection has only strengthened since. I survived for a purpose. In my travail it was revealed to me that I am called to liberate all Friends from empty forms so they may enjoy a more direct connection with the Almighty. My life's mission is to lead my lambs to follow their consciences in this matter rather than a proscribed form; therefore, we meet when God Within dictates, as we did this day."

"But the Bible clearly bids us cease our labors and devote ourselves to worshipping God on First Day," Mary reiterated. Since Allie had opened this opportunity, she would not waste it. "Why gainsay that?"

She looked carefully at each of the men's faces, as she spoke. Luke, Levin, and Thomas Browne were wavering, but Perrot and his companion bristled.

"Why adhere to an empty form?" Perrot shot back his face flushed. "Wouldst tether the spirits of my lambs, because some self-important Friends across the sea dictate how and when we worship?"

Now Mary understood. The man was embittered by the attitude of the London Friends upon his return from Rome. Acting upon his "revelations" was Perrot's revenge against prominent members of the Society who had spurned him.

"Our tenets are not empty forms," Allie answered calmly. "They organize and unite all Friends in fellowship."

At that moment Susannah appeared.

"Food is on the board. Come sit, and it please you," she smiled, oblivious to the tension.

Perrot rose immediately and went in with John Browne on his heels, but the Denwoods and Thomas got up more slowly, politely indicating Mary and Allie precede them. Their faces were grave, considering the missionaries' words and Perrot's reaction. It gave Mary hope.

Throughout the meal, the talk was superficial. Perrot did not address Mary or Allie and avoided eye contact with them, instead conversing charmingly with Mabel and Susannah. They hung upon his every word and treated him like royalty. There was no further opportunity to speak with him that evening, as the Brownes and Perrot took their leave soon after eating. Thomas and Susannah Browne led the way in their wagon, the baby asleep in her mother's arms. Perrot and John Browne followed with their cart. They had brought lanterns but hoped to be home before full dark.

It had been a long, eventful day, and the Denwood household retired soon after. Mary and Allie slept on a pallet in the loft they shared with Mabel, so they could not discuss John Perrot freely. As she settled back-to-back with Allie, Mary determined to talk with Luke on the morrow about holding a meeting for worship on the next First Day. They could use the meeting house that his father Levin had built for the community. Reestablishing regular meetings at that location seemed a good start, but she had no doubt Friend Perrot would prove a formidable challenge.

Chapter 25

NASSAWADOX, EASTERN SHORE OF VIRGINIA

August/September (6th/7th Month) 1663

They did not see John Perrot again for several days. At breakfast Luke agreed to a First Day meeting at the cabin his father had built for that purpose. Mary persuaded the young Denwoods and Mabel to spread word of it in the community. It was easier than she had feared.

"How dost thou know of our little meetinghouse?" Luke asked, once she introduced the idea.

"Doctor Hack told us of thy father's generosity," she answered. "We would like to put it to good use."

"Father supplied the materials, and Friend Dixon helped build it, along with others in our community. I daresay, I was sorry when we stopped using it," Luke admitted.

"How did that come about?" Allie asked innocently, though Mary was sure her friend knew.

Luke and Levin looked sheepish, but Mabel answered for them.

"Everything changed when Friend Perrot came. We said we must meet when the spirit moves us," she said.

"Moves you or moves Perrot?" Allie asked arching an eyebrow.

Their three hosts exchanged a guilty look.

"Did no one question that assumption?" Mary asked gently.

Luke cleared his throat. "Some did, privily. I, myself, was reluctant at the first…" he trailed off then straightened. "But last evening when thou didst remind us of God's rule for the Sabbath, Mary, my misgivings returned."

"I persuaded thee, Luke," Mabel said quietly. "We were so grateful that someone of Friend Perrot's spiritual status concerned himself with our humble settlement. We wanted him to stay as long as possible. It is years since an English Friend visited here." She sighed audibly. "Now I am confounded. Are we wrong to heed Friend Perrot?" she asked, frankly.

Mary answered her question with another. "Didst thou experience fellowship at the meeting yesterday?"

The Denwoods and Mabel looked confused.

"Friend Perrot is an accomplished speaker but have ye remarked that the subject is ever himself?" she went on, "*His* suffering, *his* enlightenment, *his* definition of 'forms.' Do ye find fellowship in that?"

Luke and Levin slowly shook their heads, but Mabel temporized.

"But he is so saintly!" she argued. "He proves there can be revelation in our time, not just in the Bible. Certes he has God's approval to survive three years of torture at the hands of the Inquisition! And his speeches are so, so—" she groped for the word, "—inspiring!"

"Would they seem so were he not comely?" Allie asked. "What if he were small and rotund with a lisp?"

They all laughed at this image, easing the tension, but Allie had made her point, and Mabel said no more in Perrot's defense.

On First Day a meeting for worship was held at Levin Denwood's legacy to the Nassawadox Friends.

Things began well. Everyone was eager to hear news from the Mother Country, and in the days after Perrot's meeting word had spread of the two female missionaries who made the perilous crossing (unescorted!) to bring them spiritual refreshment. Mary and Allie, gratified by the turnout, patiently answered questions about life in England under the restored monarchy. Inevitably, folk asked for news of family members, none of whom the missionaries knew. Luke finally broke up the informal gathering outside the little meeting house and announced that further discussion could continue after worship. Everyone squeezed into the tiny log cabin. Some had to stand along the walls or listen from the doorway, as there were no windows. Candles lit the gloomy interior but failed to mask the odor of bodies packed into the small space on this summer day. Mary counted near thirty, including children. They were singing an opening hymn when there was a commotion at the open doorway.

Voices faltered, as John Perrot pushed past the men standing at the entry. By the time he made his way into the only clear space between the women's and men's benches, there was silence. John Browne stayed by the door, and both wore their hats.

"What passes here?" Perrot asked, spreading his arms and turning in a slow circle. "Why do ye sing like Anglicans?" he smiled, as though amused by fractious children.

Mary was furious at the interruption, but she spoke politely and remained outwardly calm.

"Greetings, Friend Perrot and Friend Browne. Ye are welcome to join us in this meeting for worship; however, if ye stay, I beg ye remove your hats before God."

Perrot looked around, chuckling. "Think thee the Almighty remarks whether my head is covered or no?" he said lightly. "Removing the hat for worship is a mere form," his tone became censorious, "*as are regular meetings.*" He glowered and none met his eye. Then his smile returned, and he addressed Mary. "My lambs know this, for they are upright in their hearts. We gather when the Light prompts us."

There was a heavy silence, as the worshippers looked to Mary for direction. She was loath to debate with Perrot in public, but she saw some folk surreptitiously don their hats and felt compelled to speak.

"Hat-honor is a basic tenet of our faith," she began, looking at everyone but Perrot. "As Friends we do not remove the hat to any temporal authority in accordance with our belief that no man is better than another. Only Our Father in Heaven is above us, thus we remove our hats during worship to show God the respect that is given to no other." She met Perrot's eyes. "Many Friends have suffered imprisonment and flogging on this point. Wouldst thou belittle their sacrifice by saying it matters not?"

Hats hastily came off again, and Perrot's mask of easy amusement slipped. He had not expected an eloquent adversary, particularly this small, plain woman. His face darkened, and he glared at Mary.

"I would say they need not have suffered at all!" he shot back. "Wouldst thou bind people to empty forms that lead to conflict and punishment? I bid them listen to their consciences, to verily connect to the Light Within. Wearing hats or meeting at such-and-such a time and place are superfluous."

Mary breathed deeply, avoiding the emotional whirlpool Perrot was creating. She would not be drawn in. "Fellowship is not superfluous," she countered evenly. "It is the core of our Society. Worship is not solely for the individual to connect with God Within. Worship is sharing that divine connection in company with others of our faith. That is fellowship, and it cannot exist without regular meetings that consistently bring us together."

"Enough talk!" John Browne bellowed from the doorway, startling everyone. "Those who cleave to John Perrot, come with us now!" he pronounced and pushed his way out. Perrot stayed, staring at Mary.

After a moment's hesitation, some began to leave. A triumphant smile lit Perrot's face, then he touched his hat brim to Mary in mock salute and left. Half the crowd remained. There was nothing for Mary to do but continue the meeting for worship.

For the next several weeks Mary and Allie labored to reestablish regular meetings and to correct the damage John Perrot had wrought among the Nassawadox Friends. The Denwoods became staunch supporters and helped by hosting discussions at their home, but attendance grew in small increments and included old friends of the family for the most part. The man's charisma made him a formidable opponent, and once his adherents chose to embrace Perrot's version of truth there was no convincing them otherwise. Luke's good-brother Thomas Browne informed the missionaries that Perrot was holding more impromptu meetings than usual among his supporters and spreading rumors that questioned Mary and Allie's authenticity as spiritual guides.

"What is he saying about us?" Mary asked.

Thomas hesitated and looked uncomfortable.

"We shall not take it to heart, Friend Browne," Allie assured him. "We need to know."

Thomas nodded and plowed on. "He questions why ye are unmarried, insinuating that ye are tainted women. He doubts your training at Swarthmore Hall, as well as the suffering in the northern colonies, saying we have only your word for it."

"'Tis no more than I would expect from him," Mary replied calmly.

"How kind of him to ignore this," Allie quipped, gesturing to the scar on her face.

The men smiled, accustomed now to Allie's wry sense of humor, but Thomas sobered and went on.

"There is also a rumor that Perrot has visited with powerful landholders in the area like Edmund Scarborough," he said.

"Who is Edmund Scarborough?" Mary asked, noting the men's worried expressions.

"He is the Royal Surveyor for Virginia and one of the wealthiest men in the colony," Luke answered.

"He also holds the rank of captain and leads the militia when the Indians threaten the outlying settlers," Thomas added.

Luke snorted. "When he *says* they threaten the outlying settlers," he said sourly. "When I was yet a boy, Scarborough called for volunteers to join his militia in a raid against the nearest Pocomoke village, claiming they planned to attack us. Many from Nassawadox followed him, including my father and Ambrose Dixon. It was '51, and Virginia had just passed a law protecting the local Indians on the land that had been allotted for them. The settlers were only to defend themselves if attacked. Eventually we learned that the Pocomokes had no such intent, thus all who rode with Scarborough were called to court, reprimanded, and fined. The Captain got off scot free, mind ye, because of his connections, but those who believed him suffered for his lies. My father suspected that Scarborough was selling firearms to the Pocomokes on the sly and contrary to the law, thus he stood to gain both ways."

"Abuse of power here as in New England," Allie commented.

"I fear it is a common problem the world over," Luke added. "Scarborough also encouraged the Anglican Reverend Teackle to issue the summons to court in '59 that drove so many Friends to remove to Maryland—my father and Ambrose Dixon among them."

"Perrot is drawn to men in power," Thomas went on. "I have heard him speak with my brother of his friendship with Thomas Modyford, the Governor of Barbados, although 'tis possible he exaggerates."

"Perrot and Scarborough have much in common," Luke agreed. "Each makes his own way with little regard for laws or tenets."

"I do not understand how people can be so blind to self-serving tyrants," Mary said.

"As Allie reminds us, folk are swayed by comely looks and a glib tongue," Luke replied, smiling ruefully. "Levin and I sought his approval, and Mabel was smitten, as well. It took ye missionaries to open our eyes to Perrot's true motive—his own personal power."

"He is unlike most Friends," Thomas mused. "His fondness for physical comforts is suspect."

"Worse, he lusts for dominance over people," Luke added. "His 'lambs' he calls us."

"Allie and I were alarmed by his fondness for spirits when last he was here," Mary said.

"And his apparent love of fine dress," Allie put in.

"More Friends attend thy First Day meetings each week, Mary," Thomas observed, "but a deal of folk yet cleave to him. How do we open their eyes?"

"With the truth," Mary answered.

"And love," Allie added.

Chapter 26

NASSAWADOX, EASTERN SHORE OF VIRGINIA

September (7ᵗʰ Month) 1663

Seventh Month came. The days were still hot, but the nights were cooler, and the autumn rains began as the prevailing wind shifted from southwest to northwest. The final tobacco harvest was in full swing, and the *infimaria* was busier than ever with laborers suffering the inevitable injuries—slips of the knife, skin rashes from the green tobacco leaves, aching backs, and heat exhaustion. One young man fell off a cart and broke his collar bone; another's foot was crushed when a loaded wagon rolled over it. Mary, Allie, and Mabel went daily, replenishing supplies, brewing teas, mixing salves, and binding wounds. Attendance to their First Day meetings increased with those who were grateful for their care.

The missionaries had held three meetings at the little cabin on the creek. At the last the benches were full, and some of the men had to stand. Twenty-eight Friends attended, but Mary was concerned for those who still followed Perrot. It was as if they insisted on boarding a leaky boat, but only she knew it would inevitably sink. The only antidote for her frustration was to keep busy.

The three women usually walked the two miles to and from the *infimaria*, but one day Luke came early to fetch them with the wagon.

"Well met, Luke!" Mabel greeted him cheerily. "How kind of thee to come for us."

"I have news," Luke answered, unsmiling. "Susannah sent a message, and I came straight here."

The women stared at him, realizing he had come of necessity rather than kindness.

"What is it?" Mabel asked, all cheer gone.

"John Perrot has quit the area," he said.

"Where did he go?" Mary asked at the same time Allie said, "When?"

"Yesterday." Luke answered. "He has gone across the Bay to visit the Friends on the Patuxent River."

"Well, that is a relief!" Mabel exclaimed.

Mary did not agree. She felt her business with Perrot was unfinished. It did not comfort her to think the man was freely spreading his false beliefs to other communities of Friends. She felt she had failed.

There was no time to fret over Perrot, however. When they reached the Denwood farm, Susannah's husband Thomas Browne was waiting for them.

"I fear there may be trouble," he said, rising from a bench at the table as soon as they entered the house.

"I got Susannah's message about Perrot and thy brother leaving," Luke replied, "but how is that trouble?"

"Luke, I fear this is another matter entirely," Thomas told him heavily.

"Best tell us straight off then," Luke urged.

"We were cutting firewood on the northwest quarter this morn when a company passed going north—four riders and two packhorses. The lead rider was Edmund Scarborough."

"What does that signify?" Mary asked in the heavy silence that followed this pronouncement.

"I am unsure," Thomas said slowly, "but I remarked surveying instruments on one of the pack horses, so I assume he plans to use them."

"He cannot be going to his plantation. It is the other direction on Occahannock Creek is it not?" Mabel asked confused.

Luke nodded. "Yes, but his son Charles has property on the Pungoteague, and Scarborough has more land on the Atlantic shore. His glassworks and shipping yard are there. Mayhap he simply has business at one of those places, Thomas."

Mary did not understand Thomas Browne's anxiety. "Then there is naught to w—" she began.

Thomas interrupted her gently. "We are ill at ease because Scarborough is yet rankled that the Friends he attempted to prosecute in '59 eluded arrest by removing to Maryland. He cannot stand to be bested and nurses a grudge. Furthermore, Calvert granted him three thousand acres for acting as Land Commissioner, apportioning the building lots at

Annemessex and Manokin, but that grant of land is in Maryland. No doubt Scarborough would prefer it be in Virginia, and the only way he can accomplish that would be to move the line further north."

"Certes the authorities shall not permit it, shall they?" Mary asked appalled.

"He *is* the authority," Luke answered grimly. "Scarborough is the Royal Surveyor for Virginia. He answers only to the King, and his brother is Charles's physitian, so the rogue is well connected. No colonial authority can touch him for his brother intercedes whenever Edmund gets in trouble."

"It would not surprise me to learn that he has the approval of Virginia's Governor for this gambit," Thomas added gloomily. "Berkeley is an old royalist and ever hungry to enlarge his colony."

"Yet another perversion of justice," Allie commented.

"There is none to oppose Scarborough, since Captain Robbins died last year," Luke said mournfully. "He was the last of the old Puritan faction to stand against the Royalists up here on the peninsula. He hated Scarborough in particular. They had adjoining properties but were sworn enemies. Scarborough set a line south of his land, creating the county of Accomack so his property would not be in the same municipality as Robbins's in Northampton. There are two counties where once was one, due to their feud. Scarborough may intend to pull a similar trick with the boundary between the colonies now."

"The Old Conjurer, at his tricks yet again," Thomas commented, shaking his head.

Mary and Allie looked confused by the name.

"The Indians dubbed Scarborough 'Conjurer,' since he conjures the truth to suit himself," Luke clarified. He turned to Thomas. "If he moves the boundary, dost think he means to harass the Friends on the Annemessex?" he asked.

"Yes. Once they are under Virginia's authority, I fear he shall take his revenge," Thomas affirmed.

"Then we must warn them," said Mary.

The next morning Luke left sixteen-year-old Levin in charge of the farm. He had asked Thomas Browne to check on his younger brother in a couple of days. The missionaries and Luke left at first light, sailing back to the Annemessex River in his skiff. Mary felt an unexpected lift at the prospect of reuniting with the Dixons.

In his younger years Ambrose had been a caulker by profession, and it had served him well providing coin for his passage from England and establishing a holding in the colonies; however, his wealth had come through the headright system. With a wife and 6 children, Ambrose gained one hundred acres of land for each "head" in his family, as well as himself—a total of seven hundred acres. His quick mind and steady temperament inspired trust in his neighbors. He saw through John Perrot immediately, which was why the latter had had little success with the Annemessex Friends. People listened to Ambrose Dixon. He was the unofficial leader of the river community, and Mary was eager to hear his thoughts concerning the events of the past month.

It was a long day's sail, but the wind was with them. Luke knew the way well, and his small craft was swift. They set out in the cool pre-dawn and reached the mouth of the Annemessex in the gloaming. The lanterns at Dixon's Choice were a welcome beacon in the gathering dark. As they approached the landing, they reefed the two sails, and Luke guided them in with a sculling oar, maneuvering around a merchant ship with *The Dove* painted on her transom.

"Ah, Captain Groome's ship!" Mary exclaimed. "Samuel is here!"

Laborers were rolling hogsheads from the warehouse up a ramp onto the vessel and into the hold. Storm lanterns and torches cast macabre shadows that distorted the activity. It was the third week of September, and the tobacco leaves were harvested, dried, and packed in hogsheads ready to ship. Activity was brisk, and the work of loading the precious crop continued after daylight. Henry was on deck, tracking the process with a slate and chalk. Ambrose was on the pier, talking to Captain Groome with twelve-year-old Thomas at his side, but he broke off when the skiff bumped the dock.

"Luke Denwood with Mary and Allie! Well met!" Ambrose exclaimed, approaching them.

"Greetings, Friend Dixon, young Thomas," Luke answered, shaking hands with the big man and his son.

Allie tossed Thomas the stern line, and Ambrose helped the missionaries onto the dock.

"'Tis good to have you back!" Ambrose smiled, shaking the women's hands warmly. "Friend Groome is here, as ye can see. He is come to take our first yield of tobacco to New Amsterdam."

Ambrose turned to rejoin the sea captain, but Luke put a hand on his arm, stopping him. "We come with disturbing news, I fear," he said quietly.

Ambrose sobered, peering at their faces through the flickering light and shadow of the lanterns.

"We are near done here," he said slowly. "Ye have had a long day from the look of it. Young Tom here shall see to your skiff. We can talk when ye have had some refreshment. Samuel and I shall join you at the house forthwith."

Samuel Groome greeted Mary and Allie cordially, but it was obvious that the men were occupied and could not stop their work to chat. Mary thought the Friends were fortunate to have a skilled mariner of their own faith to trust with the fruits of their labor.

The travelers retired to the house for they were bone-weary and hungry. Half an hour later Ambrose, young Thomas, Henry, and Captain Groome found them finishing a meal in company with Dixon's wife and thirteen-year-old daughter. When the children retired to the loft to join their younger siblings, the adults were able to talk. Luke related his concerns about Scarborough.

"Certes he would not make so bold as to fiddle with the colony's boundary!" Mary Dixon exclaimed.

Ambrose snorted. "'Tis verily what Conjurer would do! In any case, we must make no assumptions," he mused. "The questions are, where is he going, and what is his intent? We need a scout, and I know just the man for it."

Chapter 27

ANNEMESSEX, EASTERN SHORE of MARYLAND

September (7ᵗʰ Month) 1663

S tephen Horsey immigrated to Virginia at the age of twenty. Like many laborers wish-ing to leave England, he could not afford the passage price of six pounds—a year's wages for a young cooper; therefore, it was paid by Captain Obedience Robbins in re-turn for seven years of Horsey's service. Because the captain was an established resident of Virginia, he was awarded one hundred acres for every laborer he brought to the New World by means of the headright system. For colonists with means it was a fine way to procure cheap labor and add to their land holdings.

Stephen had been lucky. Once his obligation to Robbins was met in 1650, his employer treated him justly, awarding him an ox, a plow, and ten acres on the north bank of the Nassawadox River for his years of service. Despite his fair treatment, Horsey vowed never to work for another man again for he was fiercely independent. The first thing he did as a free man was to marry Sarah Whitlock, a widow with three children. They built a modest house and set to clearing their small holding. During his indenture, Stephen had learned to cultivate tobacco, and two years later, when Stephen Jr. was born, the Horseys harvested their first crop.

Their neighbor Ambrose Dixon helped the young couple. Both men hired Pocomokes for the Indians understood the land and were happy to be paid in English goods. Although Stephen was not inclined to join the Society of Friends, the two men found they had much in common and became close friends. They agreed no person was better than another, particularly in the workings of colonial government. Horsey believed any willing landholder was capable of service in public office and was a primary instigator of the Northampton Protest in 1652, addressing this issue. As a result, he represented his county as a Burgess the next year.

Unfortunately, this duty acquainted him directly with the members of the court at James City, who looked down their well-bred noses at him and treated him like the common laborer they deemed him to be. He referred to them publicly as "asses and villanes" for they were all Cavalier gentlemen of means who sought to maintain the status quo. His temper cost him his appointment.

In '59 he stood with the Friends of Nassawadox when they refused to pay church tithes to the Anglican Reverend Teackle of nearby Hungar's Parish. The Horseys subsequently joined their Quaker neighbors in the exodus to Maryland. This time the headright system worked in Stephen's favor, for as head of a family, he was able to claim fifty Maryland acres for his wife and each of their five small children—three hundred acres in total.

Now at forty-three Stephen was an established landholder in his own right with a capable wife and six children—four boys and two girls—all healthy and thriving. They ranged in age from eleven to two. Sarah was expecting another in January, but pregnancy suited her, rather than slowing her down. When her first husband died, leaving her with three small children, Captain Robbins had employed her as a housemaid. She was no beauty, but her industry and good humor attracted Stephen from the first. Mistress Robbins wept when she left. The Horseys prospered well enough to add three-hundred-fifty acres to the original grant, and they called their Maryland plantation Coulbourne for Horsey's uncle.

Most of the colonists feared the wilderness, but Stephen loved it. During his indenture, he had befriended the Pocomokes employed by Captain Robbins, and they taught him to read animal sign, to move through the woods silently, and to use his ears and nose as well as his eyes. His friendship with them did not end with his indenture to Robbins. He continued to hunt with them in winter when the demands of running a plantation eased. As a result, the Horseys had more fresh meat than most, and contrary to the law, the door was always open to their Indian friends. Thus, it was no surprise when Stephen and Sarah took on a young boy from the nearest Pocomoke village. He was to work for the Horseys until the age of twenty-four in exchange for a Bible-based education. His exact age was unknown, but Sarah judged him to be ten, when he first came to them. According to custom she helped him choose an English name. None of them could pronounce his Indian one, in any case, and he was eager for a new name for his new life.

Jeremiah was now fourteen, and anyone might take him for a colonist but for his copper skin and blue-black hair, now cut short. He dressed like an English lad with one exception; his feet and legs were bare below his knee britches unless he was attending a meeting for worship. He had joined the Friends and wore hose with his moccasins on First Days. He could not abide English boots, and the Horseys did not press him on this point.

When Ambrose Dixon told Stephen Horsey about Scarborough, he readily agreed to be their spy.

"I shall take Jeremiah," he told his friend. "He is best at tracking. Think you they went north or south?"

"Thomas Browne said north. Four riders and two packhorses. Their trail should be easy to follow," Ambrose answered. "Ye must light no fires and keep well out of sight, mind you," he cautioned. "We know they carry survey equipment, but we need to know *where* Scarborough is using it. Do not get too close or put yourselves in danger of discovery. There is no telling what that man will do."

"Jeremiah is a capable tracker. Can he not do this by himself?" Sarah Horsey asked softly. She was kneading dough at the other end of the table while the men talked.

"'Tis only good sense, Sarah," Ambrose reasoned. "If one is injured, the other can go for help."

This failed to reassure her. "Heaven Forbid!" she said, pausing in her work.

"The safety of our community is at stake, Sarry," Stephen added.

Seeing the light in her husband's eyes, she nodded reluctantly and went back to kneading. There would be no dissuading him. Stephen loved an adventure even more than the woods.

Horsey returned sooner than Ambrose expected. Three days after he and Jeremiah set out, he appeared at the Dixons' home. It was late afternoon, and Ambrose sat at the big table, entering Henry's accounting of the tobacco harvest in his ledger. Mary and Allie were in the kitchen garden, picking the last of the pole beans for the evening meal, when Mary Dixon called them in to hear Stephen's news. The five of them settled at the table with mugs of sweet cider.

"I made a rough map," Horsey began, producing it from the pouch on his belt.

"Didst find them then?" Ambrose asked eagerly.

Horsey nodded as he smoothed the crumpled paper and pointed. "We went first to Manokin, figuring Scarborough may have stopped there, since he has sympathizers among the Anglicans. Fear not, Ambrose," he added, responding to his friend's worried expression. "I did not speak direct with Elzey or his like. We went to thy Uncle Wilson, Mary," he told Dixon's wife. "He said Scarborough was there two days past and was entertained at Almodington—Elzey's place. Wilson knew no particulars, but he said the surveying party went north when they left. Jeremiah and I picked up their trail easy enough. They crossed the two fords at the Manokin River and continued north. Some five miles further on we found the first markers. Scarborough is setting a line from here," he indicated with a finger, "at the river's mouth up to the first northerly bend then due east to Wicomico Creek. We caught up with them here," he said, tapping the spot. "They made enough noise for twenty men and did not remark us watching them." He straightened and looked at each of them. "In short, it appears the scoundrel is setting the boundary between the colonies some thirty miles north of the existing line."

"Thirty miles!" Mary Dixon exclaimed.

"God save us!" Ambrose said grimly. "That puts our holdings here on Virginia soil."

"Certes he cannot prevail in this," Mary Tomkins said, looking from one to the other.

"I fear he can," Ambrose answered. "Remember, he is the Royal Surveyor for Virginia; he is colonel of the militia; he is the largest landholder on the Eastern Shore; his brother is physitian to the King; and Governor Berkeley and all the Burgesses support him now Robbins is gone."

"But Maryland's Governor Calvert shall protest, one assumes," Allie suggested.

"Calvert is across the Bay at St. Mary's City, and he is ever reluctant to 'waste' coin by sending help to the Eastern Shore. Any action on his part shall take months. We are on our own," Horsey told her bluntly. "Also, Calvert hired Scarborough as one of the land commissioners to apportion lots at Annemessex and Manokin and paid him in property." He shook his head in disgust. "He trusts the rascal and does not realize how far Conjurer will go to further his own interests."

"He is about to find out," Ambrose said grimly. "Likely 'tis as we thought. Scarborough wants his Maryland patent to be on Virginia soil, and he wants us and our holdings at his mercy again."

Horsey nodded. "It rankles him that we ignored that summons to court in '59 and removed to Maryland out of his reach. He is hot for revenge."

"But certes Governor Calvert will not stand for this once he learns of it! Even if it takes months, can he not treat with Governor Berkeley to counter Scarborough's false claim?" Mary asked.

The two men exchanged a glance.

"I know not," Ambrose said slowly, "but 'tis dangerous to underestimate Scarborough."

"You had best call a meeting, Ambrose," Stephen suggested. "We should alert our neighbors of the danger. We must all be prepared for the worst."

Chapter 28

ANNEMESSEX, EASTERN SHORE OF MARYLAND

October (8th Month) 1663

The first week of Eighth Month passed without incident. The tobacco harvest was in; the drying racks were full; the days were shorter; and hearth fires blazed throughout the evenings rather than being banked as soon as food was cooked. Samuel Groome plied the numerous waterways off the Bay collecting tobacco from the river plantations, and the *Dove's* hold was two-thirds full. The young sea captain docked at Dixon's Choice and was welcomed warmly. He and Ambrose were fast friends, and Captain Groome always tried to coincide his visits with meetings for worship at the Dixons' home.

The Annemessex Friends were glad to find Friend Groome and the missionary women at First Day meeting the next morning. The Dixons' hall was crowded despite a raw, rainy day, and both fireplaces blazed. The smell of wet wool, woodsmoke, and bodies pervaded the room, but all were warm and dry. Ambrose warned the Friends about their old nemesis Edmund Scarborough moving the border, and they voiced their concerns. Mary imparted the news from Nassawadox. Those gathered were distressed that John Perrot had swayed so many of their former neighbors to follow him and relieved that he had left the area and crossed the Bay; however, Scarborough was the main topic of discussion.

The day after the meeting Mary woke to bright sunshine that burned the morning mist from the river and sparkled on the wet foliage. Mary Dixon was plagued with morning sickness, and Allie made her a pot of mint and chamomile tea and settled her near the cooking hearth with some mending. As soon as it was dry enough to work in the garden, the missionaries helped young Mary and Sarah Dixon harvest the pumpions. The girls, thirteen and ten respectively, were deft at separating the precious seeds from the pulp, some for roasting and some for next year's crop. Mary and Allie cut the orange globes in half, and Aunt Betty filled the cavities with milk and baked them to supplement the evening meal.

As they were finishing up, Ambrose came into the house with George Johnson and Thomas Price, neighbors that the missionaries had met during meetings for worship. Samuel Groome was with them. Mary Dixon had fallen asleep in her chair by the hearth, so they all spoke quietly. The men greeted the women gravely, and Ambrose asked for some refreshment for his guests. Mary Tomkins brewed tea, and Allie was putting bread and cheese on the board when twelve-year-old Thomas burst through the door, startling them all.

"Horsemen, father!" the boy gasped.

The men rose to their feet, and Mary Dixon woke up roused by her son's raised voice.

"How many, Tom?" Ambrose asked.

"A deal of them! They carry the Virginia flag and are coming apace!" the boy answered, fighting tears.

The front door stood open, and all could hear the distant rumble of hoofbeats, growing steadily louder.

Ambrose grasped his son's shoulders. "Bar the door, and take the women upstairs, son."

Thomas opened his mouth to protest, as the girls and Mary Dixon headed for the loft.

"Now, Thomas!" Ambrose barked, pushing the boy toward his mother, who was urging the children up the ladder to the loft. "You men with me," he said to his friends and went outside.

"We shall get the door, Thomas," Mary Tomkins told him. "Help thy mother now." She had no intention of cowering behind a barred door.

Allie was beside her as they stepped outside, closing the front door behind them. The sun shone brightly, and it was hard to believe anything untoward could happen on such a fine day, but the yard was unusually quiet. All work had stopped, and the laborers stood like statues, looking toward the lane. Mary followed their gaze and saw a billowing cloud of dust, staining the pristine blue sky. Then the first horsemen appeared around the bend.

They came on in military formation at a brisk trot. Colonel Edmund Scarborough led the troop in full uniform, a standard bearer carrying the Virginia flag at his side. Behind him were four commissioners from James City and a mass of mounted men. Mary tried to count them as they came into view—ten, twenty—she lost count, and still they came. Their disciplined approach was daunting, although the company was yet a hundred yards from the house. The Dixons' workers instinctively moved closer to their master, cowering fearfully.

"God save us!" Thomas Price breathed.

"Be not faint of heart, Friends," Ambrose said steadily, his eyes on the militia.

Scarborough drew rein fifteen feet from the front door. The standard bearer and four commissioners flanked him. The militia broke ranks, fanning out behind them as they could. There were so many, they could not all fit in the open area in front of the house. There was a pause as the mounted men loomed over the Friends. The labored breathing of horses, the creak and jingle of tack, and the stamp of a hoof were the only sounds. Then Ambrose spoke, breaking the eerie silence.

"What is thy business here, Edmund Scarborough?" he asked with admirable calm, Mary thought. Four men—and a cowed group of servants—against this impressive force were not favorable odds.

"This plantation is on Virginia soil, Dixon," Scarborough declared in a surprisingly high voice at odds with his daunting armaments and patrician good looks. "Ye must swear allegiance to the government of the colony or forfeit these holdings forthwith."

"We swear to none but God, as thou well knowest. Also, this land is under the proprietorship of the Calverts. The border of Virginia is well south of here at the Pocomoke River," Ambrose replied evenly.

"This warrant approved by Governor Berkeley says otherwise," Scarborough retorted, patting a pouch at his belt, and smiling sardonically. "You have usurped Virginia land without his permission. Squatters all of you! You shall not escape the righteous authority of the colony this time! Swear allegiance or your holdings shall be confiscated!"

"We know of thy perfidy, Scarborough! Thou canst not move the colony's boundary at will!" George Johnson declared.

"But verily I can," the Colonel smirked. "Governor Berkeley approved the new line, and I am the Royal Surveyor of Virginia with the authority of the King behind me." As he spoke, Mary and Allie came down from the porch to stand beside Captain Groome, Ambrose, and his neighbors. "What are these?" Scarborough pursed his lips and lifted his dimpled chin, gesturing disdainfully at the women.

George Johnson frowned at them, but Ambrose answered tartly, "Visitors from England, though 'tis no concern of thine."

Scarborough squinted at the missionaries with distaste. "More running Quakers, I wager!" he sneered. "Samuel Groome, I am surprised to find you here. You keep bad company. Have a care it does not affect your business in trade."

"The only effect to my business is that I shall not truck with thee in future, Edmund Scarborough," the young sea captain replied undaunted.

"You would join these rebels in conspiring against authority and just government?" the Colonel queried.

George Johnson emitted a bark of laughter. "'Just' government! 'Tis impossible to conspire against that which does not exist!" he declared, folding his arms across his chest.

Ambrose laid a hand on his neighbor's arm to calm him then addressed Scarborough reasonably.

"Thou knowest Charles Calvert granted us these lands, Scarborough. He appointed thee as one of the Land Commissioners for Annemessex and Manokin," he said steadily. "Thou wert paid for thy service in acres—*Maryland* acres. Thou might prefer it be *Virginia* land, but claiming the boundary is thirty miles north of its true location does not make it so. Governor Calvert shall not allow it."

Scarborough's face darkened the veneer of easy authority gone. "You shall see what is allowed this day," he snarled. "These commissioners are prepared to make a list of all tithables on this property," he stated, gesturing to the men that flanked him. "Mind you do not omit the servants, especially the females over sixteen that labor in the fields," he said to the officials.

"Women servants are not tithable!" George Johnson protested.

Scarborough smiled cruelly. "They are as of September of this year by order of the House of Burgesses at James City." He wheeled his horse around to address the militia. "Mark every building, conveyance, and tool with the yellow arrow of confiscation!" he bellowed then turned back to the Friends. "I claim these holdings in the name of the Colony of Virginia!" he announced, his eyes glittering.

"Whatever false claims are made this day shall not be countenanced by Governor Calvert on the morrow," Friend Johnson declared, but Scarborough had already turned away to oversee the claims.

Ambrose urged Johnson and Price to warn their neighbors upriver, while Scarborough was occupied at Dixon's Choice.

"Go first to Stephen Horsey. I fear he may do something foolish if Scarborough catches him unawares," he finished. "Remind him that we must not give them reason to arrest us by resorting to violence."

There were forty soldiers in the militia. Each commissioner was assisted by ten men, and they accomplished the order with efficiency. Within an hour every building, every piece of equipment, and every conveyance of the Dixons' bore the yellow arrow of confiscation, and the commissioners had recorded all the livestock, crops, and every tithable servant, according to the new law. The company was chillingly disciplined. Once done, they formed up and rode off to the next plantation without comment.

In the wake of the invasion Ambrose Dixon called a meeting of the Friends to determine the extent of Scarborough's claim. He had gone to every plantation bordering the Annemessex River. All but two families had refused to swear allegiance to Virginia; however, some Friends from the Manokin settlement related that Scarborough had gone there, as well, and met with more success. Most of the folk there were Anglicans, and only the eight families who were Friends refused to take the oath.

Stephen Horsey was furious. He attended the meeting even though he was not a Friend. The attack confirmed his suspicion of Anglicans as monied gentry that preempted the best land for cultivation. He resented their predominance in government positions, for they used their power to promote personal agendas; he bridled at their open disdain for commoners like himself; and he vowed to challenge their high-handed assumptions. He volunteered to journey to St. Mary's City across the Bay to inform Governor Calvert, the Third Baron Baltimore, that his southern boundary was compromised.

The meeting approved this proposal, but George Johnson suggested that Ambrose Dixon accompany Horsey. Two representatives would validate the report, and Dixon had a cooler head than their rebel friend, the better to make the case for redress.

"Governor Calvert must hear of this threat," Johnson pointed out. "Beyond that, we can do nothing. The issue must be negotiated between the colonies' governors to stick."

The meeting found consensus on this point, and Horsey was glad to have Ambrose accompany him. They planned to leave the next day in Ambrose's sloop.

The meeting finally ended, and the missionaries were alone with the Dixon Family and Captain Groome. Mary asked to go with Ambrose and Stephen Horsey. It was an opportunity to follow John Perrot for she worried about his influence among the Friends on the Western Shore.

"He must be stopped, Ambrose," she said earnestly. "We can at least counter his false doctrine and guide folk back to the Light, if they have strayed."

"Thomas Browne said Perrot and his brother went to the Patuxent River?" he asked.

"Indeed," she confirmed. "Near two weeks past."

"We must first go to St. Mary's City and speak to the Governor," Ambrose told her.

"I understand," she replied. "Is the Patuxent River far from there?"

"'Tis some forty miles by sea, as one must return south and go around Lookout Point before heading north to the Patuxent. But once our business with the Governor is done—which, mind thee, may take some time— 'tis two day's sail to reach the plantation of my friend Richard Preston, who lives on that river. If Perrot has been there, Richard will know, as he has held regular meetings at his home for years and is known to all the Friends on the Western Shore. Wouldst tell him of our coming, Samuel?" Ambrose asked, turning to Captain Groome.

"Certes," Groome replied. "I should be glad to help in any way I can."

"Thou art going to the Prestons' plantation on the Patuxent?" Mary asked him, straightening.

"Yes, once we are finished collecting the tobacco crop on the Eastern Shore," he confirmed.

"Might we take passage with thee? 'Twould be best to go to this community of Friends directly, if possible," she said.

"I am going there in any case," he smiled, "and I am honored to aid thy mission. However, 'twill be several days before we finish on the Eastern Shore and cross the Bay, mind you," he warned.

"We understand," Mary said. "It shall be sooner than waiting for Friends Dixon and Horsey, I wager. Thou art indeed generous, Friend Groome."

Ambrose chuckled. "And thou art indeed true to thy mission, Mary," he said admiringly.

Chapter 29

PATUXENT RIVER, MARYLAND COLONY

October (8ᵗʰ Month) 1663

The ship *Dove* was a seasoned vessel. In 1631 she had brought the first Catholic settlers to Maryland in tandem with the *Ark*. She was now over thirty years at sea, but she was well maintained and had safely carried passengers and cargo across the Atlantic many times. Samuel Groome became her captain when he reached his majority in '58, a rare achievement at the age of twenty-one. It was testimony to his skill as a mariner.

On the morning of departure, Groome broke his fast with the Dixons and their guests at the house. They finished eating as the sun cleared the eastern horizon, and the family accompanied them to the landing to see them off. Mary was energized by resuming her mission with John Perrot. Since Ambrose would be joining them at the Prestons' plantation, parting was no hardship. He promised to meet them there as soon as possible.

The sun warmed as the *Dove* was towed away from the pier. Out on the bay the wind picked up.

"We shall arrive at the Prestons' landing before dark with this blow, I reckon," Captain Groome said, eying the taut sails as they caught the southwest wind. "The plantations along the Patuxent are our last ports of call before heading for New Amsterdam with a full hold."

Mary nodded absently, her mind already grappling with the challenge of catching up to John Perrot and counter-acting his false doctrines. The far-flung vault of the boundless sky above open water always cleared her mind, and the day at sea gave her time to think and plan.

They sounded the signal cannon some fifty yards off the Prestons' landing then dropped anchor and furled the *Dove's* sails. She would eventually be towed alongside the stout pier and loaded, but for now, Captain Groome and the missionaries went ashore in the ship's longboat rowed by two of the crew. By the time they reached the dock, their host was waiting to greet them with his youngest son, Samuel at his side. The fourteen-year-old was Captain Groome's godson and namesake, and the boy's face lit with pleasure at seeing him. Mary was impressed by the warmth of their reunion. Captain Groome made introductions, and Friend Preston welcomed Mary and Allie with warm respect.

"Public Friends from England! Ye do honor us with your company!" he exclaimed, shaking their hands with both of his. He was an older man. The hair beneath his hat was silver, but his grip was strong, and his eyes were clear. "My wife Margaret shall be thrilled to entertain you. We see so few female travelers. I hope ye shall stay long enough to worship with us on First Day."

"Our thanks, Friend Preston," Mary returned. "'Tis we who are honored by thy hospitality."

Richard's smile broadened. "My dears, although we have only just met, I feel we are kindred spirits."

The Light shone in his eyes, and Mary was moved by the connection blossoming between them.

"I trust thy cargo is ready for transport, Richard?" Groome asked, addressing the business at hand.

"Verily, we have anticipated thy arrival, Samuel," Preston replied. "But 'tis near dark, and Margaret will berate me if I keep these ladies standing on the dock another moment. Let us retire to the house. No doubt ye could all do with some refreshment while the crew docks thy ship, Samuel."

Groome turned to the sailors in the long boat. "Tell Mr. Trent to bring her in, men. We can load her in the morning. There shall be an extra ration of rum this night, once ye are done."

"And a hot meal, as well," Richard added, reaching to shake each of the men's hands. "Come up to the house when your work is done. I shall inform Missus Berry, our cook. How many, Samuel?"

"There are eight—six crew, the cabin boy, and my navigator Mr. Trent," Groome replied. "But we would not inconvenience thee, Richard. We have food aplenty onboard."

"Aye, but 'tis not Missus Berry's fare, the best in the county, I wager! Conserve thy supplies for the journey to New Amsterdam, my friend," Preston urged.

"Thou art ever generous, Richard," Groome smiled, clapping the older man on the shoulder. "The crew shall be most grateful for one of Missus Berry's hot meals."

The Prestons' house was modest but obviously built with care. It was a brick edifice of one-and-a-half stories with decorative Flemish bond work around the windows and the façade at the entry. A porch with a simple arched pediment supported by four columns faced southwest affording a fine view of the river. Two large brick chimneys flanked the house like bookends. A wood-frame addition extended from the southeast corner for food preparation or other household labors.

Margaret Preston was indeed thrilled to have female visitors in addition to the pleasure of seeing Samuel Groome whom she treated like family. The young sea captain was as popular on this side of the Chesapeake as he was on the Eastern Shore. She served them tea and slices of applesauce cake in the parlor, while Missus Berry scrambled to supplement the evening meal for a dozen unexpected guests. The Prestons' daughters Naomi, twelve, and Margaret, eight, were introduced to the missionaries then sent to help the cook. The family put on no airs and ran their plantation in keeping with the Friends' principles of simplicity and integrity.

The Prestons' parlor took up half the ground floor and was warmed by a fine paneled fireplace. A hall occupied the other half, where the family lived and worked when not entertaining, as Mary and Allie would discover. A partition wall with double doors divided the two rooms. Each had its own hearth.

The Prestons had many questions about Mary and Allie's experiences in the Bay Colony, and during a lull in the conversation, Mary was surprised to note it was full dark outside, its early advent an indication of the coming winter. She was wondering how to bring up the subject of John Perrot when Margaret provided an opening.

"I find it quite a wonder that we recently entertained two other Public Friends," Margaret began. "Are you acquainted with Friends Perrot and Browne?" she asked the missionaries.

"We are," Mary answered evenly, glancing at Allie. "Verily, John Perrot is the reason we came to the southern colonies." She groped for words. "How did—what was your impression of him?" she asked.

Now the Prestons exchanged a weighty glance, and Richard cleared his throat nervously.

"I beg you, be honest in your opinions," Mary added, seeing them hesitate. "Our Founder has charged us with finding him and bringing him back to the Light."

Richard and Margaret both sighed with relief. "We are glad ye are not followers of his radical ideas!" he exclaimed. "Friend Perrot was engaging at the first," he began slowly, "but we became alarmed by his lack of respect for some of our most basic practices. He bade us cease regular meetings, said they were a mere form and that we should gather 'when called,' although just *how* we were to coordinate that call to worship with other Friends, he failed to address."

"He is comely and eloquent, impressing men as well as women," Margaret added, "but he seems too taken with his own charms and uses them to convince folk of his spiritual superiority."

"He does not subscribe to hat-honor either," Richard added. "Another empty form, he says! In truth it was disturbing. He spoke at our First Day meeting, and by the end he was ranting about being 'upright in our hearts' and breaking free of the 'bonds of form.' Frankly, he struck us as unbalanced."

The Prestons looked uncomfortable, and after a pause Richard went on.

"We were convinced by William Robinson in '57, when Friend Ambrose Dixon transported him here from Virginia. We have entertained many of our faith since, but none ever spoke so rashly." He shook his head sadly.

"Do ye know if they are yet in the area?" Mary asked.

"They stayed here some days," Margaret said, "but after his rant about forms, most of us became wary of him. I fear we parted at odds. He had hard words with Richard about our lack of faith before they left."

"Dost know where they went?" Mary asked, her heart sinking.

"They did not say," Richard answered, "but Perrot talked of returning to Barbados. He mentioned it several times. Folk appreciate him there, he said."

"I am ashamed to say we were relieved to see them go and did not ask," Margaret admitted.

Mary could not imagine anyone accusing these fine people of lack of faith, but disappointment overwhelmed her. The hope of finding Perrot and initiating a resolution was crushed again.

Chapter 30

PATUXENT RIVER and THE CLIFTS, MARYLAND COLONY

October (8ᵗʰ Month) 1663

Mary and Allie did not see much of Samuel Groome, his namesake, or their host the next day, as the men were up at dawn to supervise the loading of the *Dove*. Margaret Preston was good company, and she devoted the day to helping the missionaries in their search for information of John Perrot.

"May I suggest an outing to the Clifts?" she proposed as they broke their fast in company with the Prestons' two youngest children, Naomi and Margaret. The girls squealed with delight at the prospect but quickly quieted with a stern look from their mother.

"There is an active community of Friends there, and 'tis not far," Margaret went on, turning back to her guests. "If we take the trap, 'tis less than an hour. John Perrot visited there, too. Mayhap our good friends the Sharpes know where he went."

"May we take a picnic, Mama? Please?" little Margaret begged.

"Yes, we may," she answered, "and you girls may ready the basket." The children leapt to their assigned task. "And put in a crock of the apple butter we made last week, as a gift for the Sharpes," Margaret added, as they headed for the kitchen ell.

It was a perfect autumn day with bright sunshine and a light breeze, requiring only a shawl. They were on their way within an hour.

"Dr. Sharpe is known by folk hereabouts as 'the good Quaker Doctor,'" Margaret told the missionaries, as the trap rolled along the lane. "He is a treasure for few physitians in Maryland share our faith."

Judith Sharpe greeted them warmly, but predictably, the doctor was out on a call. The house was a two-story edifice, with a lovely prospect, situated near a pond fed by a freshwater stream. Some fine old oaks and loblolly pines shaded the house. A fenced pasture surrounded the pond, where a dozen cattle grazed.

Upon arrival the Preston girls ran off with the Sharpe children Mary and William, who were the same age. Judith drew cups of cider for her guests, and they settled on the porch. The four children were clearly visible at the edge of the pasture, tempting the cattle with handfuls of fresh grass from outside the fence. Their mothers kept an eye on them as the women talked.

"Contrary to appearances, my husband has no inclination to farm," Judith confided. "Verily he has no time for it, as he is constantly busy with his patients. My son John manages the beeves and is making a fine job of it. He went to look at a neighbor's bull this morning, but he shall be back for the noon meal."

"John is Judith's grown son from her first marriage," Margaret clarified. "He is a deal older than Mary and Will."

"Yes, we came from Cornwall in '51, but my first husband John Gary did not season well, and the fever took him within months of our arrival," Judith informed her guests.

"What a trial for thee," Mary murmured, curbing her inclination to ask about Perrot immediately.

"Ah well, 'tis more than a decade gone now," Judith replied unfazed, "and fortunately, my good-brother Stephen immigrated with us. We managed better than most, thanks to him. I do not believe I could have gone on alone with four children, though they were all in their teens by then. The Lord works in mysterious ways for I met Peter when he tended my husband, and we married a year later."

At that moment, a rider appeared trotting up the lane to the house.

"There is my Johnny now," Judith said with obvious affection, raising a hand in greeting.

The figure lifted his hat in a jaunty gesture to the ladies on the porch and turned in at the stable. The children left the cattle and ran to greet him, and their hostess stood up.

"Time to lay out the board," she said.

"We brought a picnic. Shall we eat out here in the sun?" Margaret suggested.

"We have a fine dinner on the board," Judith answered. "'Tis already prepared for my Johnny is up early of a morn and appreciates a full dinner at noon. Let us allow the children a picnic on their own, and we shall be free to talk and deepen our acquaintance," she smiled warmly at her guests.

Mary agreed with alacrity, as it would be easier to talk about Perrot without the children present.

John Gary was unusually tall. When Judith introduced the missionaries, he bowed as he shook their hands, his brown eyes twinkling merrily. Mary judged him to be of an age with her and Allie. His dark brown hair was short and straight, and he seemed unaware, or did not care, that it stood up in random tufts, when he removed his hat. Over his work clothes he wore a deerskin coat that looked native-made. He smelled of leather and horse and fresh air. He assessed the women with lively interest, and talk flowed easily in response to his perceptive questions. The Sharpes' indentured couple came and went from the table, but the missionaries barely noticed, so engrossed were they in conversation with the young man, his mother, and Margaret Preston. Judith insisted they use Christian names, which generated a feeling of comfortable informality. Long after they had eaten, the five of them sat at the table, and Mary was at last able to tell her new friends of their mission to find John Perrot.

"He was here briefly," Judith told them, "but when he bade us cease First Day meetings, none of us could countenance it."

"I tried to reason with him several times," John added earnestly, "but 'twas like talking to a post. He speaks well but seems unable to listen."

"Did he say where they were going, when they left?" Mary asked.

Judith and her son shook their heads.

"Once he parsed that we would not adore him without question, he wanted nothing more to do with us," Judith said.

"Likely they went to James City to take ship for Barbados," John offered. "He oft spoke of returning."

"So we thought, too," Margaret Preston confirmed.

There was a pause in the conversation, and Mary realized Allie was more than usually quiet, even for Allie. Perhaps John noticed too, for he posed his next question directly to her.

"That scar looks somewhat fresh. May I ask what happened, Friend Ambrose?" he asked gently.

Margaret's eyes widened at this personal probe, but Judith seemed as curious as her son and did not reprimand him. Mary was surprised by the change in topic, but she knew Allie was not sensitive about it. John's attitude was sympathetic and clinical. His stepfather was a doctor, after all.

Allie straightened and met John's eyes for the first time. She did not answer immediately, and Mary felt something pass between them. Judith and Margaret glanced at each other. They felt it, too.

"We were arrested at Dover in the Bay Colony," Allie said at length, still holding his gaze. She paused, and he waited patiently for her to elaborate. "We were flogged at the cart tail, and when I turned to look at Mary beside me, the whip went high and opened my cheek," she explained calmly.

"How dreadful!" Judith exclaimed.

"Ye did not tell us they flogged you in the Bay Colony!" Margaret Preston said, distressed.

"How many stripes?" John asked evenly.

"Ten at Dover and ten more at Hampton," she replied. "We were released at the third town, Salisbury, thanks to the intervention of our friends and an influential man of the town named Robert Pike."

"When was this?" Margaret asked, looking from Allie to Mary.

"Ninth Month past," Mary murmured. She avoided talking about their suffering as it made people uncomfortable.

"Ninth Month? In a northern winter?" John asked outraged. It was common knowledge that whippings were administered on bare flesh.

"Oh, certes they did not, they *could* not have—" Judith began.

Mary nodded. "Yes. We were stripped to the waist," she supplied gently, sparing Friend Sharpe from using the word. "We walked behind the cart for more than a mile through frozen slush before they took us on to Hampton, another twenty-three miles ahorse. We were served the same there."

"How ever did ye survive it?" Margaret asked appalled and impressed in equal measure.

"Our friend Doctor Walter Barefoote accompanied us. He treated our wounds and tried to keep us warm and fed. 'Twas he arranged our release along with Friend Edward Wharton from Salem." Mary paused. Saying Edward's name released a wave of longing that made it hard to speak. She cleared her throat and went on. "Once we could travel again, they took us back to the Shapleighs on the west bank of the Piscataqua River. The Territory of Mayne is somewhat removed from the Bay Colony authorities."

"For the nonce," Allie added. "We would have died but for them," she said gravely.

"I had no idea ye had suffered so!" Margaret Preston exclaimed. "God love you!"

"We do all verily owe you our respect and gratitude!" Judith Sharpe added. "I hope ye will speak at our next First Day meeting. The Friends here should know of your experiences in the Bay Colony."

The older women were lavish in praise and sympathy, but John was speechless, gazing at Allie. Mary noted his eyes shone with more than admiration. She recognized it, for she had seen that expression many times on Edward Wharton's face.

Chapter 31

PATUXENT RIVER AND THE CLIFTS, MARYLAND COLONY

October (8th Month) 1663

Richard and Margaret Preston hosted the next First Day meeting for worship. Word of the visitors spread quickly, and the parlor was so crowded with Friends that the paneled doors were folded back to afford more space. Outside gusts of chill wind ripped leaves from the trees, but the rain held off, and both fireplaces blazed, making the house cozy. The busy harvest season was over, and after the slaughtering was done, the colonists looked forward to the quieter winter months. Spirits were high.

As people arrived, they greeted the missionaries warmly, but Mary and Allie felt a special bond with the Sharpes. The doctor came with Judith, their two younger children, and John Gary, hair combed and wearing a clean brown suit. When the physitian learned that Allie had some knowledge of healing, he peppered her with questions. He knew of the Friends' *infirmaria* at Nassawaddox and became animated, when she spoke of the work being done there.

"Fevers and flux are so common to new arrivals here. Didst thou encounter many cases?" the doctor asked her.

The subject was of particular interest to him as his wife's former husband had died of fever soon after immigrating. Judith and her four children had not been afflicted, and Peter Sharpe was intrigued. Why did some immigrants season well while others perished? He and Allie were soon deep in conversation, oblivious to the crowded room. John Gary hovered near the tall missionary, hanging on every word, as his stepfather drew her out. Mary noted his improved appearance and wondered if Allie remarked it too.

Mary stood nearby, talking with Judith Sharpe who was as forthright as her son. No one could accuse the doctor's wife of reluctance to communicate her opinions.

"It is unusual for women of thy age to be single," she opined, "but I was thirty-seven when I remarried, so one never knows. You girls are right to be discerning and wait for the right man. My first marriage was a practical arrangement, but Peter is the love of my life."

Mary followed her gaze and saw it rested on John rather than the doctor. Was the mother hoping that her son would find that kind of love? Judith turned back to her and lowered her voice.

"I did not know if I could yet bear children, but I managed to give the doctor two healthy babes ere my courses ceased entirely. Many women bear into their forties, I reckon, though likely 'tis not their first."

Mary wondered if Judith was musing about Allie's prospects for bearing children.

"And do your older children hold with the Society?" Mary asked, deftly changing the subject.

"Oh yes," Judith answered definitively. "We entertained Friends Coale and Thurston when they visited in '57. The family entire was convinced by them, including Peter. Our convincement did save my eldest daughter Elizabeth as she was sore conflicted about marrying young Robert Harwood. During their betrothal, she did claim he forced himself upon her, and Peter took him to court over it."

So much for safe topics. "How distressing for all of you!" Mary exclaimed. She found Judith's willingness to speak of more than the weather wonderfully refreshing if a bit of a challenge.

"In truth, 'twas a misunderstanding," Judith responded cheerfully. "Elizabeth did consider it all in contemplation and realized she had overreacted. Young Harwood was more than usually ardent, but he was lectured on the dangers of lust and was contrite. He apologized, and they were married the next spring. They live north of here, further up the Patuxent, with two little ones now, thus they attend meetings closer to home."

Richard Preston appeared at Mary's side.

"Pardon the interruption, but shall we begin, Friend Tomkins?" he asked politely.

Although they had left Devon more than a year ago, Mary and Allie's news of England was relatively fresh for the isolated colonists. The Friends were dismayed to hear that persecution against their faith was undeterred in the mother country, despite the restored monarch's mandamus of 1660 that stopped the executions in Boston. In the mother country meetings for worship were still interrupted by clerical students, the military, and general mischief makers—often violently. Friends were yet being fined, imprisoned, flogged, and ridiculed as enemies of government and order.

"We have traveled from the Piscataqua Region in the north to the Eastern Shore of Virginia in the south," Mary told the gathering, "and we did suffer for our faith in the Bay Colony. But we were also encouraged by the many steadfast communities of Friends we visited.

"In the Colony of Rhode Island Freedom of Conscience is the law, and a number of Friends are active in the government. In June they held the Third Annual Meeting of Friends at Newport, and near two hundred attended. There are also well-established communities of our faith on Long Island, despite Director General Stuyvesant's disapproval. On the Eastern Shore regular meetings are held by Friends in both Maryland and Virginia, and we are heartened to see that is true on this side of the Bay as well," she added, smiling at her hosts.

Now was the moment to bring up John Perrot. Mary sobered and took a deep breath. "But we must all strive to uphold the tenets put forth by our Founder George Fox. The greatest threat is within our faith from those who would deviate from the practices that define us. Hat-honor, oath-honor, and the fellowship of First Day Meetings for worship are basic to our Society. We must guard against those who would divide us from within for there is our downfall. Of late this threat is realized in the person of John Perrot, who disparages these tenets as empty forms and encourages Friends to abandon them." She indicated Allie, standing at her side. "We are charged with finding him and healing the division among Friends that he creates. It may be that he and John Browne are bound for James City to take ship for Barbados. We humbly ask your advice as to where they may have put in along the way. Perrot must be found, and his false doctrines corrected."

Richard Preston spoke up. "It is customary to take ship for Barbados from James City," he said. "I also believe Friends Perrot and Browne are likely headed there."

"Are there communities of Friends on the way, where they may have stopped?" Allie inquired.

"The nearest settlement is on the southern part of the Elizabeth River," Richard answered, "However, the latest news from there is disturbing. They are plagued by an overzealous sheriff. Colonel John Sydney is his name, the High Sheriff of Norfolk County. We recently heard that he did arrest and fine a number of Friends who met at the home of Richard Russell—Sydney's own daughter among them!"

"She is wife to John Porter the younger," Margaret Preston elaborated. "His elder brother is also named John, for a wonder, thus they call him John Sr. Just this past autumn the elder John lost his seat in the House of Burgesses for refusing to swear the new Oath of Supremacy. It is considered treason for one who holds office not to pledge the oath to the King as Supreme Governor of the Church of England. Thus, Porter was dismissed and stands accused of being a 'lover of Quakers.'"

"Sounds like the Bay Colony," Allie remarked.

"They also reward folk for reporting Friends," Richard said grimly. "Half the fine goes to the informer."

Peter Sharpe spoke up. "I would advise avoiding Virginia, but if ye must go, I shall give you a letter of introduction to Friend Mary Emperor. Her husband Francis died at sea last year, but she continues to manage his shipping business. She is a woman of influence in the Elizabeth River community."

"Our thanks, Doctor Sharpe," Mary said. "That sounds like a good place to begin."

"How shall ye travel there?" Margaret Preston asked.

"Friend Ambrose Dixon is currently at St. Mary's City, informing Governor Calvert that his southern boundary on the Eastern Shore is compromised," Mary said.

She briefly related Edmund Scarborough's attack on the Friends' plantations along the Annemessex and his attempt to move Maryland's southern border thirty miles north. They were amazed.

Samuel Groome had stayed for the meeting and now spoke. "I would take you to the Elizabeth River myself, but the *Dove* must go north to New Amsterdam once her hold is full."

"We understand, Captain Groome," Mary said. "We are already indebted to thee for thy help twice over. Friend Dixon intends to meet us here when his business with the Governor is completed. I hope he may help us."

"How far is the Elizabeth River from here?" Allie asked the young mariner.

"Two- or three-days' sail, depending on wind and weather," Groome replied.

"Mayhap in the *Dove*," John Gary commented. "'Twould be longer in a smaller craft."

"Friend Dixon has a fair-sized sloop," Mary said.

"Aye, I know it well," John nodded. "He has transported many Friends from Virginia to the safety of Maryland over the past six years, but it cannot match the *Dove* in speed."

"We shall consult with him, when he arrives," Mary finished.

Their new friends were glad that the missionaries were not leaving immediately, and Mary promised they would return for an extended visit on their way back north.

None of them realized how soon that would be.

Part IV

WINTER/SPRING 1663-64

November 1663. 'People commonly called Quakers were seized for holding an unlawful meeting aboard ye Shipp Blessing, *riding at anchor in the southern branch of the Elizabeth River. John Porter, junior, was speaking. They were all fined 200 pounds of tobacco.'*

—Lower Norfolk County Antiquary, iii. P. 36

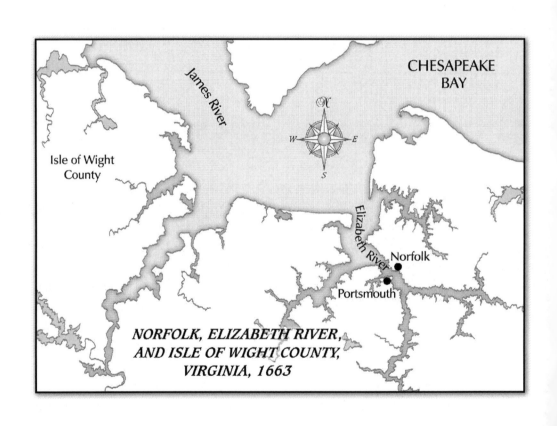

CHESAPEAKE
BAY

James River

Isle of Wight
County

Elizabeth River

Norfolk

Portsmouth

*NORFOLK, ELIZABETH RIVER,
AND ISLE OF WIGHT COUNTY,
VIRGINIA, 1663*

Chapter 32

PATUXENT RIVER, MARYLAND AND ELIZABETH RIVER, VIRGINIA COLONY

November (9th Month) 1663

Three days later Ambrose Dixon and his stepson Henry Pennington arrived at Preston on Patuxent. Mary was relieved. Much as the missionaries were enjoying the company of their new friends, with every passing day she felt the likelihood of catching up to John Perrot slipping away. The reunion with Ambrose was mutually warm, and the depth of her relief at their reunion caused Mary to realize how much she had come to depend on him. She forced herself to wait for the right moment to ask him about continuing south to the Emperors' plantation on the Elizabeth River.

"Where is Friend Horsey, Ambrose?" she asked instead, once they exchanged greetings.

"He went home with George Johnson, who joined us two days after we arrived," Ambrose told her. "He had more accounts of the attack from other Friends, and he could not sleep for fretting over the incident. There was nothing for it, but he must meet the Governor with us. He and Stephen went back this morn."

Over dinner that night Richard Preston questioned Ambrose about his meeting with Governor Calvert.

"Calvert was livid—more about the threat to his southern boundary than any hardship to us, but the wheels of governance turn slowly," Ambrose said wryly. "God knows when he will take action. At least he is apprised of the situation."

The men spoke of possible courses the Governor might take, while Mary waited for an auspicious moment to bring up her request.

At last Ambrose turned to the missionaries and asked, "Did ye learn anything of John Perrot's whereabouts?"

"Nothing for certes," Mary answered, putting down her knife. "He and John Browne left this region over a week ago, the general consensus being that they plan to take ship for Barbados at James City."

"They may have left already then," Ambrose said bluntly.

"Even if we cannot find the man himself, it is our mission to undo the damage he may have wrought along the way," Mary persisted. "Dr. Sharpe suggested we journey south to the Elizabeth River, as 'tis possible Perrot stopped to visit the Friends there on the way to James City. He gave us a letter of introduction to a Friend named Mary Emperor. Dost know her?"

"I knew her husband Francis. He was a sea captain and business associate of Samuel Groome," Ambrose replied. "I met him at James City back in the '50s. We had adjoining slips at one of the piers, and he invited folk to board his ship the *Francis and Mary* to hear the latest news. We found we shared many of the same opinions, including our religion. Francis was a devout Friend and a fine fellow."

Mary glanced at Allie, who nodded her head slightly. Mary drew breath and plunged in.

"'Tis possible John Perrot is yet in that area, Ambrose," Mary said. "We must go there. Wouldst thou consider transporting us?"

Friend Dixon's eyebrows shot up, and he looked from Mary to Allie. They looked back steadily.

"We have been gone near two weeks already," he said slowly, glancing at his stepson Henry.

"The tobacco is in, and Friend Cummings is managing things while we are gone, sir," the boy said, eager to prolong his first extended voyage at sea with his stepfather. Henry was in no hurry to go home.

"I suppose he is," Ambrose allowed. "We shall be at least three days at sea, mind ye," he told the women. "'Tis an hundred miles south of here."

"Yes!" Henry exclaimed, realizing his stepfather had agreed to the journey.

Mary had been holding her breath and let it out in a rush of gratitude. Not only did she value the transport and their friend's extensive knowledge of the local waters, but also his steady wisdom. Her relief at securing his help was so profound words failed her.

Allie smiled her rakish smile. "Our thanks, Ambrose," she answered for them both.

⁓

They left the next morning. The Prestons saw them off at the landing with reluctance.

"Virginia is a dangerous place, and I cannot say we shall not worry about you," Richard said, clasping each of the women's hands in turn. "Your mission is an important one, however. We shall pray for you and wish you Godspeed. Give this letter to Friend Mary Emperor, when ye arrive. I pray she can help you. Certes, she shall welcome your company. Friend Dixon is likely known to her by name from association with her late husband Francis, as well."

Mary smiled up at him. "Our thanks, Friend Preston. Our time with thee has refreshed our spirits, and we hope to return on our way back north."

"I would advise ye not to challenge the authorities of Norfolk County directly," he said gently. "Virginia is much like the Bay Colony concerning members of our faith—particularly visitors who own no property. The Emperors are a family of influence. Ye should be safe under their protection."

"Has Friend Emperor been a widow for long?" Allie asked.

"It is scarce two years, since Francis was lost at sea in a tempest enroute to Barbados," Richard answered. "He was active in the local government before the laws against our faith prohibited him holding office. Francis was wise enough to invest his earnings in land, as he had some skill as a surveyor. Such a loss! He was just over thirty," he finished, shaking his head.

"We are all in God's hands," Ambrose said quietly with a meaningful look at the women.

"Amen," Mary and Allie chorused.

⁓

Ambrose was relieved that the English missionaries were familiar with sea travel. They did not need to be coddled; in fact, they were an asset. As usual, Allie was adept with the jib, and Mary kept the ropes neatly coiled and tied off with the proper knots. The women delighted their companions by singing and relating stories of their ten days with Mary Dyer and their subsequent training at Swarthmore Hall. Ambrose told them of his convincement by William Robinson and the many Public Friends he had smuggled into Virginia by way of the Eastern Shore on the pretext of taking them to St. Mary's City in Maryland. Their friendship deepened, and the days at sea flew by.

They reached the Elizabeth River late in the morning of the fourth day. The mouth of the river was so wide Mary assumed they were still in the Bay, until Ambrose informed them otherwise.

"We are nearly there," he explained. "Mind ye, the Elizabeth has three tributaries—west, south, and east. The Emperors' landing is but another hour's sail down the south branch."

As the riverbed narrowed, boat landings and cultivated fields appeared on both sides. Just before the east fork of the river split from the southern tributary, they passed a merchant ship at anchor. *Blessing* was painted in gold on her black transom.

"'Tis a fine deep-water anchorage here," Ambrose told them. "I wager a proper town shall develop one day. That is James Gilbert's ship. He is a Friend, as well."

The two ships hailed each other from a distance as the sloop passed the merchant ship. Henry blew the signal horn, and they all waved until they rounded a bend and lost sight of the *Blessing*. A few miles further on fields dotted with grazing livestock appeared to port, and Ambrose told them the land belonged to the Emperors. Around the next curve they came upon the dock with a warehouse close by. Young Henry blew the horn, alerting those onshore of their arrival. The landing extended into the river far enough for Ambrose to dock easily, being designed for larger vessels. Henry and Allie secured the bow and stern lines, while Mary and Ambrose reefed the sails.

The pier jutted from a long sweep of cleared land that sloped gently up to a brick manor house with a colonnaded porch and several chimneys. Four children appeared running along the pier toward them—three boys with a little girl trailing behind. Two women followed at a more sedate pace.

"Halloo! Welcome!" the boys cried, approaching the newcomers apace. The little girl hung back, alternately staring at the strangers and glancing over her shoulder to ensure her mother was coming.

"Hello, young fellows!" Ambrose greeted the boys heartily. "Your father did speak of you, so let me see if I remember your names. Francis... Tully... and William, is it?" he said as he shook each boy's hand.

The eldest looked about ten years old and regarded Friend Dixon solemnly. "Thou wert acquainted with our father?" he asked, his eyes widening.

"Indeed, and a finer man and mariner I shall not meet again," Ambrose said warmly. "Thou art his namesake and favor him, as well, I see. He would be proud to see how thou hast grown."

The women were close enough to hear this last statement. "True that!" the taller of the two agreed in a surprisingly deep voice. She took the little girl's hand, guiding her along to meet the guests. "We must let down the cuffs of his pants daily," she quipped approaching and holding out her hand. "I am his mother, Mary Emperor, and this is my companion Ann Godby. Well met!"

As they shook hands and exchanged names, Mary Tomkins produced the letter of introduction from Richard Preston. Their hostess barely looked at it, saying "Ye are Friends and ever welcome here."

As they walked up to the house, Mary realized their hostess and her companion were women of some quality. They wore the unadorned attire customary to Friends, but the material was fine gray bombazine, and Mary Emperor's outfit was trimmed at collar, cuffs, and hem with a darker shade of velvet. Likely the material had come from England by means of the widow's late husband, Captain Francis Emperor. His widow's attire was a testimony to his success before his untimely death at sea.

"I prefer to use Christian names, and it please you," their hostess was saying, as they drew near the house. "'Friend Emperor' is something of an oxymoron and engenders images of despotic rulers, does it not?" she said, arching a shapely eyebrow.

Allie laughed outright surprised and delighted that their hostess's sense of humor matched her own. "I suppose it does!" she replied merrily.

Mary Emperor's smile broadened for she was relieved as well. Over the years since she and Francis were convinced, she had encountered Public Friends who were so devoted to their mission that they frowned on levity of any sort. She was glad these guests were not so constrained.

⌒

The three boys doted on Henry Pennington and hauled him off to show him their favorite haunts, while Mary Emperor led her other guests into the house. A negro woman met them at the door and took their cloaks and headgear.

"We shall have tea in the hall, Wanny," their hostess said. "Is the fire lit?"

"Yes, Mistress," the woman answered in a voice like velvet. "There be a fine blaze."

Mary and Allie smiled and thanked the woman then followed the others. Mary was reminded of the Sylvesters at Shelter Island, who had brought negro slaves from Barbados. It seemed likely their hostess had emigrated from there, as well.

They made small talk as they waited for the refreshments. Wanny and a younger woman set a silver tea service and a platter of gingerbread on a small table next to their mistress. Once they left the room, Mary Emperor's tone changed.

"It has been an exceedingly eventful autumn," she declared, stirring the teapot. They sat in the radius of warmth around the hearth. The November day was chill, and Allie held her slender hands out to the blaze. Her hands and feet were more sensitive to the cold since her ordeal at Dover.

"The Friends here shall be encouraged by your visit," Anne Godby added, passing Ambrose the platter of gingerbread. "God has sent you at an auspicious time."

"Oh? Do tell," Ambrose encouraged, placing a fragrant piece of cake on the handkerchief spread across his knee and passing the plate along to Allie. The gingerbread was dark with molasses and still warm.

"Verily, it all began last Ninth Month, when Colonel Sydney interrupted one of our meetings for worship. He was high sheriff at the time, and he even fined his own daughter, who was present."

"Aye, we did hear of that from the Prestons," Ambrose said. "We came direct from their place on the Patuxent. Sydney's daughter is wife to John Porter the younger, is she not?"

"Indeed," their hostess confirmed. "Predictably her Puritan Cavalier father did not approve. The elder John Porter was a Burgess, until John Hill replaced Sydney as sheriff last spring. Hill accused Porter of being a 'Quaker lover,' but Friend Porter maintained the sheriff had no proof. Then did Hill press him to swear the Oath of Allegiance, which, certes, as a Friend, Porter refused. He was removed from office."

"Mind ye, Governor Berkeley has appointed a new commission to eradicate Friends in our county entirely," Ann Godby explained. "Informers receive half the fine, thus arrests have become quite lucrative. Sheriff Hill enriches himself, while posing as the savior of the Baptist Church."

Mary Emperor went on as she poured cups of steaming tea. "This past Sabbath Day we met for worship at the home of our friend Richard Russell, and Sheriff Hill broke in and arrested everyone present. We are called to court next month," she informed them calmly, passing the first cup to Mary.

"There is nothing for it but to protest the new law by continuing to meet," Ann declared stoutly.

Mary Tomkins agreed heartily. "Is anything special planned for the coming First Day?" she asked.

"Yes!" Ann replied, her eyes shining. "There is to be a meeting aboard James Gilbert's ship *Blessing*. She is at anchor in the river a few miles north."

"Aye, we passed her on our way here," Ambrose affirmed, accepting a steaming cup of tea.

"Captain Gilbert was an associate of my late husband and is also a Friend," their hostess smiled. "He deems that since the ship is not on Virginia soil, whatever takes place aboard is under his authority and no business of the government."

"Are ye able to stay for it?" Ann asked eagerly.

After a glance at Allie who nodded, Mary replied, "We shall, indeed; however, we do have a mission. It may be that ye can help us," she added, pausing to form her thoughts. "We are charged with finding a Friend named John Perrot. Have ye heard aught of him and his companion John Browne?"

"Oh, Richard Russell did speak of him last week at meeting," Mary Emperor said. "Richard received a letter from Thomas Jordan, a Friend who lives at Isle of Wight—a neighboring county to the northwest, not the English one," she clarified for her guests. "Friend Jordan wrote that this Perrot fellow convinced the folk there to renounce hat-honor and First Day meetings, but I find that hard to credit," she smiled.

"I do not," Mary Tomkins said gravely. "'Tis as we feared. We are on a mission for the Founder to correct the falsehoods and dissension Perrot is spreading among Friends."

"Verily, Richard was disturbed," their hostess allowed sobering. "Apparently Perrot persuaded folk that the authorities would not be able to arrest Friends so easily, if we did not hold regular meetings."

"But the point is not to avoid arrest!" Ann Godby said indignantly. "The unjust laws shall never change, if we do not protest by breaking them and holding our meetings regardless."

Mary Emperor waited for the chorus of agreement to subside then went on. "According to Richard's friend, meetings have ceased at Isle of Wight altogether thus he allows that the effort to shirk persecution has done the Society more harm than the persecution itself."

Mary's heart sank. She had tried to guess Perrot's destination, but apparently, he had chosen to go directly up the James River stopping at Isle of Wight on the way and ignoring the community of Friends on the Elizabeth River. She and Allie must go there, but would Ambrose consent to yet more travel?

He met her eyes and seemed to read her thought. "I reckon ye both should stay for the meeting on the *Blessing*. Henry and I can sail up to Isle of Wight on the morrow and talk to the Friends there," he said.

"I fear 'tis too much to ask of thee, Ambrose," Mary demurred.

The big man shook his head. "'Tis an easy day's sail, and I am acquainted with Thomas Jordan. I shall speak with him, as we know he was not taken in by Perrot. He can give us an account of things. It should only take three days. Then we can all return to Isle of Wight after First Day, if we deem it necessary to help the folk there," he finished, popping a last bit of gingerbread into his mouth.

"Thou wouldst do that for us, Ambrose?" Mary asked amazed and humbled by this generous offer.

Ambrose finished chewing then dabbed his mouth with his handkerchief. "Verily, I do it for all of us, Mary," he answered earnestly. "Perrot's influence on our faith is not solely thy responsibility. It concerns us all. He creates disharmony when we most need unity among Friends."

Mary Emperor spoke up. "Amen, Ambrose!" She turned to her female guests. "Ye are most verily welcome to stay with us as long as ye wish," she said. "The Friends shall be thrilled to hear your news of England, and I should be insulted, if ye do not stay at least a week or more."

Mary and Allie exchanged a look. "Our thanks, Mary, but our stay shall depend upon what is learned at Isle of Wight," the former replied. "We are in your debt, Ambrose."

"If all goes well, Henry and I may be back in time for that meeting on the *Blessing*," he smiled.

Chapter 33

ELIZABETH RIVER, VIRGINIA COLONY

November (9th Month) 1663

Ambrose and Henry were not back from Isle of Wight by First Day.
"I pray no harm has come to them," Mary said to Allie, as they prepared for the meeting on the *Blessing*.

"It does not serve to worry," her friend answered.

Ann Godby joined them later that morning, and they left after a light meal at noon. The November day was chilly. The sun made fitful appearances between fast-moving clouds, herded out to sea on a brisk northerly wind. Everyone wore their warmest cloaks and shawls and did not tarry on the walk down to the landing. Mary Emperor had the finest shallop the missionaries had yet seen. Two of the Emperors' servants rowed them upriver as wind and current were against them. The three boys crowded into the bow, and the four women sat on the wide stern bench, little Elizabeth on her mother's lap. About an hour later they came alongside the *Blessing*. The merchant ship towered above them as the men shipped the oars. One grabbed a rope ladder dangling from the port side to steady the shallop and hold it in place.

"Ye can return for us in two hours' time," Mary Emperor told the men, "We shall want to be home before dark."

The rope ladder was the only access aboard since the ship lay at anchor some three hundred yards offshore. It was a first for the missionaries, who had usually boarded large ships by gangplank from a dock. One of the rowers bore little Elizabeth up on his back while the other steadied the bottom of the ladder. The boys scampered up like monkeys, and the four women followed slowly but without mishap. Captain

James Gilbert greeted them warmly and assisted them on board. They were not first to arrive.

Mary Emperor and Ann Godby knew everyone. The common room was crowded and buzzed with conversation, but it felt wonderfully warm after the chilly trip upriver. A flurry of faces and names ensued, and flagons of cider were pressed into the missionaries' hands. Mary and Allie conversed with Richard Russell the elderly Friend their hostess had spoken of. They were soon joined by the younger John Porter and his wife, another Mary. Friend Russell had hosted many meetings for worship in his home on the western branch of the Elizabeth River. He had been summoned to court several times and fined in pounds of tobacco as a result.

"Governor Berkeley seeks to eradicate our faith from the colony, but it has only served to make us more determined," Friend Russell said with a gentle smile.

Young Porter was not so philosophical. "My brother's dismissal from the House of Burgesses was a call to resist. That scurvy Sheriff Hill accused him, and I wager he profited by it," he growled.

The room was becoming more crowded as others arrived, and Mary Emperor squeezed in at Allie's side.

"Captain Gilbert suggests we go to the mess now," she said quietly. "There are not seats enough for all."

The ships' crew took their meals in the mess, and it was the largest space below deck, barring the hold. It seemed spacious after the common room. There was no natural light, but lanterns hung from hooks on the ceiling. Two long benches and some crates served as seating, but the table was bolted to the floor and could not be moved. The meeting would have to take place around it. The women used their folded cloaks to cushion the hard benches and sat on one side, while the men arranged themselves on the other. By the time everyone settled, Mary counted nine Friends in addition to their small party. There were no other children, but during their stay with Mary Emperor the missionaries had learned that the widow always included them. The three boys perched on the crates, and Elizabeth sat on her mother's lap.

Young John Porter spoke briefly, encouraging the Friends to remain steadfast despite the Virginia Colony's increased persecution against their faith.

"The authorities are motivated by fear and greed," he stated, "but we are inspired by the Light Within. Once lit, it cannot be extinguished for there is no returning to ignorance once knowledge is acquired. Stand fast, Friends, and we shall prevail!"

Mary did not doubt it. The Elizabeth River Friends were strong in their faith and unafraid of challenges. There had been arrests at recent meetings, yet here they were again, risking more fines to worship together. Although their community was small, they were as committed to protesting the unjust laws as any Public Friend. Her heart swelled with admiration and fellowship, as the silence deepened.

The first sign of trouble was the sound of heavy boots overhead. James Gilbert's head snapped up, and he quietly slipped out to investigate. Soon after there were raised voices and more thumping. John Porter rose to follow the captain, but before he reached the door, it burst open. Three men stepped into the room with Captain Gilbert on their heels.

"Ye have no authority here!" he was insisting. "The *Blessing* is at anchor, not on Virginia soil."

The officials ignored him. "Here be a whole nest of 'em hidden away!" one of the deputies exclaimed.

"You are all under arrest," the leader declared with an evil smile. "Take down their names, Maitland," he added. "No one leaves this room until we have the name of every person present."

"Ho! We shall be rich!" the third man crowed.

Mary Emperor handed Elizabeth to Ann Godby and made her way toward the men. She did not speak until she was standing before the leader.

"John Hill, thou dost exceed thy authority," she intoned in her deep voice. "This ship is out of thy jurisdiction. Captain James Gilbert is in charge here, and thou canst not gainsay him."

"Well, well. Mistress Emperor," the high sheriff drawled. "I am not surprised to find you here."

John Porter joined her. "Have the keepers of the law no other wrongs to right? Why must ye harass honest folk at worship except to enrich yourselves with a share of the fines?" he challenged.

"Add John Porter Jr. to that list," Hill ordered the deputy who had sat at the table and was opening his writing box, "along with Mistress Mary Emperor." The sheriff smiled, but his eyes were steely.

"No one leaves until all yer names are recorded!" the third man shouted, blocking the door.

Ann Godby stood in a corner with Mary, Allie, and the Emperor boys. Elizabeth clung to her neck, and she spoke over the little girl's shoulder. "I fear for you," Ann whispered. "They shall fine us who live here, but you own no property. They shall treat you as vagabonds."

"'Twill not be the first time," Allie answered quietly.

"We shall not hide behind a lie," Mary added, lifting her chin.

Ann's warning proved correct. When it came time to give their names, Sheriff Hill seized upon the fact that the two Public Friends had no permanent residence in the colony.

"What are you about here but to make trouble in our county, inciting these folk to resist the law, eh?" he said with narrowed eyes. Mary started to speak, but he cut her off. "By the king's order ye must swear the Oaths of Allegiance and Supremacy or be taken to gaol and stand trial."

"These women are my guests," Mary Emperor stated icily. "They are under my protection."

John Hill laughed. "You promise what you cannot deliver, Mistress. They are vagabonds who break the law by attending this meeting in our colony. They must be publicly punished, or more shall plague us."

"But I urged them to attend," she insisted. "The responsibility is mine. Increase my fine to compensate. I give thee my word I will ensure they do not foment rebellion."

"The word of a heretic! Hah!" Hill laughed then scowled. "How daft do you think me?" he snarled. "Read them the oath," he ordered the clerk at the table, jerking his head toward the missionaries.

"Our religion forbids swearing oaths to any but God," Mary Tomkins stated calmly.

"Then you refuse to swear?" Hill asked. He looked at Allie, "Both of you?"

"Yes," Mary answered. Allie nodded.

The sheriff turned to the man guarding the doorway. "Fetch some rope!" he barked.

The Friends protested, but even Richard Russell's gentle reasoning could not dissuade the sheriff. Rope was procured, and the missionaries' hands were bound in front so they could manage the climb down the rope ladder to Hill's skiff. Mary Emperor draped their cloaks around the missionaries' shoulders. Her eyes shone with indignation and unshed tears.

"Where are you taking them?" Friend Russell asked, as the Friends followed the prisoners on deck.

"'Tis no business of yours," Hill said over his shoulder.

Mary Emperor gripped Richard Russell's arm. "They must not go to James City," she whispered hurriedly. "Remember, Friend Wilson died in the gaol there last year!"

Russell drew the sheriff aside. "Certes, the courthouse near Elizabeth Parish Church is closest, is it not?"

The sheriff nodded grudgingly, and Friend Russell pressed some coins into the man's hand. "See our friends are fed and have blankets and a candle this night, I beg thee," he said quietly.

Hill grunted noncommittally as he pocketed the money.

"Do not despair!" Mary Emperor called as Mary and Allie clambered down the rope ladder. "We shall come to you on the morrow! And we shall discover the day of your trial and attend!"

"We shall do everything in our power to help you!" Richard Russell added, as the skiff pushed off from the *Blessing*.

It was the last time Mary and Allie spoke with the Elizabeth River Friends.

Chapter 34

ELIZABETH RIVER, VIRGINIA COLONY

November (9ᵗʰ Month) 1663

Mary did not know how long they sat in the stern of John Hill's skiff, as the deputies rowed upriver. The sun had set by the time they docked, but Mary could make out a church by its steeple, an ordinary with light in its windows, and a few other dark buildings, obscure in the twilight. Her fingers were numb, and everything seemed vague and unreal. Allie shivered beside her with hands clutched between her knees to warm them. Mary realized their things were still at the Emperors' manor, including Allie's bag of medicaments, and hoped their friends would remember to bring them on the morrow.

As soon as they landed, John Hill went directly to the tavern to refresh himself and celebrate his success. Mary noticed a well-worn sign above the front door that identified it as Shipp's Tavern, as the deputies marched the women past with unnecessary roughness. They were hustled to the back of the building and pushed through a basement door into the office of the under-sheriff Thomas Lovell who took them into custody.

"Puts me in mind of New Amsterdam," Allie said, as Lovell lifted the heavy bar at the door of their cell.

His lantern revealed a small, windowless room. The air was musty and smelled of mold and urine. Only then did Lovell set down the lantern and cut the rope binding the missionaries' wrists, as the knots were too tight to untie. Mary winced and flexed her hands gingerly as the blood rushed back into them.

"In with you," Lovell grunted with a jerk of his head.

As soon as the door closed, the darkness was absolute but for the meagre light of the lantern outside, shining through the cracks. Then Lovell moved off, and even that meagre illumination was gone. The fetid air seemed more potent in the dark. It was chill but not severely cold. Still, Mary was grateful for the comfort of her cloak and shawl. She burrowed her face into the material, which still smelled of the river and fresh air. Allie groped for her hand, and they embraced.

"I suppose we shall get used to the stink," Allie said bravely.

"Let us hope we shall not be here long enough to get used to anything," Mary sighed into her shoulder.

For an indeterminate time, they held each other in the relentless dark, reluctant to abandon this small comfort. The scrape of the bar being lifted alerted them, but the lantern still made them squint when it opened. Lovell had a bundle under one arm and set down an empty bucket.

"For yer business," he sneered. "Count yerselves lucky. Somebody paid for yer keep." He dropped the bundle on the dirt floor and left, plunging them into darkness again.

Still holding hands, Mary and Allie groped for it. A thin blanket was wrapped around a loaf of bread, some hard cheese, and two-thirds of a candle with striker and flint. Allie held the candle and after several attempts, Mary got a good strike and the wick caught. She held it up, and they looked around. The brick walls were damp, streaked with black mold and illegible scratches. An impressive succession of lines filled one section—a tally of days? The women were not inclined to count them. The bread was stale, and the cheese was dry, but it was better than nothing. They had not eaten since the light meal at the Emperors' home before the meeting. It seemed days ago rather than hours.

"We had best save the candle," Mary said with regret once they finished the food and used the bucket.

There was no bench, so they spread one of their cloaks on the driest bit of floor they could find, wrapping the blanket and the other cloak around them both. Then Mary blew out the candle, and they attempted to sleep.

Ambrose and Henry returned from Isle of Wight by late morning on Third Day to find their hostess distraught. She told them of the missionaries' arrest and her subsequent attempt to pay their fine.

"Sheriff Hill would not allow it," she fumed. "He is fanatical as well as greedy. Arresting Friends is a calling fueled by his religious zeal. I fear he means to make a public spectacle of them! I shall carry this guilt to my grave," she finished mournfully.

"Where are they?" Ambrose asked, calm as ever in a crisis. They stood on the dock, as Mary Emperor had been waiting anxiously and hurried to meet them as soon as she heard Henry's horn. Dixon was ready to go to his friends immediately.

"They took them to Shipp's Tavern. The gaol is in the basement, and their trial will be above stairs on the morrow," she answered. "I tried to visit the day after their arrest, but Hill would not allow it. I left coin for food and blankets, but I fear he shall keep it for himself. I am relieved thou art here, Ambrose."

"Henry and I shall go there now," Ambrose said. "We can sleep on the boat and attend the trial on the morrow. Our friends shall need transport from the colony, once the authorities are done with them."

"I fear they shall suffer, and 'tis all due to me," the widow lamented.

"There is no profit in berating thyself, Mary," Ambrose said gently. "Thou couldst not know how this would fall out." He turned to his stepson. "Cast off, Henry."

"Do ye not want some refreshment before ye go?" Mary asked anxiously.

"Our thanks, but we have some provision onboard, and I would get there before dark. I hope to see them this day." Ambrose took her hand in both of his. "Be stout of heart. Our friends are strong and have endured much suffering ere this. I shall take them back to Maryland and the care of Doctor Sharpe."

"Dost believe they shall be flogged then?" she asked, blanching.

"In the light of recent events here, I fear so," he admitted. "They are vagabonds in the eyes of the law."

Tears threatened, but Mary Emperor rallied. "I shall bring as many Friends as I can muster to the trial," she promised then waved Ambrose and Henry off with a heavy heart.

The locals referred to the harbor at Shipp's Tavern as Norfolk, although the name would not be official until its incorporation in 1736. It was a fine market center due to the natural deep-water harbor which could accommodate large ships of trade. These catered to the many plantations along the tributaries of the Elizabeth River, bringing cargo from Barbados, England, or New Amsterdam and loading up with tobacco and livestock. As early as 1636 Adam Thorowgood had seen the potential and established a ferry across the Elizabeth River. Four years later, William Shipp built his ordinary, catering to the increasing nautical traffic as well as the local folk. Shipp was an Anglican, and he designated a plot on his land for the Elizabeth River Chapel. The courthouse was added to the site by order of the Ports and Markets Act of 1655—an aborted attempt by the government at James City to organize the scattered plantations into serviceable towns where taxes could be collected, and justice dispensed more efficiently. However, the planters resisted losing their autonomy to a distant centralized government, and the Act failed miserably and was tabled the next year. The courthouse remained, but there were no funds for its maintenance, and it was falling into disrepair. Better to hold the court at Shipp's Tavern, which was warm with refreshment close at hand and the gaol conveniently located in the cellar.

The prisoners tried to keep track of time, but the constant darkness was oppressive and disorienting. Twice a day Thomas Lovell brought stale bread and cheese and a jug of tepid water for both drinking and washing. He emptied the waste bucket once a day. Mary Emperor's coin was more than enough for this rough fare, but, as she feared, the officers of the law pocketed the difference. The sheriff reckoned the heretics did not deserve the comforts it could provide. The women tried to talk to Lovell, but he was suspicious of their wiles and remained taciturn and hostile. The trial was set for the morrow above stairs in the tavern, but the under-sheriff knew it was mere form. The women refused to swear the Oath of Allegiance to the king and to the Colony of Virginia. They were Quakers and guilty as sin. Their punishment would make fine entertainment.

Ambrose and Henry arrived before dark. They reefed the sails, set the anchor, battened down the hatches, and rowed to shore in the dinghy. Ambrose wanted to see Mary and Allie for himself to parse their condition, but John Hill would not permit it.

"What are they to you?" the Sheriff asked suspiciously. He was on duty as Lovell had gone home to eat.

"They are my friends," Ambrose answered, "and I am prepared to transport them from the colony, assuming they shall be banished after their trial and whatever sentence is put upon them."

Hill grunted noncommittally. "The prisoners are not permitted to speak with anyone," he growled. "You can see them at the trial."

The sheriff was holding out for coin, but Ambrose refused to oblige him. There was no help for it but to wait. Ambrose and Henry went upstairs to eat. There they learned the names of the justices who would pass judgement at the trial—Lemuel Mason, Adam Thorowgood, William Moseley, and William Carver. Of the four he was acquainted only with Thorowgood, the ferry master, but Ambrose knew they were all Anglicans and established landowners. He doubted they would be sympathetic to vagabond Quakers.

The next morning Ambrose and Henry found the common room at Shipp's Tavern already crowded. The trial was the most exciting thing to happen since John Porter had been ousted from his position as Burgess the year before. The Elizabeth River Friends came in force, and Mary Emperor and Ann Godby made room on a bench for Ambrose and Henry.to sit with them. For once the Emperor children had been left at home, but Ann's friend Joan Sturges who had some skill at healing had come.

"Didst thou see Mary and Alice?" Mary Emperor asked anxiously.

Ambrose shook his head and began to answer, but a stir at the entry cut him off.

John Hill and Thomas Lovell escorted the prisoners. The women's hands were bound, but they appeared none the worse for their imprisonment. They walked steadily and looked alert, if a bit rumpled. When the missionaries saw Ambrose and Henry with the Friends, they stood straighter. The minister read an opening prayer then Sheriff John Hill stated the charges.

"Your Honors, these women are a danger to the colony, running loose and spreading heresy. We interrupted them at an illegal meeting on the ship *Blessing* in company with more some dozen other heretics. They refuse to swear the Oath of Allegiance and are vagabonds with no residence in this colony. They seek to sow disruption in our midst. I urge the court to make an example of them to discourage others of their ilk from coming here and poisoning these good folk." Hill gestured to the crowded room.

After establishing their names, Lemuel Mason addressed the women. "Mary Tomkins and Alice Ambrose, ye stand accused. Do ye deny these charges?"

As usual, Mary spoke for them both. "It is true that we were among those on the *Blessing*, but we met solely for worship," she answered. "We counsel peace not disruption."

"What is your place of residence?" Mason asked.

"We reside in the Love of Christ," Mary answered.

The justices whispered briefly, and Mason went on.

"Come now, you know well what we ask. Where do you dwell?"

"Our names are writ in the Book of the Lamb, and we dwell in the Lord," Mary persisted.

"What presumption! You do blaspheme!" Mason exclaimed, reddening.

"How is faith in Jesus considered blasphemy?" Mary posed.

"We shall ask the questions here," Adam Thorowgood warned, scowling.

"You do evade the issue!" Mason declared. "It is clear you are vagabonds!"

"Where are your husbands?" Thorowgood demanded. "Certes, they cannot approve this behavior."

"We are not married," Mary replied evenly.

The room buzzed at this revelation. The justices were shocked and consulted among themselves. When they turned back to the prisoners, their expressions were stony.

"Small wonder you have strayed without a husband's discipline to correct you. 'Tis unnatural!" Mason declared, shaking his head. "Well, here you be, and now we must deal with you."

He turned to his peers to consult on the sentence. The tavern was quiet, awaiting their verdict. It did not take long. Again, Mason spoke for the justices.

"Mary Tomkins and Alice Ambrose, based upon your own testimony and that of John Hill, High Sheriff of Lower Norfolk County, we find you guilty on all counts. You shall be returned to the cub from which you came. On the morrow at nine of the clock you shall be flogged at the pillory. Ten stripes for attending an illegal meeting; ten for refusing to swear the Oath of Allegiance; and ten for being vagabonds and encouraging honest folk to rebel against the established church. Furthermore, you are banished from the Colony of Virginia and shall be served worse should you return. May God have mercy upon your souls. Court is dismissed."

The room erupted in conflicting reactions. Thirty stripes apiece! The Friends were appalled at the severity of the punishment, but most of the crowd approved the sentence. Sheriff John Hill wore a triumphant smile, as he and Lovell led the prisoners out. The residents involved in the incident on the *Blessing* would not be tried until a later session of the court, when he and his deputies would reap half the fines from their arrests; however, Hill was not motivated by greed alone. He would also have the supreme pleasure of publicly stripping these arrogant women to the waist and applying the whip to their bare backs. His manhood stirred at the thought. He intended to mark the Quaker women for life.

Chapter 35

ELIZABETH RIVER, VIRGINIA COLONY

November (9th Month) 1663

Mary and Allie were not surprised by the verdict, but the Elizabeth River Friends were distraught. As residents of the colony, they were fined for their meetings, but none of them had ever been flogged. They were usually banished, as well, but they ignored the order, continuing to live, work, and contribute to the local society as always. The banishment of citizens with money and influence was rarely enforced, but there was no leniency for vagabonds.

After the trial Mary Emperor appealed to the local Friends for bandages, salve, and fresh clothing. They would be needed after the flogging on the morrow. Ambrose knew he must remove his friends as quickly as possible after their punishment, and he set Henry to the task of provisioning the sloop and preparing the forward berths for the missionaries then he sought out Sheriff John Hill.

"I shall remove the prisoners from the colony, after their sentence is carried out," he began.

"Where to?" the sheriff asked, squinting suspiciously.

"To Maryland," Ambrose answered evenly. *Where did the man think?* Verily, it was the only option, but he bit back a sarcastic response. It would do his friends no good to pique the sheriff's choler. "They shall trouble thee no more," he added with a tight smile. In truth, he wanted to throttle the man.

Hill pretended to deliberate for some moments, hoping to provoke Dixon's impatience. He could sense the Quaker's outrage, simmering beneath his calm. There might be another arrest in it, if Dixon snapped and assaulted him, but this did not happen, and at length Hill gave his consent.

"I wish to see the prisoners and inform them of this course," Ambrose added.

Hill shrugged. "I shall allow it, but only for a few moments." He hefted a lantern and started for the cell. "Mister Lovell, do not let any others follow," he said to the under-sheriff. "I shall be listening, Dixon," he added, as they reached the heavy door. "You shall not be alone with them."

Ambrose was appalled by the condition of the cell. Hill's lantern was the only light, and the sheriff set it on the floor just inside the cell and stood at the door with arms akimbo.

"Have they kept ye in total darkness down here?" Ambrose asked, after they embraced.

"We have a candle," Mary said, pulling the pitiful stub from her belt pocket.

"We have no coin to supply prisoners with such comforts!" Hill said indignantly from the doorway.

"Thou wert given coin by Mary Emperor," the big man shot back. "No doubt it lines thy pocket yet."

He ignored the sheriff's blustering retort and turned to his friends. Ambrose's solid presence was a comfort, and the women were heartened to know he would take them back to Maryland on the morrow.

"Didst thou discover anything of Friend Perrot at Isle of Wight, Ambrose?" Mary asked.

He shook his head, marveling that she was yet concerned with her mission. "No, Mary. I fear we were too late. The Friends at Isle of Wight said Perrot and Browne left for James City the week before. They are well on their way to Barbados by now."

Allie put an arm around her companion. "It is done then," she said gently.

"I have failed our Founder," Mary murmured, crushed.

"Thou didst help the Friends at Nassawadox and brought many there back to the Light," Allie soothed.

"But how many more are yet misguided?" her friend mourned.

"There is no help for it, Mary," Ambrose put in. "Best prepare for the morrow now." He peered around the damp room. "I shall fetch more candles. Is there no bench? Tell me ye have not been sleeping on this damp floor." His expression darkened, and he rounded on the sheriff, but before he could speak, Mary put a hand on his arm.

"Do not anger him, Ambrose," she said softly. "Please. 'Tis just one more night."

Dixon sighed as he curbed his rage. The missionaries' fortitude under such duress impressed him. "I shall bring more blankets and food as well," he said, glaring at the sheriff.

"Yer time is up," Hill sneered, picking up the lantern.

The three Friends embraced again, and Ambrose left, promising to bring the necessaries right away, but it was his emotional support that heartened the women most.

⸙

The next day was gray and chill. The damp river air nipped at exposed skin, a foretaste of winter. Mary shivered at its touch and tried to steel herself against the ordeal to come. The deputies did not bother to bind them, and when they left Shipp's Tavern, Allie grasped Mary's hand. Quakers were dangerous and must not be allowed to speak to God-fearing folk thus Mary expected the drummer that led them from the gaol to the pillory. She and Allie ignored the racket and sang a hymn as they walked. She knew the crowd was largely hostile for people hissed at them as they passed, but a group of Elizabeth River Friends stood near the whipping posts with Ambrose Dixon, and they joined in the hymn, singing bravely.

The missionaries remained stoic as Sheriff Hill's deputies cut the back of their dresses open and pulled the ruined material down to their waists. There were audible gasps as their scarred backs were exposed. The raw air bit at Mary's bare skin and the weight of dread on her chest increased. She struggled to breathe normally and control her shivering. Then the deputies bound the prisoners' hands with running knots to metal rings high over their heads, and Mary realized this flogging might be worse than the others. Their puckered skin was stretched taut in this position, and if they fainted or lost their footing, they would hang from their wrists.

John Hill relished flogging. Arresting Quakers was lucrative, but an opportunity to flog them was a rare benefit. Most resided in the colony and had some influence, so they got off with fines and token banishment. These two would not. Hill used a nine-cord whip which he maintained with care. It had three knots on the end of each strand, allowing twenty-seven points of contact with each blow. The missionaries bled on the first strike.

Whenever either of them fainted, Under-sheriff Lovell revived them with smelling salts. John Hill wanted the women to feel every one of the thirty-two blows. He added two to the proscribed number ostensibly for the bother they had caused him. Hill wore a coarse apron to protect his fine blue suit from bloodstains. It also conveniently hid the evidence of his pleasure, which was hard to conceal as his excitement increased.

Ambrose feared for his friends' lives. Watching the spectacle was an ordeal he fervently hoped never to experience again. It took nearly two hours for all sixty-four stripes to be administered, with Hill reviving the women whenever they fainted and dangled from their bound wrists scraped raw by the rope.

It seemed much longer to Ambrose Dixon.

Each crack of the whip and the resultant cry of agony pierced him like a blade. Mary Emperor wept throughout. Ann Godby could not watch and staggered off to empty her stomach behind a bush. Blood and skin flew with every blow, but Ambrose forced himself to watch. He was a fool to bring the women to Virginia. He would gladly have taken their punishment on himself, were it possible. It would have been easier than watching them suffer. He silently thanked God he had insisted Henry stay on the boat, ready to set sail as soon as they were aboard.

At long last, it was over, and the missionaries were cut down. The agony was such that their screams had ceased long before, and they crumpled to the ground as though dead. The Friends rushed forward. Mary Emperor, Ann Godby (pale but present), and Ann's companion Joan Sturges wrapped the missionaries in clean linen bandages, which instantly bloomed red with blood. Four Friends tenderly carried each of the women to Dixon's sloop at the landing.

Mary Emperor was still weeping as she followed with Ann Godby clinging to her arm. Sheriff Hill had removed his gory apron and donned his hat again, and he stepped in front them.

"Why do you weep for these vagabonds?" he sneered contemptuously.

Mary had been crying so long, she had forgotten her tears. It seemed they would never stop, but she straightened to answer the high sheriff.

"I weep in sympathy for their pain. I weep because I put them on the path to this agony. But I also weep for thee, John Hill," she said, holding his eyes.

Hill laughed uneasily. "I need no tears. Why weep for me?" he asked suspiciously.

"For the damage thou hast done to thy immortal soul. Thou hast committed this atrocity against God-fearing women, and thy reckoning shall find thee, John Hill, in this life or the next," she said.

He could find no retort, and they left him gaping at their backs.

Once onboard Ambrose's sloop, Joan Sturges took over preparing the invalids for travel. They were settled face down on the berths which Henry had covered with oil cloth. Thankfully, both were unconscious. Joan had encountered gruesome wounds during her years of healing, but she had never seen such damage. There was no skin left intact on the missionaries' backs. Her salve was useless. She removed the temporary bandages and cleaned any scraps of clothing or dirt clinging to the wounds. The biggest threat was corruption, and Joan carefully blotted their oozing backs with a liquid tincture of honey, yarrow, and feverfew then covered the wounds loosely with fresh bandages soaked in the mixture. Once they woke, the invalids would be in agony, and she left a strong concoction of willow bark and yarrow, though she wished for laudanum. She instructed Ambrose to dose the missionaries with the tea if they woke during the voyage north. It was all they had to combat the pain.

"Do not change the dressings until they are in a doctor's care," Joan added, as she prepared to leave.

"Is there anything else I can do for them?" the big man asked her with commendable calm.

She looked at him gravely. "Go swiftly, Friend Dixon," she said.

Chapter 36

THE CLIFTS, MARYLAND COLONY

December (10th Month) 1663

Ambrose and Henry took turns at the helm and sailed without stopping. They ate and slept fitfully, bent on getting their precious cargo north to Doctor Sharpe. Ambrose deemed it the longest voyage of his life. The Public Friends he had transported from Virginia in the past had all been men, banished and betimes flogged ten or fifteen stripes, painful but not life-threatening. In this case the court officials had been affronted by the women's unmarried status, and the new laws were harsher than Ambrose had imagined—especially with High Sheriff John Hill applying the sentence. At the rare instances when the invalids awoke, Ambrose tried to administer Joan's tea, but both were delirious with pain. It was difficult to get them to swallow, and the concoction seemed to do little to relieve their agony. Henry could not bear it and would escape aloft. As Joan Sturges said, the best way to help the women was to reach the Clifts as quickly as possible.

Thankfully, the weather warmed their second day at sea, and a steady following wind sped them north. Ambrose's skill and knowledge of the waters allowed them to sail through the night taking turns at the helm. They reached the Clifts in twenty-eight hours, only to face another obstacle. The Sharpes' dock was half a mile from the house. Ambrose sent Henry for help and waited onboard. The boy returned within an hour accompanied by Judith Sharpe, her son John Gary, and three laborers. They carried the invalids back to the house, face down on blankets.

"My husband is on a call," Judith explained as they walked, "but when Henry arrived, I sent Mister Allen to alert him. He shall be here presently, I warrant."

The missionaries were in dire condition, but Judith maintained a calm efficiency, even when they cried out in their delirium at being moved. Ambrose told her what had happened in Virginia, as they went.

When they reached the house, Judith settled the patients on two cots flanking the fireplace in her husband's *infirmaria*. It was a one-story, two-room ell off the main house with a central chimney and a two-sided hearth. It was warmer than the main house, as it was snugly built and small with low ceilings. One window on the south wall of each room provided light. Missus Allen had the hearth roaring by the time the invalids arrived, and the warmth made Ambrose drowsy after the grueling trip north.

Judith had some basic skills from assisting her husband during the past decade, and the first thing she did was to soften the bandages, which were stiff with congealed blood and stuck to the wounds. She enlisted Ambrose, Henry, and John to lay warm, wet cloths soaked in yarrow over the material to soften it and retard the bleeding. She left it for the doctor to remove them. Once the missionaries were settled face down on the cots, Henry lay on a bench and promptly fell asleep. Judith covered him with a blanket, and they let him be.

"Dr. Sharpe has a tincture that will ease their pain better than willow bark," Judith assured Ambrose, whose face was drawn with strain and exhaustion. "The base is opium from the Orient dissolved in wine," she went on. "It is very potent thus I dare not administer it myself. We must wait for Peter."

Ambrose sighed and ran a hand through his hair. Where was his hat? He felt dizzy and disoriented. Judith turned from covering Henry and read his face.

"Friend Dixon, thou hast endured much to get these women here so speedily. Come, there is a pallet for thee in the loft." She tilted her head toward the main house. "I shall watch over thy friends and wake thee when my husband returns."

Ambrose had no energy to argue. He was asleep as soon as he lay down.

As a ship's doctor in his younger years, Peter Sharpe had dealt with the results of flogging, but he had experienced nothing that matched the severity of Mary and Allie's condition. In truth he feared for their lives. It would take all his skill and many weeks, if not months, to heal them.

Ambrose and Henry stayed another day, resting and answering the doctor's questions. They assisted him along with Judith and her son John as the doctor tended the wounds. When he first removed the stiff bandages, what little skin was left on the invalids' backs came away, and fresh blood welled. Sharpe was unperturbed, saying a normal flow of blood would help to keep their backs from mortifying. He did not bind the oozing wounds but gently blotted them with wet flannels soaked in a healing mixture of goldenseal, honey, garlic, and cayenne. Once the bleeding slowed, he covered the area with fresh flannels soaked in the mixture, changing them often before they dried. The missionaries were unconscious much of the time, but they managed to sip enough of the laudanum mixture to bear Dr. Sharpe's ministrations.

"*Thirty-two* stripes each!" Sharpe murmured as he worked, shocked and troubled by the knowledge.

"And their hands were bound high above their heads, stretching the skin," Ambrose added, sickened by the image now burned into his memory. "Hill revived them each time they fainted, so they would feel every blow."

His eyes misted with anger and sympathy. He realized he had come to love these feisty, independent women who flaunted convention to dedicate their lives to the Society of Friends.

Sharpe laid a hand on his shoulder. "Methinks thou hast saved their lives by bringing them here so speedily, Friend Dixon. Corruption is the major concern now," the doctor said. "I can apply salve once the wounds begin to scab over. It will take time, but I warrant they shall recover."

Judith was the only one to know of his doubts.

Ambrose and Henry left the next day. There was no more they could do for the women, and Ambrose had been away far longer than originally planned. The Sharpes would give the missionaries the best possible care, and they urged him to visit whenever he might; however, with winter coming on, the possibility was unlikely.

The day they left John Gary predicted snow was coming, and he and Mister Allen drove the cattle in to the pasture around the pond for the winter. A large lean-to shelter protected them from the worst of the weather. Two days later the first snow fell, softening the contours of the land and curtailing outdoor activity. John was confined to projects in the house or barn, and he assisted his mother and stepfather in the missionaries' care. One of them was always with the invalids who now slept most of the time.

By the end of the first week Allie showed marked improvement. Her pain, though still constant, was bearable, and Peter Sharpe reduced the strength of her opium dose. Her appetite returned. She sat up at intervals then walked around a little, grateful to use the commode without help; however, she was still weak and slept most of the day. By the end of the second week, she took only strong willow bark tea to ease her pain at bedtime.

Disturbingly, instead of improving Mary developed a fever and was either delirious or unconscious. Dr. Sharpe was concerned. He saw no evidence of infection on her back and feared she might have internal damage that he could not see. In addition to the salve, he made a tea of boneset, bee balm, honey, and crushed juniper leaves to control her fever. It was administered in turns with the opium tincture. Missus Allen, the Sharpe's cook, made fortifying soups to build up the invalids' strength. As Allie became stronger, she took over much of Mary's care, spooning broth into her mouth, applying the salve three times a day, and pressing cool flannels to Mary's burning forehead, always talking or singing softly.

One afternoon just before Yule, John Gary went to look in on them and was transfixed by the scene. Allie's long, dark hair was bound in a thick braid that hung over her left shoulder, off her back. She wore one of Peter's old shirts over a shift borrowed from Judith. Both fit her loosely, though her long stockinged calves and feet showed below, making her look small and vulnerable. She was singing, her voice low, pure, and soothing. He had been drawn to the reticent missionary since their first meeting, but his acute distress at seeing her suffer made him realize how much he cared for her. He wanted Allie to share his life. John Gary was in love.

Allie continued to sleep on the cot in the *infirmaria* and watched over Mary for most of the day, but when her friend was dosed with opium and slept deeply, Allie joined the family in the main house. She helped Judith with the endless mending, and the two women were often together at the hearth, talking as they plied their needles, clouting or darning. Judith had salvaged the skirts from the missionaries' ruined dresses. She made waistbands for them. Sewing had never appealed to Allie until her condition limited her activities. Now it calmed her. It was one of the few things she could do, while her back healed, and her skill increased quickly. When Peter brought home a bolt of material given as payment for his services, Judith offered to help Allie make new dresses for herself and Mary. It was a diverting project, and Allie enjoyed the visible progress of each day.

Little Mary helped with the simpler mending, or she and Willie practiced their letters and numbers. The children often implored Allie for stories of England and her travels. Without Mary to speak for her, Allie found she could be eloquent. The room grew quiet, as she talked, and when she glanced up from her needlework, everyone was listening— the Doctor and Judith, John Gary, and their servants Mister and Missus Allen, as well as the children.

When duties allowed, the men spent their time in the warm house with the women and children. John mended tools or whittled wooden toys for his stepsiblings; Mister Allen oiled and mended tack; and Peter sat at the table balancing accounts and copying out remedies. When he discovered Allie had a fine hand, the doctor was delighted and enlisted her help.

Peter Sharpe made his rounds three days of the week and was periodically called out for emergencies. John or Mister Allen always accompanied him on horseback. The trails could be tricky in ice and snow. A horse might stumble and throw its rider, and sometimes there were wolves. It was best not to be alone or unarmed. However, this year the winter proved mild, for the most part. A week after it fell, the first snow had melted. John remarked it was a wonder that the cattle were yet able to graze the pasture.

During the third week after the flogging, Mary's fever finally broke. By Christmas Eve she could sit up and was fully conscious. They all counted it as the best gift they could possibly have. She could not join them at table yet, but they brought her small portions of roast goose and plum pudding. Though she ate little, she savored every bite. John Gary and Mister Allen placed a Yule Log on the hearth in the *infirmaria* as well as in the main house. Judith served cups of milk punch gently spiked with rum and dusted with precious nutmeg, and Peter Sharpe brought his Chaucer, delighting them all with the story of Chanticleer and Pertelote from "The Nun's Priest's Tale." Judith had finished the missionaries' skirts. She wrapped them in two new shawls knitted by Missus Allen and gave them to Mary and Allie as gifts.

"Oh, would that we had something to give you, as well!" Allie said, moved by this demonstration of care and generosity. "Ye have all done so much for us. I despair of ever repaying you!"

"Ye both suffered near to the death for our faith," Judith answered. "'Tis we who owe you a debt."

Mary was speechless, but in her weakened state tears of gratitude tracked her cheeks. She was sitting up to eat and open her present. She buried her face in the new shawl, breathing in the comforting smell of wool and clung to it, even as they helped her lie on her stomach again. It became her favorite pillow.

Chapter 37

THE CLIFTS, MARYLAND COLONY

January/February (11ᵗʰ/12ᵗʰ Month) 1663

Allie's deepening relationship with Judith and Peter and the adoration of the younger children made her feel at home with the Sharpes, but she fell asleep each night and woke every morning with John Gary foremost in her thoughts. She felt a connection when their eyes met, and she anticipated being with him.

John's father had died when he was sixteen, and as Judith's only son, he had assumed the responsibilities of a grown man early in life. When they celebrated his name day in January, Allie was surprised to learn he was two years younger than she. Outside winter held sway, but indoors they shared their thoughts and plans in the warmth of the hearth fire. John wanted to enlarge his herd of cattle and had his eye on a piece of land a mile and a half to the northwest. He proposed purchasing it in partnership with his stepfather, and they discussed the details at length.

Once this prospect became a reality, John intended to ask for Allie's hand in marriage. If she accepted, he would build a house for them there. But what if she refused? Privacy was at a premium in the open common room. It was impossible to speak with Allie alone without drawing the family's attention, but John was a patient man. He bided his time and drew Allie out with sincere interest, asking about her life in England, her beliefs, her hopes, and her realizations. No man had ever been so attentive, and Allie's habitual reticence eased with John's encouragement. Although they tried to be discreet, their growing affection was not lost on the elder Sharpes and the Allens.

At the beginning of Eleventh Month, Mary began to join the family in the main house each day for an hour or two, though she tired quickly. Allie was concerned. Her friend did not speak unless addressed directly but stared into the fire wrapped in her new shawl. Her body was mending, but Allie feared for Mary's spirit. It was not only the debilitating punishment in Virginia; she had failed in her mission to bring John Perrot back into the fold, and Allie knew that it affected Mary's sense of her own worth.

The winter was relatively mild. The first significant storm of the season did not come until after John's name day. He and Mister Allen wrapped up and forged out to check on the cattle, as the weather had turned cold enough to freeze the pond, the only source of water for the household as well as the livestock. They took axes to open the ice and buckets to draw water for the house. Willie kept a look out and opened the door for them, as they staggered in carrying the brimming pails. The snow was still falling, and it coated the men's headgear and greatcoats. Instead of cursing the weather, John laughed as he removed his hat and shook it off. His face was rosy with cold, and he looked around to share the moment with Allie. As their eyes met, she knew she wanted to share the rest of her life with John Gary.

Mary seemed not to notice their connection, staring into the fire as usual, but that night as the missionaries settled down to sleep in the *infirmaria*, she spoke into the darkness.

"The Sharpes are most kind. This is a fine place to stay for the winter while we gain strength, but we must consider where we shall go once spring comes and we can travel again. I must write Margaret Fell concerning Perrot. I assume all responsibility for that failure; however, we can yet accomplish our original mission by following Mary Dyer's lead. We can take our protest to Boston."

Allie was quiet. How could Mary be serious? She had nearly died and was recovering slowly. The thought of sacrificing themselves to Endicott for yet another arrest and whipping seemed both dangerous and futile. Allie was not sure she could survive more abuse, but certes, Mary could not. In any case, Allie did not want to leave John and the Sharpes, for any reason.

"I reckon it is too soon to make any decisions," she answered. "Spring is months away."

"Thou hast become knit into the fabric of this family," Mary said so softly Allie had to strain to hear.

"They have welcomed us both, Mimi," Allie protested gently.

"And what of John Gary?" she murmured.

"What of him?" Allie asked, stalling for time. Apparently, Mary noticed more than she had realized.

Mary sighed. "One can see he dotes on thee, Allie. The question is, dost thou care for him?"

Allie dreaded this choice between her lifelong friend and this new love. It was inevitable, but she chose to put it off as long as possible. Mary was yet weak in spirit, as well as physically, and Allie deemed it too soon to add a devastating emotional blow.

"I care for all the family," she answered lightly.

Silence.

Allie sat up. Mary's face was a white oval, barely discernible in the meagre light from the banked coals in the fireplace. "For now, thou must regain thy strength, Mary. We can discuss future plans, once thou art well again."

"Has he declared himself?" Mary's voice was so meek, Allie wanted to cry. Her dear friend knew her too well to be diverted.

Allie eased back onto her stomach. "No, he has not," she answered honestly.

"What wilt thou say, when he does?"

"*If* he does, I shall consider that path when I come to it," Allie replied.

Mary turned her head away and said no more, but it was a long time before Allie could sleep.

⌒

By Twelfth Month the missionaries were able to wear regular clothing, but their healing backs itched maddeningly. They were desperate for distraction. Mary still took willow bark tea each day, but Peter Sharpe had weaned her from the opium. She had lost weight during the weeks of fever, and the energy and conviction that drew people to her was gone. Her perceived failure with Perrot hounded her in her weakened state, and she was inconsolable. She wrote to Margaret Fell saying only that their struggle with Perrot was worse than anything they had faced from their enemies. She touched on their arrest and punishment in Virginia but not her subsequent brush with death and protracted recovery. She was a pale wraith, staring into the fire. The children were wary in her presence, and the adults exchanged guarded glances of concern.

One day while Mary was napping in the *infirmaria*, Allie sat with Peter Sharpe at the big table in the main house, penning labels for a fresh batch of medicaments. Judith and the children were up in the loft; Missus Allen tended a stew and rolled out pastry for a dried apple pie at the kitchen end of the open room; and John and Mister Allen were outside, drawing water and checking on the livestock. The missionary and the doctor had a rare interval alone, and Peter took advantage of it.

"I do not wish to pry," he began, "but I am concerned about Mary. She seems afflicted by a phenomenon I have observed in some patients during recovery from serious ailment or injury."

Allie placed her quill carefully on a blotter and gave him her full attention, nodding encouragingly.

"I have observed that pain afflicts the spirit as much as the body," he went on. "It weakens both, allowing the black humors to dominate the damaged system and retard recovery. Those who were formerly energetic are overcome by a pervasive lethargy. They loathe weakness yet are forced to acknowledge it in themselves and live with it, day by day. I fear Mary is of this type, but thou knowest her best. What is thy opinion?"

Allie was relieved to talk about Mary. She was worried, too, and the doctor's perceptive observations reassured her. Mayhap Peter would know how they could help her friend.

"I do agree, Mary is not herself," she began. "She counts our mission a failure, since we did not stop Friend Perrot. She is compelled to make up for it by assuming our mentor's cause in the Bay Colony."

"She would go to Boston?" he exclaimed, alarmed. "Certes they would arrest and flog her!"

Allie bit her lip and nodded.

"Thou didst say Mary Dyer was your spiritual mother," Peter went on. "Is she this mentor?"

She nodded again but feared she might weep if she met his eyes.

"Dear girl!" he cried, taking her hand in both of his. "Certes, Friend Dyer did not intend for ye to follow her unto death! Another flogging might be fatal for your friend and cause thee permanent damage as well. I beg thee, do not follow this course, Alice. Judith and I have come to love thee like a daughter, and John—" he broke off, realizing he had said too much.

Allie kept hold of the hand the doctor tried to withdraw. Normally she would acquiesce, but this was too important. Her future hung on Peter's answer. "And John what?" she whispered.

Peter's face colored, and he gently disengaged their hands. "Verily, he must speak for himself, my dear," he finished. Then his gaze sharpened, and he asked candidly, "Dost care for him, Alice?"

"Yes, I do," she confirmed without hesitation. It was a relief to say it out loud.

The Doctor gathered her into a gentle embrace, holding her upper arms to avoid pressing her back and laying his cheek alongside hers. His voice was thick with emotion. "I should guard my tongue, but he is completely and utterly taken with thee, dear girl. Judith and I pray he shall soon declare himself. We would love nothing better than to have thee verily part of our family."

Allie closed her eyes and hugged him back. She was home at last.

Chapter 38

THE CLIFTS, MARYLAND COLONY

March (1ˢᵗ Month) 1664

Spring came early in the southern colonies. Allie recalled the year before in New England when they had had to wait until the end of Second Month before the weather warmed reliably and the roads became passable. Here crocuses and daffodils bloomed in the beginning of First Month, and even with spring downpours, John said the roads would be passable by Second Month, if not sooner.

Willie Sharpe turned nine on March 12ᵗʰ, and Missus Allen made gingerbread in honor of his name day. Judith had made him a pair of long pants, a pair of knee britches, and a light jacket from the same bolt as the missionaries' dresses. Willie was delighted for long pants were a sign of maturity, and he had outgrown last summer's clothes over the winter; however, his favorite gift was a new knife from John.

Allie wore her matching dress and quipped, "We shall be twins, Will." They all laughed.

The warmer weather drew everyone outside away from the hearth. The kitchen garden was still too wet for planting, so Judith focused her energy on the garth around the house. The winter winds had ripped branches from the trees, and last year's leaves littered the ground. Allie helped the two children pile the debris up for a bonfire at the edge of the pond. Although the Society of Friends did not encourage celebration of the Anglican holidays, the Sharpe family observed Christmas and Annunciation Day as they had done throughout their lives. Like Mary and Allie's singing, they retained these small pleasures from their former religion.

"There is little comfort in this wilderness," Peter maintained. "I warrant the Almighty shall not begrudge us the company of our neighbors and friends to welcome the new year."

Annunciation Day had originated in the Catholic Church and was adopted by the Anglicans, but it was more than a religious observance of the day the angel Gabrielle told Mary she would be the mother of Jesus. March 25th was also the advent of a new year, according to the Julian Calendar, which prevailed in Great Britain and her colonies until 1752. In any case, the return of longer days and warmer weather lifted everyone's spirits and invited celebration. The Sharpes marked the occasion annually by inviting everyone they knew, and the preparations took a full week.

When it was warm, Mary sat in the sun with a basketful of mending. She helped readily with light chores but still seemed distant. Each day Allie feared her friend would broach the subject of leaving again, and she dreaded the confrontation. John had not declared himself, and she was beginning to fear he never would. Then a few days before the New Year celebration John and Peter decided to walk the land they would purchase in partnership. John invited her to accompany them, and she accepted readily.

They took some refreshment with them, as they would be gone for several hours. It was a fine day, and the horses were eager for an outing, trotting along at a good pace. They reached their destination in less than an hour. The lot was bordered on two sides by a tributary of the Patuxent called St. Leonard's Creek, so water was no problem, but the land was completely forested.

"Thou shalt have thy work cut out for thee, John," Peter commented as they crested a rise and wound their way through budding beech, poplar, and oak down to the riverbank.

"Yes, but it flattens out near the river," John responded over his shoulder. "I shall start with a few acres of pasture along the bank and leave some of the largest trees for shade." He was ebullient, talking on as he led them. "The stream can be diverted for a watering hole. There is a prime spot further along."

Allie turned in her saddle to exchange a smile with Peter, riding behind her.

"I discovered a good location for the house, as well," John continued, oblivious to their shared amusement. "The river runs north to south predominately, and we are on the east bank here, thus the house can face southwest for the best light and the finest prospect of the river."

When they gained the top of the next knoll, Allie could see water glinting through the budding branches.

"There's the river," John said, halting his mount. Allie and Peter rode up beside him. "A season of cutting and burning with four fellows, and we can plant pasture down to the bank with a house lot near that big oak where the ground levels out."

He looked at Allie, his eyes shining, and she smiled back, engaged by his enthusiasm; however, it was unclear whether the "we" meant John and the laborers or John and herself.

"Capital choice! That is verily a prime spot for the house, John," Peter said. "But ye must excuse me a moment, as Nature calls," he added dismounting and looping the reins around a stout branch. "I shall rejoin you shortly."

The good doctor made for a grove of rhododendron some fifty paces away, leaving the two young people alone. He hoped John had included Allie to propose marriage, and he did not wish to inhibit him.

John and Allie tethered their horses with Peter's mount and walked down the gentle slope to a relatively level area about a hundred yards from the river.

"I see the house here," he told her, pacing it off. "There will be more sun, once most of these trees are cleared, but I reckon we should leave a few to keep the house cool in summer." He stopped in front of her and smiled. His eyes held a question.

Was this a proposal? There was that "we" again. Was he including her in his plans, or was it a more general reference? She dared not ask outright and stared back at him wordlessly.

John stepped closer and took her hand. His face was serious, his expression intent. "What say thee, Allie?" he asked softly. "I am offering my hand in marriage. Wilt thou have me?"

The blood rushed to her face and pounded in her ears. Allie squeezed his hand and nodded, struggling to speak through a flood of relief and joy. "Yes, John," she managed.

John closed his eyes briefly then broke into a wide smile. He cupped her face in his hands. "We must seal our pledge with a kiss then, I reckon," he said and did so.

His lips were warm and gone all too quickly. As he began to pull away, Allie wrapped her arms around him and kissed him back. He stiffened briefly in surprise then responded with a passion that made her knees buckle. They broke off but held each other close for some moments, collecting themselves.

Peter was the first to hear the news. He found them holding hands and gazing at the river view that would be both comfort and inspiration for the remainder of their life together.

⸺

Allie asked that the engagement be kept secret, until she could talk to Mary. John wanted to announce it at the celebration on Annunciation Day, so she must tell her friend before then. She feared Mary's reaction. They had been together from birth, grown up as virtual sisters, been convinced and trained as missionaries, crossed the Atlantic, endured imprisonment and punishment, and celebrated triumphs side by side. Although Allie loved John Gary, she could not imagine life without her dear friend. Most like, Mary would not abandon her call, but it would be an emotional hardship for her to go on alone.

Allie did not delay. After the evening meal on the day John proposed to her, she asked Mary to walk with her. The sun was low as they took the path to the Bay. There was a chill breeze off the water, but they found a sandy spot sheltered from the wind at the base of one of the cliffs.

Allie was unsure how to begin, and the two friends sat in silence for a time. Mary drew circles in the sand and sifted it through her fingers. Allie studied her thin features. The lines around Mary's mouth and on her forehead had deepened since her illness. For the first time Allie could imagine what her friend would look like as an old woman. Mary looked up and met her eyes.

"Thou didst not walk all this way to stare at me, Allie," she smiled. "Art thou in mind to plan our next mission?" she asked hopefully, brushing sand off her hands.

Allie retied her shawl, delaying a response. "I am in mind to speak of our future," she said at length.

Mary's smile faded. "I am listening," she responded cautiously.

Allie took a deep breath. "John Gary proposed to me this day," she said. There. It was out.

Mary's face paled. She stared at her friend, and Allie suppressed the urge to babble.

"What was thy answer?" Mary managed through stiff lips.

Allie steeled herself against the dread in her friend's eyes. "I accepted."

Mary winced and looked out over the water. Allie scooted closer and took up her limp hand.

"Mary, I want this more than anything I have ever wanted in my life. I love him, and I love this family. I feel I belong here. I can assist Peter in his practice and be of use—"

"What of our calling?" Mary interrupted. Two spots of red had bloomed on her cheeks.

"'Tis not an easy decision, nor a hasty one," Allie protested. "I have pondered this since Yule."

"So long! Yet thou hast kept it from me." Mary's eyes flashed with hurt. She withdrew her hand and stood up. "So, I shall face our greatest challenge alone."

Allie rose with her. She had feared this reaction, but it did not make it easier to bear the reality. "There is an alternative, Mary," she said gently. "John will build on the land we saw this day. It borders a fine river and is beautiful! It is my fondest hope that thou might stay and live with us."

Mary's expression was incredulous, and her voice rose with each bitter phrase. "Stay and live on John's charity? Each day remark thy marital bliss, while I wither and grow old? We swore to carry on Mary Dyer's mission, Allie! We vowed not to marry so we could make a difference in the world! *I* shall not abandon that promise for a life of safe tedium."

Her expression was fierce. Allie wanted to shrink from her dear friend's wrath, but she lifted her chin and bore it stoically.

"No, Allie, I cannot!" Mary went on. "I *will* not! Boston is the cradle of injustice, and I must fight it to my last breath."

"Consider thy health, Mary, I beg thee," Allie answered earnestly. "This last near killed thee, and Peter fears we could not survive another flogging."

"Peter fears," Mary scoffed. "What does he know of answering a call? God is my strength, and if I die fulfilling His purpose, at least my death shall serve a righteous cause!"

"Thou wert near death for weeks!" Allie protested. "Many times, I feared thou wouldst not see the morn, but Doctor Sharpe saved thy life!" Mary turned away, but Allie persisted. "We have brought the Light to many folk. We have fought injustice and suffered near to death *four times*. It is enough, Mary. We are more use to the Almighty alive than dead."

"I am God's instrument," her friend insisted. "He shall use me as He sees fit. If I must die in His service, so be it, but *I* will not abandon our mission." She turned and made for the path.

Allie felt terrible. It was the first time she and Mary had seriously disagreed, and she feared there was no way back to the solid friendship that had sustained her throughout her life.

Chapter 39

THE CLIFTS, MARYLAND COLONY

March/April (1st/2nd Month) 1664

W hen Allie told him of the conversation with Mary, John was sympathetic about the rift between them, but inwardly he was relieved that Allie had chosen to stay with him. Once Mary knew of it, John shared the news with his family as they broke their fast the next morning. There was a chorus of joyful comments.

"Thou shalt be my true sister then!" Little Mary exclaimed, clapping her hands.

"And mine, too!" Willie added anxiously.

The children flanked her at every meal, and Allie put an arm around each of them. "Yes, we shall be proper siblings," she assured them both.

"Shalt thou stand witness with her, Mary?" Judith asked gently, noting her silence.

Mary was staring at her trencher but looked up at the question. "Have ye chosen a date?" she asked.

Allie and John exchanged a look. "The second First Day in Seventh Month," John answered.

"I shall not be here by then, I fear," Mary said quietly, looking at Allie.

"Where wilt thou be?" Peter asked, his brow creasing with concern.

Mary straightened. "I shall be at Boston."

The mood at the table changed drastically. No one spoke for several moments, but the silence was eloquent. Sensing the tension, Missus Allen rose and began to clear the table. She wanted no part of this confrontation. Her husband went outside to smoke his pipe. The two children clung to Allie's arms, looking from her to Mary and back again, as though afraid Allie would float up into the air and disappear if they let go.

Peter spoke first. "'Tis such a fine morning, wouldst thou walk with me, Mary?" he asked lightly.

Mary knew the doctor wished to dissuade her, but it would be rude to refuse out of hand. She inclined her head and stood up. Her face was set, and she did not look at Allie as she tied her shawl and followed Peter outside.

They strolled down to the pasture, and Peter leaned on the top rail of the fence, watching the cattle nibble at the new grass. In another week or so, John would move them to their summer pasture. Mary followed and stood stiffly at his side. The rising sun cast long shadows and enhanced the soft green of new growth with unnatural brilliance. The winter was truly over, and it would soon be time for her to leave this lovely refuge. She swallowed a tinge of regret.

"I admire thy dedication, Mary," Peter began.

She smiled ruefully and lifted her chin. "But..."

He sighed, his eyes on the beeves. "Thou art an intelligent woman of great courage, ergo I shall put it to thee bluntly." He turned to face her. "Thy recovery is precarious for I cannot determine the extent of the damage thy inner parts; however, I have little doubt another flogging would be fatal. I fear this latest abuse has injured a vital organ, mayhap thy spleen or a kidney. An inflammation from within caused thy fever, and 'tis only by God's Grace thou didst survive. I beg thee, reconsider going to Boston."

"Doctor Sharpe, I am grateful thou didst save my life," she said, "and I intend to stay and work until that debt is paid, but I believe God did spare me for a greater purpose. I cannot abandon my mission."

"There is no debt incurred here," he protested. "Healing folk is *my* mission, Mary. We have all come to care deeply for both thee and Allie. Stay with us a few months more and allow—"

"Prithee, say no more," Mary interrupted. "The Friends here are well established in their faith and require no encouragement. I must follow my conscience and go where there is need."

She turned abruptly and started back to the house. Peter shook his head and followed her.

The meeting for worship before Annunciation Day was held at the Prestons' home on the Patuxent, as the Sharpes would be hosting the New Year celebration in just two days.

Samuel Groome had come up from his plantation on Drum Point to visit the Prestons for several days and to join in the festivities at the Sharpes'. He greeted the missionaries warmly.

"I am glad to see you both in good health! I was dismayed to hear from James Gilbert of your arrest on the *Blessing*," he said. "Virginia is not kind to Friends."

"We are quite recovered now, thanks to Doctor Sharpe," Mary responded crisply. She did not want to talk about their latest ordeal and asked, "What is thy next port of call, Captain Groome?"

"I shall be home at Eltonhead until the end of Second Month. There is much work to be done there, improving the house and grounds. My partner Francis Canfielde has made a good start of it, and our first shipment of livestock shall soon be ready for transport to New England, but I try to be present each year for the celebration at the Sharpes'." He grinned at John Gary.

At the mention of New England Mary was instantly alert, but John spoke first. "It shall be a celebration twice over this year," he smiled. "Allie and I shall announce our betrothal that day."

"Congratulations!" Samuel enthused, shaking their hands. "That is fine news!"

"Where in New England, exactly?" Mary asked the young sea captain.

"I beg thy pardon?" Samuel asked, confused by the sudden change of topic.

"What port shalt thou land at in New England?" she repeated patiently.

"A settlement of Friends in the Plimouth Colony called Sandwich. Dost know of it?" he asked.

"I do. We anchored there one night on our way to Rhode Island the spring past," Mary answered. "Might I take passage with thee?"

Samuel glanced at Allie, and she understood the question in his eyes.

"I am not going," she supplied briefly. John squeezed her hand, and she returned the pressure.

"Thou shalt travel alone, Friend Tomkins?" Samuel asked, unable to hide his surprise.

"Yes," Mary said, lifting her chin. "If 'tis inconvenient, I can seek passage elsewhere, Captain Groome."

"No, no! It is no trouble," Samuel amended. "'Tis only I hesitate to leave thee alone among strangers."

"If there are Friends at Sandwich, I shall not be alone," Mary replied. "And 'tis not far from Boston, as I recall."

"Boston!" Samuel exclaimed. He glanced at John and Allie and would have said more, but Friend Preston called everyone to meeting, and conversation stopped.

During the social time after worship, all talk was of the coming celebration on Third Day and John Gary's betrothal to Alice Ambrose. Mary felt like the only one present who was not thrilled by either prospect. She pursued her goal to confirm passage on the *Dove*, and Captain Groome's misgivings were overcome by her determination. Departure was set for the end of Second Month. She was only sorry they were not leaving sooner. Somehow, she would have to get through another month, but at least she knew she had passage north with a captain she trusted. It made her feel more tolerant of Allie's choice, and she had to admit, her friend glowed with happiness and had never looked more beautiful.

On March 25th, the household rose early. Breakfast was unusually hurried and simple, as there was so much to do. Mary concentrated on being cheerful for Allie's sake and found it easier than she feared.

Morning clouds burned off, and the day warmed. People began arriving late in the afternoon for the party would go past midnight to see in the New Year of 1664. John and Mister Allen had moved the herd to the south pasture the week before. The gate stood open, and the unlit pile for the bonfire had grown to the height of a man. It was near the pond with plenty of buckets at the ready in case of errant sparks. The ground was damp from recent rains, but Peter Sharpe was a stickler for safety.

Indoors the table was ladened with food, and although the Sharpes were not habitual drinkers, this day was an exception. Wine, rum, and sack flowed freely, as well as sweet cider. Outside a cask of ale was breached, and the guests filled their own cups, knowing Judith could not supply them all.

The afternoon flew by. Spirits flowed, lubricating conversation and games while it was light. At dusk John lit the bonfire. Some of the Friends brought musical instruments, and the revelers danced and sang by its flickering light. Richard Preston had a rare pocket timepiece and declared the arrival of midnight. After a toast to the New Year, Peter and Judith announced the engagement of their son John Gary to Alice Ambrose, making it official, although everyone knew of it already. There were cheers and congratulations and more toasts to the happy couple and prosperity for all in the New Year.

Mary was tired, but she stayed up to toast Allie and John, catching Allie's eye as she raised her cup of cider and smiled. Allie made her way through the throng of well-wishers to her friend. They looked at each other for a moment then embraced.

"Oh Mimi," Allie whispered. "Canst thou forgive me?"

"There is nothing to forgive," Mary assured her. She pulled back and took Allie's hands. "I am glad thou hast found happiness, dear Allie."

Although it broke her heart to part with her dear friend, Mary was surprised to find that she meant it.

Chapter 40

THE CLIFTS, MARYLAND COLONY

April (2nd Month) 1664

Mary tried to savor her last weeks with Allie. She sought out chores involving light exercise to build up her stamina and was more engaged with the others in the household at the Clifts now she had a plan. In mid-April a meeting for worship was hosted by the Sharpes. She was sweeping the front porch when the Prestons arrived with Samuel Groome and his partner Francis Canfielde, who was curious about the Society of Friends. Mary lit up when she saw the young captain, setting the broom aside and ushering them indoors. As soon as greetings were exchanged, Mary asked Samuel the question that dominated her thoughts each day.

"Have we a date of departure as yet, Captain Groome?"

"I am glad to see thy health has improved, Friend Tomkins," he responded, "but I fear the lambs need another two weeks before transport to Sandwich. I shall send a message when the date firms up."

Mary nodded and smiled through her disappointment. John and Allie heard their exchange, and he spoke up. "Samuel, I can bring Mary down to Eltonhead, on that day if that would be a help to thee."

"Why, yes," the captain agreed. "I must admit sailing up here is out of our way, as we make for the Atlantic. Does that suit thee, Friend Tomkins?" he asked, courteous as ever.

Mary looked at John dubiously for it would take him away from working on his land, but Allie reassured her. "I shall come, as well Mary. We want to see thee off properly."

Mary was touched. She nodded and squeezed Allie's hand. "I would like that," she admitted.

In truth Mary was surprised how quickly the two weeks passed. Planting, husbandry, and spring cleaning indoors and out kept everyone busy. John's crew was making progress in clearing the land he had purchased with Peter's help. When Captain Groome's message came at the end of the month, the entire household helped Mary prepare for her voyage. John gave her a new satchel of sturdy leather made from the hide of one of his herd slaughtered in the autumn. Mary was impressed that he had worked on it secretly all winter. Judith had garnered summer clothing from friends and family to fill it, but Peter's gift moved her profoundly. The doctor gave her his copy of Chaucer, and when Mary tried to refuse, he cut her off.

"It will comfort thee like an old friend and remind thee of our love," he insisted.

Mary embraced him and forced herself to smile. It would not do for the family to see her cry. They might think she did not want to leave.

On the day of departure, Allie, John, and Mary left the Clifts at first light. The family rose with them and saw them off from the landing. It was a fine day with a brisk offshore breeze from the west. The majestic cliffs marking the community of Friends that had harbored her for five months receded, as the skiff moved south. Peter Sharpe had saved her life, and this place would ever remain special in her heart.

Captain Groome's plantation at Eltonhead was twenty miles south on Drum Point, but with the brisk wind John's skiff arrived within two hours. The anchorage was deep off Drum Point, and the *Dove* was tied up at the sturdy pier, bustling with last minute preparations. John tied upA s opposite the merchant ship.

"Good morrow and well met!" Samuel called from the *Dove's* deck, as the crew rolled barrels up the gangplank and into her hold. "I am glad ye are here so early! The livestock are loaded, and we can set off in an hour or two as soon as the provisions are on board. Hast thou baggage, Friend Tomkins?"

"Just this satchel," John answered, holding it up.

"Ah," the captain laughed. "No bother there! We shall soon board, so prithee do not wander off."

The three Friends stayed on the skiff, out of the way but within earshot. John went aft and busied himself so that Mary and Allie might have a last interlude alone. They sat close to each other, arms and hands linked.

"I never thought to say good-bye to thee, Allie," Mary said softly. "I know not how to go about it."

"Shalt thou return? After Boston, mayhap?" Allie asked.

Mary met her eyes and slowly shook her head. "I think not."

The full force of their parting hit Allie then, as she realized she would never see Mary again. Still, she clung to a last shred of hope. "Thou art ever welcome to return here. I shall look for thee every day," she said softly, squeezing the hand that had led her throughout her life.

Mary did not answer. After a small silence she began to sing, and Allie joined in, harmonizing through the ache in her chest. John paused at his work in the bow and closed his eyes to listen. Their voices were beautiful together, but sorrow permeated every note.

Captain Groome's call interrupted their singing. The women stood and embraced while John hefted Mary's satchel. He helped her onto the dock, and they headed for the gangplank of the *Dove*. Allie was struck with foreboding. Mary was leaving, walking out of her life forever, and her reaction was visceral.

"No! Wait!" She clambered onto the dock and ran to her friend, grasping Mary's arm. "This is wrong!" She turned to John, who stood stunned. "I beg thee understand, John. I love thee, and I want to marry thee, but I must be with Mary for this. It is why we came to the Colonies. I cannot let her go alone!"

John was speechless, and Allie took his hand. "I promise I shall return to thee!" she said fervently. "I know not when, but it shall be as soon as I am able. If I do not do this, I shall despise myself forever."

"But thou art not prepared for travel," John protested weakly. "Thou hast no clothing or—"

"I have my bag of curatives," Allie interrupted. "'Tis all I need in truth." She put her arms around him, hugging him tightly. "Please say thou wilt wait for me!"

John was dismayed and looked over her head at Mary, but she had moved away in deference to the seriousness of the situation. This was Allie's decision, and she did not want to appear to influence her. Also, her elation at Allie's change of heart shamed her, and she did not want John to see it in her eyes.

Samuel Groome met them at the top of the gangplank. "What passes here?" he asked, sensing the tension as the three Friends came aboard.

John set down Mary's bag and straightened. "It appears thou shalt have two passengers to Sandwich," he said heavily.

Part V

SPRING 1664

*When it came to dealing with those deemed ungodly—be they Native
"heathens" or Boston heretics—Massachusetts could repeatedly defend
its interests in ways at once harsh, autocratic, and outside the law.*

—John Winsser *Mary and William Dyer*

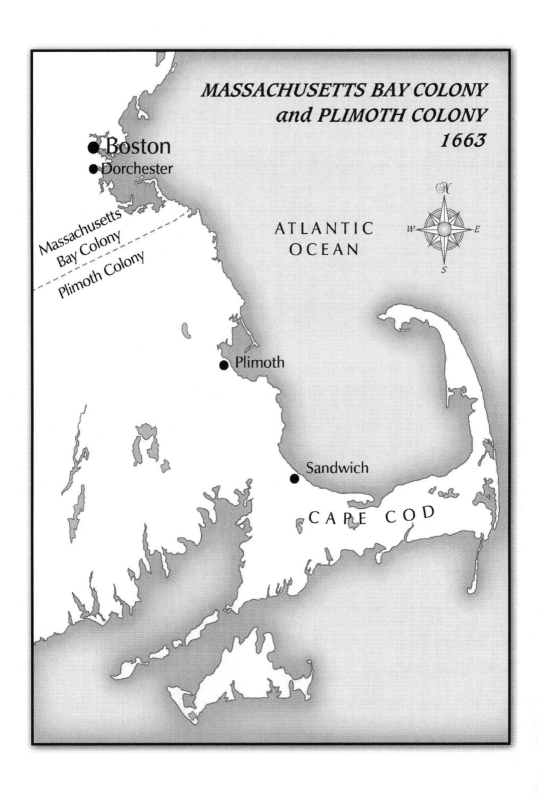

MASSACHUSETTS BAY COLONY
and PLIMOTH COLONY
1663

Boston
Dorchester

Massachusetts
Bay Colony
Plimoth Colony

ATLANTIC
OCEAN

N
W   E
S

Plimoth

Sandwich

CAPE COD

Chapter 41

SANDWICH, PLIMOUTH COLONY

May (3rd Month) 1664

Captain Groome was an exemplary host. He insisted the women share his cabin as they had on their first voyage with him from Hack's Point to the Annemessex River. A screen made from sailcloth curtained off the berth, and Samuel had hung a hammock to sleep in on the other side of the small room.

"Certes ye cannot bunk with the crew," he said reasonably when the missionaries politely demurred. "Trust me, Friends, my cabin is best."

Mary was in no mood to argue. She was elated by Allie's change of heart. The melancholy she had wrestled with for months lifted, and she felt energized. The *Dove* and its crew were familiar, and during the two and half weeks at sea the missionaries sang and held meetings to the delight of all aboard. They had long discussions at table with Captain Groome, the First Mate Mister White, and the Bosun Mister Stark. Mary slept well at sea, and as the *Dove* traveled north, she felt eager to meet this challenge.

On the nineteenth day the *Dove* reached Sandwich in the Plimouth Colony. Captain Groome received a warm welcome for he was well known in the community. A boy was sent to alert Ralph Allen that his cargo had arrived. However, the young sea captain had other ports of call on the Cape. Once the lambs were herded off the ship and into a holding pen, he shook the missionaries' hands and bid them farewell.

"I fear we shall never be able to repay thee for all thy help, Captain Groome," Mary said.

"I am right glad to have been of use to such accomplished Public Friends," he replied, smiling. "Ye are the strongest women I know. God keep you."

 ⟶

Ralph Allen was a devout Friend, wheelwright, and planter, who had been convinced by Christopher Holder and John Copeland in '57. His wife Susannah had given him eight healthy children, seven sons and a daughter, but only the three youngest still lived at home. Patience was ten; Zachariah was eight; and Increase was four years old.

The Allens were well established. They survived the precarious years of 1658-61, when the Plimoth Colony authorities hired a clergyman from the Province of Mayne called George Barlow to "clean up the Quaker problem" in Sandwich and Scituate. Like John Hill, Barlow cloaked his greed in religious zeal. As a result, eighteen families were prosecuted for nonpayment of tithes to the Puritans' First Congregational church. Many did not have the coin, and Barlow helped himself to their best livestock, the family pewter, or anything of value to the point of financial ruin. During the purge, the Allens were able to help their less fortunate neighbors for as a wheelwright, Ralph always had work. The livestock on the *Dove* was for his son Joseph, recently married and living nearby with his wife Sarah and their one-year-old baby girl.

Susannah and Ralph Allen were engaging and intelligent hosts. Ralph had helped to establish the settlement at Sandwich in '37, and he continued to be a leader in the seaside community. He knew the Wright brothers and their families and was dismayed to hear that Peter had been lost at sea. On their first night Mary and Allie stayed up talking with their host as he described his convincement by Christopher Holder and John Copeland.

"Did ye know them?" he asked his guests.

"Certes we know of their good work and their courage, but we never met," Mary replied, "We trained for missionary work two years after they were at Swarthmore Hall."

"Thus, ye know they were brutally flogged and had their ears cropped at Boston." Mary and Allie nodded, and Ralph went on. "Their hair covered the scars, but Christopher showed me his." He shook his head admiringly. "Their suffering did not deter them. Not one whit!"

"Public Friends are trained to endure suffering. There is solace in the Light," she said.

"Have ye two also suffered for our faith then?" he asked.

The missionaries exchanged a glance. "We have known our share," Mary said briefly.

"Certes ye did not travel alone. Which of the other Public Friends accompanied you?"

"We made the crossing alone, but we were on one of Nicholas Shapleigh's ships. We stayed with them on Kittery Point once we arrived in Fourth Month of '62. Two Salem Friends, Edward Wharton and George Preston met us at Dover and took us there."

Ralph sat up straighter. "I am well acquainted with Friend Wharton!" he said. "He has come to Sandwich several times and encourages the Friends here greatly."

Mary smiled and nodded, unsurprised. She had not forgotten her promise to contact him when she came north. "Many people aided us in our travels," Mary went on, "as thou art helping us now, Friend Allen. It may appear we are alone, but in truth we have been uplifted by the companions we met along the way and could not have succeeded without them."

"Ye show rare courage, coming to this wilderness. What is your mission?" he asked, intrigued.

"Our mentor was Mary Dyer." Ralph's eyebrows rose for all Friends knew of her execution. "We came to the colonies to carry on her work against the unjust laws at Boston," Mary told him.

"Boston!" Ralph sat back, shocked. "Certes, they shall arrest you on sight, two female Friends."

"We fully expect that, but a perversion of justice must be publicly challenged lest it continue unremarked and unimpeded," she replied calmly. "Friend Allen, we require safe lodging, when we arrive in the city. Dost know where we might be entertained? We can work for board and lodging."

Ralph regarded them silently then said, "Thou art cut from the same cloth as Holder and Copeland, methinks. I admire you for it, but 'tis disturbing to think what they may do to two tender women." Mary met his gaze unflinchingly, and he sighed. "Well, I, myself, stay away from Boston, but I know a family in Dorchester who might entertain you, and they have connections in the city. They follow the Puritan faith, but they are good folk, nevertheless. Captain John Capen is head of the household, and his sister Dorothy Upshall has a tavern called the Red Lyon on River Street in Boston."

"Is Dorchester far from Boston?" Mary asked.

He shook his head. "About six miles by land, but ye cannot just walk through the gate, mind ye. The guards scrutinize every soul going in or out of the city. They arrest Friends on sight!" he scowled then brightened. "Ye might prevail upon Captain Capen to take you though. He delivers foodstuffs from their farm to the Red Lyon regularly. Also, Dorothy's husband Nicholas Upshall resides with them now. He is a fine old gent and a devout Friend, though he is much reduced by the years in prison, we hear. I can write a letter of introduction if ye like," their host offered.

"Our thanks, Friend Allen," Mary responded warmly. "That would be a great help."

Allie spoke for the first time. "Nicholas Upshall. The name is familiar, but I cannot recall his circumstances."

"Back in '56 the Society's first missionaries came to Boston, Mary Fisher and Ann Austin. They were arrested as soon as they arrived—even before they got off the ship," Ralph related. "The authorities thought to starve them in the prison, but Friend Upshall heard of their need and would not countenance it. He provided coin for their food, although that is not why they arrested him."

"Why did they then?" Allie asked.

"They kept the women in prison for eight weeks, confiscated all their belongings— even their bedding, mind ye—then sent them back to England. Days after, Endicott announced the first of the so-called Quaker Laws, forbidding Friends from coming to Boston and fining ships captains an hundred pounds each for transporting them. The marshal read the new law publicly outside all the ordinaries in the city, including the Red Lyon. Nicholas commented that it was a 'sad forerunner of some heavy judgement to fall on the country.' Mild speech, in truth, but they deemed it rebellious. He was arrested and banished—a sixty-year-old man and respected member of their society for over twenty years!" Ralph raised a finger, emphasizing his next statement. "And winter was coming on!" He shook his head and continued more quietly. "He came to us here at Sandwich. My brother William and his wife Priscilla entertained him. He is a godly man, and we welcomed his fellowship. That spring he went on to Rhode Island and stayed there for more than a year, but he missed his family." Ralph shook his head. "He should not have gone back to Boston, but he did. They arrested him, as he had gone against the order of banishment. It took Dorothy two years to get him out, and they only relented when John Capen said he would stand surety for his sister's husband, being of the Puritan faith, y'see. Thus, Friend Upshall is living out the rest of his life in his good-brother's custody at Dorchester."

"At least he is out of gaol," Allie commented.

Mary was intrigued. "We shall welcome the opportunity to meet Friend Upshall," she said.

Chapter 42

SANDWICH, PLIMOTH COLONY and DORCHESTER, MASSACHUSETTS BAY COLONY

May (3rd Month) 1664

Although under the authority of the Plimoth Colony, Sandwich was a refuge for dissenters since its settlement in 1637. It was small wonder that Public Friends found a warm welcome there two decades later. Unlike those who had established Boston, the Puritans of the town were not Separatists, and they observed reformed Anglican practices rather than discarding them altogether. Against all odds, the town was a rare bastion of religious toleration in New England.

For two weeks Mary and Allie enjoyed the fellowship of Friends in a relatively secure environment. A bout of rain in the second week of Third Month delayed their departure, but the two women were not restless. Once word spread that Public Friends were staying with Ralph Allen, people dropped by at all hours of the day, bringing gifts of food or drink and staying to talk and worship with them. The Sandwich Friends were heartened to hear of their counterparts worshipping freely in Rhode Island and Maryland. The missionaries' struggle with John Perrot and their suffering in the Bay Colony and Virginia earned everyone's respect.

When the women heard that Allie had no extra clothing, they brought whatever they could spare from stockings to dust caps. No one matched her height, but hems were lowered, and cuffs let out, and they soon supplied her modest needs. Susannah Allen made a bag from an old rug to carry Allie's new wardrobe. The missionaries almost regretted the return of clear weather, allowing them to leave Sandwich.

Ralph penned a letter of introduction to John Capen and insisted the missionaries accept ten shillings donated by the local Friends for their travel expenses. The Allen's eldest son Phillip was unmarried with few responsibilities, and he agreed to take the women to Dorchester in his skiff, as he had friends there.

"It is my custom to overnight at Scituate," he explained as they discussed the route. "'Tis a full day's sail, mayhap less, if the wind is southerly. There are Friends there and an inn there, as well. Ye can get a decent meal and a bed for three shillings. No bugs. I shall sleep on the *Polly*."

"How much farther is Dorchester from there?" Mary asked.

"About another day's sail. We should arrive sometime after midday, I reckon," he replied.

After a last meeting for worship with the Sandwich Friends, the women took their leave of the Allens. It was chilly for Third Month for although the winter had been mild, it was a reluctant spring. Still, they enjoyed a following wind. Phillip was a skillful sailor, and they docked at Scituate before dark. Mary insisted on buying him dinner at the inn then the weary travelers bid each other goodnight.

"Come break thy fast with us on the morrow, Friend Allen," Mary said when they parted.

As she and Allie prepared for bed, Mary had trouble removing her boots. She had ignored the pain, although her feet bothered her all day. Now she saw why. They were red and swollen past her ankles. Allie was concerned and tried massaging them, but it was too painful.

"I just need to rest," Mary told her, crawling under the covers. "I shall be fine by morn."

"No doubt," her friend replied, but Allie's doubts were legion, recalling Doctor Sharpe's warning.

Captain John Capen's house was one of the first built in Dorchester. It sat on the corner of Pleasant and Pond Streets, and the town had grown up around it. At fifty the Captain still led the militia and had two grown children by his first wife, Redigon, who had died of a fever in 1645. His second wife, Mary, was fifteen years younger than he, and they had seven healthy children. Samuel, the eldest at sixteen, was apprenticed to the ship-building concern at Gulliver's Creek. His six younger siblings still lived at home, ranging in age from fourteen to two years old.

Twelve-year-old Merry opened the door to the travelers on a busy, boisterous household. Everyone was active, working on one spring chore or another, except for an old man who sat in a cushioned rocking chair by a south-facing window, a blanket across his knees. As the only stationary person in the melee, Nicholas Upshall appeared to be the eye of a tempest. The sun lit his fine white hair creating a nimbus of light around his head, but when he greeted the newcomers, his eyes sparkled with intelligent interest.

Two years before, Nicholas was released from prison at Boston, but the abuse aged him. Although John Capen was not a Friend, he was appalled by his good-brother's decline and disapproved of the Bay Colony's harsh laws against Friends. Dismayed by the executions at Boston, particularly that of Mary Dyer, the Captain was a gentle and sympathetic warder; however, as a deacon of the First Church of Dorchester, he dared not express his opinions publicly lest he be branded a Quaker lover and arrested.

The Capens knew the Allen family, yet their hostess greeted them distractedly. She was preoccupied with the sheep shearing, which was late this year due to the cool weather. The family coordinated this task with neighbors, and Mary Capen had no time for pleasantries with unexpected guests.

"Your pardons if I do not sit with you," she apologized hastily, knotting her shawl. "Next week is the feather and down harvest, thus this chore cannot be put off. Merry shall fetch some refreshment for you, and Nicholas enjoys company."

"That I do!" Friend Upshall declared in a surprisingly strong voice that contrasted his frail condition. "Come sit and tell me of your travels. Have ye come from afar?"

Mary was exhausted. Even the short walk from the town dock made her feet throb. She sank onto the window seat near Nicholas' rocker, propping them on a stool with a sigh of relief. Allie helped Merry bring cups of cider and the morning's cornbread drizzled with molasses then sat with Mary. Their young hostess hurried off to help her mother. The pungent cider was slightly hard and eased a thirst Mary had not remarked, until she allowed herself to rest.

"Friend Upshall," she began, "we are glad to make thy acquaintance. My name is Mary Tomkins, and this is my companion, Alice Ambrose. We are Public Friends who lately came north from Maryland."

"Well met, Friends!" Nicholas reached for their hands eagerly, and each of them clasped his gnarled fingers gently. "Well met, my dear girls!" he repeated, his eyes watering with emotion. "Forgive me, but I see so few fellow Friends." He chuckled and dabbed at his eyes with a handkerchief. "I fear I am easily overwhelmed, these days. Pay an old fool no mind."

"The Allens of Sandwich told us of thy courage and thy suffering on account of our faith," Mary said gently, warming to Nicholas immediately. "Friends Fisher and Austin did sing thy praises, as well. We were training for missionary work at Swarthmore Hall when they returned from their ordeal in the Colonies. Thy generosity didst save them from starvation, and thou wert the first to protest Endicott's bloody laws. Many strive to follow thy example."

"I could not bear to let them suffer so," Nicholas murmured. "They came with love in their hearts and no intention to do harm. They led me to the Light. Certes, 'twas not the Will of the Almighty that they should starve." He looked up. "I would do it all again, though it cost me my family and my livelihood."

"We understand," she said. "We, too, have dedicated our lives to the Society."

"I would hear all ye would tell of it," their new friend said, leaning forward.

Mary and Allie did not realize how long they spoke with Nicholas Upshall, until they noticed the light at the window had faded. They looked up with surprise as young Merry came to help the old man to the table, and the three of them joined the family for the evening meal. Mary had no appetite, and once she was not distracted by talking with Nicholas, she realized how exhausted she was. She was not alone, and the household retired soon after eating. The missionaries shared a pallet in the loft next to those used by the six children.

They were awakened early the next morning when two-year-old Hannah crawled onto their pallet to investigate these new people. She cuddled between them, and Mary recited finger rhymes she thought were forgotten from the days of caring for her nephews. Hannah was delighted, as her busy family rarely found time to play with her.

Mary felt refreshed. Every time she looked at Allie, gratitude warmed her heart. Her swollen feet recovered after a good night's sleep, although there was a persistent ache in her lower back. Mary ignored it. She and Allie helped Hannah down the ladder to the main room, where the household was gathered at the table, breaking their fast. Mary and Allie sat on either side of Nicholas at the table, and Hannah crawled into Mary's lap and scooped up porridge from the trencher with her pudgy fingers.

The family spoke little, ate efficiently, and soon headed out to finish the shearing. Allie went with them, and the chore was finished before noon. Merry guided her in separating the high-quality wool on the back and sides of a sheep from that on the legs and belly, and Allie helped the children sort and pack the raw wool into sacks. Even six-year-old Joseph was enlisted in this chore.

However, shearing was only the beginning of the process. After the Capens ate a brief meal at noon, the raw wool was washed in a huge cauldron over an outdoor firepit. Their three young sons collected wood, and Mary and little Hannah kept the fire burning. The toddler was respectful of the blaze, pointing and saying "Hot! Hot!" repeatedly for which Mary was grateful. The boys were then put to the task of hauling water from the well to the cauldron. Twelve-year-old Merry, Mary Capen, and Allie soaked the wool, changing the water three times over the course of the afternoon before their hostess deemed it clean enough to spread on the racks. Once dry, it still needed to be combed, carded, and spun before the clean raw wool would become usable yarn.

When Hannah became tired, Mary Tomkins took her back inside and set the child on the window seat with her poppet. She chatted with Nicholas as she cleared the remains of the morning meal from the table and wiped the trenchers. By the time this task was done, Mary turned to find Hannah had fallen asleep. It was a rare opportunity to talk with Nicholas without interruption.

"Friend Upshall, dost know where we might stay in Boston?" she asked, sitting on a stool by his chair.

He gazed at her a moment before answering. "I fear for thee going there, Mary, but I know thou art determined." He sipped his tea and sighed. "My wife Dorothy keeps the Red Lyon now, as she has since my arrest. Our girls Susannah and Ruth assist her. If I send a message, they shall entertain you both."

"We do not wish to endanger thy family," she demurred.

"As long as ye hold no meetings there, the authorities shall not be alerted. It is a public house." His gaze sharpened. "What dost thou intend to accomplish in Boston, may I ask?"

"We shall appeal to Governor Endicott to rescind the laws against our faith," she said.

"Verily, they shall arrest you out of hand," he warned softly.

"Yes," Mary said, lifting her chin, "but we will add our protest to the others, and one day, God willing, the persecution shall end."

"So we hope," he said, "but I remark thy companion hardly speaks of it. Are ye both prepared for this?"

"We are," Mary affirmed. She was moved by Allie's loyalty in coming north with her. How much harder this would all be without her steadfast company.

Nicholas nodded unsurprised. "When shall ye depart?" he asked.

"Since thou hast helped us find a place to stay, as soon as possible," she answered.

"Have you transport or shall ye walk?" he asked. "'Tis six miles."

"I am unsure," Mary answered, thinking of her sore feet.

Nicholas grunted and patted his mouth with a handkerchief then spoke carefully. "My dear, might I suggest waiting until thy strength returns?"

Mary colored, embarrassed that her weakness was apparent to him.

Friend Upshall's keen eyes noted this and went on. "When ye first arrived, it was evident that the journey from Sandwich taxed thee, my dear. 'Tis doubtful ye could get past the gate, and even if ye do, public protest leads to arrest, and they shall abuse thee with hard labor and daily beatings in the prison. The cubs are dark and dank, the air and food noxious. Two years of it near killed me, and I was a hale man at the start. I fear for both of you, but especially for thee, Mary, if thou art unwell."

"We hesitate to overstay our welcome here," Mary said quietly. "I fear we are a burden to the Capens at this busy time. We must spare our coin, as we shall have need of it at Boston. We cannot linger here."

"My good-sister has a sharp tongue, but she will not turn you out," Nicholas assured her. "John has means, and he is generous. I wager they do not expect payment from you. Also, I shall tell Dottie—my wife—thou art a Friend. We do not charge Friends at the Lyon, although few come there anymore. I beg thee, consider resting here until thou art stronger."

The next morning Phillip Allen stopped to say farewell, as he was returning to Sandwich. Allie accompanied him to the dock, while Mary bid him goodbye at the gate with little Hannah. The Capens were grateful to be freed from watching her, and Mary found it no hardship. When Allie returned, she found Mary and Hannah playing in the garth between the house and barn. The toddler had bonded with "Maywee," and the two seemed happily occupied, so Allie joined the family in their labors.

The missionaries need not have worried about overstaying their welcome. At supper Mary Capen thanked Allie profusely for her help that day and asked the missionaries if they might stay another week. They were glad to be of use. Allie worked with the family while Mary spent her days with Hannah and Friend Upshall. Her feet and ankles did not swell, if she was careful not to walk about too much, and she bore the ache in her lower back stoically and did not speak of it to anyone.

The kitchen garden was dry enough to work the soil, and Hannah "helped" to plant peas and greens. Mary made sure she got plenty of fresh air and exercise to encourage afternoon naps, and Hannah was a quiet child for the most part. She could amuse herself with rocks and sticks for surprisingly long periods, but her sturdy little legs worked quickly, when she spied something of interest. More than once, Mary was grateful for the fence that bordered the garth.

At supper on the first day of the feather and down harvest Mary Capen held Hannah on her lap, while she cut some tender boiled mutton into small pieces for the child.

"Our Hannie behaves for you?" she asked Mary Tomkins.

"Oh yes," Mary answered, smiling at Hannah who grinned back. "We are merry, are we not, Hannie?"

The child nodded vigorously as she chewed.

"Canst thou count for Mama, sweetling?" the missionary urged.

Hannah held up a greasy hand. "Wan, too, tree!" she said, raising a thumb and two fingers for each number. She and Mary had worked on this during the afternoon, and the family praised them both, laughing with delight.

"She shall be keeping the accounts ere ye leave us!" the Captain chuckled.

"We are indeed grateful for your help, both of ye," Mary Capen added with unusual warmth. "It commonly falls on Merry to watch her little sister," she continued, "but she is a fine helper with the labor at hand, and we would miss her. I hope ye shall stay with us a while yet."

Young Merry blushed at her mother's rare compliment, and Mary Tomkins felt a surge of relief. She and Allie were of use and need not beg charity from the busy family.

"We do hope to stay another week or so before going on to Boston," she ventured.

"Stay as long as you wish!" John exclaimed. "We are ever in need of extra pairs of hands."

"Adult hands especially," his wife amended, gracing her guests with a rare smile.

Chapter 43

DORCHESTER AND BOSTON, MASSACHUSETTS BAY COLONY

May/June (3rd/4th Month) 1664

During the final week of Third Month, the tentative New England spring turned cool and rainy, but the Capens were a force of nature in and of themselves. Inclement weather was no obstacle to finishing the work at hand. With two major spring chores accomplished, the mood in the household was calmer.

"We have plenty of clean, dry wool," Mary Capen said as they all broke their fast on the first of what would prove to be a series of raw, rainy days. "We shall have a spinning circle this day, I reckon," she finished.

Merry's face lit up. "Shall I invite the neighbors, Mama?"

"Yes, Merry," her mother smiled, and the girl leapt to her feet. "Finish thy porridge first, daughter!" she laughed, gesturing to Merry's half-full trencher.

Spinning circles were social gatherings, as the women talked or sang while working at the tediously repetitive task of turning wool into usable yarn. It went so much faster with extra hands and good company. By mid-morning eight women sat in a circle before the open door of the Capens' barn, carding and spinning the new wool as they chatted and laughed over the steady drone of rain on the roof. The adult women could spin in their sleep, but young Merry was still acquiring the skill. After some practice, her mother relented and let the girl go back to carding.

When conversation lagged, Mary and Allie started up a round. Mary Capen joined in with a fine strong voice, and the others followed suit. When the women had exhausted their repertoire of rounds, the local ladies sang a colonial tune popular since the '30s called "Forefathers' Song."

New England's annoyances you that would know them,
Pray ponder these verses which briefly doth show them.
The place where we live is a wilderness wood,
Where grass is much wanting that's fruitful and good:
Our mountains and hills and our valleys below,
Being commonly covered with ice and with snow;
And when the north-west wind with violence blows,
Then every man pull his cap over his nose:
But if any's so hardy and will it withstand,
He forfeits a finger, a foot, or a hand.

But when the Spring opens we then take the hoe,
And make the ground ready to plant and to sow;
Our corn being planted and seed being sown,
The worms destroy much before it is grown;
And when it is growing, some spoil there is made
By birds and by squirrels that pluck up the blade;
And when it is come to full corn in the ear,
It is often destroyed by raccoon and by deer.

And now our garments begin to grow thin,
And wool is much wanted to card and to spin;
If we can get a garment to cover without,
Our other in-garments are clout upon clout:
Our clothes we brought with us are apt to be torn,
They need to be clouted soon after they're worn,
But clouting our garments they hinder us nothing,
Clouts double are warmer than single whole clothing.

If fresh meat be wanting to fill up our dish
We have carrots and turnips as much as we wish:
And if there's a mind for a delicate dish
We repair to the clam-banks, and there we catch fish.

Instead of pottage and puddings and custards and pies,
Our pumpkins and parsnips are common supplies;
We have pumpkins at morning and pumpkins at noon,
If it was not for pumpkins we should be undone!
If barley be wanting to make into malt,
We must be contented, and think it no fault;
For we make liquor to sweeten our lips,
Of pumpkins and parsnips and walnut-tree chips.

Now while some are going let others be coming,
For while liquor's boiling it must have a scumming;
But I will not blame them, for birds of a feather
By seeking their fellows are flocking together.
But you whom the Lord intends hither to bring,
Forsake not the honey for fear of the sting;
But bring both a quiet and contented mind,
And all needful blessing you surely will find.

That night at supper John Capen proposed a plan to transport Mary and Allie to the Red Lyon Inn without drawing the unwanted attention of the authorities.

"As ye know, Nicholas' wife Dorothy is my sister," the Captain began. "We supply her tavern with meat and fresh produce when we have it, and we have some salted mutton ready for delivery now. I thought to take the wagon myself and visit her, once the road is dry. If ye ride with me, I shall say you are my wife's cousins hired to help the Upshalls at the Red Lyon for the summer. Thus, ye shall not be bothered at the gate. Also, the guards know me, and they are ever glad to see food coming into the city."

Mary and Allie exchanged a glance. Ralph Allen had suggested this very thing, and now John Capen was offering it of his own accord. They could not ask for a better escort. John would take them straight to the Red Lyon's door, introduce them to his sister, and Mary would not have to walk six miles.

"Our thanks, Captain Capen," Mary answered gratefully. "That sounds a fine plan."

"Orange Street—that's the road along the Neck—is apt to be marshy after a rainy spell, especially at high tide, so our departure must be planned to cross at low tide in dry weather," he explained. "We want no mishaps with a loaded wagon."

"Take all the time you need, husband," his wife put in, "Parting shall be a hardship for us all, I fear." She smiled at her guests, who were gratified by the compliment.

The salted mutton was already packed in firkins ready to be loaded onto the wagon. During their last week with the Capens, the missionaries took every opportunity to sit with Nicholas Upshall, when they were not helping the family with chores or watching little Hannah. After four days of rain and drizzle the weather broke, and three days later John Capen deemed the roads were dry. Mary felt ready.

Parting was indeed a hardship. Nicholas put a brave face on, but Mary Tomkins knew he would miss them terribly. They were his only connection to the faith for which he had lost everything. In turn, he had provided a place for them to stay in the city and inspired them anew.

Little Hannah tried to climb up on the wagon with the missionaries. When her mother held her back, the child pitched a rare fit. She was accustomed to going everywhere with Mary Tomkins, and she did not understand why this day was different. Mary Capen bid a hasty good-bye and carried her into the house.

"May-wee! May-weee!" Her plaintive little voice begged tearfully, tugging at Mary's heart until it faded with distance.

⌒⟩

Two horses pulled the wagon, and they made good time; however, half an hour into the trip the dull ache in Mary's lower back became more pronounced as the wagon jolted along the rutted road. The odor of mud flats at low tide reached them well before they got to Boston Neck. When Mary saw how narrow it was, she understood the Captain's careful planning. The track was yet soggy and deeply rutted by the continuous traffic going in and out of the city. There were few trees on the Neck, but one stood out. It was a lone, gnarled elm tree on a rise at the side of the road, and Mary shivered at the sight of it.

"Is—is that…?" she stammered.

The Captain nodded grimly. "Aye, 'tis the Gallows Elm. They did hang thy fellows there."

Mary groped for Allie's hand, and they passed the place in silence for the pall of death was pervasive. Their dear mentor had been hanged from that branch. Here she had given up her life to God.

Progress stalled as they neared the gate at the narrowest point on the Neck. Even at low tide the water was a stone's throw away. The wooden edifice was ten feet high with walls of earth and rock extending to the high tide mark on either side. The guards took their job seriously, monitoring entries and exits from the city, and Captain Capen waited his turn with weary patience.

Mary saw the wisdom in his plan as they made their slow approach. Two unescorted women could never have slipped past the gate. In fact, the guards recognized John Capen but asked the identity of his two passengers.

"Cousins on my wife's side," the captain answered casually. "My sister needs help at the Red Lyon this season. She has hired them for the summer. 'Tis ever busy in the warmer weather, is it not, lads?"

They agreed heartily, confirmed his load with a cursory glance, and waved him on. The wagon rattled through the gate, and the three of them breathed a sigh of relief.

Barring the short time at New Amsterdam, the missionaries had not been near a city for more than a year. The early June day warmed quickly, and as the wagon progressed, the miasma of animal and human refuse overcame the rank odor of low tide. When they reached the business district, the way was paved with cobblestones, and the vibration of the iron-bound wheels rattled their teeth. Mary gripped the wagon bench and suppressed a grimace of pain. There was no ignoring the ache in her lower back now. Short as the trip had been, she prayed it would soon be over.

The Red Lyon was a sturdy, two-story edifice with its own wharf across the lane on the south bank of the Charles River. Captain Capen drove the wagon down a side alley that accessed the tavern's storage area and stable. Before they could climb down, a rotund, rosy-cheeked woman appeared at the back door, wiping her hands on her apron.

"Well met, brother!" she sang out, as her eyes took measure of the strangers with frank curiosity.

"Greetings, Dottie my dear!" John replied, securing the reins, and jumping down from the wagon.

They embraced warmly, and John turned to help the missionaries down from the high wagon seat. As usual, Allie was managing on her own, so he offered Mary a hand. When her feet hit the ground, the ache in her back spiked to a sharp pain, and she could not contain a gasp. The Captain's face creased with concern, but she turned to his sister before he could comment.

"Good day to thee, Mistress Upshall," she said, managing a thin smile.

John took the hint and made introductions. "They are visitors to our colonies, lately come from Maryland," he elaborated after names were exchanged. "They have been with us for some weeks, and we consider them part of the family. They require lodging, and Nicholas suggested here."

"Ah, so you met my husband, did you?" Dottie inquired, neatly skirting the issue of lodging, as she assessed the strangers with an innkeeper's eye. "How fares he?"

"He perked up greatly in our guests' company," her brother asserted.

"We enjoyed excellent conversation and shared silent worship each day," Mary added. "Thy husband is an example to us all, Mistress Upshall."

Dottie's smile fled, and she glanced around the yard. They were alone. "You are practicing Friends then?" she asked quietly.

"We are," Mary answered without hesitation. "Captain Capen suggests we pose as his wife's cousins come to work for the summer, and verily, we should be glad to work for our room and board. We shall not trouble thee for long, Mistress Upshall."

They had come into the city discreetly, but Mary had no intention of staying hidden for long. Best to be open with this woman who had suffered so much concerning her husband. The missionaries would not stay where they were unwelcome, letter or no. She withdrew Nicholas' message from her pocket pouch and gave it to Dorothy.

The innkeeper's wife went on without reading it. "Certes we will entertain you, ladies, but I caution you. There can be no 'thou' or 'thee' with the other guests, and there can be no meetings here, you understand. John spoke surety of us in the court, and 'twould go hard with him, as well, if they find we harbor Quakers. We cannot afford to be arrested."

"We understand," Mary affirmed. "We are grateful for a place to stay and can pay coin."

Dorothy held up a work-reddened hand. "No friends of my husband or my brother need pay coin here," she pronounced. "Now John, let us get this meat in the cold cellar."

In the end two hired men unloaded the wagon, while John and the missionaries took some refreshment with Dottie and her two daughters. The eldest, Sarah, was several months pregnant. She and Joseph Cocke had been married five years and longed for a child. She was due in September and hardly showed, but she was radiant. Sarah was tall and thin like her father with dark blonde hair peeking from her dust cap. Her sister Ruth was the youngest of the Upshall daughters. She was unmarried at twenty-two and favored her mother, being small and rotund, but lacked Dottie's confidence. She rarely spoke.

John left soon after eating. Mary and Allie thanked him profusely, and the women waved him off. Ruth showed them to a small room off the back stairs to the kitchen in keeping with their ruse as servants. When she had gone, Mary lay down with an audible groan of relief. She still had her boots on, and Allie sat on the edge of the bed.

"Is all well with thee, Mary?" she asked, sensing her friend's discomfort.

Mary smiled weakly. "Just need to rest after all that jouncing on the wagon." She took Allie's hand. "I am so glad thou art here, Allie," she said fervently.

Allie put her other hand on her friend's brow, feeling for fever, but it was cool. "Let us remove your boots, at least," she suggested, untying the laces.

Mary hissed, as Allie worked the boots off her feet with difficulty.

"They are swollen again," Allie said, lifting a foot to remove Mary's stocking. "Do they pain thee?" Mary nodded, looking miserable. "I shall make a tea to ease the inflammation," the tall missionary said, fetching her bag of medicaments. She turned at the door. "Rest now, Mimi."

Mary was worried. Even without walking much that day her feet and ankles were swollen, and the pain in her back was ominously persistent. She did not want to believe Peter Sharpe's warning that the beating in Virginia had injured more than the skin on her back. She only needed to rest, and all would be well. It had to be. She could not be ill on the brink of her final and most important protest to confront the man responsible for Mary Dyer's death.

Chapter 44

BOSTON, MASSACHUSETTS BAY COLONY

June (4ᵗʰ Month) 1664

Mary did not sleep well. Her feet and ankles throbbed, and the ache in her lower back kept her from finding a comfortable position. On top of that, River Street was never quiet. Outside their small, shuttered window the rattle of iron-bound wheels and the clop of shod hooves on cobblestones continued even after dark. The Red Lyon Inn was a busy establishment with guests thumping along the halls and banging doors above stairs, while others caroused in the ordinary directly below their room—all prevented sleep. She drowsed fitfully, and as the rising sun poked fingers of light through the shutter, Edward Wharton came to mind. She must contact him, and Salem was not far, less than a day's sail from Boston if she remembered correctly. Edward might advise her on making their protest effective. He had opposed the Boston Puritans numerous times during the past five years. The hope of seeing him propelled her out of bed. Allie woke when Mary got up.

"Dost feel better this morn?" Allie asked sleepily.

"Yes," Mary lied, determined to overcome this pain that threatened to interfere with her plans. "I must send a message to Edward at Salem," she said, pulling her stockings on quickly. Her feet and ankles were only slightly swollen. She eased on her boots, tying them loosely. "We must ask Mistress Upshall how best to go about it."

They found the Upshall women already hard at work, feeding their guests. The smell of corncakes sizzling in lard usually appealed to Mary, but this morning her stomach roiled at the heavy odor. The two women paused, glancing through the doorway to the common room. Except for one middle-aged couple the guests were all male—sea captains and officers, merchants on business, and three nattily dressed gentlemen visiting the colony from England. Dorothy beckoned to Mary and Allie.

"Best to let the other guests think you work here, as John suggested," she cautioned quietly. "One 'thou' or 'thee' from your mouths could set the marshal upon us. If anyone asks, you are cousins of the Capens come to help out."

"In truth, we would be glad to work for our room and board, Mistress Upshall," Mary said.

Dorothy responded with a dismissive wave and handed them each a trencher with corncakes and ham.

"Sit you down and break your fast," Dorothy replied. "No need to fret about that, if Nicholas sent you."

By midmorning, the common room was empty of guests. Despite Dorothy's protestations, Mary and Allie helped the Upshall women clean up. Once done, they were all able to sit, and their hostesses took some much-needed refreshment themselves. Mary asked them how she might get a message to Salem.

"Richard Fairbanks has a fine system at his tavern," Susannah answered, sipping her tea. "It has ever been the place to send or receive letters, especially overseas. There are two large posts on the porch—one for outgoing missives, and the other for those coming in. But for local letters 'tis likely quicker to find a boat from Salem at Dock Square and send it direct."

"Have you friends in Salem?" Dorothy asked.

"Yes," Mary answered. "Edward Wharton and George Preston. They met us at Dover on the Piscataqua when we first came to the Colonies."

"Edward Wharton!" The innkeeper was impressed. "My husband spent some months in prison with him, among others. Nicholas spoke highly of him."

"He removed us from danger several times, last year when we were in the Bay Colony," Mary said. "We parted at Gravesend on Long Island last autumn, and we have not seen him since." She turned to Susannah. "Is Dock Square far from here?" she asked.

"Nothing is far in Boston," Dorothy laughed, "but pay no more than a penny," she warned. "Ever since the court named him Master of Posts, Richard Fairbanks set the charge at a penny so do not let anyone on the docks fun you for more than that."

"Thou dost not object, if he comes to visit us here?" Mary asked to be sure.

"As long as you are quiet and hold no meetings," Dorothy answered.

"I shall accompany you to Dock Square," Susannah stated. "Cook requires fish for supper tonight, and the boats sell their catch right off the pier, fresh as can be."

"An excellent idea, daughter," Dottie agreed, giving Susannah some coins from her pocket pouch. "Just ensure that it *is* fresh. Do not take any offscourings, mind you."

"The nose knows," the young woman smiled, a feminine version of her father.

Mary penned a quick message to Edward, and Allie moved closer to her, as Susannah prepared to leave.

"Mimi, let me take the letter for thee," she suggested gently. "Thou shouldst mind thy feet."

Mary opened her mouth to protest. She wanted to see more of the colonial capitol, but her friend was right. Her feet throbbed already. She must save her strength for the day of protest. She sanded the wet ink, blew off the excess, and handed the folded note to her friend.

"My thanks, Allie," she said, embracing her.

Susannah linked arms with Allie, and they walked south on River Street to the Common then turned east on Beacon Street. As they approached the business center, Allie was overwhelmed by the sheer volume of traffic—people, beasts of burden, a tangle of conveyances from handcarts to plush coaches-and-four—and on every street a myriad of store front displays, coffee houses and ordinaries, market stalls, and peddlers calling out their wares as they moved through the throng. It seemed the street sweepers could not keep up with the morning's fresh deposits of horse dung and refuse tossed from windows, and the women placed their feet with care. Susannah pointed out landmarks such as the First Church, King's Cross Cemetery, the Boston Town House, and Governor Endicott's dwelling. Allie took keen notice of the latter. Directly south of the Town House, King Street led onto the Long Wharf, where fishermen docked alongside merchant ships to sell their wares.

"'Tis not uncommon for Salem boats to be here," Susannah told her, as they made their way along the crowded pier. "We shall find one to take your letter. But I wager 'tis best if I speak," she added quietly.

Allie nodded. Keeping her mouth shut was no chore.

They joined a group of women haggling prices over some fine cod, and Susannah elbowed her way through, ignoring the protests. Allie had no choice but to follow, smiling in mute apology. Susannah selected a fish that was long as her arm. It was too heavy to carry home, so she paid an extra thruppence to have it delivered to the Red Lyon.

"Do you know of any craft out of Salem here this day?" she asked the man, as his young apprentice wrapped their fish in damp linen.

"That would be this one," he smiled.

"Oh excellent!" Susannah exclaimed. "Might you take a letter to one who lives there?"

"I might," he agreed, "for the right price." He grinned, enjoying an exchange with a pretty lass.

Allie got out the letter, and Susannah held up a penny.

"We pay the going rate," Susannah smiled back. "One penny."

"I am bested by beauty!" he exclaimed, clapping a hand over his heart, even as he took the coin and the letter with the other. "Fair enough then. Who is it for?" he asked, glancing at the writing. Being illiterate, he could not decipher the name himself.

"Edward Wharton," Allie told him.

His easy expression sharpened. "Y'keep dangerous company, Missus. He be a Quaker heretic, mind ye."

"Mayhap there is another going to Salem," Susannah mused, casting her gaze along the pier.

"Be not addled!" the man protested. "'Tis nothing to me! I shall deliver it into his hands."

The two women thanked him and headed back to River Street.

Chapter 45

BOSTON, MASSACHUSETTS BAY COLONY

June (4th Month) 1664

Edward came two days later. He wanted to leave the moment he received Mary's message, but there was a shipment of tools, and he could not abandon his partner George Preston until it was offloaded and stored in their warehouse. It was planting season, and the goods were in demand. At least now they had the help of Edward's fifteen-year-old nephew, John Windett. His sister's eldest boy had immigrated to Salem in Second Month to apprentice with his uncle, and he proved strong and willing.

Friend Wenlock Christison was staying with the Salem men and volunteered to help Edward crew the *Sea Witch* to Boston. Wenlock was a quiet man, but when he spoke, he was eloquent. He was well educated in the law and had nearly died in 1660, when he ignored an order of banishment from Boston and walked into William Leddra's trial before the Great and General Court. He questioned the legitimacy of the Bay Colony's law to execute Quakers, enacted by Endicott and his ministers without the King's approval. He also warned the officials of shedding innocent blood for the sake of their own souls. They dismissed his arguments and arrested him, sentencing Christison to hang; however, he was reprieved by the mandamus from King Charles II. The executions were stopped by royal order, and the restored monarch declared no more of His subjects should die on account of religion in the American Colonies.

Edward had told Wenlock about his adventures with Mary and Alice, and Christison was impressed by the women's courage. He wanted to meet them. Both men were banished from the Bay Colony, but Edward ignored the order and continued to live in Salem and run his import business. No one outside of Boston troubled him. He was well respected, and many people depended on his wares. Now Mary's letter brought both Friends back to the lion's den.

Dorothy greeted the two men in the entry hall, and Edward introduced Wenlock Christison. The innkeeper glanced out the door, looking up and down the street before closing it.

"I am glad to meet you, Friend Wharton. My husband speaks highly of you, but you take great risk coming here against an order of banishment. I hope you were not seen, for they shall arrest you as they did my husband," she said quietly. "Your friend Mary is not well," she continued, leading them up the back stairs. "I thought she looked poorly when she arrived three days ago, and she took to her bed yesterday." She stopped in front of a door, her face grave. "Also, I must tell you, when Ruth last emptied the chamber pot, there was blood in the urine." She sighed, a busy woman with a good heart but burdened by endless responsibilities beyond sheltering a heretical invalid. "Let us hope your company shall revive her somewhat," she finished.

The innkeeper knocked softly and opened the door. The room was small and dim, the shutters on the only window closed to the early June sun. Allie sat on the bed next to a small form that must be Mary. The latter was curled on her side facing away from them. When she saw him, Allie stood up, and Edward crossed the room in two strides.

"Edward!" she exclaimed. They embraced warmly. "Thank God thou art here," she murmured.

"It is good to see thee, Allie," he replied, keeping his voice low, "but what passes here? What ails her?"

"I am unsure," Allie answered. "She never fully recovered from the flogging in Virginia."

"When was that?" he asked dismayed.

"This Tenth Month past," she told him. "Thirty-two stripes each," she added, knowing he would ask.

Edward winced. "Dost think this malady is a result of the whipping?"

Allie nodded. "Peter Sharpe, a physician and a Friend, saved our lives. For weeks Mary was fevered even though there was no infection in her wounds. She nearly died, Edward. It took all winter for her to recover, and even then, she was not fully restored. The doctor fears she suffered damage that cannot be seen, mayhap to a vital organ. He thinks another flogging might kill her. We tried to dissuade her coming to Boston, but she is determined to answer her call and plead with Endicott to rescind the Quaker laws. We left the Clifts in Maryland at the end of Second Month."

Edward knelt beside the bed on one knee. "Mary, I am here," he said, touching her shoulder.

She stirred and slowly turned over. Edward was alarmed at her appearance. Her eyes looked huge and glittered with fever. The skin underneath them looked bruised. Her cheek bones and the lines around her mouth were more prominent than he remembered, and she grimaced in pain as she moved.

"Edward." The grimace became a smile. "Thou hast come." She reached for his hand, and he clasped hers tightly, fighting tears. He felt her forehead with his free hand. It was burning.

"I am dosing her with willow bark tea, but the fever is not responding," Allie told him.

"We must bring in a physician. Mistress Upshall, dost know one we can trust?" he asked over his shoulder.

"I shall send for Doctor Clarke," she answered from the doorway. "He is returned from England now and is the best in the city," she added and hurried from the room.

Edward bit back a flood of questions and stroked Mary's hand. Wenlock stood behind him next to Allie as she briefly told them of all that had passed since their parting at Gravesend—the pursuit of John Perrot from the Eastern Shore to the Elizabeth River; their arrest and flogging in Virginia; the long recuperation in Peter Sharpe's care; and her betrothal to John Gary. Before Edward could respond, Dorothy's voice came from downstairs, raised in protest.

"Stop! You have no business up there!"

Heavy boots pounded the stairs, growing louder as they approached, and Edward stood up. The door opened, and two grim-faced men entered with the innkeeper at their heels. She pushed past them and blocked their way with arms akimbo.

"Richard Baker and James Humphrey, what calls you to disturb our peace?" she demanded.

"We are on official business. Now, step aside, Mistress Upshall, or we shall count you complicit with this lot," the taller of the two said, raising his chin toward Edward and Wenlock.

"'Tis the heretic Edward Wharton there," the other added, pointing at the Salem man, "and this one almost hanged back in '60. He is banished, too." He frowned at Christison, who gazed back impassively.

"Well, they break no law here," Dorothy stated. "They have come to comfort a sick friend, is all."

"'Tis not reason enough to flaunt the order of banishment," Constable Baker replied.

"Mistress Upshall did not invite us," Christison put in. "We are come of our own accord to visit our friend, who is too sick to come to us." He gestured to Mary in the bed.

Baker snorted. "And who is this 'invalid'?" he sneered, moving closer to the bed. "Another heretic?"

Edward blocked him. "She is fevered and weak. Leave her be," he asserted emphatically.

"These women are my good-sister's cousins from Dorchester, come to work here," Dorothy protested.

"We must know if they are Quakers," Humphrey declared. "We are charged to apprehend all such that break the laws of our city, which you do by being here, Edward Wharton and Wenlock Christison. It is up to the Governor and his Court to decide yer fate."

"Will you come quietly or must we use force?" Baker demanded, laying a hand on his truncheon.

"We have broken no King's law," Christison replied calmly.

"But you have broken the Colony's law and no mistake." Baker was losing his patience. This was the standard heretic's excuse, always hiding behind the King, and he would not stand for it. "I parse you are all heretics. Get her up."

"What! Ye would drag a sick woman from her bed?" Edward asked appalled.

"She is a Quaker thus she is under arrest, sick or not," Humphrey declared, stepping forward.

No protestations or reasoning would change the constables' minds, and the Friends realized resisting would only incite violence. Dorothy and Allie helped Mary to dress, while the men waited in the hall. Her face was flushed with fever, but she was conscious. They gave up lacing her boots and stuffed the untied ends into the tops. Mary could barely stand on her swollen feet, and the two women all but carried her down the stairs. The constables had tied the men's hands behind them, and they bound Mary and Allie's, as well.

"Is it verily necessary to bind her, constables?" Dorothy asked. "The poor thing can hardly stand!"

"Standard procedure," Humphrey answered curtly, tightening the knot so that Mary staggered.

"No doubt she exaggerates her illness to play on our sympathies," Baker said, leering at the invalid. "These Quakers are a deceitful lot."

Susannah and Ruth appeared to see what all the commotion was about and stood helplessly by with their mother as the four prisoners were hustled out into the street. There was no opportunity for good-byes.

It was a beautiful day in early June. Colonel Thomas Temple decided to walk to his luncheon engagement with the Governor and left his house in the North End of Boston on foot accompanied only by his trusted valet Francois. Thomas was relatively new to the Colonies, having immigrated in the spring of 1657, but he embraced his adopted home whole heartedly. His Uncle William Fiennes, Viscount Saye and Sele, had influence with Cromwell and had secured the proprietorship of Acadia for his nephew the autumn before. The fifty-three-year-old bachelor had docked at Boston in his own ship with his usual retinue of servants; however, after one foray into the wilds of the north country, the Colonel, as a gentleman of means with refined tastes, elected to settle in Boston. Impressed by his connections, the New World Puritans welcomed him. He hired Thomas Breedon, an English merchant familiar with colonial trade, to manage the Acadia interests, leaving Temple free to enjoy a reasonably comfortable life in the colonial capitol on the erratic profits. Fortunately, his credit was good.

As Thomas and his valet approached the Common, the perfect day was marred by a bizarre scene. A cluster of people blocked the way, the usual foot traffic diverting around them like water around a rock. As he neared the group, the Colonel realized two of the men were constables, and the other four—two men and two women—were prisoners, bound and in their custody. Most striking, one of women lay prone on the cobbles, apparently senseless. Thomas Temple stopped.

"Ye cannot leave her to lie in the street!" one of the prisoners exclaimed, kneeling awkwardly beside her with his bound hands. "Help her! She has swooned!" he implored the constables—most sincerely, Thomas thought. Certes the Colonel was moved by his plea, but the enforcers of the law were not.

"She funs us, I wager," one of the constables sneered, "I doubt the truth of it."

"We shall wait until she tires of it," added the other, crossing his arms over his chest.

"Thou art mistaken. Verily, she is gravely ill and should be abed," the tall woman objected with admirable calm. She would have been a beauty but for the ragged scar on her face.

The kneeling man groaned with frustration.

Thomas was intrigued. From the woman's speech, he surmised the prisoners were Quakers and was instantly alert. Much as he loved his adopted home, the Colonel had never concurred with the Boston officials on their harsh reaction to religious dissenters. In '59 when Endicott sentenced the first two Quaker men to hang, Thomas had offered to take them into his own custody rather than see them executed, but the Governor refused to consider it. Here was more evidence of Puritan brutality, even against tender women. He could not tacitly condone it by pretending not to see.

"What passes here, gentlemen?" he asked, adopting a tone of authority.

The constables recognized him and snapped to attention.

"Colonel Temple! Good day to you, sir," Humphrey said, removing his hat. Baker did, as well, and both men touched their brows in respect. "I am Constable James Humphrey, and this is Constable Richard Baker. These Quakers have broken the law of banishment against them, and we take them to the governor," he asserted proudly.

"I have no doubt you are doing your duty, Constable," Temple responded, raising an eyebrow, "but one wonders if 'tis entirely necessary for a woman to lie prostrate in the street in order to accomplish it."

"'Tis all play-acting, sir," Humphrey told him. "They are a wily lot, these Quakers, ever pandering to our sympathies, especially the women."

Temple gently prodded Mary's shoulder with his walking stick and got no response. "Appears sincere enough to me," he said dubiously. "She is verily in a faint."

"Do not bother yourself with these offscourings, Colonel sir," Baker spoke up. "Certes, you are about some important business. We have the situation under control."

Temple knew he was being put off but arguing on a public street was not the way of a gentleman. He turned away from Baker and addressed Humphrey. "You go to the governor, Constable?" he asked.

"Indeed, sir," Humphrey answered.

"Then I shall see you there," Temple said and went on his way.

However, he did not intend to dismiss the issue. If the woman was sick, the officials should not imprison her. She might die in her cub, and that would reflect very badly on the Bay Colony. He must make John understand that. He did not agree with Endicott's laws, but he loved Boston and hoped to see the colonial capital become more tolerant. The constables were mere minions of Endicott, but the Governor's attitude of cruelty validated their harsh treatment of prisoners. Thomas did not believe the Almighty condoned this behavior even if the governor did, and he intended to do what he could to help the prisoners and their sick friend.

Chapter 46

BOSTON, MASSACHUSETTS BAY COLONY

June (4th Month) 1664

Thomas Temple arrived at Governor Endicott's home well before the constables and their charges. He stationed Francois outside with instructions to alert him when they came into view. The governor was not alone. Deputy Governor Richard Bellingham, and Edward Rawson, Endicott's trusted Secretary, were also present, but the plan for a convivial meal was not realized that day. Once Temple described the scene on the street and the prisoners involved, Endicott prepared to hold court in his study. The three officials were familiar with both Wharton and Christison for the two Friends had appeared before the Great and General Court in more formal circumstances on several occasions. Both were banished from the colony, and the court had sentenced Christison to hang, but the King's mandamus had prevented his death by the halter. In addition, John Endicott knew Edward Wharton personally, for they had been neighbors in Salem before Endicott moved to Boston to take up the position of governor upon Winthrop's death in 1649. When Francois reported the constables were approaching the house, the officials were ready for them.

Reviving from her faint, Mary felt more alert. She realized they had been arrested and were on their way to the governor. This was her opportunity to confront the man responsible for executing her spiritual mother. She had prepared for this moment for years, and her determination to confront him at last dispelled the fog of her illness.

Francois led the entourage directly to the study where the governor and his friends sat behind his large desk. Rawson, as secretary, had quill, ink, paper, and sand at the ready. As their hands were untied, Mary focused on Endicott. His expression was stony, but two spots of red colored his cheeks above his neatly trimmed goatee and moustache, revealing a bilious nature. He wore a black suit of fine material adorned with a white linen cloth from neck to shoulders and matching white cuffs. The clothing might be plain, but the man who wore it was fastidious.

Mary took his measure and waited for an opportunity to speak. Edward and Wenlock stood with their hats on in defiance of the authorities. Although familiar with this behavior, the governor was peeved.

"Remove your hats before this court!" he barked.

"We do not recognize thy temporal authority," Edward replied calmly. "There is One higher."

Mary was appalled that this cruel murderer was concerned with such a trifle. It was almost laughable. Four people had died at his order, and hundreds of others had been imprisoned, tortured, and financially ruined by his so-called laws, yet he was concerned with this small show of defiance to his authority. She and Allie wore only dust caps, as their hats had been left with their belongings at the Red Lyon. She plucked Edward's hat from his head, dropped it on the fine India carpet, and set her foot on it.

"There is thy honor under my foot!" she declared, glaring at him.

Everyone in the room—even her companions—stared at her open-mouthed, dumbstruck by the blatant taunt. In the shocked silence Mary addressed the four men behind the desk with scathing contempt.

"Ye officials of this so-called court whine about trifles like hats and oaths when good people have suffered and died by your order. Many have entreated you to rescind your bloody laws for your own souls' sakes, yet ye remain set in your cruelty. Ye deserve no respect!" She glared at each of them, her eyes bright with righteous indignation and fever. "Ye should get down on your knees and beg God's forgiveness for all the innocent blood ye have shed. Your day of reckoning is at hand!" she finished.

Rawson was first to recover. "More pronouncements of doom. How predictable," he drawled.

Endicott blinked and squirmed in his chair. The woman could not know of the mysterious and painful sores that had recently appeared on his back, yet her keen gaze pierced his soul as though she could see them. He suppressed a shiver of dread and attempted to ignore her by focusing on Wharton.

"Edward Wharton, why do you continue to flaunt the order of banishment upon you? Why can you not stay away from this city?" he asked, as though personally affronted.

"I came because I am concerned for my friend, who is gravely ill," Edward answered, indicating Mary.

"Ill, is she? There is nothing wrong with her tongue," Rawson observed.

"But certes you knew you broke the law by doing so," Endicott complained.

"Is it now a crime to visit a sick friend?" Wenlock Christison asked.

Endicott huffed, dismissing the comment. "What must we do to be rid of you? Would that I could hang you all and be done with it, but the Crown forbids it," the governor opined with a sigh. "Well, since you seek punishment as others seek sustenance, we shall feed you. You shall all be confined to the prison and publicly flogged at the cart tail ten stripes each at Boston, Lynn, and Salem. The sentence shall be administered at nine of the clock on the morrow."

Colonel Temple had stayed silent thus far, but this pronouncement prompted him to speak.

"Gentlemen," he said to the officials, "before we pass sentence, might we take a few moments to deliberate privily?"

"Whatever for?" Rawson asked blandly. "Their guilt is assured."

Temple did not deign to look at him. The man was an upstart with no manners. "A moment only, I prithee, John," he entreated Endicott quietly.

The governor respected Thomas Temple and nodded reluctantly. He ordered the constables to take the prisoners out into the hall. Edward and Wenlock supported Mary between them on her tender feet. Once they were gone, Temple moved his chair closer to his friend.

"John, although the woman seems recovered from her faint in the street, I do believe she is indeed fevered. Certes, she is too weak to perform forced labor, and if she dies in the prison, her death will reflect badly on you, and might cause a public outcry—"

"I do not pander to public opinion!" Endicott interrupted brusquely, holding up a hand.

"Wharton has no regard for the law!" Bellingham put in. "He has ignored our authority too many times! He shall be a cautionary example to all heretics and vagabonds."

"Edward Wharton is no vagabond, Richard. He resides at Salem and runs a brisk import business, as we all know. But I speak of the woman," Temple said patiently. "She is in danger of expiring, and if she is in our custody, we shall bear the blame. Wharton is strong and can take a beating. Make an example of *him*, if you must, but 'tis in the best interest of the colony to let the other three go."

"He has a point," Rawson acceded. "What gain in flogging her if she dies? It may indeed sway folk against us, and if it gets back to the king…"

He left the dread thought unspoken. Charles II could revoke the Massachusetts Bay Colony's Charter if He chose. It was the officials' greatest fear, the perpetual axe hanging over their heads.

"But what shall we do with the other three? We cannot just let them go!" Endicott protested.

"Certes not, but I have a solution," Temple assured him. "My business associate Thomas Lake has a ship leaving on the morning tide for Bermuda. I know as I have cargo on it. I shall personally arrange passage for the other three. I give you my word as a gentleman, they will be gone on the morrow."

Rawson cocked his head then nodded. "Wharton gets what he deserves, and we are rid of the others."

Endicott's face cleared. "Yes, that will serve. My thanks, Thomas, for finding a solution to this thorny problem. Call them back for sentencing."

The prisoners returned, and Rawson wrote out the order—flogging through three towns for Edward Wharton and deportation for the other three. The pronouncement was swift, and the Quakers were not allowed to speak, but as they were herded from the room, Mary turned to address the governor.

"God's judgment did smite thy priest Norton, and it shall visit thee as well, John Endicott," she intoned. She raised her arm and pointed at him. "Mark thee, thy own bloody reckoning is at hand, and thou shalt atone for all the innocents thou hast caused to suffer and to die."

All color drained from Endicott's thin face, and he shrank back into his chair. Her words sounded prophetic, and Mary had the satisfaction of seeing fear blossom in his eyes before she was hustled out.

Then they were in the entryway to the governor's house, preparing to leave. No longer galvanized by her mission, Mary swayed as her pain reasserted dominance. Allie and Edward steadied her, but Constable Baker pulled them apart to bind their hands again. Edward turned to Colonel Temple, who had followed them out, his faithful valet close behind.

"I beg thee, let us say farewell before we are bound again!" he said to the Colonel.

It was obvious Wharton cared for this sick woman who now appeared barely able to stand, and Thomas Temple was moved. One of the reasons he had left England was due to a woman. She was the love of his life, but she was married and unattainable thus Thomas tended to be sympathetic in matters of the heart.

"A moment more shall make no difference, Mister Baker," Temple said to the constable. "You shall have your way with him on the morrow. Allow them this small courtesy."

Baker glared at the Colonel, but Constable Humphrey caught his fellow's eye and shook his head, and the man stepped back grudgingly.

Edward gathered Mary close and whispered in her ear. "God keep thee and give thee strength for this journey." He kissed her forehead. "I love thee, Mary," he said with quiet intensity. "I shall never cease to love thee. I shall find thee and bring thee home no matter how long it takes."

Mary hugged him tightly and rested her head on his chest, breathing in the smell of the sea and of his dear self. Tears wet her cheeks. There was so much she wanted to say, but there was no time, and she could not speak past the ache in her throat. She looked up at him with eyes full of love and anguish, and their lips met for the last time.

"That's enough then," Baker growled, grasping Edward's arm and pulling them apart.

"Goodbye, Edward," she whispered, as his hands were roughly bound.

"Take care of her, Allie!" Edward called, as the constable led him off to prison.

"I will!" Allie called. "God keep thee, Edward!" Her voice broke on his name.

Once again, he had saved them from brutal punishment, taking the wrath of the authorities upon himself. She put her arms around Mary, as much to keep her from falling as to comfort her. All of Mary's energy seemed to depart with Edward, and she slumped against her tall friend.

Thomas Temple sent Francois to collect the women's belongings at the Red Lyon, and the five of them made their slow way to the docks. Wenlock Christison's hands were bound, but Constable Humphrey let Allie support Mary for the short walk. Although he hid it behind a stony countenance, Humphrey was moved by the love these people showed for each other. In any case Colonel Temple was there to assist him, in the unlikely event that any of them made a run for it.

When they reached the wharf, Colonel Temple spoke to the captain of Thomas Lake's frigate, while the prisoners waited on the pier with Constable Humphrey. At first the man was reluctant to take on three unexpected Quakers, especially one who was ill, until Thomas paid him generously in coin. Then the mariner not only relented but also arranged for them to have the First Mate's cabin near the galley. Allie could conveniently brew her medicinal teas, and the invalid would have a berth and privacy. Her companions could make pallets on the floor to be near her at all hours.

The ship was ultimately bound for England, carrying Temple's furs from Acadia as well as barrels of molasses and hogsheads of Virginia tobacco. It was scheduled to stop in Bermuda enroute to add rum to the hold. The miscreants would be put ashore there. Once Mary and Allie's belongings arrived, they thanked him warmly for his intervention. Colonel Temple bade the Friends a safe journey, and he and Francois took their leave.

Wenlock Christison helped Allie make Mary as comfortable as possible and took turns sitting with her. He was both strong and gentle. Their shared ordeal at Boston had bonded them. They used each other's Christian names and shared the burden of ministering to Mary and praying for her recovery.

After three days at sea, Mary was rarely conscious. Nausea plagued her, and she could not even stomach the clear broth Allie tried to feed her. The retching exhausted her, leaching what little strength she retained, and it worried Allie as her friend had never been plagued by sea sickness. Allie feared it was something much worse. Mary seemed to slip away more each day. Allie sat up with her throughout the night, and Wenlock did what he could to help, replenishing cool flannels and bringing Allie tea and food to sustain her. In the quiet intervals they talked or prayed together, deepening their friendship. Allie told him about Maryland and confided her hope to return there one day. She was grateful for his calming presence and capable help.

On the fourth morning at sea Mary awoke coughing but more lucid than she had been since they boarded. Allie was dozing on her pallet next to the berth but was instantly up and alert.

"I am here, Mimi," she whispered, bending over her friend. Wenlock was sleeping on the other pallet, and she did not wish to rouse him. She helped Mary sit up, steadying her as she coughed. She caught the mucus in a basin and wiped Mary's clammy face with a clean, damp flannel. When the fit finally passed, Mary's breathing was labored and rattled in her chest.

"Are we underway?" she wheezed when she could speak.

"Yes, dearest," Allie answered. "The Captain says we shall reach Bermuda in another week. He says the island is wondrous temperate. We shall—"

"I am so glad thou art here, Allie," Mary interrupted, squeezing her friend's hand. Her eyes were intent and dominated her thin face. "I saw our Mary," she whispered.

Allie's blood froze at this statement, and dread stopped her tongue.

"I shall join her soon, but there is something I must say first," Mary labored on.

"Nonsense! Thou shalt recover, and we—"

"List now, Allie. No time for pretense," her friend insisted. She gripped Allie's hand with surprising strength. "Thou must return to the Clifts and marry John Gary."

Allie smoothed a strand of hair from Mary's face with her free hand. "All in good time, when thou art well again—"

"No," Mary sighed. Her head moved slowly back and forth. "Promise me thou shalt return to John."

Allie met her eyes and nodded, her heart sinking.

"Say it!" Mary whispered intently.

"I promise," Allie managed. Unshed tears burned.

Mary closed her eyes briefly then went on with effort. "One more thing. I know thou shalt write to my father and sister, but thou must also inform Edward. I would not have him wait for me in vain. I pray he shall find another love and be content."

Allie's tears spilled over then. She climbed into the berth and wrapped her arms around Mary, laying her cheek against her hair. "Do not leave me, Mimi," she begged, cradling the thin body.

Mary reached up and stroked her friend's cheek. "Dearest Allie." She smiled. "We have had some adventures, have we not? When we were girls, I never thought to travel the world and touch the lives of so many. My life is a wonder to me, and I could not have managed without thee. I count myself fortunate indeed."

Allie held her and sang softly as Mary sank back into unconsciousness. Allie fell asleep praying her dear friend would recover, but Mary did not rouse again. Her bruised kidneys ceased to function, and fluid built up in her body and her lungs. Mary Tomkins never saw Bermuda. She died two days later at the age of thirty-one.

Wenlock helped Allie prepare the body for burial. They made a winding sheet from sailcloth, and Wenlock helped her stitch the tough material, binding up the small, thin form and weighting it with bricks. Allie was grateful when he offered to lead the ceremony, as she could not speak through her tears. Mary's body sank quickly beneath the gray, heaving swell of the Atlantic.

After the ceremony, the crew dispersed quickly, but Allie stayed on deck, staring at the water. Wenlock stood with her, understanding that his silent company was enough. The sun's warmth was small comfort. It seemed mockingly bright compared to the aching darkness of a world without Mary.

Wenlock knew the heartbreak of loss, as all Public Friends did. In dedicating themselves to the Religious Society of Friends, they risked their lives and sacrificed comfort, safety, and family to bring the knowledge of God Within to others. During the past decade he had worked ceaselessly and suffered beatings, deprivation, and the loss of close companions. His unwavering faith had sustained him, but Mary's illness and death left him feeling sad and drained. Brutal ignorance had caused her untimely demise. He had had his fill of it and felt he was at a turning point.

"Dost know where thou shalt go now, Allie?" he asked at length.

She shook her head slowly. "No. If I had the coin for passage, I would return to the Clifts in the Maryland Colony to my betrothed John Gary." She paused as a fresh sadness assailed her, thinking of John. "We were to be wed this autumn in Seventh Month," she added quietly, realizing it was unlikely that she would be there in time.

The Allens had given her and Mary ten shillings for travel expenses. There were six left, but passage on a ship to Maryland would cost pounds. In Bermuda she might heal folk with her herbs or work in a tavern as she had as a girl in Kingsweare, but it would take months, even years to save such a sum.

Wenlock studied her tear-streaked face. Even in her grief and despite the livid scar on her cheek Alice Ambrose had a quiet beauty and a calming presence. He respected her courage, and his heart ached for her loss.

"Thou hast spoken of the Friends in Maryland. Tell me more of them," he responded, hoping to distract her from sorrow if only for a moment.

"Maryland is a haven from religious persecution, and our faith thrives there," she answered, slowly warming to the subject. "There are strong communities of Friends, and it is especially beautiful at the Clifts. It felt like coming home. They hold regular meetings and enjoy such fellowship as we—" she broke off and took a breath, "—as I have rarely experienced," she amended, the pain of loss flaring. There was no "we" anymore.

"I have coin," Wenlock said, "and I would be glad to escort thee there, Allie."

In her grief for Mary and longing for John, Allie could not manage the usual polite refusal. She stared at him amazed.

"Thou wouldst pay my passage back to Maryland?" she asked stunned by the generosity of the offer.

He nodded. "We can travel together. Thou canst not make such a voyage alone and grieving, and I would meet these Maryland Friends. It sounds a fine place."

Fresh tears gathered, but this time they were prompted by Allie's relief and gratitude. She took both of Wenlock's hands in hers.

"I swear to thee, John and I shall repay thee!" she promised fervently.

Wenlock shook his head, smiling. "Nay, helping thee would be my greatest pleasure," he responded. "Mayhap I shall come to love it there, as well. I have had my fill of being a vagabond, I warrant."

Allie agreed.

The End

AFTERWARD

The Friends who suffered and died for their faith during the first forty years of the new religion did not do so in vain. In 1689 King James II passed the Act of Toleration officially ending the persecution practiced against Quakers and other nonconformist sects in England and the American Colonies. Arrests and whippings on account of religion became rare by the end of the 1670s; however, prior to that Rhode Island and Maryland were the only outposts of toleration in the New World until the settlement of Carolina (1663), New Jersey (1664), and Pennsylvania (1681). In England alone historians estimate that 15,000 Friends had been imprisoned by 1689. Some like Edward Burrough died in the noxious condition of the jails. Hundreds suffered beatings, forced labor, branding, and disenfranchisement in the Colonies, and four were executed by the Puritans of the Massachusetts Bay Colony. Freed of persecution the Society of Friends flourished in the American Colonies, and by the late 17th Century one-third of New Hampshire's population were practicing Friends. Despite decades of harassment these brave people kept their faith and instilled the concepts of religious freedom and equality under God in the governing of our nation in its infancy.

The overwhelming majority of the people in the Vagabond Trilogy were real, but 17th Century records are sketchy, particularly for women. Below is the information I was able to find about the fates of the major characters featured in books 1 and 2.

Mary Tomkins No record of birth or death. Although her illness and death at sea are fictional, they are within the realm of possibility, considering her documented whippings.

Alice Ambrose Gary returned to the "Clifts" of Maryland and married **John Gary.** They had a daughter named Mary (no DOB). There is no record of Alice's birth or death, but she was mentioned in Peter Sharpe's will.

John Gary passed in 1681 at the age of 46. The cause is unknown.

Edward Wharton died in 1677/78. His birth date is estimated around 1620. He never married.

William Reape served as a Newport deputy in 1667 and was a member of the General Court in 1667-68. He was a member of the court at Monmouth, New Jersey Colony in 1670, although he never lived there. He died in Newport in 1671 at the age of 43 (cause unknown). His wife **Sarah** and their son moved to Shrewsbury after his death. She died in 1715 (age at death unknown due to no birth date).

Nathaniel Sylvester died in 1680 at the age of 70. His wife **Grissel** passed in 1687 in her 50s.

Catharine Marbury Scott died at Providence, RI in 1687. She was in her 70s (birth date unclear). Some sources claim she had a change of heart and left the Society of Friends in her old age.

Augustine Herman was born in 1621 and died in 1686 at the age of 65. His charts of Chesapeake Bay were used well into the 18th Century. His wife **Janet** died in 1674 (age at death unknown due to unclear birth date).

John Perrot returned to Barbados, arriving on October 18, 1663. He still called himself a Quaker but was favored by Governor Thomas Modyford, who sent him on a diplomatic mission to Hispaniola the next year to persuade others in the Society of Friends to be more worldly like him. Perrot built a large house and was said to wear a velvet cloak, gaudy apparel, carried a sword, and enforced the law to take oaths. In 1665 he served as clerk to the magistrates of Barbados, and later that year Modyford gave him land in Jamaica and a ship to travel there with several hundred settlers. His attempts to amass a fortune by trading in tobacco failed, and he died in debt there in 1671.

Ambrose Dixon continued to ferry Public Friends from Virginia to the safety of Maryland, most likely meeting the Founder George Fox when he visited the American Colonies in 1672. Ambrose died in 1687 at the age of 69. His wife **Mary Dixon** died a year later at age 68.

Samuel Groome died in 1683 at the age of 43, probably at sea. He had a wife and two children.

Wenlock Christison was embraced by the community of Friends in Maryland. He settled in Talbot County on 150 acres of land given to him by **Peter Sharpe** named "End of Controversie." He first married a woman named Mary (no information), and his second wife was **Elizabeth Gary** (her second marriage) sister of **John Gary** and stepdaughter to

Peter Sharpe. Several sources say Wenlock was originally from Sotland. He died in 1679 at the age of 59.

Peter Sharpe (aka the Good Quaker Doctor) died in 1671. **John** and **Alice Gary**, **Wenlock Christison** and **Elizabeth Gary Christison** are mentioned in his Will. No information on **Judith Gary's** death (birth date estimated around 1614).

Nicholas Shapleigh was arrested in 1668 along with **Richard Nason** and **John Heard** for being Quaker sympathizers. They lost their positions as selectmen for the Town of Kittery, and the Great and General Court at Boston fined them severely. Nicholas' sister Katherine went to Boston to plead his case before the court and secured his release. He died in 1682 at the age of 65 at Peter Diamond's shipyard in Kittery, Maine, when a spar broke and fell on his head at the launching of a ship. There is no record of his wife **Alice's** birth or death.

Richard Walderne died in June,1689 during the Cocheco Massacre. Indians broke into his house, tied him to a chair, and took turns cutting the Major, saying "I cross out my account." This was in retaliation for all the times Walderne had cheated them in trade or made false promises of peace. Finally, they killed him with his own sword. He was 75 years old. His only surviving son, Richard Jr. changed the spelling of the family name to Waldron.

Eliakim and Lydia Wardell moved to Rhode Island in June of 1663. They invested in the Monmouth Project and moved to Pootapeck Purchase south of the Shrewsbury River in 1665. They were instrumental in establishing the colony of New Jersey and Eli participated in the government. They had ten more children after Joseph. Lydia died in 1699, and Eli passed around 1710.

Walter Barefoote served as a deputy collector of customs during John Cutt's administration when the Province of New Hampshire was chartered in 1680. He was appointed a councilor of the province when Edward Cranfield was governor in 1682, and the next year he was appointed deputy governor and became acting governor when Cranfield left the province in 1685. He served as acting governor for one year until the province was absorbed into the Dominion of New England, on whose council he also sat. His will was written in early October 1688 and was formally proven in February 1688/9. His exact date of death is presumed to fall between these dates. His will mentions neither a wife nor children.

Robert Pike achieved the rank of Major General by 1668 and was the commander of all the Massachusetts Bay Colony forces east of the Merrimack River by 1670. He continued to serve the Town of Salisbury as magistrate and was well loved. In 1676 Pike refused to subordinate his civil authority as magistrate to **Reverend John Wheelwright**, who retaliated by excommunicating him; however, the Major General was so loved by the townsfolk, the Reverend was forced to allow him back into the church by popular demand. Robert Pike was one of the few Puritan officials who spoke out against the witch trials of the 1690s. He died in 1706 at the age of 90.

John Endicott died on March 15, 1664, less than a year after the final trial scene with Mary Tomkins. Early historian William Sewel described the cause as "a loathsome disease." Other sources refer to "suppurating sores" that appeared on his back. He was 77 years old.

What's next?

Book 3 of The Vagabond Trilogy will be *Vagabond Apothecary*. It is a prequel to books 1 and 2 and tells the story of David Thompson, who was the first European to bring his family to live on the mainland of what is now New Hampshire. He established a fishing enterprise on the Piscataqua River in 1623 in company with William and Edward Hilton and seven other Englishmen. Thomas Roberts was one of the latter. Roberts attended the London Fishmongers College with the Hilton brothers and eventually married their sister Rebecca. More of these people and the early history of Seacoast New Hampshire will be featured in book 3.

CHARACTER LIST

Characters' ages in 1663 are included when date of birth was available. If this information was not on record or with fictional characters, I estimated. Fictional people or dates are in italics.

MAJOR CHARACTERS

Mary Tomkins, *30-year-old* missionary for the Society of Friends

Alice Ambrose, *same age*, missionary Friend and Mary's lifelong companion

Anne Coleman, missionary Friend, *age late twenties*, traveling with Mary and Allie

Edward Wharton, 43-year-old merchant of Salem, owner of the *Sea Witch*, an unofficial missionary for the Society of Friends in the Colonies and *in love with Mary Tomkins*

George Preston, *in his mid-30s*; Edward's life-long friend and business partner, also a Friend

PISCATAQUA REGION

Captain Nicholas Shapleigh, 46-year-old Anglican friend of Mary and Allie from their hometown of Kingsweare, Devon, living on Kittery Point and managing the Shapleigh Family shipping and property interests in the American Colonies

Reverend Seaborn Cotton, 30-year-old Puritan minister at Hampton

George Walton, 46-year-old proprietor of the inn on Great Island in the Piscataqua River

Alice Walton, his 44-year-old wife

NEWPORT, RHODE ISLAND

William Reape, 35-year-old Friend, owner of a successful shipping business based at Newport, RI, and recruiter for investors in the Rhode Island Monmouth Project that settled New Jersey in 1664/5.

Sarah Reape, his *29-year-old* wife

William Reape Jr, the Reapes' 6-year-old mentally handicapped son

Sarah Reape the younger, their 3-year-old daughter

Enna, the Reapes' Dutch nanny, 18 years old

Nicholas Easton, 70-year-old Friend, living in Newport, RI, and active in local government

Christiana Barker Easton, his 62-year-old third wife; *communications coordinator for Friends*

John Easton, Nicholas' eldest son by his first wife (Mary Kent), age 42

Mehitable (Merry) Gaunt Easton, John's wife, age 22

Peter Easton, Nicholas' 41-year-old son by his second wife; married to Ann Coggeshall Easton, daughter of John Coggeshall, first Governor of Rhode Island Colony and Providence Plantation

William Coddington, 62-year-old Friend; one of the founders of Portsmouth (Pocasset) and Newport; magistrate and leader in colony politics

Ann Brinley Coddington, his 35-year-old third wife

Mary Coddington, their 9-year-old daughter

Francis Brinley, Ann Coddington's brother, 31 years old; investor in the Monmouth Project

Hannah Carr Brinley, his 27-year-old wife; daughter of Caleb Carr, 16th Governor of Rhode Island and Providence Plantation

Catharine Marbury Scott, 56-year-old sister of Anne Marbury Hutchinson (killed by Indians in 1649) and close friend of Mary Dyer; living in Providence, Rhode Island; *a key enabler of communications for Friends in the Colonies*; *corresponded with Mary Tomkins for three years (1660-62)*

Richard Scott, her 58-year-old husband, cobbler, and land investor

The Scotts' daughters: Mary (21 in 1663), married Christopher Holder in 1660, lived in England; Hannah (19 years old); Patience (16), engaged to Henry Beere; and Deliverance (14)

SHELTER ISLAND

Nathaniel Sylvester, 53-year-old owner of a provisioning plantation near Long Island for the Sylvester holdings in Barbados; in partnership with his brother Constant and Thomas Middleton (the latter bought out John Rouse who was an original partner in the enterprise)

Grissel Brinley Sylvester, his 27-year-old wife and mother of their children Grissel (9 years old), Giles (6 years old), Natty (2 years old), and Peter (an infant)

Hannah, the Sylvesters' Barbadian housekeeper; married to Jacquero (*ages late 30s/early 40s*); both came to Shelter Island with Grissel in 1652

Hope their teenage daughter, a house slave and *the children's caretaker*

OYSTER BAY AND HUNTINGTON, LONG ISLAND

Hannah Wright, daughter of Peter Wright (deceased in early June 1663 at age 68), in her late teens; never married

Anthony Wright, age 63; Hannah's unmarried uncle (Peter's brother)

Alice Wright, 49-year-old mother of Hannah and Peter Wright's widow; they had 9 children, 7 of which survived; 3 youngest living at home in 1663: Mary, age 20 (engaged to be married in September); Hannah, 17; and Elizabeth, 10

Nicholas Wright, age 54, Anthony and Peter's younger brother; married to Ann. They had 7 children, all survived; 3 girls still at home: Sarah, age 16; Mercy, 13; and Deborah, 11

Reverend William Leveredge, age 60, first Puritan minister of Huntington and former minister at Dover (1635-37) and Sandwich (1638-54)

Ellin Leveredge, *his 58-year-old wife*

Caleb Leveredge, their *25-year-old* son

Eleazar Leveredge, their *23-year-old* son; married to Rebecca Wright

Rebecca Wright Leveredge, age 21; Ann and Nicholas Wrights' eldest daughter; married to Eleazar

GRAVESEND, LONG ISLAND

William Goulding, 50-year-old Friend; *Mary and Allie's host at Gravesend*; investor in RI Monmouth Project; part of exploration party of *June 1663*

Anna Cathryn Goulding, his 40-year-old Dutch wife

Will and Joseph, their young sons, age 12 and 9 respectively

Joseph Nicholson, a missionary Friend, age 23; formerly traveling with Anne Coleman

Jane Millard, his wife *also in her early twenties*; Anne Coleman's former companion

John Liddal, a missionary Friend *in his twenties*, traveling with Joseph and Jane

John and Mary Tilton, among the early founders of Gravesend; hosted Anne Coleman's three companions (listed above) on their way south in autumn 1662; imprisoned at New Amsterdam with nine other Friends in June 1663; held for unpaid fines after the others were released

Penelope Stout, 41-year-old Friend living at Gravesend

Richard Stout, her husband, age 48; a Friend and investor in RI Monmouth Project; *leader of the exploration in June 1663* across Achter Kol

Four Stout children out of seven at home in 1663: Mary, 13; Peter, 9; Sarah, 7; and Jonathan, 3

FLUSHING, FLATBUSH, AND NEW AMSTERDAM

Pieter Tonneman, Dutch *schout* (sheriff) of New Amsterdam who arrests John Liddal

Govert Loockermans, provost and *jailer* at New Amsterdam

Petrus Stuyvesant, Director General of New Amsterdam, employed by the West India Company; presiding judge at the trial of the eleven Friends in June 1663

Augustine Herman, 42-year-old sea captain, businessman, and cartographer; originally from Bohemia; owner of plantation at Bohemia Manor *who transports Mary and Allie to Maryland*

BOHEMIA MANOR ON THE BOHEMIA RIVER, MARYLAND

Janet/Jannetje Varlet Herman, Augustine's 43-year-old Dutch wife

Their three children Ephraim, Casper, and Anna (*estimate ages 11, 7, and 3 respectively*)

Samuel Groome, 23-year-old sea captain and owner of the *Dove*; a Friend

EASTERN SHORE of MARYLAND, ANNEMESSEX RIVER

Ambrose Dixon, 45-year-old Friend; a leader in the Friends' community of plantations and farms along the Annemessex River established in 1661; known to transport Public Friends from Virginia to the refuge of Maryland or to the Eastern Shore

Mary Wilson Pennington Dixon, his 43-year-old wife

Henry Pennington, Mary's son by her first husband; age 15

Dixon children: Mary, age 13; Thomas, age 12; Sarah, age 10; Elizabeth, age 6; Grace, age 4; baby Alice due in February 1663 (by the old Julian Calendar) so Mary was pregnant in the summer of 1663.

Thomas Price, 39-year-old Friend; neighbor of the Dixons; moved to Maryland with them in 1661

George Johnson, 35-year-old Friend and neighbor who also moved with the Dixons

Stephen Horsey, 43-year-old neighbor who also moved to Maryland with the Dixons

Sarah Horsey, his wife; *age 38*

Jeremiah, Pocomoke Indian lad living with the Horseys; 14 years old

EASTERN SHORE of VIRGINIA

Joris/George Hack, 43-year-old physician born in Cologne, Germany; emigrated to Amsterdam then to New Amsterdam with Augustine Herman and eventually to the Eastern Shore of Virginia

Anna Varlet Hack, his 39-year-old Dutch wife and younger sister of Janet Varlet Herman

George Jr and Peter, their sons; age 8 and 4 respectively

John Perrot, age 43; renegade Friend and Mary Tomkins' biggest challenge; Irish origins

John Browne, age 40; a Friend and Perrot's companion and supporter; *unmarried*

Thomas Browne, age 35; John's younger brother; a Friend

Susannah Denwood Browne, his 21-year-old wife; a Friend and Luke Denwood's twin sister

Luke Denwood, age 21; unmarried; Susannah's twin; *managing the Denwoods' original holdings in Virginia*; a devout Friend and son of Levin Denwood who moved to Maryland with the Dixons in 1661

Levin Denwood Jr, 15-year-old Friend; Luke's younger brother *who also stayed in Virginia*

Mabel Waters, widow in her late 40s; Luke and Levin's *housekeeper at the Denwood farm*

Edmund Scarborough, age 46; Puritan entrepreneur; Royal Surveyor for Virginia; one of the richest landholders on the Eastern Shore of Virginia; enemy of Friends and Indians

WESTERN SHORE of MARYLAND at PATUXENT RIVER and THE CLIFTS

Richard Preston, age 58; a leading Friend; established a settlement of 70 families named "Preston on the Patuxent" along the Patuxent River around 1649-51; originally a Puritan who was convinced in 1659 by Friends Coale and Thurston; hosted meetings in his home

Margaret Preston, his *40-year-old* wife; a Friend

5 Preston children, 3 boys, 2 girls between ages of 20 and 8 years old; 2 youngest, Naomi (12) and Margaret (8). at home in 1663

Judith Gary Sharpe, age 49; wife of Peter Sharpe (1st husband John Gary) and mother of John Gary Jr

Peter Sharpe, "The Good Quaker Doctor," age 48; Judith's husband

John Gary, age 28; Alice Ambrose's fiancée; living with Judith and Peter Sharpe

Mary Sharpe, *age 11*; Judith and Peter's daughter

Will Sharpe, 8-year-old son of Judith and Peter

Mister & Missus Allen, employed by the Sharpes

ELIZABETH RIVER, VIRGINIA

Mary Emperor, age 36; widow of Francis Emperor; a devout and active Friend

Emperor children: Francis, Tully, William, and Elizabeth; *ages 11, 9, 6, and 4 respectively*

Ann Godby, *in her thirties*; a devout Friend and close companion of Mary Emperor

Joan Sturges, *age early forties*; a healer and friend of Ann Godby

Wanny, *in her 40s*; Barbadian slave who came with the Emperors when they immigrated in 1650

James Gilbert, *in his 40s*; Captain of the ship *Blessing* who allowed the Elizabeth River Friends to hold a meeting for worship onboard his ship

Richard Russell, *in his late 60s*; an Elizabeth River Friend who held meetings in his home in defiance of the Virginia laws of the early 1660s; fined multiple times in pounds of tobacco

John Porter, *mid-late 20s*; Lower Norfolk County Friend who protested when his bother (also John Porter) lost his seat in the House of Burgesses (1662) because he "loved Quakers"

John Hill, *early 40s*; high sheriff of Lower Norfolk County who arrests and flogs Mary and Allie

Thomas Lovell, *mid-30s*; Hill's deputy and *the jailer at Norfolk, VA*

Justices in Mary and Allie's trial in Virginia: Lemuell Mason, Adam Thorowgood (ferry master at Norfolk), William Moseley, and William Carver

SANDWICH, PLYMOUTH COLONY

Ralph Allen, 48-year-old Friend *who hosts Mary and Allie*; a wheelwright and farmer

Susannah Allen, his 46-year-old wife

Phillip Allen, their 27-year-old son; unmarried

DORCHESTER, MASSACHUSETTS BAY COLONY

Captain John Capen, 51-year-old Puritan *who hosts Mary and Allie*; farmer and Captain of the militia

Mary Capen, his 36-year-old wife; also a Puritan

7 Capen children (6 at home): Samuel age 16, apprenticed out; Bernard age 14; Mary (Merry) age 12; James age 10; Preserved age 8; Joseph age 6; Hannah age 2

Nicholas Upshall, 67-year-old Friend; husband of John Capen's sister Dorothy; savior of Ann Austin and Mary Fisher (first Public Friends to visit Boston in 1656); banished from the Bay Colony for mildly protesting the Quaker Laws of 1657; jailed for two years when he returned to Boston to see his family against an order of banishment

BOSTON, MASSACHUSETTS BAY COLONY

Dorothy Upshall, Nicholas Upshall's 61-year-old wife and proprietor of the Red Lyon Inn at Boston

Sarah Upshall Cocke, their 25-year-old daughter; married to Joseph Cocke; *helps her mother* at the Red Lyon and eventually inherits the inn

Ruth Upshall, their 22-year-old daughter; lives at the Red Lyon and *helps her mother*; *unmarried*

Wenlock Christison, 43-year-old Public Friend and companion of Edward Wharton; a Scot

Boston Constables: Richard Baker and James Humphrey; *ages late 30s/early 40s*

Colonel Thomas Temple, 50-year-old English gentleman; Puritan; Governor of Acadia, living in Boston

Francois, his valet, late 40s

John Endicott, 75-year-old Governor of Massachusetts Bay Colony; instigated increasingly strict laws against Quakers, culminating in the hanging of 3 men and a woman (Mary Dyer)

Richard Bellingham, 72-year-old Deputy Governor of Massachusetts Bay Colony who became Governor at Endicott's death in 1664

Edward Rawson, 49-year-old Secretary to the Governor

GLOSSARY

Online Sources: colonialquills.blogspot.com; macmillandictionary.com.us; mental floss. com

Thee subjective form of you singular/familiar

Thou   objective form of you singular/familiar

Thy/Thine   possessive form of yours singular/familiar

Ye subjective form of you plural/formal

You objective form of you plural/formal

Apothecary   physician, healer, pharmacist, doctor

Anon   soon

Bever a snack, a light meal (noun)

Breeches/Britches   men's pants, usually (but not always) knee-length

Certes   certainly, sure

Clout(s), to clout patch(es), to patch as in sewing

Convincement conversion to the Society of Friends

Cooper   barrel maker

Cub   prison cell

Discomfitted/to discomfit upset, uncomfortable in a situation/to cause discomfort

To entertain/be entertained by   to host or be hosted by someone (usually overnight)

Forsooth indeed

To fun to cheat, to swindle (fun did not mean "amusement" until 1727)

Gaol jail, prison

Garth yard or garden (archaic)

Glazier one who makes glass windows and installs them

Good-brother, good-sister, good-daughter brother-in-law, sister-in-law, daughter-in-law

Husbandman, Yeoman farmer, one who keeps animal stock and/or works the land

Infirmaria infirmary, medical clinic

Muskeetos mosquitoes (archaic spelling)

Naught nothing

Nonce now

Ordinary tavern, inn, public house dispensing alcohol, food, and sometimes lodging

Peltry furs, cured animal skins

Physitian physician, doctor (archaic spelling)

Privily secretly, in private

Public Friends those on a mission to minister to all humanity in the Quaker style, usually traveling

To remark to notice, to see (not to comment)

Salat archaic or dialectal spelling of salad

Small clothes underwear

Verily truly

17th Century Shipping Containers

Firkin = 8 gallons

Kilderkin = 16 gallons

Barrel = 32 gallons

Hogshead = 64 gallons

Pipe = 128 gallons

Tun = 256 gallons

Note: barrel measurements vary according to product (wine, beer, or dry goods), English vs American gallons, and historical time periods. The containers listed above are simplified to give the reader a sense of relative size.

ACKNOWLEDGMENTS

Many people and organizations assisted with resources and historical information during the four years of research and writing that went into the creation of *Vagabond Quakers: Southern Colonies*, book 2 of The Vagabond Trilogy. I am deeply grateful to each of them for contributing to the authenticity and accuracy of this fictional version of actual events and people in early American History.

Thanks go to Kenneth Carroll, President Emeritus of Friends Historical Association and Associate Professor of Religion at Southern Methodist University, for answering all my questions and giving invaluable feedback on the early planning of book 2; Molly Burgoyne Brian of the Third Haven Friends of Easton, MD (thirdhaven.org) for arranging the meetings with Professor Carroll and for her friendship; Quaker historian Betsy Cazden of New England Yearly Meeting (neym.org) for sources on the Perrot Schism; Jocelyn Ozolins, Director of the Shelter Island Public Library (shelterislandpubliclibrary. org); the staff at the Sylvester Manor Educational Farm (sylvestermanor.org) who allowed us to explore the grounds even though the facility was closed; Amelia Viars, Reference Librarian at Cecil County Public Library in Elkton, MD (cecilcountylibrary.org); the Enoch Pratt Free Library in Baltimore, MD (prattlibrary.org); the Worcester County Library Pocomoke Branch, Pocomoke, MD (worcesterlibrary.org/branches/pocomoke); Chateau Bu-de Winery site of Bohemia Manor Farm, Chesapeake City, MD (chateaubude.com); Monika Bridgforth and Kristen Dennis at the Barrier Islands Center, Machipongo, VA (barrierislandscenter.org); the Jefferson Patterson Park and Museum, St. Leonard, MD (jefpat.maryland.gov); the Maryland State Archives, Annapolis, MD (msa. maryland.gov); and Sandra Glasscock, Special Collections Archivist at the Maryland Historical Society, Baltimore, MD (mdhistory.org). On the local front Barbara Lord was invaluable with information about raw wool and the process of making it into yarn.

Additional thanks to my editor Marina Kirsch for her sharp eyes and for creating the maps that illustrate book 2; to John T. Kingman for the cover art (jtkingman.com/my-art); and to Susan Eldridge, Sandy Brown, and Beverly Nelson Elder for their help in editing early versions of the manuscript. Their perceptive feedback and corrections are greatly appreciated.

Last, but certainly not least, my undying gratitude goes to my husband Steve Morrill for his enthusiastic encouragement and support throughout the process of creating The Vagabond Trilogy.

BIBLIOGRAPHY

Adams, Brooks, *The Emancipation of Massachusetts: the Dream and the Reality*, Riverside Press, Cambridge, 1899 (original publication by Houghton, Mifflin and Company, Boston & New York, 1886).

Austin, John Osbourne, *The Genealogical Dictionary of Rhode Island: comprising three generations of settlers who came before 1690: with many families carried to the fourth generation:* Albany, J. Munsell's Sons, 1887.

Besse, Joseph, *A Collection of the Sufferings of the People Called Quakers*, London: L. Hinde, 1753.

Bishop, George, *New England Judged by the Spirit of the Lord*, London: printed and sold by T. Sowle, 1703.

Bowden, James, *History of the Society of Friends in America*, London: Charles Gilpin, 1850.

Carroll, Kenneth Lape, *John Perrot early Quaker schismatic*, Journal of the Friends Historical Society, Suppl. No. 33. London: Friends Historical Society, 1970.

Gragg, Larry, *The Quaker Community on Barbados*, Columbia, Missouri: the University of Missouri Press, 2009.

Hallowell, Richard, *The Pioneer Quakers*, Riverside Press, Cambridge, MA, 1887.

Harrison, Samuel Alexander, "Wenlock Christison and the Early Friends of Talbot County, Maryland" in Maryland Historical Society Magazine, March 9, 1874: Print

Hatfield, April Lee, *Atlantic Virginia: Intercolonial Relations in the Seventeenth Century*, University of Pennsylvania Press, Philadelphia, PA, 2004.

Hayes, Katherine Howlett, *Slavery before Race*, New York University Press, New York and London, 2013.

Hinman, R. R., *A Catalog of Names of the First Puritan Settlers of Connecticut*: Hartford, Genealogical Publishing Company, 1968.

Janney, Samuel M. (Samuel McPherson), *History of the Religious Society of Friends from its Rise to the Year 1828*, Philadelphia: T. Elwood Zell, 1867.

Johnson, Robert Leland, *The Good Gene Pool of the Eastern Shore of Virginia and Maryland*, Baltimore, MD: Gateway Press; 2006.

Jones, Rufus M. *The Quakers in the American Colonies*, London: MacMillan & Company, 1911.

Mason, George Carrington, "The Court-Houses of Princess Anne and Norfolk Counties," the Virginia Magazine of History and Biography, Oct. 1949: 405-415. Print.

Neill, Edward Duffield, *Virginia Carolorum: The Colony under the Rule of Charles the First and Second, A.D. 1625 – A.D. 1685,* Baltimore: J. Munsell's Sons, 1886.

Ogden, Evelyn H., Ed. D. (and descendants of founders) *Founders of New Jersey: First Settlements, Colonists, and Biographies by Descendants*, 3rd Edition, 2016.

Parramore, Thomas C. *Norfolk the Frist Four Centuries*, University Press of Virginia, Charlotteville and London, 1994.

Pelletreau, William S. A. M. *A History of Long Island From Its Earliest Settlement To The Present Time*, New York: Lewis Pub. Co., 1905.

Powning, Beth, *A Measure of Light*, Toronto, Canada: Alfred A. Knopf Publishing, 2015.

Reynolds, Sarah J. "Hurricane Sandy Disaster Relief Assistance Program for Historic Properties." Historic Architectural Resource Survey, Eastern Shore, Accomack and Northampton Counties, Virginia, M.H.P. Richmond, VA: Virginia Department of Historic Resources, 2014.

Salter, Edward, *A History of Monmouth and Ocean Counties*, Bayonne, NJ: F. Gardner & Son Publishers, 1890.

Sewel, William, *The History of the Rise, Increase and Progress of the Christian People Called Quakers*, Philadelphia: Samuel Keimer, 1728.

Shorto, Russell, *The Island at the Center of the World*, New York: Vintage Books (a division of Random House), 2005.

Torrence, Clayton, *Old Somerset on the Eastern Shore of Maryland: A Study in Foundations and Founders*: Richmond, VA, Whittet & Shepperson, 1935.

Troth, Samuel, "Richard Preston Sr. Puritan Quaker of Maryland, Grandfather of Samuel Preston, Mayor of Philadelphia": *The Pennsylvania Magazine of History and Biography* Vol. 16, No. 2 (Jul., 1892), pp. 207-215 (9 pages) University of Pennsylvania Press.

Waller, Henry D., *History of the Town of Flushing, Long Island, New York*, Flushing, NY: J. H. Ridenour, 1899.

Weddle, Meredith Baldwin, *Walking in the Way of Peace: Quaker Pacifism in the Seventeenth Century*: Oxford University Press, 2001.

Weeks, Stephen, *Southern Quakers and Slavery*, Baltimore, Maryland: Johns Hopkins Press, 1896.

Wertenbaker, Thomas Jefferson, *Planters of Colonial Virginia*, Princeton, Princeton University Press; 1922. Retrieved from the Library of Congress, <lccn.loc. gov/23003542>.

Whitelaw, Ralph T., *Virginia's Eastern Shore: a History of Northampton and Accomack Counties*: Virginia Historical Society and Picton Press, Rockport, Maine, 1951.

Winsser, Johan, *Mary and William Dyer*, Charlestown, NC: CreateSpace Independent Publishing Platform, 2017.

Woodard, Colin, *American Nations: a History of the Eleven Rival Regional Cultures of North America*. New York: Penguin Books, 2011.

Zwierlein, Frederick J., *Religion in New Netherland, 1623-1664; a history of the develop-ment of the religious conditions in the province of New Netherland 1623-1664*, Rochester, NY: John P. Smith, 1910.

HISTORIC ARCHITECTURAL RESOURCE SURVEY, EASTERN SHORE, ACCOMACK AND NORTHAMPTON COUNTIES, VIRGINIA Hurricane Sandy Disaster Relief Assistance Program for Historic Properties by Sarah J. Reynolds, M.H.P Prepared for Virginia Department of Historic Resources, 2801 Kensington Ave, Richmond, VA 23221.

WEBSITES and ONLINE SOURCES
"Forefathers' Song" www.americanlit215.weebly.com/colonial-song-lyrics.html

"Historical Geography of Long Island: sequence of settlement":

www.geo.hunter.cuny.edu/courses/geog383.33/PP8-LIHistoricalGeog.pdf

North Fork History Project: www.riverheadnewsreview.timesreview.com

"The Life of William Leverich": https://leverichgenealogy.org/rev-leverich/#life

About Barbados: www.bbc.co.uk/history and www.barbados.org/history

About Sharp's Island and Kent Island: www.lighthousefriends.com

About the original tribes that lived on and around Manhattan Island: https://nmai.si.edu/sites/1/files/pdf/education/Manahatta_to_manhattan.pdf

About people and their families: https://www.findagrave.com/memorial and https://www.geni.com/people and https://www.wikitree.com and https://www.myheritage.com/name and https://www.newenglandhistoricalsociety.com/1662